THE PROOFREADER

Mark Rasdall

Copyright © 2024 Mark Rasdall

All rights reserved

The characters and events portrayed in this book are fictitious. Any similarity to real persons, living or dead, is coincidental and not intended by the author.

Published by Burwell Web Communications Ltd

No part of this book may be reproduced, or stored in a retrieval system, or transmitted in any form or by any means, electronic, mechanical, photocopying, recording, or otherwise, without express written permission of the publisher.

CONTENTS

Title Page
Copyright
Chapter One — 2
Chapter Two — 41
Chapter Three — 72
Chapter Four — 105
Chapter Five — 143
Chapter Six — 180
Chapter Seven — 216
Chapter Eight — 249
Chapter Nine — 273
Chapter Ten — 309
Chapter Eleven — 341
Chapter Twelve — 368
About The Author — 410
Mailing List — 412

'... Yesterday don't matter if it's gone
While the sun is bright
Or in the darkest night
No one knows, she comes and goes...'

From *Ruby Tuesday*, The Rolling Stones

CHAPTER ONE

"There you are. I told you I'd look after you, didn't I? You'll be quite safe now.

Can you see the stars? I thought we might be able to; it's such a clear night. There's Orion's Belt; see the three stars in a little line? Further over is the Great Bear. I've always called it that but my grandad told me its real name was The Plough! If you move up and over to the right it will lead you to the North Star. That one sits directly over the North Pole but it shines as brightly as it does (like a torch, isn't it?) so that it can see all of us and not miss anybody out.

You mustn't worry about the dark either. The stars won't give up on you, ever, and the man in the moon will come out to play shortly. Maybe he'll play hide and seek with you behind those wispy clouds that are coming in from the southwest? Just remember that if he winks at you, you must wink back, or he'll think you've grown too old for such games.

I have to go now but I'll be back in the morning to see how you are. I promise that the pain will go away for good, but I won't; I'll come and visit you as often as I can. Then you can tell me all about your days, and I'll tell you about mine."

***

'Nothing is as it seems at first; look more closely.' Andrew Patch places his paperback on the table in front of him, face down. It is early April 2017, and he is heading back to the place from which he and his family ran almost 40 years ago.

The train has already deposited most of its passengers at Oxford, so - in the absence of a working train indicator board or announcements from a driver who clearly cannot multi-process, only drive in a straight line - he has calculated that Moreton-in-Marsh must be the next stop. The familiar countryside of rusty brown fields rolls past, separated haphazardly by creamy golden stone houses that rush past between crumbling ghosts of platforms: halts that once connected these sleepy communities with the get-up-and-go of the outside world.

When he was just a boy, Andrew had assumed there would be no going back, but the train proved him wrong. He has been wrong about so many things since then, he thinks, as he quickly empties the Styrofoam cup of its remaining contents that might once have been living plants in Colombia. He places it carefully in the bin underneath the set of seats over the aisle from him, so as not to drip anything on his new 'casual' grey jeans. 'My life didn't end in Castle Upton as I thought it had - thought it might,' he reasons internally.

Nobody knew him in Acton Town. They still don't really. Collier's offered him financial security amid relative social obscurity, which is just how he likes it.

There had been a marriage but of course never any

question of children. Now there are no unanswered questions at all. No more secrets. His wife - that small, blonde epicentre of all that was once so promising in his life – had been revealed. He hadn't read too much into her seemingly lofty ambition to achieve an A-level in English Literature, attending two-night school classes each week. Perhaps he should have taken her more literally when she had told him she needed to broaden her horizons.

In the event, she had been relieved to be rid of the guilt as much as a life sentence. The divorce came through just over ten years ago now, though he has never celebrated it. The void which had always tried to pull him over its edge in the long years before Vivienne is even deeper and darker than he remembers it being.

"See all tickets please!"

The demand is made in a much louder voice than is necessary, especially (and somewhat ironically, he considers) as he is seated in the designated 'quiet coach.' The first inspector was older and calmer. There must have been a change of staff or roster at some point in the journey since then. What absurd phrase had that train strike been about? 'Flexible rostering.' That was it. Except there doesn't seem to be much room for manoeuvre with this younger, uniformed officer of the Iron Horse. Fresh out of big school failure he is clearly on a mission to get his own back. Perhaps they all are?

Andrew obligingly shows him his papers which the officer peruses for just a little bit too long before handing them back.

"Evesham is our next stop after Moreton, sir, but you'll need to move forward as these last two carriages overhang the platform."

'Overhang the platform!' Thank goodness they are unlikely to stop over a cliff edge. The railway is losing enough passengers as it is.

He'd barely been on a train back then. Once, they had been down to visit an aunt in Bristol who still lived with his grandparents. He had remembered the old couple with wrinkled skin and jagged teeth who had sat opposite them, more than the rest of the day. His dad had argued with his sister over something to do with money and so it had only been the once.

Today there is just a teenage girl in some kind of red jumpsuit, three seats ahead of him, listening to music on tiny headphones that still resolutely refuse to stay in her ears. Perhaps the buds are keen to share the music with other passengers. Or doing their best to escape her tuneless accompaniment.

It risks incurring the wrath of everyone else, except there is only one other person in their carriage, as far as he can tell. Behind him, he knows there is a white shirt-sleeved businessman of some kind who very deliberately and ostentatiously walks past him to the connecting area between their carriage and the next one. He then proceeds to bellow into his mobile phone as if to make up for the relative silence he has just left behind.

No, he hadn't roamed far as a child; none of them had. Most of their time was spent in and around Castle

Upton. Usually in shorts, plimsolls and cheap T-shirts - emblazoned with the names of beaches they had never heard of nor would ever visit for themselves - they had roamed the nearby woods and hills, scrumping apples and plums from the orchards that seemed to cling to every slope overlooking the Vale of Evesham.

A rustle in the hedge, or the familiar whine of a tractor coming up the hill, meaning they often had to make a run for it, and quickly! Leaving a trail of broken promises behind, they would leap over fences and race around the edges of tree-lined fields until, breaking cover, they hurtled across meadows and streams to safety.

It wasn't always so straightforward. Andrew had once been leaning out towards a cluster of purple fruit that had remained stubbornly out of his reach. One final lunge secured the plums but detached his fingers from the branch he had been holding on to. Unceremoniously, he had fallen about six feet to the leafy ground below. He had simultaneously been unable to move and barely breathe. Like every criminal before him, he was immediately and acutely aware that he couldn't shout out for help, nor could he help himself. The others had of course fled the scene, not waiting for him to recover or wanting to be found as accomplices to stealing, or even witnesses to death.

There were the four of them - the Famous Four - inseparable once out of school. He'd always known though that this couldn't last forever. Even as a child, there had been a part of him that weighed things up and managed to keep things in separate 'boxes.' Home occupied a quite different and not especially happy part of his life.

Watching his father working on the car engines in blazing sunshine and then asking people repeatedly to pay what they owed him was like a serious brake on playtime running and jumping. Being owed money became even more of a teatime topic (not that he was expected to contribute) than the Queen's Silver Jubilee. Quite soon one or other of life's downward spirals would entrap each of his playmates in turn, but they didn't know that then.

To confirm the time of day they could rely on dandelion puffs; each one blown away would equate to an hour. They somehow left all of this behind once Stuart was given a new wristwatch for Christmas. Rainy days would mean picnic lunches and colouring books at the far end of Stuart's old barn. It always smelled of damp straw but at least it was dry, apart from the persistent drips over by the huge door. Sometimes Stuart's mum would quietly bring out glasses of blackcurrant juice and ginger biscuits, but only if his dad was out in the fields. Even now, Andrew remembers him shouting. Always shouting.

Julie had been his favourite. Perhaps she had been his one true love, or would have gone on to have been? Games of kiss chase in the playground usually ended in breathless hugs and awkwardness, especially if their hot cheeks had accidentally brushed together. She had beautiful dark hair then. Silky and shining in a ponytail with an assortment of grips and slides that held everything together for no more than five minutes at a time, it seemed, before urgent remedial work was required. Like her hair, her clear blue eyes always seemed to be shining out of a face that was suntanned all year round.

A faint sheen of sweat has formed on Andrew's head. Even now he can remember, no, relive those pangs of jealousy when she was with somebody else - anybody else. Playing games that he wasn't allowed to be a part of. Sometimes those feelings became more than just longing. The hurt turned as quickly and unexpectedly to anger as a pan of tomato soup boiling over on his mother's small stove. There was nobody else to explain it all to then and, besides, where would he have begun his story? It's a small world, especially so when you're a child.

An aeroplane is visible through his window; quite big or quite low (he has never really got his head around physics). Naturally, he can't hear it above the sounds of the train: the wheels gliding effortlessly over fish plates connecting steel rails; the engine's diesel motor at the front. The regular hum of the air conditioning above.

They must be getting very close now. He sees the ridge lines of familiar hills in the distance, manned by occasional trees, some still skeletal to the naked eye. A flash of sunlight bounces off a windscreen and, shielding his eyes, he can just make out a miniature stream of cars heading slowly down to the village below.

He sits back in his seat and takes a deep breath. Sleep always eludes him on rail journeys, as it does even on long-distance flights. To be perfectly honest, he has never been a very good sleeper, full stop. Without the mental fatigue of work, any sleep he does get is fitful, interrupted by the same memories he is facing now. Only this time he is going back voluntarily; hoping, if not quite allowing himself to believe, that he will find some kind of resolution in this familiar place, and maybe even peace. He's too tired for any more games.

**

'This 737 was one of the newer MAX models so could handle up to 200 passengers, though only 190 had featured on the manifest. Not that she could believe that now. There were at least three of them and probably two others on the flight deck. The tall one in the dark blue balaclava stood at the front of the cabin. That was Jana's place. Her position from whence she tried so hard to capture everyone's attention during the safety drills. Well, she had their attention now alright. The blood on her forehead would see to that.

It was impossible to know the nationality of these people, though the 'blue balaclava man' had a distinct African accent. They were all burly or did it just seem that way when, clad in various shades of black, they had swarmed all over the cabin, terrifying everyone present? She looked across at the three empty seats on the far side where two of them had been sitting. There had been a space between them. She remembered that now. Two vegetarian meals.

At first, she had been expecting the plane to change course; not just continue the route she knew. Or thought she knew? How could she be sure up there above the clouds that they hadn't been gradually turning to either port or starboard? Port would have been less likely as it would have taken them out over the Atlantic. They always had much more fuel than they required on the run up from Tripoli but not enough to take them to either the States or Latin America.

At least the MAX was one of the safest planes around. If they started messing around with the navigation systems, the response times from the aircraft were usually good and should be able to cope. That is assuming they knew what they were doing. There had to have been some kind of training to take this on. No chance of support from the ground. Not at over 30,000 feet.

She didn't know much about guns but this one looked bigger than most. It wasn't a rifle but bigger than a handgun. Perhaps it was an automatic of some kind. It wouldn't take long to wipe out everyone on board if so. Bullets in the fuselage would kill the air pressure. Those that survived would be sucked through the tiny windows. Which would be the better way to die?

The control tower at Heathrow would have picked them up on the radar while they were still over western France. They must be making their descent now, turning to follow the Bristol Channel before steadily falling towards the Cotswold Hills. Nothing unusual about that. Had their attackers made contact? No doubt there would be demands. Or, if they were working hard to disguise what was happening then maybe they would get closer first. When the threat was more real. When the cost to human life would be easier to calculate, and no longer just including all of them in the air. They would soon be forgotten in the aftermath of such an atrocity.

The turbulence they had been told about before take-off finally appeared from below. Jana followed the tannoy advice delivered by a voice she no longer recognised, strapping herself in as they prepared for their final descent. It all seemed so pointless now. She needed to quickly adjust her belt as Bruce had originally been on that side of the plane and he wasn't toned like she was. Nor did he refuse leftover food as she did. She closed her eyes and thought about when she was a little girl; how she'd looked up into the bright Yugoslav skies and dreamed of travelling in an aeroplane.'

Suddenly, there is a sharp knock on the door. Somebody is outside. There it is again.

Daniel looks up from the screen and quickly comprehends that there really is somebody at the door.

"Yes," he answers, trying not to sound as weary as he feels.

His wife enters, wearing some kind of voluminous white dress and not at all like a member of the cabin crew.

"You said you wanted a second cup!"

"Ah, yes, sorry. Did you not want to finish it?"

"You know I never have a second cup. It gets too stewed. You ask the same pointless question every time."

He saves his comments in the PDF as she places a large cup of coffee beside his laptop.

"Don't let me stop you."

"Sorry? Oh, no, no you're not. I just lost track of time a bit."

"It smells in here. Why don't you open a window?"

"Because then the flies pile in."

"Perhaps it's the smell of shit that attracts them!"

He doesn't rise to it, only answers quietly and perhaps too patiently. "I hadn't noticed. I suppose I'm used to it."

"You could open the door. I wouldn't disturb you; you know."

This he knows.

"How is it?"

"A bit formulaic to be honest and she's spelling everything out rather than letting the suspense build, allowing her readers to engage on their terms."

"Sounds like an ITV drama adaptation?"

"That's about right. Dumbed down, though she claims to be aiming for a more discerning reader. There's been a major incident and yet her key character is supposedly allowing herself to drift off gently and re-live her childhood daydreams, even as she straps herself into the dead man's seat - a man she remembers for his over-eating rather than what must have been a pretty horrible death."

"But she'd be frantic, wouldn't she? Looking for any kind of sanity, whatever form that might take?"

"True, and I know that looking back - considering the adult before us as the child she once was - is a device used to make us empathise with her and her plight: to will her to survive. And yet, it's a bit like experiencing an explosion and worrying about what's for tea."

"I don't agree. I think that in moments of that kind of terror, our minds would try to find some kind of safe place. Where better than in the past, especially childhood where bad things generally don't happen, to attempt to restore some balance?

People walk, do make cups of tea after unimaginable horrors even though afterwards they cannot begin to imagine how they did it. I suppose it's like muscle memory when your mind and body have otherwise shut down to low-level processing."

"You learned all of this in personnel, did you? A lot of individuals traumatised by lack of overtime or appreciation of company loyalty, but at least they'd enjoyed their days in the sunshine?" He regrets the question almost as soon as it is out in the open, but nothing can be done. Perhaps tiredness is playing its customary role.

"Employment law may not have taught me lots of things, but I have read pretty widely too, you know."

"What kind of stories have you been reading?"

"These aren't stories. It's been widely proven. You may call it daydreaming but without memories to draw on we'd all be lost. Nothing to compare today or tomorrow with; no sense of where we came from or what we've done with our lives. How would we ever build up the confidence to face unexpected challenges if we cannot say to ourselves 'come on, you've faced worse and managed to get through it.'

"Not that many of us mere mortals have ever been involved in a hijack in midair and survived it!"

She ignores the sarcasm bordering on a pomposity she has noticed more and more since he left the newspaper. "In a case like this, I think it would be more important than ever: like being in a sort of protective bubble I suppose. Perhaps it's based on a natural desire to want to return to an embryo state, to amni…

"Amniotic?"

"That's the word! Yes. To amniotic safety, away from anything the outside world can throw at us. Isn't that the ultimate escape?"

"Sounds a bit West Coast though. I'm not sure that our author has done the kind of research that you have."

He sees that her jaw is set now, the muscles around her mouth tightening as the anger brews.

Her tone is grudging (or is it goading?) as she asks, abruptly. "What's the grammar like in this book?"

"Generally OK but far too many split infinitives."

"So, all things considered, you're not enjoying it?"

"I'm here to proof it, not to prove its worth."

"That sounded just a little bit worthy?"

She would know. "Did it? Yes, I suppose it did, but

you know what I mean. It is a bit of a struggle. I'm understandably not that good with air disasters either."

"Oh, let's not raise that old chestnut again." She does understand.

"Fine by me."

With a familiar ping, a new text announces its arrival on her mobile phone.

"Anyway, that coffee should keep you going. I'm off to bed to read. I might even learn something new. See you in the morning."

And then she is gone.

***

It is a cold, bright day, not raining at least. They've had rain off and on since mid-January it seems to him. The earth is still soft underfoot and smells dank when it really should be drying out and hardening by now.

A couple of jackdaws swirl on the light-blue horizon while a crowd of pigeons hurry from hedge to hedge. 'Making house calls' his mother used to say as they watched them out of the grubby window of their cramped flat. He could see enough then though, as he does now.

Tubby Mike from the pub, and Jan, trying her best not to look around them all to see if anyone is looking at her. Why would she do that? Why today would she do that? He knows that Jan was kind to his mother in the latter days, but she'd been marking time for much longer than anyone had expected her to do when she first arrived in the village. Just hanging around, waiting to get her hands on that room. Waiting to be accommodated.

His mother had also lingered for a long time and for what? To be surrounded by the likes of Frank and Stuart and all the other barflies that flew in when they smelled a victim. Eager to help themselves. What would his thousands of followers make of the life he has led? Maybe one day he'll write his own story.

The vicar has stopped speaking. Perhaps he did so a while ago? Duncan crumbles the clod of earth into the box below and turns to walk quickly away. He has nothing more to hear and absolutely nothing to say.

***

Stuart Fairhurst is standing at the top of the garden. In reality, this is only about fifty feet from the French windows, but they've always called it 'the top' as though their small patch merits such a boundary marker. It had been a big concern when they'd moved here that the outside space would never be big enough for children to play in. That no longer applied.

It's four in the afternoon but he has knocked off early. There are no pick-ups due until tomorrow and, besides, it's difficult to phone from work. He is holding his phone in his right hand - a seemingly miniscule object against a giant palm. Stuart has always been a man who has worked with his hands. The cracks and small scars bear testimony to this fact.

He is absent-mindedly running the fingers of his other hand through his shock of hair. Grey now, it is still as bushy as anyone can remember. "It will all be fine.

Just leave it to me ... have I ever let you down before? As I said, she knows nothing."

The other person must be talking now because he says nothing for a while, just gazes towards the house, wearily dragging the hair-grooming hand across his forehead.

"When he's gone, it will be like a new start for us. We've got to stay positive. We've come too far not to. Like I've always said, I'll look after you no matter what."

He is momentarily distracted by a movement towards the closed glass door and isn't sure whether to move nearer or further away. Except he can't move further away as there is a six-foot wooden fence blocking his way. Straining his eyes, he can't see anything moving exactly but something has changed. Then it happens again. He feels his lungs expel the breath he has been holding. The crow flutters upwards and away - a dark shape against the early spring sky - before clattering into the branches of next door's fir tree. Rather than being exposed on a spying mission, it had probably just been seeking out a bedtime snack.

Even so, Stuart's nerves have been put on edge because of it.

"She's not here, she's out at the shop."

The voice at the other end is clearly not convinced.

"She is. She is!" He hears the unusually firm tone his voice has now taken but, sometimes, the softer approach doesn't work for him ... or her. Certainly not at this moment in time.

"Just now. She'll be at least ten minutes."

The light is fading, and he can feel the cold creeping under his jacket. Still holding the phone, he pulls it more tightly around him, not taking his eyes off the house and simultaneously listening out for the front door closing.

She has been talking in the intervening seconds, but he has missed most of it.

"Sorry. You broke up for a bit there! What did you say?"

This time he doesn't miss a single word, the weight on every individual syllable is clear.

As he pockets the phone and begins to walk back towards the house, a hidden figure quietly pulls the door towards them before quickly moving away from the curtain and switching the light on.

***

DS Gabriella Taylor locks her car outside the 'compact' Victorian terraced house that has been her home for almost three months now. The tower of the old power station from the same period looms up behind them as if on guard: making sure they all stay in line, even though it has long since been converted into posh residential flats.

Her boss DI Harcourt was thrilled to hear that she had finally managed to move out of the tiny, rented flat just up the road in St John's, and down here to Powick. He talked quite a bit about the war of course.

So many older people still do that for a reason she finds quite odd. In his case, it's even odder – although, of course, she'd never mention it – as it's stories from the English Civil War he is so happy to share with her. The 'Battle of Powick Bridge' was apparently one of the first skirmishes in that conflict. It sounds to her much more like one of the Bob Dylan tracks that her cousin, Doreen, plays endlessly back at home – and much more accessible.

She wonders if this will ever be 'home.' She does still get a thrill each time she turns the key in the lock of her own front door, and even more so when she closes that door behind her and shuts out the passers-by who still stare at her for a little bit too long.

She owns two bedrooms now. 'Progress!' Her dad had clapped his hands together and congratulated her with one of his biggest hugs when hearing that she'd completed. It took him nearly thirty years to get to the same point. People down at the station and some of her friends (is there any real difference these days?) call her 'mumsy.' Some do it in a disparaging way to hide their rejection, others are kinder.

Both Gabriella and her dad understand that his own life will never be complete unless or until she manages to bear him a grandchild. That much is clear, and it makes him sad and she sadder still, each time she passes the empty room on her way to an empty bed.

***

Annabel Fairhurst reluctantly places her book face down on the little table beside her after hearing the crash of the front door (as she imagines most of her neighbours have). The inevitable heavy footsteps follow, as surely as night follows day. Not tiptoeing, plodding.

It is her husband who appears, of course, invading her space as usual. His face is red - much redder than the falling temperature would have caused.

"You're back from The Beaver then!" It is a statement more than a question, as the answer – as unarticulated as he is - is quite obvious, as is the source of the inflamed blood vessels. She resists the temptation to add 'at last' as that would just be as predictable as he is. Annabel doesn't like predictability, and doesn't want to feel that life has settled into a pattern that will not substantially change now until one of them dies.

True, her whole world is based on the certainty of nature's changing seasons, no matter how blurred their boundaries have recently become, and she knows that she is undeniably entering the winter of her life, yet she remains determined that there is still more to learn, more to know.

"I don't suppose you missed me," he barks, "Not lounging around in here with your true loves."

"No lover stands a chance if there should be love to repel him!" She rather likes this, has surprised herself, in fact. She can't remember where, from the multitude of books by her side of the bed, it had recently come from. However, she has remembered the quote and, perhaps fortified by the fresh spring air that had entered through the open doors and made itself at home, has had no hesitation in expressing it. It's completely lost on him of course. If the confusion in his eyes isn't evidence enough, his body language of useless hairy arms hanging by his side, not knowing what to do next, is confirmation. Even if his brain had sent any signal of recognition, the beer would have blocked it.

"What time were you planning on tea?"

By this, he means 'While you've been in here fantasising all afternoon, I've been putting the world to rights, so now I'm hungry.' She hasn't been planning anything. Even more incredibly, hasn't even given it a thought.

"Only I've got to be back at eight. Our visitor is only staying here for a couple of days. Would be a shame to miss him."

Yes, wouldn't it just. I've only been here every day for nearly 40 years – even longer if you count the early years at the farm. Usually, they've been taken; there's been very little giving.

"I'll get on to it shortly. Just let me finish this chapter."

He turns, hands in pockets now, apparently satisfied that all is as it should be. Equilibrium has been restored and he hasn't even needed to raise his voice for once.

The increased birdsong from the trees beyond the wall indicates that the day is almost over. So different from the chorus which wakes her almost every morning. If she had sorted things out properly, all those years ago - made the right choice instead of that proposed to her - it could have been so different, she broods for the umpteenth time. At least she also has an outside space she can escape to when the stories don't work. There would have been blood on the walls of a flat or apartment - and it wouldn't have been hers.

***

Andrew is gazing out of the window and down the village's High Street for the first time from this angle. How often had they raced towards The Beaver, with its dark wooden Elizabethan framework and whitewashed walls, and then veered off to the left and on into the woods? One of them - Grace probably - had always said the pub was haunted by a young girl called Edith.

Edith's father (the landlord) was a relatively easy target for those suspicious of and uneasy over the unknown. He had a pronounced limp, caused by complications at birth, and, to make matters far worse, was supposedly also a Royalist sympathizer. He was caught by Cromwell's forces as they marched mercilessly towards the city of Worcester and victory. Given the village's strategic position out to the east, the man had also been serving as a part-time lookout, reporting back to Charles's forces in the city itself. Unfortunately for him, he had been ambushed one night as he galloped out from Castle Upton, intent on delivering urgent news of the enemy's advance.

In these last days of the war, atrocities were not uncommon, even from soldiers who counted God among their exclusive number. The man was hung in the village square before being horribly mutilated, while his daughter and wife were made to watch from the windows of their home. His head was then tied up below the sign of the pub, destined to swing in the breeze before being mercifully cut down and buried in the Christian churchyard opposite once the soldiers had departed to earn their ultimate victory. The little girl was supposed to haunt all visitors to the pub thereafter, apparently carrying her father's head and seeking out the rest of his body.

Perhaps they looked out of this very window, muses Andrew, before pulling himself together and conceding the story for what it no doubt was. The 'ancient tale' was transcribed in scrawly, gold 'Olde English' writing on fake parchment and encased behind glass in the main bar downstairs. Presumably, the power of suggestion, no doubt washed down with strong beer, had conjured up Edith's questioning face before one of the more recent visitors in the dead of night and they had subsequently sought out the history of the village after breakfast.

Constructed in 1588, the pub was named after the many beavers that flourished in the nearby streams and rivers but here was a story that would give the whole village an unnatural notoriety. For those tasked with inward tourism to the county, the tale had been quickly upgraded to that of 'legend.'

For his part, no ghosts interrupted his sleep in the basic but adequate room under the eaves, or at least none that he can now remember. Indeed, a passable 'Full English' breakfast of Danish bacon, German eggs and mushrooms imported from France had set him up for a day of, if not exploration exactly, then re-acquaintance with history: their history.

The 'waiter' - who he had also seen behind the bar when he had first arrived - flounces around, rearranging the salt cellar, teapot and cups on his table, quite unbidden. He must be trying to convince himself that order is being restored after the 'chaos' of the previous evening that he keeps talking about (quite unbidden) when a wake had taken place for one of the barmaids who they had buried that day. He professes to be exhausted even as his little acts of correction are exhausting.

Later, takeaway coffee in hand, Andrew wanders slowly through the village. Careful to avoid being seen by anyone who might have known him, he walks past the old family bungalow next to the garage. Tattier than the one that has always appeared in his mind's eye, a couple of slates have slipped on the grey roof and the low hawthorn hedge shielding it from the road has long outgrown its original shape. The front lawn on which he had taken his tentative first steps is now a concrete off-road parking space for a grubby transit van, white before its new owner had driven it off the garage forecourt.

A little further on, to his right, he spies a small collection of maybe five or six fruit trees, their stunning blossom providing a natural dark-pink canopy above an old wooden seat. Apple or plum he thinks. Probably the former as the pink is so deep. He remembers this much but not the trees themselves. Indeed, he's fairly sure that they occupy a patch where there had just been a low, stone wall he used to climb over and into the field beyond.

Opposite the trees, a woman about his age is digging what looks like peat into a border of rose trees, failing as yet to challenge their counterparts in the colour stakes. The remaining compost sits in a tatty sack on a rusty wheelbarrow – watching her, as he does, momentarily. With thinning blonde hair and a short, dumpy body given in to middle-aged spread, it isn't an adult version of anyone he remembers from childhood, so he moves on.

The village square looks the same, with its blue plaque reminding the public of the seventeenth-century hanging and the upright post of the old gibbet just in front of it. He remembers the gallows (every schoolboy for miles around knew about that) but not the plaque.

The old row of terraced houses - alms houses his mother had called them - had gone. Mr and Mrs Lang had lived in one of them. He recalls them walking slowly, his back a non-returnable stoop, up to the church each Sunday morning, whether raining, snowing or fine weather. White-haired Mrs Arbon lived in another. She would sit by one of the tiny windows - a testament to the window tax - for hours on end. Stuart once suggested that she had already died and been stuffed for appearance's sake.

Although such residents would be long dead by now, Andrew is surprised that permission has been given for what would surely have been listed buildings to be pulled down. Perhaps the building contractors, who have replaced it with a housing estate, were seen by the Council as being more forward-looking than those wanting to preserve historical buildings. The village has plenty of history of its own, after all.

Certainly, the estate is far from being new. At least nine large 'executive' properties with double garages fill the plot, where four or five might have sufficed. Not that garden space comes into developers' calculations these days, provided there is enough room for fences. Though still young, trees and bushes are well established, as are the neatly trimmed lawned frontages which no resident would dare to neglect.

Reaching the end of the High Street he steals a glance at Grace's bungalow. The garden is landscaped now, whereas then it had been just a lawn with busy, often overgrown borders: a green stage for that day's re-enactment or new creative enterprise. Each day had been so different in those days - unique really - before maturity had conferred uniformity, or is that just how getting old feels?

Several dark benches, all curves and latticework, provide resting places between empty flower borders and little islands of shrubs, some bare and some still fully clothed. Does she need to sit and rest that often? What has happened to all that youthful energy? Or is the whole thing just an ornamental facade presenting visitors and residents with what they would expect to find in a historic village on the edge of an Area of Outstanding Natural Beauty? Rustic charm dutifully playing its part in the illusion.

He has no desire to linger outside the bungalow. He'll see her again soon enough. Instead, he tracks back and ascends the public footpath that joined the road just beforehand and is soon surrounded by trees. Largely conifers now, he notices, and not as tall as he had remembered them to be. Confusingly, he also finds himself in a clearing, facing the early afternoon sun, which he has no recollection of whatsoever. Again, saplings have been planted at regular intervals, protected by wire cages, but there is evidence of further deforestation on either side. Some logs lie where they have fallen, or been felled, and long strands of dark-green ivy have them surrounded.

The sheer white and orange sides of the old quarry come into view down in the valley below. He can almost smell the dust. A wonder it hasn't been filled in by now, he considers. Turned into a water park or fishing lake. The quarry hadn't been in use when they were children and probably not for several years before that. The stone for the new houses in the village is of a different hue and certainly doesn't look as if it has come from a local source, although it has been dressed to look that way.

He almost convinces himself at one point that he can hear the familiar refrain of a cuckoo, but that cannot possibly be the case - not if the rhyme is still true. Other birds whistle and call to each other overhead, less alarmed now by his unexpected appearance, yet still preferring to circle rather than land. Perhaps an oral history has been passed down through the decades of how Stuart had once removed the eggs from a Blue Tit's nest leaving its family planning in tatters. Creamy eggs with little brown specks all over them. Eggs so fragile that three of the four had smashed in his hand as he had held them far too tightly when he had been in such a rush to show them all his illicit hoard.

Still disoriented, Andrew has seemingly come around in a complete circle. Yes, it has been many years since they had played there, but it just looks so completely different. Duncan's wooden shack is still there on the next hill, but you would never have seen it from that point; not until you were almost right on top of it. He finds himself wanting to hit an 'undo' button which usually gets him out of spreadsheet troubles when a new formula has similarly led him astray, except, naturally, there isn't one. Gradually and somewhat sadly, he realises what has happened.

The orchards that had lain in wait for them each morning - and just for them, obviously - are no more; line upon line of fruit trees have been grubbed up and are now being replaced by a whole new year group of young pretenders. Black pears may have made the county's name, but people still following the 'Blossom Trail' these days might be disappointed at so much of their passing.

Now he is preparing to meet them all again downstairs. He wonders if they have noticed the changes as he has or if that is the privilege of returning natives alone. Unlike him none of them have ever left; never escaped. He isn't sure either whether they have produced new children. Without the pioneering excitement of youth, are their own cries in the woods destined to remain a collective veil forever?

***

He is the first of course. Each of the other guests' short walks will be counted in more steps than the two flights of stairs offer up. In other ways, though, he has made much the longest journey to be there and almost certainly the hardest.

A younger woman had signed him in when he'd first arrived, and this is his first time in the public bar where 'breakfast bar man' has now relocated to. Eventually, he stops dusting invisible mites from the counter and walks slowly towards him. Andrew takes in the dark shirt below the off-green cardigan even as his tailored blue shirt over grey chinos is being similarly and unfavourably appraised. A slight upward tilt of the head indicates that the man is, after all, there to serve.

"I'm meeting a couple of old friends tonight. Grace Beech and Stuart Fairhurst - you might know them?"

If he does, he says nothing, neither is there any change in the barman's entirely disinterested expression. No non-verbal clues.

"It will be Grace's 50th birthday on Friday and I believe she booked a table for us?"

"Why didn't you come on Friday then?"

The question is reasonable he supposes, yet impertinent as an opening 'welcome to our beautiful little village' presentation.

"I have to be away on a weekend's residential course," Andrew hears himself adopting the same deadpan tone, "So this was the closest to the actual date I could get away." He feels himself blushing ever so slightly, yet there is no need. It is none of this unfriendly man's business after all.

"She booked a table over by the window, just beyond that wooden trellis." He is pointing without enthusiasm as if his work there is now done.

Noting that it is at the furthest point from the bar itself, Andrew assumes this is so that they can have a quiet catch-up, but he cannot resist testing his theory.

"Are you expecting many in tonight?"

The man sneers, openly. "On a Wednesday?"

Andrew is undaunted. "No midweek crowd; no gathering of locals to discuss the week's progress now that the weekend is finally in sight again?"

The man is conspicuously unsure over whether Andrew is being sarcastic, ironic or any other word to describe not being 'normal.' He settles for a bland rebuff. "I sincerely hope it isn't busy. With Mrs Harewood gone away, I've got to cope here all on my own."

"Duncan's mother? It hadn't occurred to me that she might still be alive."

The pause in the conversation is uncomfortably long and soon becomes permanent.

Andrew had hoped that Grace would arrive first so that they could have a few moments alone before the others muscled in. So that he could hand over her birthday card and present without causing either of them embarrassment. They've kept in touch of course - he has sent a card every year - but he hasn't physically seen her in person since her ninth birthday.

Naturally, things don't quite work out that way. The bulky frame of Stuart Fairhurst soon fills the bar. Andrew is certain he would have known him anywhere. He still has a full head of hair (though mostly grey now) and the slow, dry delivery followed by a nervous chuckle is pretty much exactly as he has remembered it.

The woman beside him is also familiar, but only from that morning's short walk around the village. Close up, he takes in the scruffy, washed-out blonde hair that is also receding. The lumps and bumps below her maroon jumper and black leggings belie the 'trendy' image she has no doubt wanted to project. The 'gone to seed' reality is what he observes before him.

They had headed straight for the bar but now, clearly advised by their host (who cleverly managed to offer up directions at the very same time as wiping his sweaty forehead with a surprisingly clean handkerchief) they turn and walk hesitantly towards Andrew's corner.

Stuart is subconsciously undoing the top button of his white shirt and no doubt regrets the choice of a dark woollen tie to go with his fawn jacket and dark trousers - especially when he sees that Andrew has opted for relaxed smart casual. Conciliatory rather than combative.

"Well. Well. Hello, my old friend" Stuart booms while holding out a huge, calloused hand which looks as though it is attached to the rest of him via a long, sinewy boom. "Why are you hiding right over here in the corner?"

Andrew feels immediately intimidated, and not just

because there are two of them. He splutters an explanation about the table being reserved just for them.

"But there's nobody else here!"

"I know. I know - just following instructions." He attempts a watery smile. "Please have a seat. What would you like to drink?" He has turned his attention to the woman who takes up one and a half stools opposite.

"Ah, sorry. Not sure if you would have known Lisa?"

"I don't ..."

"No, I thought perhaps you wouldn't. I said that on the way over didn't I, Lisa?"

She nods knowingly at Andrew, for some reason, rather than Stuart.

"I think I may have seen you earlier today, feeding your rose trees?" Andrew offers, politely.

Her shoulders relax only slightly. "That will have been me. I spend as much time as I can outdoors at this time of year. It's the one thing that Stuart's mum and I have in common; not that my little scrap is anything compared to her beautiful back garden. Frank – Stuart's dad – brought me a bag of mulch from the woods. He usually does at about this time of year."

"God's beauty is never so apparent than in his garden?" Andrew doesn't wish to appear pompous and certainly not give the impression of being a religious person, but the woman before him unnerves him with her intensity like no other he can recall."

"I didn't expect you to find religion?" Stuart smiles, hungrily.

"I haven't. I don't even keep to a faith, but, if I did, it would be despite religion, not because of it."

"Phew. Much too heavy for me."

"Nick Cave's words which I'm happy to endorse."

Thankfully, Lisa isn't interested in either divinity or divine music. As if someone has suddenly pressed a button on an old-style cassette recorder, they can each hear her delivering her back story - like a witch reading a diary - slowly and deliberately, as if fearful of mistaking anything that could be used against her.

"I lived up in Lenchbury so went to All Saints Primary School then the De Montfort Middle School where I met up with Stuart (and Grace of course). We all went to Evesham High School together... it's all the same now - The De Montfort School that is - the Middle School got a caning from Ofsted and never really recovered. It all merged about three years ago."

"We did Simon de Montfort at school, do you remember?" Stuart is either eager to join in or keen to add some colour to proceedings that his wife's monotone and monochrome historical review is never going to achieve. "We drew pictures of the Battle of Evesham."

"And you placed a tank on the hill above the town!" Andrew beams in memory of the medieval versus the modern talk that Stuart's picture inspired.

"I was never that good at History," Stuart grins broadly, "nor most anything else for that matter."

"And your children: did they go to Evesham High too?" Andrew is feeling a little more relaxed now, but nervousness over meeting Stuart again has been replaced by Lisa's still unwavering stare.

She shifts uncomfortably on the stools. Stuart answers his question.

"We couldn't so, no, there were no children."

"I'm sorry."

Still, she stares at him or, rather, right through him, yet seemingly keen not to minimise small talk for now. "Do you have children?"

"No. Never seemed to find the time, nor a wife who stayed for long enough!"

They all laugh, a little too loudly before the door to the bar opens and all turn expectedly, choreographed for the occasion. Only this isn't Grace either. A tall, willowy man - even taller than Stuart but about ten or fifteen years older - enters. He pauses for a second or two in the doorway and glances briefly in their direction as their laughter quickly confirms that they are the room's only other occupants, before heading, with a slight limp, straight to the bar and accepting the glass of beer already waiting on the counter.

"Must be a regular!" Andrew finds himself lowering his voice below the level required for mere politeness.

The other two nod and smile.

"You surely recognise him?" Stuart raises his eyebrows but doesn't wait for an affirmation. "That's Duncan."

Andrew gazes past his companions and, surely enough, the huge beak of a nose below wide, alarming eyes confirms it.

"He looks so old!"

This time it is Lisa who responds, drawing her unlovely, podgy head slightly nearer to Andrew's. "Well, he is, isn't he? Turned fifty five a couple of years ago."

The fact that he is only seven years or so older than they are is either lost on them or not a state of affairs they wish to retrieve. In truth, Duncan always did seem much older, being seventeen or so when they were just nine or ten. Positively a lifetime of difference at that age and, seemingly, now too.

"Is he still working, do you know?"

The last part of the question is superfluous, he realises almost immediately. Of course, they know. They probably know everything there is to know about everyone there is to know in the village.

"He still helps me on the pumps some days. Dad gave him a job when he sold the farm. Felt guilty I suppose. Duncan's dad had worked for Grandad and so he was a bit like one of the family."

"The weird cousin, more like!" Lisa stifles a laugh for Andrew's sake if not Stuart's, but she needn't have bothered. If he remembers one thing about Duncan it is that he had always seemed otherworldly, even to their young, impressionable minds.

Andrew is just as I remember him, thinks Stuart, though changed physically of course: mainly in the face which has become lined and pale and so serious despite his best efforts to appear relaxed. Not at all like the mischievous, grinning playmate of old who would do anything just to be part of their games. Whereas he has grown more solid around the waist, Andrew is still quite wiry and looks in good shape for one who works in an office.

"Do you go to the gym then, up there in the big City?"

Andrew pauses slightly, assessing whether Stuart is being sarcastic. Unsure he answers anyway. "I wouldn't even know where the nearest one is!"

"They're on every street corner in London, aren't they?" Lisa feigns mock surprise. She is pleasantly surprised to see Andrew on the back foot, nervous even.

"You don't want to believe everything you read or see on the TV, Lisa. Not all execs start their days on treadmills and then breeze into work, latte or cappuccino in one hand and briefcase in the other." Was that a bit patronising? Is it because he doesn't know this Lisa at all, or because she has assumed some imaginary superiority over him? Perhaps she is encouraged by 'safety in numbers.' Why hasn't Grace arrived yet?

Stuart notices the familiar tightening of his wife's lips and her body rotating slightly, arms folded across the chest he had once been so aroused by. Andrew in turn has shifted, unsmiling, back into the red, plastic booth padding.

"I suppose we have a very different way of life down here," he attempts. "Not often we get to spend time with someone we know - an old friend - who lives up there. We get plenty of visitors, of course, what with the history and Broadway just over the hill, but they're here today, gone today." He sits back himself, watching to see if his small attempt at clever wordplay will be rewarded. It isn't.

"Good for business though?" Andrew is pleased to see Stuart shrink a little. "You'd be lost without the tourist trade I imagine?"

"Has its benefits in the summer months, certainly. Causes a good deal of congestion too, mind. People get very impatient about that; want everything to always be the same."

"Things change though, don't they?"

They both stare at Andrew, waiting expectantly for him to continue but he leaves the statement hanging in the air for the time being. He often uses this technique in business meetings as it bestows on him a certain gravitas, whilst at the same time giving him time to plan his next move.

Voices from his left indicate that more people have entered the bar from the side entrance which serves the small car park. He doesn't even bother to turn his head as he senses that she has arrived at last.

Grace uses the time it will take for her to walk to their table to assess both Andrew's appearance and body language. He has aged more than she had imagined; looks a bit pasty and uncomfortable - ill at ease even. The indecent haste of his standing up, ready to greet her, suggests relief in the face of attack.

"There you are! We'd almost given up on the birthday girl."

"It's not until Friday, is it?" Lisa asks the unnecessary question. Perhaps she just wants to be noticed or to remind the other guests that she's there.

Andrew sees not just Grace's lined, sunburned face but also a glint of excitement in her still startling green eyes that he has rarely experienced since he was a boy. She is wearing a dark, woollen jacket and an even darker dress (naturally). Her hair is short and steely grey, neatly cut. If Stuart's wife has gone to early seed, Grace is positively blooming.

Naturally, after so long, there are few meaningful words at first but then, over the next hour or so, with the help of glasses of house red (Grace refused the offer of champagne on the grounds of it being far too ostentatious, much to Lisa's obvious dismay - although she bravely accepts the collective responsibility of the decision) and bar snacks of chicken, scampi and surprisingly good chips, they reminisce.

Stuart and Lisa watch and nod politely, knowingly sometimes, amid eager mouthfuls of food washed down with cider, but they know that Act One is long past, and they are merely supporting actors now: warm-ups for the main event.

Andrew gradually becomes aware of a loud voice

towards the bar area but is concentrating hard on Grace explaining why she never married. It seems that, quite understandably, she has found relationships difficult and there has been nobody to fill the void as such. He has strived throughout to steer the conversation away from his own marriage. It seems unwanted here by any of them especially Andrew himself but, eventually, he hears himself describing the moment when another part of him died inside, as his wife lay naked on their bed but with the inner knowledge of another.

"She wasn't moving at all. Her eyes were wide open but not even a flicker of recognition when I spoke to her. Honestly, I didn't know what to do next ..."

What did happen next was that there was an unexpected roar in his left ear from the man whose voice he had known from the past and would never have mistaken. He had been listening to Andrew's every word from his new position behind them. Rearing up like a dark, menacing tide out at sea, he had stopped him in mid-sentence with accusations about his father and calling him a 'fly by night' among other choice epithets. Spittle flew in all directions for all the world to share.

The other three had looked surprised, initially, but then the dullness of recognition had blunted their reactions. As the tirade finally came to an end Andrew raced across the room and exited by the main door, ostensibly to get some fresh air.

He headed down the familiar High Street again. It was pitch black. Why weren't there any streetlights apart from the one in the distance? There always used to be. He needed help and quickly; she too had needed help but what could he do? Where was she?

He walked quickly but not quickly enough to outrun fate. The pain was indescribable at first, then it eased, slowly but reassuringly, until he felt nothing at all. Just lay there, eyes wide open but no longer seeing. His last memory of the sleepy village of Castle Upton was surprisingly like one of his earliest.

CHAPTER TWO

The mobile phone has almost vibrated itself off the bedside table, having somehow expertly avoided the pristine paperback which was sitting in its way.

"Martin!" A voice from the other side of the bed is calling him, but that can't be right as he hasn't answered the phone yet.

"Martin. For pity's sake - your phone is ringing!"

This finally wakes him, and all confusion is extinguished. Early morning clarity presents a much harsher reality.

"It's been ringing for ages."

Noticing the offender's precarious position on the edge it registers that this must indeed have been the case and snatches it up.

"Harcourt! Yes, yes, I am. No problem at all. Go ahead. Where was this? When? Have SOCOs arrived at the scene yet? Great. Thanks. No, no problem. I'll be there in about three-quarters of an hour. Yes, yep. see you there."

"Gabby?"

"Yup." He rubs his eyes before placing the phone back on the table and climbs purposefully out of his side of the bed. Fully awake now. Focused.

"Well?"

"Well, what?" For some reason, he whispers the question as he heads towards the shower, or 'en suite' as she still insists on calling it, some nine years after they moved in.

"It's only five past seven so it must be serious."

"Evesham Police were alerted to a body on the edge of woodland earlier this morning."

"So why involve you?"

"Well, they're South Worcestershire, same as us. Depends on what it is. If it's just a homeless or wanderer they'll probably be able to handle it. Either way, there'll no doubt be a sensitive and informed discussion about territory, but one of our crews was out that way and got wind of it. Gabby thought it might be worth us taking a look."

"The scent of blood eh!"

"Something like that."

"You ought to put the ringer back on at night; it was buzzing for ages."

He smiles darkly. "I thought it was your suggestion to take it off in case it woke you up before me?"

"Well that didn't work, did it?" She turns over, away from him, pulling the blankets over her head. He often wishes that he could do the same.

***

He beeps the Skoda and jumps in, energised now after a shower, bowl of cornflakes and a strong cup of Yorkshire Tea. Debbie prefers Taylor's but he did the shopping last week and pretended they had run out. He's not convinced she believed him, but he got a result, which was the main thing. He took a cup up to her and she didn't complain, although, in her defence, she was probably still asleep - or pretending to be.

Their three-bed detached backs onto a leafy lane that was once surrounded by fields and paddocks before the builders extended town planning to the countryside. Nearly three years ago they were among the first phase of owners on the estate which has since sprawled way beyond the original boundaries that had been excitedly revealed to them at the 'show home.' To be fair, Debbie had been more than excited too. The house represented pretty much all she had ever wanted and was a far cry from the semi in Droitwich she had grown up in.

Already knowing by then that they would only need a minimum amount of space, he would have been just as happy in an apartment on the Diglis Basin - perhaps with a little balcony - and from which he could have walked along the riverbank, letting his mind get back to equilibrium as the Severn flowed peacefully and reliably next to him.

Now he diligently mows the front and back lawns most weekends during the summer, if other duties don't call him away, and there is still plenty of greenery around to make him think he is further away from other people than he is. He still has to deal with the break-ins but these are people from the past, determined to climb into his mind. He can't escape them but by making them smaller – as the doctors advised – they find it more difficult to see in, and him to realise that they are still there.

Fernhill Heath is about three miles north of Worcester's city centre and easy to get in and out of the station or elsewhere within their region which extends just beyond them to Droitwich, or down to Malvern, Pershore and Evesham in the south.

Proceeding over the M5 he soon finds himself on the A44 (or Evesham Road as travellers would once have called it) and 'phones his DS via a button on the car's built-in navigation system. Fleetingly, a memory stirs him of his father having to park on the hard shoulder of the A1 and walking to a lay-by more than a mile away, AA Kiosk key gripped firmly in his hand, so that he could 'telephone for help' when their Marina had mysteriously started smoking. It had become a bit of a habit and was exchanged for a dark green Hillman Hunter soon afterwards.

Gabriella Taylor - DS Taylor of course - is already at the scene and her friendly but confident voice soon fills the car.

"If you take the turning for Fladbury, sir, you then go past the pie shop and take the right-hand fork to Castle Upton which is the next village along."

"Fine. Sat Nav seems to agree with you. What have you found out so far?" He is so happy to be digging into the detail: the minutiae of moments not lost on him.

"Locals got a call to say that a body had been found

just off the main road through the village, sir. Paperboy - David Wright - had almost finished his round when he saw a foot poking out of the undergrowth."

"I suppose he didn't see anything else?"

"Not that he's been able to tell us yet. He's still a bit shaken up, as you can imagine."

Harcourt's jaw tightens. His imagination is dark enough, deep enough.

"Have you managed to keep him there?"

"I have. His mum is with him and the chap from the little cafe bought a hot chocolate over."

"How old would you say he is?"

"He's fourteen, sir. He only took the job on at Christmas when his elder brother gave it up to concentrate on his A-levels."

"OK. Please don't let him go anywhere if possible."

"Right on it, sir!"

Harcourt groans inwardly at the turns of phrases that seem to have lately overwhelmed the station, like a virus affecting verbs and vocabulary. What was so wrong with definite articles? He has noticed it on TV as well. Why can't people speak or write correctly anymore, as in the historical biographies he loves to read when his wife is snoring beside him? Too much Netflix and 'networking' he supposes - where meaning is everything and language languishes some way behind?

"Jenny's just arrived." Taylor is oblivious to his inner trials.

"Very good." He forces his face into a smile to project what he hopes is a positive voice. "I'm only about ten minutes away now. Who is the local DI?"

"Barker, but she's been alright so far."

***

Neither Harcourt nor his colleague needed to have worried about him finding the village. A series of small signs ended with a much larger brown rectangle urging him to bear right after Fladbury with the promise of food, drink and a site of historical interest.

He passes the pub and pretty village square before heading down the High Street. Small groups of people hug the pavement, deep in discussion and motioning towards the end of the village. Unlikely that the village would normally witness this number of residents so early on a Thursday morning in March, he considers, unless news of a coach tour had spread, requiring each of them to be at their newsagent, cafe and library posts (with extensive tourist information packs and second-hand books for sale). The prospect of an unexplained death to chew over is seemingly even more exciting than the beep of contactless credit card transactions or the jangling sound of hard cash being thrown into tills.

He is almost out of the village again by the time he spots DS Taylor on his right, leaning against the grey metal post with its bright green and white 'Public Footpath' instruction attached, like a finger that has been amputated and then sewn on again, but now at a slightly downward pointing angle.

She straightens up as soon as she sees his car and nods as he passes her, parks just beyond her own and gets out.

"Do you have anything new to add?" He walks briskly towards her, signing the Crime Scene Log Sheet held out to him by a young, male police officer whom he doesn't recognize before ducking underneath the blue and white police tape that now joins the post to the skeletal trunk of an ancient oak tree on his left.

Taylor quickly stuffs the creme egg wrapper in her pocket, hoping he hasn't noticed (but he probably did). "Jenny can't be sure of the cause of death. She suspects a heart attack but there's also a strange mark on the front of his neck and a contusion on the back of his head. She's not sure whether or not the latter was caused by him falling on a rock beyond the entrance to the footpath. One of the Scene of Crime officers found blood traces on it."

"And this strange mark - could it have been made by a ligature; is that what she means?"

"No, *she* doesn't." A clipped voice provides a ready answer. Dr Jennifer Graham, dressed in white from head to toe, has joined them from behind, emerging quietly from the bushes as if to conclude a successful game of hide and seek being played by angels.

"Dr Graham."

"Detective Inspector Harcourt. We meet again!"

He notices the rather sinister inflexion in her voice, as though she is trying to sound like Dr No, or some other self-assured villain for him to contend with. As usual, he is not sure if she is trying to humour him or trying to be humorous. Though only about five to five-two in height she packs a powerful verbal punch (and probably a considerable physical one too).

"Sergeant Taylor has mentioned some strange markings on the body."

"Indeed."

"Would you be able to elaborate?"

"Specifically, or generally?"

There she goes again he notices. He has felt no real fatigue since the early morning call, but now weariness is creeping in behind his eyes - or perhaps the adrenaline of the find is wearing off?

"Specifically, if that would be alright with you." He refuses to be goaded into semantics.

"Bruising to the left-hand side of his cheek, but on the face of it" ... she hesitates, presumably for comic effect but, with straight faces in the audience, continues more quickly, "it looks more as though something has been pushed or poked in his face, rather than a straightforward blunt force trauma."

"And the contusion. What can you tell us about that?"

"Impossible for me to speculate now, not that I would. Could have been caused by a blow from behind or, equally, by his falling backwards. We've taken blood samples from both the body and the stone."

"Was the body facing up or down?"

"Upwards. Gazing blindly towards the heavens."

"Are we looking at a vagrant do you think?"

"How Elizabethan your language and yet so thoroughly modern that you would assume the unfortunate victim is some kind of undeserving vagabond."

He stares into her deep blue eyes - stunning in their elfin-like way, though there have been rumours about her. "I assume nothing, I assure you."

"I am not in the least bit reassured, I'm afraid. My assumption, based solely on experience, would be that this man was far better dressed than your average tramp ... or hobo ... and the fact that we've found a leather wallet, still full of notes and a couple of credit cards would rule out a hand-to-mouth existence."

The veins in his cheeks tighten and he can feel the blood draining from his lips. "Do you have a possible time of death for us?"

"As usual, I'd want to carry out a thorough examination before playing your little prediction game, but there are some definite signs for me to start with."

He notes the usual patronising tone and also her emphasis on 'me' rather than 'us.' He wants to shout out that it's a team game, but to her, it isn't - it's a matter of her professional (and thus personal) standing. More importantly, this is not a game at all.

"Rigor has set in and there's the expected rigidity around the facial and other smaller muscle areas, but there must be some ATP left in the lower part of the body because the muscles haven't fully contracted - in the thigh area for example."

"Less than twelve hours then, all other things being equal?"

"I find that things are rarely equal, Detective Inspector, but yes, less than twelve, though most contraction is complete after about eight hours or so. We also have the benefit of lividity. Again, the contusion on the back of the head is showing as an indentation with blood pulled towards it due to gravity. This would seem to confirm a hard object coming into contact with the skin in some way. Given pooling further down the spine I see nothing at this stage to suggest the body was moved after death."

"So, we potentially have a scene of death if not where any attack may have started."

"If there was an attack? Could have been due to natural causes. The former is down to you and the latter to me. I was unable to change the discolouration pattern on the body so I'd say that lividity is now fixed and that this body became a corpse at least six hours ago."

"The two together suggest death between six and twelve hours ago then?"

"Probably more likely six and eight. I commenced my initial examination at 7.51 this morning, so I'd say your man died between around 11.30 PM and 1.30 AM, but I should be able to be more accurate than that in time."

"Thank you, Doctor, that's been extremely helpful." He takes the bundle of clothing she hands him. "Pale blue! I thought all SOCO suits were white?"

"Shortages at West Midlands HQ. These are a cheaper version, apparently; imported from China, where health is valued less."

He steps aside, onto the grassy bank, to let her pass.

"Please do let me know when you can give me an update?"

"Don't I always?"

With that, she strides past, short blonde hair like a torch lit by early morning sunlight, and heads back down the High Street towards the small knot of people that remains.

They quickly slip on the protective clothing and head up the footpath. A small white tent blocks its way about three feet further on. A young, uniformed PC stands just by their side of it and asks for ID as they approach.

"Were you the first officer on the scene?" Harcourt asks, replacing his warrant card.

"I was, sir. PC Killingsworth, sir."

"Thank you. We'll have a chat in a moment if that's OK?"

"Of course, sir." The officer nods at DS Taylor as she beams at him encouragingly while dutifully following

Harcourt into the tent."

Body odours, coupled with the vegetation beneath, make for a dank, sour aroma as they both instinctively reach to cover their noses. The body of a man is, as Dr Graham informed them, lying on its back. The unseeing eyes and mouth form a sort of grimace but not, Harcourt notices immediately, a look of fear or terror, though that expression could have been wiped off the face as it fell.

Taylor takes in the grubby blue shirt - torn in three places that she can see. Perhaps this was the result of a struggle with a human or made by a creature from the woodland on an early-morning stroll. She stares at the purple, unnatural position of the hands - one face up and one face down.

"A bit of a conundrum!" A soft, female voice disturbs their thoughts.

They both turn to see a younger but similarly blue-clad figure enter the tent, which now feels far too small. Harcourt feels awkward and claustrophobic.

"DI Barker. Good morning."

"Not really - not for this chap, is it?"

"I'll be just outside." Taylor senses the tension and has noted the blood draining from her boss's face, as if in silent accord with the victim.

"So," Harcourt relaxes slightly, "are you talking about the positioning of the hands?"

"At the end of his arms? No, not really ... I was

referring to the two of us being here together: in a small tent where nobody can see what's going on."

He ignores the sarcasm, recognising it as being entirely what he would have expected from one whose masterful, spectacular rise in the force is the stuff of local legend. He forces himself to focus on the serious business of death.

"As far as I'm aware we heard the call on the radio and came over to offer support in case it was needed."

"Very generous. It wasn't. Goodbye."

"I think perhaps we should wait and see what Jenny..."

"You mean Dr Graham I take it."

He ignores her. To get involved in an argument with Karen Barker is like facing tennis balls from Sue Barker without a racket.

"Once we know the cause of death, we can move to assign resources accordingly. If it's natural, neither of us will spend any more time on it. If it proves to be something more sinister, well, that's for Detective Superintendent Hunter-Wright to decide, not us. All I will add at this stage is that we have considerable experience of major crime ..."

"Don't come that. This is our patch and precisely why we have regional teams."

"Shall we at least talk to people for now as though we are on the same side?"

"I've already completed my initial enquiries. If you

should discover something new, do feel free to share."

"Well, that would be difficult, wouldn't it?"

She is already on her way out of the tent but turns slightly. "And why is that?"

"Because we don't know what you've already ascertained, so couldn't be sure whether our evidence is new or not?"

"One of the problems of pooling resources, I'm sure you'll agree." With that, she lifts the flap of the tent and disappears from view.

Harcourt spends a few more minutes gazing at the body but also at the flattened area all around it. Satisfied at last, he too rejoins the world of the living.

***

She is sprawled across his settee, shoes kicked off in haste lying discarded in the middle of the room. She looks forward to this now and needs it even though it wasn't always the case. Initially, it felt wrong, dirty - like a betrayal - to be spending so much time with another man - one she barely knew. Now it is a new normal she looks forward to.

"He's not a part of your life any longer. It must make you feel ... relieved? Or do you think you'll miss him?"

"A bit of both, I suppose. We went through so much together. We've known each other for years and you can't just delete that, can you?" He simply stares, unblinking, back at her, so she lays her head back and closes her eyes, like before, hoping for some response from him or some encouragement at least. "We went through so much in the early days, but he always listened to me then."

"Paid attention?"

"You make me sound like a sergeant-major!"

"Are you?"

"If you haven't worked that out by now ..."

"Go on."

"He knew we were doing the right thing - even though it was going to hurt a lot of people; ruin some people's lives, possibly for good. But we went through with it, and it worked out pretty much as I told him it would."

"What changed then?"

"He did. I mean, we all do, don't we? After a while? Some of us mature and become wiser; some of us just become mouldy. He started worrying about the ethics of what we'd done."

"What you'd advised him to do!"

"And that's what did it." Her eyes are wide open now, her voice drowning out his whispers. "Suddenly I was the cold-hearted bitch of the piece whereas he was somehow just following my instructions. He was always trying to opt out of something he'd previously been so happy to sign up to. I couldn't stand that."

She can feel her heart thumping in her chest now. Surely, he can see it rising up and down below her new white, silk blouse; will he be moved to do something about it?

"You got angry with him?"

"Too damn right I did. I can still hear the screams."

***

DS Taylor is talking with PC Killingsworth just outside the tent, both pen and notebook active in her hands. The young, uniformed officer stiffens as he stands to attention.

"At ease, Constable; we're all on the same side here, regardless of what your DI may have told you." Harcourt prefers disarmament to imaginary guns pointing at the back of the head.

"Thank you, sir."

"You were first on the scene, I believe?"

"Yes sir. At about 6.40 a call came through from the station indicating that a young boy had spotted what he thought was a body in the undergrowth just off this public footpath. I was on the way back to Evesham - my shift finished at six-thirty - and swung over here to take a look."

"And the young boy ..."

"David Wright, sir."

"How was he when you got here? Was he distressed, relieved that you'd arrived?"

"I'd say he was fairly calm, sir, but his mother was with him by then. They only live at the other end of the village, just beyond the pub. I imagine he had calmed down somewhat. Must have been a bit of a shock for him."

"Not the sort of thing you'd expect to see on the back pages at the end of your morning paper round?"

"Thankfully not, sir; not in normal circumstances anyway."

"Normal circumstances. No." Harcourt hears the words rebounding around his head, unsatisfactorily, even as the PC bows his head slightly as if in silent respect for the newly dead.

"Was there anybody else here - when you arrived on the scene?" Taylor' voice is more gentle and encouraging.

"No ma'am. The owner of the cafe just along the street there came up shortly afterwards." He temporarily pauses, consulting his notebook. "A Mr Steven Pateman, owner of the 'Cotswold Kettle.' That's the name of said establishment."

What a quaint use of words, thinks Harcourt, before nodding to the PC to continue.

"He told us that he was preparing the cafe for opening when he saw us through the front windows."

Preparing a cafe for opening before seven o'clock on an average March morning? Unlikely, thinks Harcourt but this isn't the moment or the person to query. The PC is only reporting what he has been told. He hasn't yet been taught to detect.

"Whereupon," Killingsworth continues, more confidently now that he has got into his stride, "He appeared with two takeaway cups. Coffee for the mother - 'Sunday Morning' blend - and hot chocolate for the boy. He offered me one, but, of course, I declined."

Of course!

"And I presume either mother or son – or both - were eager to tell him what had taken place here?"

"In similar words to my own."

Heaven help them! "You didn't advise caution, given that this is now a police matter."

The PC shifts uncomfortably, crestfallen that he may not have followed the correct procedure after all.

"I'm sure they would have told him anyway," Taylor kindly comes to his rescue, "Especially after having been given hot drinks on a morning as cold as this one was."

"Where are they now?" Harcourt asks softly just in case they should be sitting comfortably in the tree above their heads, listening.

"Over there, sir, in front of the cafe."

How nice. Harcourt spies two figures, huddled together under the garish purple awning, which serves no purpose on cold spring mornings. Both are staring in their direction.

"Thank you. We'll need to preserve the scene for now - at least until we get the pathologist's report back. It may be that nothing sinister happened here, but, if it did, the next stage will be a fingertip search. We just have to wait for now."

"Understood, sir. PCs Boon and Mills have just arrived to take over from me."

"Well, thanks again, PC Killingsworth. You've been a great help. Our apologies for keeping you way beyond the end of your shift."

"Not at all, sir; I'm sure I'll get used to it."

"My advice would be to think of police work as negotiating constantly shifting sands rather than shift work." He smiles mirthlessly and watches the young man head back to his police vehicle, perhaps deeper in thought than when he arrived.

Harcourt turns to his DS. "A wallet was retrieved, then: do we at least know who the victim was? A local man?"

Waiting respectfully for him to pass her and head down the footpath, she addresses her answer to his retreating back. "His name was Andrew Patch, sir. According to his driving license. 50 years old. The wallet contained £70 in cash – mainly fives but some tens – a Mastercard and a Costa Coffee loyalty card. Doesn't look like the motive was theft, sir. His address is listed as Acton Town, West London. No idea how he found himself here."

"Or perhaps more importantly, why?" Harcourt didn't mean it to sound as patronising as it possibly sounded, lost in other thoughts as he was. "Again, we'll need to wait to see what Jenny comes back with - we don't want to put a lot of resources into it if it is a case of someone just having too much to drink, falling over and unfortunately hitting their head. Either way, though, his next of kin will need to be informed. Can you suggest DI Barker follows up, please, if she hasn't already done so?"

"Yes sir."

As they reach the road, they spot Kate Shelbourne, a journalist from the local paper, waiting for them; waiting to hear the story more likely.

"Kate." He struggles to take his eyes away from her lovely face, not to mention a figure of medium height and still shapely for a woman in possibly her late forties, though running to a little fat now. Not that he can talk. Too many glasses of red wine have called time on him more loudly than the running machine Debbie had installed in the garage for both of them to use. He isn't sure whether she still uses it either. The journalist always stands just a little too close to him and he can smell her perfume - flowery with a hint of violets.

He so wishes that he didn't still have the hormonal feelings that he does. If there is such a thing as a 'male menopause' he hasn't experienced it – yet. Why does he still notice women in the way that he does? It gives him no pleasure – no fantasy interlude here – and he hates himself unambiguously for it. He'd love to talk to someone about it, but he can't. Who would listen to him? He's never once come close to being unfaithful to Debbie (never even considered the possibility) and she will always keep him straight, thank goodness. She's been his love, his lover and, perhaps more important than both of these, his life raft.

The journalist's clear, blue eyes stare directly into his, still slightly bloodshot after the unexpectedly early beginning of his day's work. "An early start!"

"Indeed. I didn't think you'd be here so soon."

"We don't get that many bodies around here."

"I thought the Horticultural Society was alive and kicking."

"I report on other things you know."

"So, it would seem." He moves away slightly but she simply follows, practically standing on his toes.

"Are you going to let me in?"

He ignores the innuendo (if that's what it was?). "All I can confirm is that the body of a male - possibly late 'forties or early 'fifties - has been discovered. There's nothing at this stage to suggest foul play. We'll know more when we receive the pathologist's report but, I repeat, we have no reason to treat this sad event as suspicious at this time."

She has been watching him intently during this little speech, scrutinising every muscle of his face as he speaks. She is aware of his discomfort though isn't sure why; doesn't yet know if it's because he is hiding something or not. "You will let me know as soon as, though?"

"Of course. I will update you personally."

Taylor begins to cross the road, but Harcourt waits for Shelbourne to head off before turning to look back up the footpath, disappearing as it winds around the hill.

"Sir?"

"Could you walk along the pavement on the other side of the road please and then cross over and walk on this side - again, past the footpath entrance but looking towards it."

She hears the roaring diesel engine of an articulated lorry in the distance, hurtling down the hill to her right. As it comes into view, so does Killingsworth's patrol car which hasn't yet departed the scene. The driver slams on his brakes in a less-than-subtle attempt to confirm that he has also seen the '30' speed limit sign and is, of course, adhering to the instruction while driving carefully through Castle Upton at least.

A few minutes later, she rejoins Harcourt on his side of the road.

"Thoughts?"

"Because of the way the road winds round, relative to the entrance to the footpath, you see less far along the path itself, if walking or cycling on the other side of the road, than if you're on this side. The mouth of the footpath seems to be wider as you get closer to it."

He nods, reassuringly and reassured.

"Good. Let's go and see what the early morning papers had to say."

David Wright is quite tall and lanky for his age. He has a grey hoodie - with hood, mercifully down, Harcourt is pleased to see - over creased blue jeans. His mother is short and stubby with what could almost pass as bleached blonde hair. She is wearing a dark purple anorak above light grey jeans with regulation knee holes for those who haven't noticed that they are no longer young.

"Good morning. David Wright? and Mrs ..."

"Wright." She eyeballs him, sullenly and with as much disdain as just the one coffee so far that day can help her to muster.

"Right." He continues without missing a beat and ignoring her attitude. "David, let me say first of all that you are not in any kind of trouble and therefore, contrary to what you might see in detective programmes on the TV, I will not be cautioning you today."

"He's not stupid!" The mother folds her arms over a bust that has never been as large as she would have liked people to think it was, continuing to stare. The boy, smelling strongly of peppermints, looks vacant and disinterested.

"So, please can you tell me what happened this morning."

"He's already said all this to the other one: the woman."

"I know, and I'm sure you're very anxious to get to school but I'd like you to repeat what happened to me please, David. If that would be alright?"

The boy glances at his mother and shrugs slightly as though it's no skin off his freckled nose. "I was nearly at the end of the round. Number 67 has three papers so ..."

"Which side of the road is number 67 on?"

"This side. Why?"

"So, on the opposite side to where the footpath begins?"

"Yeah, That's right."

"Are you able to let me know which three papers number 67 takes please?" He has chosen his words carefully: 'able to' appeals to a witness being able to prove that they can, and therefore primed to show that they can; 'will you' introduces command into speech which might be rejected simply because it can immediately alienate a witness from an interrogator.

"Course."

"What do you want to know that for? The other one didn't ask anything about papers."

Harcourt tries to picture a scene where the insufferable mother comes face-to-face with a disarming Harpo Marx and is, at last, able to acknowledge that actions really can speak louder than words. Maybe even make all of them feel a little happier. He's not entirely sure who would win the argument, though. It's never as black and white as that.

He would prefer to talk to the son alone but knows that age - and the age in which they live - make that completely impossible, even though it wouldn't strictly be against the growing labyrinth of police rules as this is not a formal interview.

"David?" He coaxes the boy gently.

"Times, Telegraph and Mail. There's only two of them - no children - so I guess the Mail's for her and he reads the other two."

Harcourt smiles, his little tests of the boy's powers of perception bearing early fruit. "That's fine. Please do continue."

"So, the bag was much lighter after the Scotts (the people at number 67) and I only have one more drop after that. Miss Beech at number 80 on the footpath side of the road."

"Ok. Thanks for that." Harcourt continues to ignore the mother who is now shuffling her feet, pointedly, and sniffing while gazing pointedly up at the sky and those few dead stars which haven't yet found a morgue to go to. "Did you notice anything on the footpath before you crossed the road to Miss Beech's house?"

"No."

"And it's a bungalow - for the record." The mother adds, unhelpfully.

Harcourt has a sudden brainwave. "DS Taylor, would you care to accompany David's mother inside the cafe for a moment - it's still a bit fresh out here - and take her statement in the warm?"

Taylor nods effusively, recognising the decoy, though

not understanding yet why he wants to set it in play.

"Mrs Wright. David and I will be right here so if that sounds good to you?"

Getting out of the cold is immediately more appealing to her than standing around listening to some copper asking her son stupid questions. She takes the bait as he had hoped, leaving the two of them alone now, but still directly outside the window of the cafe.

"Don't worry, we're nearly finished," Harcourt reassures him, although David seems entirely at ease, almost smug in his comfort zone. "So, when you finished your round at Miss Beech's did you stay on this side of the road or cross back over?"

"I crossed straight back over. There's no reason for me to stay over there - the newsagents' shop is on this side and then I stay on this path all the way home."

"Did you look back towards the footpath on your return journey?"

"Yeah, I did."

"Why did you do that?"

The boy glances almost imperceptibly over Harcourt's right shoulder. "I dunno. Fate, I suppose."

"And that's when you saw the foot of the victim poking out of the undergrowth."

"Yeah. Proper freaked me."

"Well, let me freak you a little bit more." He notices a much more obvious look of alarm flash across the boy's face and muscles tensing in his neck. "Given the position of the body some way up the footpath, it would be impossible to see anything from this side of the road. Even on the other side, you have to walk at least four paces along the footpath before the body comes into sight. So, let's start this last bit again, shall we? If you'd crossed the road, as you said, you wouldn't have seen anything untoward. If you'd just walked past the entrance to the footpath on the far side you wouldn't have seen anything either. You walked up the footpath didn't you?"

He gulps and Harcourt watches the tell-tale blush appear. "Just a little way, yeah."

"Sneaky cigarette?"

The boy relaxes and Harcourt senses, for the first time that morning, that the barriers are finally down.

"You mustn't tell Mum. Dad died of lung cancer when I was only eleven years old - just before I went to the Comp. She'd kill me if she found out."

Ordinarily, Harcourt might have laughed at the irony of his last sentence, but he is relieved to be getting to the unadulterated truth at last.

"You will have to make a written statement - as will your mother and the owner of the cafe..."

"Steve."

"Him too. It's all routine stuff. Depending on what you tell me next, there's no need for your mother to know what's in your statement, even though you're technically a minor by law."

"I didn't do anything wrong!"

"I believe you, but I do need to know what happened this morning. You delivered to number 67 and then?"

Harcourt observes the boy taking in a much larger-than-necessary gulp of air before relieving himself of the truth - the whole truth this time - glad to be rid of it.

***

Later, Harcourt and Taylor are sitting in the corner of a small tearoom, part of a farm shop just beyond the nearby village of Cropthorne.

They are the only two in there but, then again, it is only just after nine. Harcourt pours them both strong cups of tea from a ridiculously ornate pot, stirs two sugars into his cup, and sits back in his chair.

"Enlighten me on what the mother had to say, though I suspect it won't take too long!"

She smiles knowingly. "As you suspected, sir, she was just glad to get out of the cold. Didn't say much at all, to be honest. She got a call from her son's mobile at about half-past six..."

"A bit early for a paper round, isn't it? He must have started about an hour earlier than that!"

"It seems that a lot of people around here commute; the cafe owner - Steve Pateman - confirmed this. The newsagent has to be able to meet their demands or they'll just buy a paper at the station."

"Or switch on their apps."

"Exactly."

"Isn't she worried about him being up so early - on school days especially?"

"She never mentioned it but it's something we could ask later if you think it's relevant, sir?"

"Probably not. Sorry Gabby, I interrupted you as usual." He smiles as he says this, knowing how his DS operates.

"Not a problem, sir. She said that David reported seeing the foot of a body on the footpath. Naturally, he was quite shaken up."

Naturally.

"She told him to phone the police on his mobile straightaway, telling them exactly what he'd seen, and that she'd get dressed and be with him as soon as she could."

"And Pateman corroborated this?"

"He didn't see her arrive, just the two of them standing next to the footpath when he got to his cafe at about 6.45."

"Again, really early - especially at this time of year."

"Same reasoning, sir, he gets people calling in for takeaways on their way to work and, in his exact words 'you've got to be there to hoover up the worms.'"

"Sounds like a lovely man, with his finger very much on other people's pulses."

Taylor screws her nose up by way of a response, then continues. "He saw PC Killingsworth arrive, then Dr Graham. He took the drinks over to David and his mum soon after that."

"Wanted to see what was going on up the footpath most likely." Harcourt's face has returned to its unsmiling default. "Did Mrs Wright say whether she'd seen the body for herself - in which case she too would have had to have walked a little way up the path?"

"No. According to her, she was more interested in her son's welfare."

"Yeah, right." His impression of a disaffected teenager is meant to amuse her. It falls short. Probably only because she is carefully reimagining the crime scene, he tries and fails to convince himself.

"But PC Killingsworth's arrival almost certainly killed her curiosity, even if she'd wanted to see for herself. Does the son's story fit with all of this? You felt he was holding back on us?"

"On his mother, not us. He's been up for a sneaky fag and got the fright of his life. Allegedly, he threw the unlighted cigarette away and shot down the path to phone his mum."

"The dangers of smoking eh sir?"

"Can seriously damage your health if you believe everything you see!" He gratefully accepts a second cup and gazes past her to an elderly couple at the counter, extolling the virtues of some carrots they'd recently bought from the farm shop. He hated to disabuse them of the crop being locally grown, remembering his father only just sowing early varieties at about this time of year. Did people still grow their own vegetables, or were their back gardens just designated leisure areas for al fresco dining on imported crops from Tesco?

"It's all we have for now; nothing so far indicates any reason for us not to believe them or that they were involved in what happened to the victim. We'll have to report all this back to DI Barker's team. She can organise written statements, and we'll have to find the cigarette to add some depth to his story. She'll want to take his DNA too to eliminate it from the scene - probably the mother's too, in case she's lying about not heading up the footpath. Heaven forbid!"

"I'll see to it right away, sir."

"Tea first, Sergeant, and no doubt a hefty slice of that walnut cake you have under surveillance wouldn't go amiss?" He enjoys seeing her grin back at him. "And then we wait."

CHAPTER THREE

Daniel can still feel his car keys rubbing against his leg as he strolls across the King Street car park. As so often, he laments the lack of some kind of 'man bag' that would provide the same storage facility as a woman's handbag but without it looking effeminate. With his fingers he gently shifts the clump of splaying metal shafts to the other side of his jeans pocket, taking extra care not to look as though he is enjoying it.

Feeling marginally more comfortable, he crosses the main road, and turns left, then right by the cinema and into Friar Street - one of Worcester's few remaining 'old walkways.' The black and white timbered buildings of Tudor House and Greyfriars lead him back through time as he steps forward into New Street. Formerly Glover Street, it is here that some of the city's oldest buildings present themselves and King Charles House at the top end is of course one of its most iconic. He recalls the plaque telling all comers that it was from that building that Charles II began his escape to France after The Battle of Worcester - one of the bloodiest battles ever to take place on English soil. It further confirmed that though he was saved, the country was lost to Parliamentarian forces.

He spots the familiar bowed and multi-pained windows up ahead but the house immediately to his right is where he is heading to. Black and white gables lean over the road as if they wanted to witness his approach, every bit as much as they did Charles's departure more than three hundred and fifty years earlier.

"Hi. Welcome to Papa's." A bearded man of Mediterranean origin, in perhaps his early 'twenties, greets him pleasantly with a menu larger than a tabloid newspaper, which is entirely appropriate. "Is it a table for one?"

"No. No thanks. I'm meeting a couple of old work colleagues here."

"Ah. Yes. They have arrived already , I think. Please."

They head over towards the window which looks back onto the street and, sure enough, Eddie and Kev are sitting at a table meant for four, each with large mugs of something steaming in front of them.

"Thanks very much." Daniel nods to his Pathfinder. "Could I have a skinny latte please?"

"Of course, sir." The waiter leaves them with their hearty greetings and handshakes.

Daniel spots their jackets on the nearest seat and so takes the remaining place next to the window, facing them both.

Eddie - immediately opposite him - looks much the same as when they met, just under a year ago. Jowly as ever - perhaps a little more so - his eyes are small and his vision limited. His remaining hair is sandy-coloured and combed over for effect rather than to be in any way effective.

Kev is smaller but he too has put on a few pounds. To be fair, it's been quite a bit longer since Daniel has seen him. However, with his thick, dark hair, alert, brown eyes and inevitably tanned skin, he'd recognise him anywhere and at any time.

"Great to see you! It's been far too long – a bit like you: have you got even taller since we last saw you?" Kev smiles to reveal perfect white teeth, apart from the slightly tarnished gold crown which replaced one he lost when he and the editor-in-chief had an unfortunate exchange of words, none of them ultimately finding themselves in print.

"No, but it must be two years ago at least as it was in the office."

"Really? Time really does fly, doesn't it?"

More quickly for you than me, Daniel considers, with more than a trace of bitterness, given that Kev and Eddie both survived a cull that he didn't. He stops himself abruptly. He's been looking forward to meeting them both for a quick coffee and isn't going to let the past get in the way of that - not even here.

His coffee arrives in a tall, cream mug which could also have worked well as a vase.

"Coffee's always good here. Have you been before?"

Daniel is glad to have his reverie interrupted. "Yes. Well at least I've been to a cafe here before, but I don't think it was called Papa's."

"I think they took it on about four years ago." Eddie slurps a mouthful of froth, noisily and quite unselfconsciously. "Lovely on winter mornings; it's like coming straight into the warm front room of someone's house."

"Nash?"

"Who?" The others ask in unison.

"Wasn't it a Nash who had it built? It's the tallest building in Worcester with a timber frame. I do remember that."

"Wow. Not lost that attention to detail then?" This was Kev, still smiling; still being Kev.

"I don't think you ever do, do you?"

"Let's hope not." Eddie concurs but Daniel notices that he is a little uncomfortable. The coffee has certainly woken up the blood vessels in his face.

"It's nice to chat and watch the world go by, isn't it? I suppose this window would once have been a Victorian shopfront?"

"Beats me," Kev was never one for history, Daniel recalls: either remembering it or making it. He and 'Steady Eddie' were pretty similar in that regard.

"So, are you getting much work?"

Daniel isn't sure if Eddie wants the answer to be 'yes' so that he feels less guilty or 'no' so that the burden of guilt is correspondingly increased.

"A steady flow, thankfully." He assumes this update

will land somewhere in the middle.

"Fiction or fact-checking reference stuff?" Eddie asks this while looking across the half-empty room, trying to attract the waiter's attention, which just proves his half-hearted interest in answers - any answers - Daniel might supply.

"Yes, I still have a deal with that publisher in Bristol and she keeps me busy."

"Any good?" Kev nods his order for a second coffee too.

"Mixed, but there are the occasional joys."

"Beats having to battle your way into the office jungle each day though, I'll bet!" Kev smiles as Eddie does.

Daniel doesn't give him - either of them - the satisfaction of a direct reply. Instead, he gulps his coffee and goes on the attack. "How's Linda, Eddie?"

"She's fine; same as ever, you know. Still finding me endless jobs to do."

"A man's work is never done!" Kev grins as only a middle-aged bachelor can.

"I've got a picture here somewhere. It was our Pearl Wedding anniversary in January." He takes a small brown wallet out of the back pocket of his trousers and rifles through a series of credit and other store cards until he finds a small photograph of his beloved at the bottom. He hands it to Daniel.

As he takes it, Daniel feels a surge of energy running through his fingers and almost drops it onto the table or, worse, into his drink. This hasn't happened for a long time. He finds himself gripping the little piece of plastic, looking at the couple grinning benignly out of it, and yet, seeing Linda's head swathed in white bandages. Eddie's wife. No longer smiling. No more happy days to celebrate.

They haven't noticed, thankfully. Kev - presumably up to date with the state of Eddie's marriage - had chosen the moment to smirk about the latest intern and some pun about her 'dexterity.'

"And Charlotte?" Eddie returns the question, taking back the image. "How's she coping with retirement?"

Daniel takes a moment to compose himself, a gulp of smooth coffee is a good disguise for the unseen turmoil in his head. "She's well." He kicks himself mentally - he didn't ask about her health. "She finds it hard, I think. Early retirement seemed such a good idea at the time but, in retrospect ..."

"Hindsight is a wonderful thing!" Kev was always much better at cliche than originality. "I guess she misses the cut and thrust of being a lawyer?"

He ignores the sarcasm. All three of them know that his wife was effectively sidelined for the last few years of her legal career: the equivalent of an active police officer being given a desk job, he has always supposed. "Possibly. I mean she doesn't miss the toxic atmosphere as such, but perversely I often think she misses things to be angry about - people behaving badly, that sort of thing."

"Welcome to our world." Kev has certainly become

even more inane than Daniel remembers but lets him continue, even as Eddie again starts shifting in his seat. "I mean, things did improve when Newsquest came in - when was it, mid-Nineties?"

Both silently nod their agreement, though the question may well have been rhetorical as Kev has barely paused for breath. "The investment was welcome and all that but since production moved up to Oxford ... were the presses still there when ..."

Eddie has had enough. "Of course, they were; they didn't move them out until 2016! What he's trying to say is that the paper seems to be getting less support than ever. You remember when Reed bought Berrows out, what, more than 30 years ago? Has to be! Lots of changes planned and new teams for this and new teams for that. Now it's all about multi-disciplinary tasking and skills shadowing. It's a far cry from' Midlands Best Local Newspaper of the Year 'that's for sure."

"Were you still there then?"

Daniel has had more than enough of Kev's contemporary woes and faux amnesia. "I was. It was seven years ago. I remember that bash. Well, when I say, 'I remember' perhaps that's being a bit economical with the truth."

"You and almost everyone else!" Eddie is happier with this than with their more recent history. He leans forward, conspiratorially. "Some great new relationships were forged that evening, that's for sure, and you didn't read about that in *Worcester News*."

***

Detective Superintendent Rupert Hunter-Wright surveys the plain walls of his office or 'the cell' as he refers to it to close friends and sometimes his wife. He has the obligatory family photograph in a silver frame on a side table and Judith does her best with cut flowers in the vase on the ledge beneath the window, but it is the very essence of 'soulless.'

Luckily, he has his Air Pods in. Ostensibly they are in there so that he can talk quickly with callers on his mobile whilst continuing with the deception of signing important documents, folding them multiple times, or simply filing each unseen in an unexciting choice of Manila folders to one side of an otherwise immaculately empty glass desktop. Usually, the papers and reports contain information about budgets or procedures or, Heaven forbid, budgetary procedures. Occasionally there will be a human-interest story, quite surprisingly concerning real people.

Multiprocessing is the word, not Grease, he chuckles to himself, hearing a sort of deep breathing in each ear as he does so. He swivels around in his comfy office chair. Both his phone and his iPad are hidden in his desk drawer together. The mini receivers are connected via Bluetooth to music playlists on the iPad. He considers that urgent callers will leave messages that he can get back to once his flirtation with origami is at an end. Far better to enjoy the urgent, inspired lyrics of Howard Devoto's early Magazine tracks or pre-Sandinista Clash albums.

'Shot by both sides
On the run to the outside of everything...'

He is mouthing the words, certainly, but not sure if any sound is coming out of his mouth, which might of course be used in evidence.

Miriam bought him these magical earpieces for Christmas, despite them only coming out about a month before that. The wonders of having a wife glued to Amazon he supposes! In truth, the quality can be a bit in and out and the connection can sometimes drop out altogether, but then didn't Joe Strummer often experience the very same thing? He sees the red light on the main telephone console flash. How quaintly retro! How they've still got you on a lead … how annoying.

He reaches into the desk and hits pause on the music app.

"Yes, Judith."

"DI Harcourt is here to see you, sir."

"Splendid. Do send him in, and perhaps another frothy coffee?"

"For the DI also?"

"Oh, I don't think we need to over-extend our hospitality, Judith." He replaces the receiver, blows out his considerable cheeks, and hopes this conversation – or, much more likely, a monologue - will be a quick one.

There is a brief rap on the door before DI Harcourt shuffles apologetically around it and closes it behind him. Why can't the man be more self-confident, befitting his rank? Hunter-Wright waves him onto the not-too-comfortable chair in front of his desk and sits back, rotating slightly, just to show that he is the one with the wheels.

"So. Bring me up to speed, Martin. I'd be equally grateful if we could do this speedily as I have a lot to get through this morning."

Harcourt fiddles with the buttons on his jacket as he always does, then, looking suitably uncomfortable, continues quickly, almost breathlessly (as he always does).

"We've just received the lab report from Dr Graham, sir. She isn't happy with 'accidental death.'

"I don't suppose any of us are." Seeing that Harcourt hasn't got it, he continues the interview quickly. "What precisely are her grounds for doubt?"

Harcourt is pleased to be on the safe ground of data and information. He often finds Hunter-Wright to be a little off-the-wall, whereas he prefers to stay sitting firmly on it.

He refers to his notebook, reading slowly and carefully. "According to Dr Graham, sir, the victim died ultimately of a cardiac arrest."

"I did ask for precision." Hunter-Wright leans back, spinning slightly from left to right, enjoying Harcourt's struggle with the medical language their professional colleagues love to inflict on them. "A heart attack is clear cut is it not? What we need to know is the cause behind the cause, surely?"

"Not technically a heart attack, sir. The two terms are, I'm afraid, not synonymous." Harcourt watches as his superior stops spinning. Not a good sign, usually. Undeterred he continues to explain, with just the right degree of patience, he hopes. "A heart attack is usually caused when blood flow to a certain part of it stops and that part of the muscle begins to die. With a cardiac arrest, the entire heart stops beating."

"Well, many thanks for the biology lesson. Presumably, even with a *cardiac arrest,* there is a reason for it to occur?"

"Yes sir. In this particular case, it seems that electrical activity in the heart went haywire because of incorrect electrical signals from the brain. This itself was caused by a spontaneous subarachnoid haemorrhage, caused by sudden trauma. A bleed on the brain but one where blood has seeped into the cavity between the membrane surrounding the brain and the skull itself, causing immense swelling and sending those chaotic signals to the heart causing arrhythmia and subsequent cardiac arrest.

In this case, Dr Graham believes the electrical activity would have been both severe and sudden i.e. death would have been very quick. CPR might have corrected the arrhythmia, but the brain damage was probably too immense to be repaired."

And they accuse the French of speaking in a foreign language! "You mentioned 'sudden trauma.' Is she certain that this caused the process to start?"

"She is. She points out that there is no evidence of heart disease - congenital or otherwise - and the lungs and liver show no signs of either a life of smoking or alcohol abuse which might, in themselves, have led to heart weakness. Research has shown that cocaine usage can be a contributing cause of arrhythmia but there is absolutely no sign of that or any other kind of substance abuse either. He seems to have been in pretty good health for his age."

"This traumatic event undoubtedly made the difference."

"It undoubtedly did, sir."

Hunter-Wright tilts his head back, searching for – examining - the younger man's likely capacity for sarcasm. "Right. So, taking all the medical mumbo jumbo away, we have to ask whether the trauma was the result of an accident - perhaps he slipped and maybe, just maybe, on this particular occasion, he had a few drinks and couldn't stop himself?"

"It's possible, sir. He had certainly been drinking but we haven't got all the samples back yet."

"Perhaps that's why he was wandering on foot up a dark footpath, late at night; could he have been looking for a place to relieve himself?"

"Yes, sir, but there is a further problem, which Dr Graham highlights. There is severe bruising on the left-hand side of the victim's face which is as yet unaccounted for."

"OK. He encountered someone on that footpath, was punched in the face for some as yet unknown reason, fell backwards and hit his head on the rock."

"Possibly ... sir ... but Dr Graham believes the

contusion - the bruising - to have been caused by a blunt instrument of some kind, the pattern is not consistent with knuckles in a closed fist. The most confusing aspect is that it must have been effectively pushed or pressed into his face with some considerable force somehow. The neck muscles at the rear were ripped quite badly which shows a definite force from the front and wouldn't have been caused just by him falling backwards."

"I assume he couldn't have accidentally walked into a low-lying branch of a tree - you know, in the dark?"

"Dr Graham did consider that, sir, but ruled it out as, again the pattern of bruising is inconsistent with that kind of injury. There was, to be fair, a small splinter of wood in the wound, but certainly not in keeping with him colliding with a tree where we would have expected fragments of bark as well as many more wooden pieces."

Hunter-Wright doesn't do wooden. He frowns and sits forward in his chair. It is a deliberate movement, both meaningful and menacing. "You are erring towards foul play then?"

"We would need to ascertain what happened immediately before the event to better understand the circumstances, sir. We were waiting for the pathologist's report before proceeding and thus committing further police resources, as it were."

"Yes. Quite right. Let's assume that this death is suspicious, even if we do not assume that it is malicious. Let's keep this to ourselves for now and do not let the Press Office get wind of it. Get out there and talk to people, see if we can build a picture of events leading up to his death. If we still think there is any reasonable doubt, we'll launch a full-blown enquiry and go from there."

"Right away, sir."

"'Accidental death' is neat, tidy. Do you know what I mean?"

"Sir."

"Whereas no coroner wants 'unexplained.' Makes us all look as though we haven't done the job properly, and haven't finished it. If this is any way malicious - manslaughter or even premeditated murder - we need motive and we need evidence, fast."

Harcourt is inwardly reeling from so many 'm' words in a single sentence, as though they had been put together to form a memorable marketing slogan. What do they call those other made-up constructions that are used to aid memory? Mnemonics! They're the ones. He almost slaps his forehead with relief. "Should I send SOCOs back in sir, even though we don't yet know if a crime has been committed? I did also wonder whether that wouldn't alarm the villagers; there's a pretty noisy jungle drum operating as it is."

'Jungle drum?' Where does he get these terms from? Biggles? Probably racist too (Hunter-Wright resolves to check that appendix to the Met's *Verbiage* manual he'd received from Hendon a few months ago.

"Locals tend to talk when there's something to talk

about; even more so when there isn't. Let's go ahead and widen the scene of the crime. Any evidence will otherwise be destroyed or so degraded as to be declared invalid. I assume everything is still sealed off?"

"And a presence from South Worcestershire is still at the scene, yes, sir."

Why can't he just say a 'person' or even 'policeman' is still at the scene? 'Presence' is a very impersonal word for such a personal tragedy. Or maybe it's Harcourt's way of absenting himself from any emotional attachment, substituting procedure instead? God, he does need that coffee.

"I can't throw too much money around at this stage. As you correctly point out, there isn't enough yet to suggest a crime as such. It may save us a lot of time later, though, so just the basic stuff for now. Where did you say it was?"

"Castle Upton, sir; on the Fladbury road."

"Never heard of it. Isn't Fladbury where it floods?"

"Among many other places in Worcestershire, sir; especially in 2007, of course."

Why 'of course?' "So, to sum up: we'll keep this in-house for now. Is that understood?"

"It is, yes. And DI Barker, sir"

"Let her bark. Oh, and by the way, DS Flowers's overtime sheets are looking pretty thin. You know my views on police officers who consistently leave on time. Makes me even more suspicious. Do you understand?"

Harcourt does - up to a point.

As he leaves the office, all but clicking his heels and saluting at the door, Hunter-Wright stares long and hard at the now-closed door. It was forever thus, he thinks to himself.

***

DS Ian Flowers looks up from his PC as Harcourt enters the room. They are the only two officers present in a room equipped with six workstations and a large whiteboard to one side. A printer is humming efficiently as it prints out pages of information tucked away in the far corner, as far away from human beings as is physically possible, and in the certain, digital knowledge that very few of the pages, downloaded from the web, will be read by humans.

Harcourt's little 'office' situated to one side is effectively a partitioned-off space. More like a cupboard without natural light, and dominated by a tall, grey filing cabinet that merely emphasises its resident's analogue mind, it says 'static' rather than 'status.' The scratched and battered black anglepoise lamp on his desk is lit, as it always is, but his desk is tidy below piles of paper - many of which the same, much-hated printer has been responsible for.

"Any update for us, sir?" Flowers has moved to the doorway that Harcourt has just barged through, landing heavily in his office chair, and attempting to swing away from the entire office, police force and life in general, as is his usual mental state after a 'briefing' with Hunter-Wright.

Harcourt surveys the younger man's baby face with as much patience as he can currently muster before responding slowly and deliberately. "On a need-to-know basis - which means this team and the Superintendent only - we are treating the events in Castle Upton as suspicious. I'll call a briefing when DS Taylor rejoins us, which should be when?"

Flowers' mind has paused on the word 'suspicious.'

"Flowers?"

Harcourt rarely shouts out loud but the 'targeted response unit' in his head does a similar reboot job, both inside of him and anyone else found to be deep in thought or just plain 'daydreaming.'

"Around mid-day, she hopes, sir; she's in court this morning for the end of the McKennedy case."

Harcourt's mood is not improved by this update - neither the absence of the only other member of his current team, given his DC has been seconded to a county lines drug case up in Droitwich, nor the mention of McKennedy: a nasty, drunken individual from Arbroath with a penchant for regularly visiting and assaulting his ex-wife while leaving his young daughter traumatised by the experience each time. This time he had gone much too far, and the child had lost her mother. Social Services would no doubt be called upon to pick up the pieces but, for the little girl, there would now never be a happy family picture on the front of her personal jigsaw box of life's experiences.

"Right. Could you make sure that you're here when

she gets back, please? In the meantime, I need background on one Andrew Patch from Acton Town in West London."

"Sir."

"Try and dig up anything you can find, however minor or insignificant it may seem to you. Who was he? Where did he work, that sort of information? Wife? Family? What was he doing in Castle Upton, a long way from home and not the time of year for a holiday - especially not mid-week?"

They've come to respect (and rely on to a greater and greater extent, given they're so short-staffed) Flowers's research skills. He manages to regularly shine a torch on the darker sides of what they call the 'invisible web' with some really useful results. Perhaps he should have been a journalist rather than a detective? Harcourt recalls the brief meeting with Kate Shelbourne that morning and resolves to give her a ring. Or is this just fantasy, as the old song goes?

"Do you have anything else to report?"

"Not at present sir. A couple of break-ins at Warndon but nothing that would involve us. Uniformed officers have them under control."

"If there's a third, have a word."

Flowers decides not to mention his superior's poetic skills. "Because it then moves from opportunistic to planned, sir?"

"Correct. Good to see that you haven't forgotten everything you learned in preparation for your sergeant's exam."

"No sir." He learned early that back-handed praise was nearly always there somewhere if you were prepared to follow Harcourt around the houses first.

"Is the departmental filing up to date?"

"Almost, sir."

"Good. Let's make that 'yes, sir' then. It wouldn't hurt to finish it off later and get some overtime on your sheets, especially given that we have no admin help at the moment either."

"Any date set yet for DC Hanrahan's return, sir?"

"Not that I've been told. The last I heard was that the leg was healing as they hoped it would, but you'll still be acting up as sergeant for the immediate future, hence the need to get some more hours in."

"I thought we were stretched on budgets, sir?"

"We are but I would be much more stretched if they found a way for you to disappear too. If they think we don't need you, they'll soon find plenty who do. Either way, money will talk. Not common else. All I'm saying is that it wouldn't hurt for you to stay later sometimes."

But it would hurt. It would hurt both him and those he loves so dearly. He's perfectly happy to play a sergeant's role, but what if they bump him down to constable again as soon as Hanrahan returns? How would he feel then? Would he want to take the actual exam to prove that he was capable of the higher rank he has been assuming for the past six weeks already?

Flowers is sweating a little, which his matted ginger fringe always gives away. Harcourt doesn't usually notice it - or pretends not to - and today is no different.

***

As the sun swings around Worcestershire's southerly boundary Harcourt and Taylor head back to Castle Upton. Even as they return to the scene of death, everything around them seems to be coming back to life and looking forward expectantly now that the coldest days are behind them. Many trees and shrubs are wearing their spring clothes of pink, white and yellow blossom, while spring lambs on the hilly slopes above Pershore are hungrily grazing on fresh green grass, barely looking up as they pass.

They park up in the gravelled car park behind The Beaver public house. Harcourt had noticed it on their previous visit and grimaced inwardly. He doesn't much like pubs (and certainly not 'wine bars'). He has never understood why the pub was supposed to be the central point of the community: noisy, smelly and bearing witness to people's indulgences and innate weaknesses. If this makes him sound like some kind of modern-day temperance leader, it is an unfair comparison as he isn't one to judge and certainly not condemn.

However, his abstinence - or quick exits from police 'celebrations' after major results - has not gone unnoticed, especially back in Cambridgeshire where pub lock-ins were the norm in many of the more isolated villages, whether the police were in attendance at the time or not.

DS Taylor isn't a pub person either, but she has her own reasons for steering clear of such establishments. Loud or leery men, or both, are not her choice of companions and as for bedfellows: not in a million beers. Give her a nice meal in a restaurant any day.

They head into the bar area and Harcourt bristles at the faux historical references designed not to enchant but to ensnare visiting tourists. The rather rotund barman busies himself with trays of glasses, arranging them just so before eventually deciding they might be worth speaking to.

"What can I get you?" His tone is more businesslike than brusque but does nothing to lighten Harcourt's mood. They can both smell the stale beer on his scruffy green cardigan.

He also elected to do away with any undeserved pleasantries. "My name is Detective Inspector Harcourt, West Mercia Police. This is Detective Sergeant Taylor. Could you tell me your name please?"

"Mike. Mike Grady." Some of the self-confidence has left him - possibly more to do with him having his routine interrupted, possibly not.

"And do you work here full-time?" Now he sounds like the Duke of Edinburgh.

"I do."

Taylor takes it from there, softly spoken but not taking her eyes off her subject for a second. "Who else works here, sir?"

"Just Janice and I at the moment. The owner, Mr Woodbridge, is away in Spain for a few days."

"Nice!"

"He's looking to buy a bar over there, should be back at the weekend."

"And were you and Janice serving on the evening of Wednesday 20th March?"

"I was but Jan - Janice - went up at about nine. There wasn't much trade and she'd been up early that day."

"Why was that?"

"Lack of customers or her being up early?"

"Let's start with 'Jan' being up early" Taylor's tone hasn't changed at all.

"We had an event the day before; a wake for a lady who used to work here. There was still a lot of clearing up to do."

"She lives above the pub?"

"She does now. Yes. I have a flat on Broughton Street. It's just a five-minute walk away."

"So, you were on your own in here until closing time?"

"As well as a few customers of course."

Harcourt isn't sure if the man is being sarcastic, superior or just self-important but the noticeable tightening of the muscles on his face compels Taylor to continue a little more quickly.

"Regulars were they, the customers?"

"We don't get a lot of visitors in March ..." The barman breaks off suddenly and appears to grasp the meaning of death if not life.

"Mr Grady?"

He leans forward on the bar, his voice lower now – almost conspiratorial. "Of course, we did have a guest staying here: Mr Patch. He arrived the day before. By train. From London he said. Naturally, we're all very shocked by what happened."

Harcourt steps in, sensing a chink in the man's pompous armour and not wishing to be seen as one of the plotters of another man's downfall. "About what happened? Can you tell us what you mean by that please?"

"The accident - on the woodland footpath."

Harcourt quickly reasons that although neither the police nor (at least to the best of his knowledge) the press have released any details about the incident thus far, it is best to continue with the general view at large that it had been an accident. He nods to Grady to continue.

"It was all over the village yesterday. Terrible. He was here that evening celebrating a birthday. I can't believe something like that would happen here."

"Worse things have occurred in this village," Harcourt indicates the 'Olde Legend' plaque on the far wall.

"I don't believe anything can be worse than death," Grady replies calmly, "Especially if you don't believe in life beyond it."

Taylor takes up the reins again. "How do you know the unfortunate person was Mr Patch, sir?"

"Steve Pateman saw the colour of the shirt and trousers and told Saint Grace... Grace Beech; it's her birthday today. 50 she is. Mr Patch was here to celebrate it on Wednesday with her as he said he had to get back for some weekend away."

Taylor knows how much this will irritate the DI. She mentally notes that a word with Mr Pateman is needed sooner rather than later. Village gossip is something they can rarely eliminate, but they can control its spread, either through communicating the facts or reminding the communicators to mind their own business.

"Why did you call her Saint Grace?"

"It's just a name."

"So is Grace?" Taylor can hear the anger rising in her voice and tries to temper it. "Why the 'Saint' bit?"

"Just the way she is I suppose. Always wears black stuff. They've called her that ever since I've been here. She is a bit worthy. You know, 'holier than thou.' Is that how it goes? I'm not one for church myself."

She ignores his clumsy attempt at humour. Even if he was standing in front of her as a stand-up comedian, delivering a series of excellent one-liners, she still wouldn't find it funny. It is the man, not the material.

"And where was Mr Patch going back to? Did he say?"

"Not as such but he was checking the train times to Paddington when I served him at breakfast that morning."

Observant or just nosy? Harcourt hasn't decided yet. "Can you tell us who else was in here that evening?"

"Mr Patch and Grace shared a table on the far side with Stuart Fairhurst and his wife Lisa."

"Any other customers whose names you can remember?"

"Stuart's father, Frank, came in at about 9.30. Johno and Pete from the farm were in, and Duncan of course."

"Duncan?"

"Duncan Harewood. He comes in every evening and sits by the window next to the door; people joke it's in case he needs to make a quick exit."

"Did you notice anything out of the ordinary at all during the evening," Taylor isn't keen to get stuck on village tittle-tattle - that could be investigated, and likely dismissed as inadmissible, later.

"Frank did seem pretty uptight, but that wasn't unusual when he'd been drinking too much; he'd been in most of the afternoon too."

"What was he upset about?"

"I've no idea but it was most likely something to do with Stuart. They disagree a lot on how things should be done ... there was a bit of shouting, that's all."

"What time was this - roughly?"

"Just before eleven, I suppose it would have been. Mr Patch left shortly afterwards. Well, we were about to close. We don't go in for all-night licensing here; not like in some places."

"Had anyone else left before him, can you remember?"

Grady lifts his head slightly upwards as if in deep thought but then shakes his head before facing Harcourt again and looking him straight in the eyes. "I don't think so... there is something that's nagging away at me though. You know how it is when you recognise someone but just can't quite place them; or when a word is on the tip of your tongue?"

"Or immediately after Mr Patch left the pub?" Taylor probes.

"Grace and the Fairhursts must have left shortly afterwards as I cleared their table. I do remember that. Tomato sauce all over the serviettes."

"Thank you, Mr Grady. You've been most helpful." Harcourt hands him his card. "I'm afraid we're going to need you to provide a written statement of everything you've told us this afternoon. If you 'phone this number my sergeant will arrange everything. It's just for our enquiries."

For the first time, Grady seems flustered, clearly not happy with the thought of leaving his little empire. "Is that strictly necessary? I mean it was an accident, wasn't it? You don't think anyone would have hurt him deliberately. This is Castle Upton!"

"I'm aware of that, sir, and, yes, it is necessary."

They leave Grady looking much less self-assured than when they had entered. The afternoon is cool but refreshing after the low beams and dark interior of the pub.

"Shall we go and see Pateman first, sir?"

"Absolutely. It will be interesting to see whether Grady has tipped him off by the time we get there."

"What did you think of Grady's account?"

"As usual, I'm trying to keep an open mind, but I did notice how everything on his side of the bar was meticulous in its placement. Even the piles of beer mats were exactly the right way round."

"How do you know that?"

"They had pictures of local scenes on them - Broadway, Boughton on the Water, Stow-on-the-Wold. Not one of them was upside down or on its side. The coffee spoons by the espresso machine were all lined up neatly; each one the right way round and placed with the same space between them. That's not normal, is it? It's like something the catering staff at Buckingham Palace would take time to measure before an important banquet. It might just be the way his mind works but if he is that tidy - and we know he may well be nosy too - he'll eventually remember everything about the evening in minute detail."

"You think he's holding something back?"

"As I say, I have an open mind at this stage."

***

"Apparently, there was some kind of incident in Castle Upton last night."

Daniel is skim-reading his next book, appalled at the grammatical short-cuts in favour of the authentic 'voice' of the main protagonist. Before each commission, he reads through a manuscript first, albeit briefly, allowing his brain to fill in the gaps between words his trained eye will later scrutinise much more closely.

"When you say 'apparently' do you mean it may or may not have happened - as in seemingly or allegedly - or that it has been seen and understood to have happened by someone you know?"

"It's a good job you're unlikely to ever wear a virtual reality headset," Charlotte replies crossly. "I read it in the Evesham News just now."

"Ah well, then it is apparent and must be true!"

"A middle-aged man was found on a footpath."

"Not that unlikely in this age that we live in ..."

"More so given that he was dead."

"What happened?" He understands that his reading will be on pause until she has finished reading to him.

"They're not sure yet. The police were called but

haven't issued any statements."

"It could just have been natural causes then?"

"Just 'natural causes?' A man has died and all you can do is reduce his death to three insensitive words - small ones at that, which is quite surprising for you."

He knows that acerbity is often synonymous with the early skirmishes of a fully-blown argument these days, or at least that seems to be the pattern of how things develop.

"I'm not being insensitive." He tries to dampen things down quickly and hopefully effectively. "When I said 'just' I suppose I was relieved that there had been no foul play."

"But they don't know that yet. This is just saying his death is as yet unexplained."

The phone shrieks from the kitchen counter. Charlotte jumps up as if it was a starter gun.

She speaks quickly into the receiver, preventing the receiver from being able to tell her what it is all about. Daniel looks up but she turns her back on him, giving him no clues as to who it might be or why they might have phoned.

He shrugs his shoulders and picks up the newspaper, quickly finding the article and the name of the journalist. Amid all the background noise he pictures a scene just down the hill from them, but it is a scene from much longer ago that he vaguely remembers.

***

"You say you arrived at the cafe at about half past six?" Taylor is sitting on an uncomfortable wooden chair at the back of 'The Cotswold Kettle.'

"Quarter to seven, as I told the Plod."

"That's quite precise." Harcourt stands over him, not trusting the chair either.

"Not really, gov. I always glance at the clock on the wall there when I get in. I need to be ready to rock n' roll by seven at the latest and if I get here much later, I have to hang around while things come to the boil. Story of my life!"

Harcourt disliked Steve Pateman from the moment he called him 'gov.' He isn't sure if it's just the way he speaks or whether there is some intended slight that the burly, shaven-headed man sitting before them finds amusing. He doesn't like his earring either.

"And you saw Mrs Wright and her son further down the street?"

"I was just checking the sugars on each table and, yeah, you get a good view from the front windows."

"And there were just the two of them?"

"Sugars or people?" He beams at the deadpan faces on the other side of the table.

Taylor can feel her boss bristle, even as she drives down her feelings of contempt for this loathsome man. "Just Mrs Wright and David ... nobody else around."

"Well, there may well have been other people around,

yeah, but I wasn't looking for them. I'm no detective, Sergeant. I just happened to notice David and his mum."

"Then, despite the apparent urgency to get the cafe ready for opening, you managed to find time to take drinks down to them?" Harcourt hates to see other people - suspects, witnesses or otherwise - disrespecting his colleague; perhaps something deeper than that.

"It only took a couple of minutes."

"But still time to walk up the footpath to see for yourself what David had called his Mum for?"

"I just glanced over, right."

"But I was led to believe that your priority was to hoover up the worms?"

Harcourt uses his words carefully.

"What? Oh, I see. Yeah, well if I'm not on the case somebody else soon will be. They've put a vending machine on one of the railway platforms at Evesham as it is. Thin end of the wedge, right? There'll be a Costa or Nero there next."

"But you put poking your nose in ahead of profit?" Harcourt can see that Pateman is becoming edgy, moving unnecessarily on his chair now, whereas previously his arrogance seemed to have glued him to it.

"Listen. I was just being a Good Samaritan on a cold morning, right!"

"You recognised the man lying dead on the footpath though?" Taylor doesn't do religious parables.

"Only because he wasn't from around here."

"That seems a bit counterintuitive."

"He was not local." Pateman is speaking very slowly and deliberately as though to a small child. "I know pretty much everyone in this dump; incomers aren't difficult to spot. Besides he was in here the day before. Got a takeaway."

"What time was that ... precisely."

"I don't know exactly but quite early - about nine-thirty?"

"Did you see where he went - assuming you were at your vantage point by the window?"

"I do have a business to run, you know!"

"But everyone else's business is somehow more interesting?"

"You know, I don't like your tone; I'm giving up my time to talk to you as a responsible citizen, right."

"Right. So how did you know the victim's name?"

"He told me his name was Andrew."

"What. He came in - a total stranger - and said 'Hi. My name's Andrew, but you can call me Andy. Coffee to take away please.'"

"We talked a bit about the village. He said he was born here and seemed to be interested in the people who live here now, yeah. I told him my name and said he was welcome to pop in any time if he wanted a chat. Nice guy."

"Ok. But he didn't tell you his surname in a friendly, chatty kind of way? The one you then blabbed about to anyone who wanted to know, and presumably anyone who didn't."

"Mike from the pub came in soon after you lot had left. I described the dude to him, and he told me his full name, right? Said he'd stayed there the night before. Besides, I wasn't aware that free speech ended with the unexplained. Quite the opposite I'd have thought."

"How long have you lived in the village, sir" Taylor is keen to move on.

"Just over eight years."

"What brought you here in the first place?"

"In the first place? I was in a relationship and my partner was from around here. The opportunity for the cafe came along and I never left."

"You refer to your partner in the past tense?" Harcourt is also bored.

"It didn't work out."

"She moved away and yet you stayed?" Taylor is vaguely interested.

"I stayed and he moved out, yes."

Now they are both interested and not just vaguely.

CHAPTER FOUR

He loves these walks with his daughter, though, with just a couple of months to go before her GCSEs, he knows how precious her time is - much more than it is to him or Charlotte.

"It must be clear today: you can see the folly up on Bredon Hill!"

They both stop to look up and, sure enough, there it is, standing squarely against the pale blue skyline. Known locally as *Parson's Folly* it had been built for an MP of the same name in the mid-eighteenth century. This much, they had found out for themselves.

"Remember when we went up there to see the Iron Age fort?"

"I remember being so glad to get to the top I'd have been happy to see anything, even your Gran!" He laughs out loud. She smiles and then joins in happily.

"Great views though!"

"They were. Did Mum come with us that day?"

"No, just you and me. The dream team ..."

"She does love you, Claire." He very often feels the need to say the words his wife has rarely been able to articulate, or at least express openly.

"I know she does." Her voice trails off as she relives a scene from earlier that day.

"Mum wants the best for you as well, or at least the best that you can be. We both do and that's all we've ever asked of you."

"So why does she make it so difficult? All I was saying was that I needed some fresh air. She shouldn't jump to conclusions and go off on one; especially not as an ex-lawyer."

"She's retired now," he corrects, not wanting to think his wife was somehow thrown out of the profession for doing something bad. He'd proofread a 'crime fiction' book the previous Christmas where the author continuously got the nuances of 'former' and 'ex' mixed up (very annoyingly so). "It makes her a bit reflective I think of what she had to do to get to the top of her field."

"Is that why she retired early?" She knows it sounds mean and instantly regrets it.

He hears it too, but continues in the same, friendly tone. "There were lots of reasons behind it but one of them was undoubtedly that things had become pretty toxic at work. She doesn't doubt that you've been revising round the clock though, particularly since the mocks, although I did hear the music quite late last night ..."

She jerks her head around at him before just as quickly relaxing as she sees he is just joking. Trying to lighten the mood as he has always done.

"I do want to do well but sometimes I need a break,

that's all."

"I know."

"I just don't understand why she feels the need to shout when she's worked so closely with people all her life. For a 'people person' why has she always felt the need to raise her voice to get her message across?"

"I'm not sure it was always like that, though, obviously, I was working late much of the time – most likely one of the reasons why it took so long for you to come along. We were both in our early forties by then!"

"Worth waiting for though..." She doesn't phrase it as a question; doesn't need an answer and they both know it.

"Worth every minute and even more so now. Going back to Mum, she was always quite forceful, but then you have to be in that line of work; she had to deal with people far more difficult and devious than her. One thing Mum isn't is devious. Maybe that just got to her in the end."

"I suppose I'm just quieter; gentle. More like you."

"It takes all sorts to make a liquorice."

They both laugh again - it's a long-standing joke from a Christmas morning when she was just a small child - but not for long. She quickly becomes serious again.

"Do you still miss the newspaper?"

"I do but not just the work. Being part of a team makes you feel part of something much bigger and you feel, I don't know, more alive. When I'm alone with a book I can fall into it and believe I'm part of a process again. That bit's fine. It's when I stop to make a coffee or walk around to get away from the screen that I appreciate how alone I am now. It's great to be able to use all of these digital platforms like you all do, but there's no real substitute for a chat is there? I mean a proper talk with someone, not messaging."

"There's FaceTime - a lot of the people at school use that I think."

"FaceTime is pretty good, and you can also blame the signal whenever you've had enough! Just raising your eyebrows at something someone's said though, or instinctively understanding what the groans or sighs of relief - or those sudden intakes of breath - all around you mean. Those signs and sounds can only be human. They're what I miss."

"At least you're still surrounded by words. Mum used to tell me they were your real true love when I was younger."

"I remember never being allowed to join in your games of Scrabble."

"We played for hours in the evenings when you were at work. Mum often used to say: 'If Dad was here, he'd know how to use these useless letters.' She was always so proud of that."

"She had to put up with a lot you know, but never complained about it. She practically brought you up on her own."

"Don't say that! You were always around. Besides, you

had to work. Mum couldn't have afforded everything on her own, could she?"

"She couldn't. But she often worked late too. When she came home from work, she probably just wanted someone to talk to - to offload to - especially when you were very little and tucked in upstairs. I often didn't get back until two in the morning."

"I remember that time when Grandad Malcolm came to stay with us and had to look after me on my own. Mum was at some do in Birmingham and you were at work."

"I dread to think what might be coming next!"

"Mum had left him instructions on how to cook baked beans on toast for tea."

"Tough gig, that one!"

She giggles. "He got a telephone call from Gran. She was worried about the sky falling in."

"Not like her at all then?"

"Shh. Listen. He could hear the thunderstorm in the background! We called her Henny Penny after that – it was our secret name for her. He'd completely forgotten about the beans though; they'd stuck to the saucepan and we had to throw it out. We put it in the bin next door. He made me promise to tell Mum that I had no idea where it had gone or what had happened to it. At least she was a lot more understanding back then?"

"She's just readjusting. I suppose both of us are. Her time of life might still be a factor. You know ..."

Claire laughs and raises her hands. "It's Ok Dad. I get it and no doubt will go through it all myself. Hopefully, it won't last so long. She should be through all that by now though, shouldn't she?"

"Nobody truly knows. Mood swings can last for years, apparently, and I can't believe it hasn't been a factor. Anyway, in a couple of years, you'll be off to Uni and rid of us."

She puts her arm through his and pulls him close. "Don't ever say that, Dad. Leaving you for a few weeks at a time is going to be bad enough as it is. Who is going to be there to listen to you?"

"Your mum listens. She just doesn't hear very often!"

They reach the crossroads with Rous Lench and head left.

"What did you say 'Lench' stood for again?"

"A good job you're not doing Geography!"

"Or would that be History?"

They laugh as he explains. "There are six Lench villages in total. The word is a variation of the Anglo-Saxon word 'linch.' It means 'rising ground' and even today it describes well these hills we always seem to be at the bottom of."

"But our little hamlet - Wood Lench - is the smallest?"

"It is. Ab Lench is pretty small as well; don't ever describe it as Abbot's Lench though. The village has never been called that, despite what the road signs might tell you."

"Not always a good plan to follow the signs then!"

"Depends on where they're leading you to, I suppose... so, are we going to walk over to Church Lench before it gets dark, or not?"

***

Harcourt has not enjoyed a night of good quality sleep. He knows this not because Debbie tells him crossly that he has kept her up 'all night' but because his neck muscles are still tight, the tautness of the previous day not departing with a decent amount of relaxing sleep. The tiredness behind his eyes never really goes away but his neck and sometimes back muscles have always been reliable indicators that a long day, physically and mentally, lies ahead.

Flowers's voice comes on the phone as he drives into the station after just the three mugs of tea.

"DS Hollyoak from the Met came back to us, sir."

"About Patch?"

"Yes, sir. They've been round to his flat in Acton Town."

"Where's that?"

"West London, sir. Our side of Chiswick and close to the North Circular Road. No sign of anything untoward so no reason to enter at this stage. He isn't known to them or appearing on any local police files, just as the main police computer threw up blanks."

"Do we know who his next of kin is yet?"

"No family to speak of. There was a wife - Vivienne - but they were divorced in December 2005. She was accused of adultery and had moved out of the family home about 18 months beforehand. She now lives in Hammersmith which isn't a million miles away from Patch's home. She's been informed."

"How did she take it, did they say?"

"A bit feisty at first. Said something to the effect of 'That's probably the most exciting thing that's ever happened to Andrew' but then she seemed genuinely upset about it. Family Liaison are in touch and they're going back to see if they can get more background unless you want me to go up?"

"I think you should, being careful to 'assist' rather than tread on anyone's toes. We do need to know more about him and what he was doing here."

"I can help you a little bit there, sir, piecing together what I've managed to pull out so far."

Harcourt pulls up to a junction, waits and then turns left. He is still waiting for his DS to continue. What does he want him to say: 'No, I'm not interested. How was your evening? Did you do anything nice?'

"Please do go ahead, Ian." He tries to hide his growing impatience amid the caffeine failing to kick in yet.

"His father, Peter, owned the garage in Castle Upton. It's on the High Street. The only one in the village. I expect you passed it yesterday, sir. Anyway, when

Andrew was eight years old the family moved away, first to Bromsgrove and then Leicester. His father re-trained as a postman before retiring to a small village near Melton Mowbray. He and Andrew's mother died there within six months of each other two years ago."

"OK. And what did Andrew do - what was his occupation I mean?"

"He went to university in Nottingham and trained as an accountant. Moved down to London and worked for Bendell's in the City. A pretty prestigious firm that one, sir; he must have done well to get in there."

"That's useful to know. Was he still working for that firm?"

"No, sir, he left them in 2008 and moved to a company called Collier and Co which is based in Bayswater. They specialise in auditing small business accounts."

"And small fry after working for one of the big City firms?"

"That's my impression too, sir."

"Interesting. Do you have anything else at this stage?"

"Only that the garage was sold to a local farmer called Frank Fairhurst who still lives in the village. His son lives there too."

'Both of whom spent the evening - or at least part of it - with Andrew Patch just before he died' thinks Harcourt before accelerating and overtaking a learner driver. He has long ago learned not to believe in coincidences.

***

Daniel hears the distant tell-tale 'ping' of a text message coming in. He always leaves his mobile phone in the kitchen so as not to interrupt his thought process (even with the sound lowered and his phone upside down on the desk he is working at, the text alerts seem determined to do their job and provide little flashes of light against the dark wood).

Only it isn't his phone this time, it's Charlotte's. She is upstairs and the shower is still on full pelt as it has been for at least the last ten minutes. Tom – Charlotte's ancient ginger cat who took up residence by the cooker when he was just a kitten – is sitting up in his basket, his eyes still full of sleep but his ears upright; as alert as he will ever be now. Curiosity has also been seriously lacking in the book Daniel is still proofreading, especially now that the plane has landed, so he finds himself gently tapping the screen. He stiffens at the message in tiny black type overlaying her Home Screen image of the happy three of them on a long-ago woodland walk:

'Really enjoyed our session and looking forward to next week.'

***

Harcourt and Taylor draw up outside the Fairhurst family bungalow in Castle Upton. Situated in a quiet cul-de-sac just off of the High Street, it has the look of a 1960s build - all light brick and white panelling - as do the other two houses completing a small (or 'exclusive' in the meaningless parlance of vacuous estate agents up and down the country) triangular development.

A small, slim woman dressed in a cream jumper and neat, beige slacks answers the doorbell. "Hello. May I help you?" She is wary but not unfriendly.

Taylor takes in the lines on her face and tied-back grey hair and estimates her age as late sixties or early seventies. "Mrs Fairhurst? DI Harcourt and DS Taylor. We are making some enquiries in the village and would value a few moments of your time. May we come in please?"

"Of course. Come through."

The bungalow is warm and comfortable but basic. Harcourt also notices the lack of pictures or photographs in the hallway or corridor walls, or in the cold, sober living room they are quickly led through.

They arrive at a large room at the back of the property which serves as a kitchen/diner with double doors leading to decking and a garden beyond. To the right of the main kitchen and eating zone lies a subtly separate area with a comfy brown sofa and fitted bookcases filled to the ceiling with books. There is a further large picture window here too which also looks straight out onto the garden.

The transformation from front to rear is astonishing. Full of light, the room is at once alive - with lush green ferns and spiky cacti adorning shelves otherwise filled with pans and canisters of sugar or jars of spices. It gives the illusion of far more space than there is, with the beautiful garden beyond promising so much colour and quite seamlessly appearing to become part of the internal space. The doors are open and a gentle breeze - cool but not cold - wafts in from time to time.

They sit at a gnarled wooden table on wooden chairs that are much more comfortable than they look like they're going to be.

Taylor is genuinely impressed, already wondering whether an extension into her pocket backyard might deliver a similar effect one day. It does face towards the southwest after all. "This is a beautiful room, Mrs Fairhurst."

"Annabel, please. Thank you. Yes, this is very much my space. We had a rambling old farmhouse before we moved here and I wanted to bring the feeling of that but, of course, in a much more modern setting. This table, for example, was cut down from a big old table we had there."

"The garden is lovely too!"

"Thank you again." She blushes slightly. "If I'm not reading in here I'm usually to be found out there somewhere. There's nothing like being outdoors in the fresh air is there; less alone somehow?"

"There certainly isn't," Harcourt affirms, with an unforced smile on his face. "How long have you lived here?"

'It must be nearly forty years now. The house was quite new still but this bit out here was just laid to lawn, so it's changed quite a bit over the years, even if we haven't: just got older!"

Her last comment is surely meant as a joke, but Harcourt notes that it doesn't reach her eyes that seem sad. He moves the conversation on. "Is your husband around by any chance?"

"He's with Stuart - our son - this morning. Down at the garage. We own it but Stuart pretty much runs everything. Frank, my husband, often goes down to 'help' but I think he just gets in the way more often than not." She glances at Taylor as if expecting to find some kind of womanly appreciation of such an observation but finds none.

"That's fine," Harcourt continues. "We'll pop down there afterwards."

"He isn't in any kind of trouble, is he?"

"Not at all. We're just making general enquiries at this time."

"Is it about the poor chap who was found on the footpath?"

"It is, yes."

"Terrible. Lisa - my daughter-in-law - told me that he'd only been in the village for a few days."

"He used to live in the village, though. Taylor takes up the conversation. "Many years ago. You might remember him. His family owned the garage before you took it on?"

"Yes, Lisa said. I do remember him: Andrew. A group of them used to play out in the fields together, as children do. Or did then!"

"He was friends with your son I believe?"

"Yes. Younger than Stuart though. I don't think he was in the same class at infant school. His family moved away before they all went off to De Montfort. Old Mrs Rogers would know. She still lives in the village, but she must be in her eighties now. She taught them all. A bit of an institution you might say!"

"And Andrew's parents: do you remember much about them?"

"Not really. Frank handled most of it - the purchase, solicitors and so on. It was quite a straightforward transaction. The Patchs were keen to sell and didn't quibble much over the price as I remember. He wasn't well. Something to do with his nerves. I think they wanted to make a fresh start somewhere else. I don't remember Mrs Patch at all I'm afraid, but I hope it worked out for them."

"As far as we know, it did," Harcourt offers, gently, sensing that there is much more to this than she is prepared to discuss at this stage. "They have both sadly passed away now, so we'll probably never really know."

"A mercy they weren't alive to see this happen to their son, I suppose."

"Indeed. You say you owned a farm previously. Was that local to here?"

"It was, out on the Pinvin road. It had been in Frank's family for generations. He was much more concerned about that side of things. It was a difficult time for all of us."

Harcourt opts to dig more deeply into this once they have more information. "And on Wednesday evening, when the incident occurred with Mr Patch, Frank was in the pub - The Beaver?"

"Without a doubt!" She sniffs and flicks her head dismissively. "It's been far more of a home to him than this building has. Quite surprising really when you consider he feels claustrophobic just about everywhere else."

"He is a regular drinker?" Taylor adopts a deliberately neutral, non-judgmental tone.

"Far too much and it will certainly kill him one day." There is distaste rather than any element of distress in Annabel Fairhurst's voice as she continues, "As I say, he doesn't generally like to be indoors. It's unnatural to him, I suppose, having spent pretty much all of his life outside in the fields or even serving on the pumps when we first bought the garage. Drinking helps him to deal with being 'hemmed in' as he puts it. I think it probably helps him to come to terms with much else besides."

They wait patiently for a further explanation, but none arrives. Harcourt spots a squirrel in the far corner of the garden, nibbling at something and listening to their every word. No doubt it had been wary of him first.

He turns back to their hostess who is now examining the rough, calloused fingers in her lap. "Was Frank aware that Andrew had returned to the village?"

"Oh yes. They were all in there, I believe. That's why

Andrew had come back here, you see: for Grace Beech's birthday party. She turned 50 yesterday."

"So Frank was invited to that?"

"I very much doubt it, Inspector. People don't tend to like Frank very much."

***

"No love lost there, sir!"

Harcourt and Taylor have left the car outside the bungalow and are now walking back down the High Street.

"I've encountered many women who are effectively living their lives alone, even though they've been married for years. She's undoubtedly one of them. She was holding back on the farm sale as well."

"Must have been traumatic if it was the family business. Perhaps that's why he turned to drink?"

Harcourt nods his head "Could be. Unlike Patch's parents who sold their business and looked for a new life elsewhere rather than one at the bottom of a glass."

"Lovely house though."

"It was, is. It felt like the back of that house was her creating a nice little world of her own, didn't it? Maybe that's as far as she can get without escaping altogether. Not so different from drinking when you think about it like that."

***

Duncan Harewood sees them approaching, long

before they see him. He's only part-time on the pumps - all they said they could afford at the time, and times haven't changed that much.

Old man Fairhurst has been quite off with him these last couple of days, but Stuart has been OK. No great conversationalists either of them, but they'd clubbed together for the do in the pub which Duncan could never have afforded himself. He was grateful, although he didn't have much choice in the matter. Does that amount to gratitude then or just plain relief that it is all over?

He bends away, out of sight. He's had to improvise of course, for now. He'd soon be sorted though, as they all would, and things would get back to normal. Seeing Andrew's body lying there brought back so many thoughts from the past. Like then, though, he'd let things lie. There wasn't anything more he could do.

***

Ian Flowers exits Acton Town's tube station quickly, not wanting to draw attention to himself. Everyone around him seems to be, if not exactly in a hurry, walking deliberately, heads down, knowing exactly where they're going. Momentarily, Flowers envies them as he moves to one side and surreptitiously scans the section of map DS Hollyoak has printed out for him, along with a key to Patch's flat.

He is standing on Gunnersbury Lane which either leads to the North Circular in one direction or the centre of Acton in the other. He spies Bollo Lane off to his right and is soon in the whitewashed Art Deco building so recently inhabited by their victim. Taking the ancient lift, complete with a second sliding door made up of black iron grilles, he arrives on the fifth floor and enters the flat, arriving directly into a bright, tidy living room.

The first thing he notices isn't a thing at all - it is precisely the lack of 'things.' The white walls are clean and had probably been re-painted at most only two years previously, but nothing hangs on any of them. On a plain, non-patterned light grey carpet a cream two-seater sofa sits opposite its single sibling with just a small glass coffee table separating them. Again, no pictures nor books, pens, paper or any other kind of paraphernalia.

A black TV of average size and age watches his every move from its stand in the corner of the room. There appears to be no radio, CD player or streaming devices. Nothing to generate white noise. Just silence.

Similar carpets appear in the two bedrooms - one much smaller than the other and containing only a single bed and chest of drawers. In the main bedroom, a black portable TV is perched on a white, wooden cabinet beside the bed. Its partner on the other side of the bed hosts only a black reading lamp. There are no pyjamas in the bed nor dirty clothes strewn across the floor. There are none in the small, grey laundry basket either; no slippers or glasses cases on the cabinets. Not only is there no colour contrast as such, but there is also no colour out of place.

Though not a crime scene, Flowers has donned white plastic gloves and looks through the drawers of each cabinet. He isn't sure what he's expecting to find but, in the event, he finds nothing at all. Even in a hotel room, he'd have found a Bible!

'Is man alone lonely?
The corners of his world seem stark.
Does the locked door only
Hold the key to every start?'

Was that one of Rob's? He'd have to ask him when he got home.

The cabinet in the bathroom contains only basic toiletries and is, like the rest of the house, clean and tidy. The white face cloth hanging beneath the sink is dry, but it gives off no stale smell suggesting even semi-recent use. The white towels are not exactly fragrant, but neither are they marked or stained.

The kitchen is neat and purposeful: chrome between white tiles, and a small breakfast bar in the corner with, naturally, a single white stool below. The fridge contains a single tub of low-fat margarine and a carton of long-life cream. No milk going off or excess food on a plate to be eaten later or, more likely, thrown in a bin. Apart from a single upturned glass on the inbuilt drying rack, there are no real signs of human life. Flowers pauses to remind himself of the irony of that comment before entering the living room once more. He stands by the large window looking east towards the huge sprawl of mismatched buildings making up that (and every other) side of the capital.

Beyond the double-glazing tiny spots of white light are moving silently across the dirty grey clouds to his left drawing his attention, puzzling him. They look like snowflakes caught in winter sunshine but are travelling diagonally rather than vertically. As one of them gets nearer to him, filling more of his field of vision, he can see now that these are aircraft heading into what must be Heathrow Airport. Relentlessly they traverse the morning sky, delivering yet more thousands of visitors or residents into the metropolis, just as he - a mere speck himself - had been transported by train earlier. Where do they all go to, he wonders, as stargazers might once have wondered about the planets each time the sun turned away from them.

Quickly correcting himself, he turns to look back into the room. This hadn't been in any way an extensive search; there was still no hard evidence that foul play had been the cause of Andrew Patch's death anyway. However, it felt as if he was standing in a modern, minimalist white space, but without the latest technology or gadgets to complete the illusion: like walking into Apple with no core.

He takes the Piccadilly Line once again for the short run up to Hammersmith. It has started to rain but few people in his carriage seem to notice; either engrossed in paperbacks, paid-for newspapers (why on earth wouldn't they take out a digital subscription, like he did?) or listening to music or mindfulness sessions on headphones.

The train stops at Turnham Green - a break from the weekday tradition if the tube map opposite is telling him the truth - and a middle-aged man with bleached blonde hair streaming from a red, bulbous head jumps on at the last minute. Dressed in a crumpled tweed jacket and sodden brown corduroy trousers, he initially struggles to release his frayed orange backpack from the closing door. Then, to nobody in particular, announces, "It's rough out there today! I'm just going up top." Nobody else appears to take the slightest notice of him, but Flowers considers that their unfortunate fellow passenger believes he has just caught a bus.

A few minutes later he is standing outside another tower block on a similarly quiet road near the river. There the comparisons end. Though much newer - possibly Seventies - there are more than double the number of storeys of Patch's block. This building's concrete walls hold little charm and neither does Vivienne Stanhope when he knocks on her (mercifully as the only lift seems to be malfunctioning) second-floor door.

Scruffy and overweight, her dirty blonde hair is platted around the side of her head making it seem as though an old pastry crust is clinging to the side of her face. She is dressed in a faded fawn tracksuit which most likely hasn't seen much exercise other than plodding to the front door and back.

She somewhat reluctantly deposits him in 'the room' before shuffling off to make tea in the adjacent galley kitchen. Books and magazines adorn every surface - perhaps reading bedtime stories to the many empty cups and glasses that aren't yet grown up enough to reach the kitchen sink by themselves.

One of the magazine covers features a view of the Empire State Building, except it seems to have been shot in landscape mode and looks more like a rocket, or post-modern cannon.

Arty prints of Parisian life have made their chic journeys across faded wallpaper, along with what he knows to be Impressionist impressions. Rather than whisking the viewer away to scenes beyond the reality of a Hammersmith high-rise, the ugly juxtapositions of the collection only have the effect of drawing the walls further in. Careful not to stare, he takes in the slightly peeling paper in the two far corners with its tell-tale damp patches, refusing to hide. Flowers sits upright on the hard dining room chair, notebook in hand, resolving to concentrate.

His hostess carefully deposits green cups (he'd have expected mugs) of a suspect steaming liquid on the two square inches of space that the groaning wooden coffee table permits, before sitting back in a much comfier maroon chair, judging by its threadbare fabric and multiple stains.

"Once again, I am so sorry for your loss." Flowers unfortunately spots a chocolate stain just above her ample left breast and resolves to look directly at her unlovely face, and nothing but her face.

"It was a bit of a shock at first, you know. I haven't seen Andrew for many years, but you don't forget, do you?"

He picks up on a slight West Country twang. "How long were you married?"

"Six years."

"No children?"

"No chance."

"You grew apart?" Flowers is aware that this is sounding more and more like a counselling session than a police enquiry.

"We were never really that close, you know?"

"Can you tell me a bit about Andrew? I've been to his flat and there isn't much to go on!" He smiles encouragingly but is nevertheless aware that this is a woman who was once married to a man who has just died.

"Well, there wouldn't be, would there? Andrew was never at home much."

"Work you mean?"

"Not really. He wasn't a home bird. A nest in the trees would have suited him a lot better. He just wanted to be outside - in the fresh air. It didn't matter to him if it was raining or not. I don't think he noticed when it did, you know? That's what first attracted me to him. He was sort of 'transcendental.' Is that a word?"

Flowers nods encouragingly (at the existence of the word if not its usage in this context).

She takes the cue. "I didn't mind that he was always a bit, you know, detached from everything. I thought we'd travel, and see the world ... but I soon found out that he just wanted - needed - space. It was being inside four walls that he hated most, especially at weekends. Not being cooped up inside was enough for him. He never really wanted to go anywhere, you know. He walked round that Gunnersbury Park for hours, just going round in circles; didn't even take photos or anything like that."

"I can see that you like to read."

"I do. If you can't go out to different places, you can still bring them home can't you?"

"I didn't see any books at Andrew's flat?"

"No, but that's more to do with the money I expect. He was an accountant remember! Always looking after the pennies. He used to borrow books from the library, and I guess he might have moved on to e-books by now."

Flowers does indeed remember that they'd found a Kindle reader among Patch's possessions at The Beaver. Apart from his wallet, nothing else of significant interest unless you counted some used dirty underwear, a dark grey T-shirt and a navy blue jumper, along with the usual travelling toiletries including a battery shaver. Other than that, there were just the clothes he had been found in. Not much for the sum total of a man's life experiences.

They had also retrieved a bent, scratched black and white photograph - most likely from a shop photo booth - from his wallet. The girl's face beaming out of it, though at least forty years younger, was most definitely not that of Vivienne Stanhope. At least Flowers had been able to detect that.

"What sort of things did he read; can you remember?"

"Crime novels mostly. Nothing too flowery."

Flowers considers the poetry collection in his

rucksack which is certainly not for public consumption. He could well imagine Harcourt reminding him that he was a policeman, not a poet if he ever found out.

"Was something bothering him do you think? Something he couldn't talk to you about?"

"Not that I ever knew. Not that he would have told me anyway."

"Was he ever violent towards you?"

"Andrew! No, of course not. It might have been better if he had: been a bit rougher, you know ..."

Flowers does know. "He just couldn't settle?"

"I never really found out what was in his head. You can live with someone for what seems like forever and yet you never really know them, do you? Not completely understand them, I mean. What exactly goes on inside them? It was like that with Andrew. The idea that he could ever be violent is (was) laughable but, then again, he could have been a secret serial killer for all I knew, providing it didn't make a mess on the carpet." She shakes her head and Flowers instinctively moves slightly backwards.

"Did he ever mention Castle Upton - where he used to live - or anyone from there; anyone who might still be living there?"

"No. Not really."

"Were you from the same part of the world, originally?"

"Gloucestershire? At least we had that in common.

I was further south than him though - just outside Cheltenham, you know."

"Did you ever visit Castle Upton?"

"Why would I do that?"

"I meant either of you - for old time's sake maybe?"

"I don't believe in old times. I did go back to my old house once in a while, but my mum died last year so no point now."

"You wouldn't ever want to move back?"

"And leave all this behind?" She beams and spreads her arms to remind Flowers of the space that is now hers and hers alone.

"And Andrew hadn't been back home since childhood, as far as you can remember?"

"Home? Both of Andrew's parents had already moved north, long before we got married. Leicestershire I think, but I might be wrong about that. Wherever it was, we never visited them there either, before you ask."

"There doesn't seem to be much love lost?"

"You can only lose love if it was there in the first place, you know. Andrew didn't feel comfortable around other people, at least not for long. Anyone - including me. I know it's a real cliche, but he had his head in his accounts every working day and seemed to have his head in the clouds the rest of the time."

Flowers knows what that feels like too but presses on. "You said he wasn't violent but did he ever get into any serious arguments at all? People trying to take advantage of him maybe."

"Andrew was passive, but he wasn't pathetic if that's what you mean. He just quietly got on with his life." She can see that the detective isn't convinced and sighs. "Andrew found me in bed with my lover one day. I hadn't tried to hide it; I knew he'd be coming home at around that time. He said nothing. Just left - went for another walk round that park I expect." She looks around in vain, presumably imagining a lover - or lovers - who had left her.

"Can you think of anyone who might have had a grudge against him; might have wanted to harm him?"

"No. Nobody. What possible reason could there have been?"

**

Daniel normally allows himself a lie-in on Saturdays. He could do so on every day of the working week, and Sundays, if he now chose to do so. For him there are just 'days' now; no distinctions, just one after another after another. Because no external institution retains its control over him, be it an employer or government organisation or media-led overseer, he is effectively free to do what he likes, when he likes. However, the structure is important - vital - to him and so he prefers the conceit of 'working' Mondays to Fridays and relaxing on Saturdays.

Sundays are effectively 'floating' and influenced by whether his wife or daughter has plans (and if he is included in them). Lately, Claire is living in a seemingly never-ending world of revision and so he often does extra work on that day too.

Last night's sleep had been restless though. He feels more washed out than after reading a fiction-by-numbers piece by a first-time author, and similarly frustrated. He had gone to bed facing a challenging grammatical conundrum, but the main cause of his broken sleep was a dream that has run through his mind repeatedly during each of the last three nights.

He had seen a small orchard of apple trees – little more than a copse really - in a beautiful, peaceful setting, somewhere in the Vale. He knew it was local yet could not place exactly where it was. This unresolved struggle for recognition made him anxious and was at the heart of his wakefulness. It was compounded by a lady's long, bare arm reaching up to pick fruit from the tree but each time her hand reached the branch - even the lowest bough - the apple disappeared.

He hears his wife shuffling past his door, presumably taking a cup of tea back to bed. She must have heard him lifting his phone from the bedside cabinet because the door opens slowly. Tom – all fur and bushy tail - slips between her legs and jumps onto the bed beside Daniel.

"I see that you've found a better sleeping partner. Is that how it is now?"

Both males stare back at her, seeking irony, finding only the usual ire.

"Did you sleep well?" She asks without raising her head to look at him, her tousled hair forming a veil between them. She doesn't believe in dreams.

"Not really. I've been struggling with synesis."

"Perhaps you should get out in the fresh air more often; clear them out?"

"No. Well, yes, possibly. But my problem is synesis, not sinuses."

She moves to leave rather than discover more, but he continues quickly. "There's a phrase in the book which is 'she wondered what share of the terrifying voices was malignant.' It sounds wrong somehow, even though the subject - 'share' - is singular. However, synesis tells us that if the sense of the sentence is plural, then you are allowed to use a plural verb form, even though it flies in the face of the normal rules of grammar. I do think 'she wondered what share of terrifying voices were malignant' sounds better, but it pains me to say so."

"On second thoughts, perhaps you should stay there until you get better!"

He doesn't add that synesis is derived from a Greek word meaning 'understanding.' There doesn't seem to be any point.

***

Some two hours later, Flowers is on the main concourse at Paddington Station, waiting for his platform number to come up. He is relaying everything back to Harcourt, lowering his voice whenever others get too close. One or two people glance over at him, then quickly look away again. Nothing new in that.

"His flat was just devoid of any character, sir. He

could have left it that morning, never expecting to return, or he could have just popped out for a pint of milk."

He pauses to point in the direction of the ladies' toilets and watches as a tall Japanese lady in a grey fur coat thanks him profusely before rushing away, fishing in her shiny silver handbag for small change as she does so, just in case it is needed.

"The contrast between the two homes was about as great as it could have been and it's very hard to imagine the two of them living together, to be honest. His boss - a Marvin Sixsmith - told me that Andrew worked hard, rarely made mistakes and always met his deadlines. If something untoward came up in any audit he rarely made a fuss about it, just corrected it and advised the client accordingly.

Sixsmith said Patch was never really invested in any of the jobs emotionally, but then he was an accountant, wasn't he? He didn't know much about the figure behind the numbers even though he'd worked there for nearly ten years. Andrew never went out with them after work and avoided social events like Christmas parties, apart from those with clients that he couldn't get out of."

As he says this, Flowers spots five men in a group on the concourse, just a few feet away. Four are wearing dark grey suits, the other a dark grey anorak. When one of them moves even slightly outside of his space, each of the others shifts too, as in a group of penguins, trained to toe the line at all costs. The platform number for his train flashes up on the huge indicator board almost immediately after that and Flowers is practically swept along by a tide of people eager to leave with him or, equally, without him.

Forced to shout now, to make himself heard, Flowers concludes "I'm afraid he was a bit of a mystery man, sir, but nobody can imagine there being much mystery in his life either."

***

Scowling, Harcourt puts his phone back in his jacket pocket. "Not much to go on, I'm afraid."

Taylor is munching determinedly through a 'jumbo' sausage roll, her fingers sliding on the grease that has soaked through the paper bag.

"Have you always had a big appetite?" He asks her with only the slightest hint of frustration, as though eating time is the greater sin.

"Always. No matter what's going on in my life, I'm always hungry. My stomach probably needs its own Post Code."

"But nothing going on in your life that is making it worse?"

She knows what he is suggesting but the word 'worse' seems inappropriate. "Nothing for you to worry about, sir. Just high metabolism I guess."

She seeks to change the subject, unwelcome as it is on every level. "Did DS Flowers glean anything at all that we can use?"

Harcourt is also relieved to get back on track,

terminating a conversation which he wishes he'd never started in the first place. "Not really, no. Either people are covering up a lot about Andrew Patch's past or there just isn't much to cover."

"No joy at the accountancy firm either?"

"Typical accountants from what I can gather. Spreadsheets and financial planning while all around them is depreciation."

"My father trained as an accountant, sir."

"I'm sorry, I didn't mean to fall back on stereotypes."

"It's fine. He certainly wasn't stereotypical in any way!"

"Does your family still live in Birmingham?"

"They do, sir; thankfully neither of them is having to work so hard these days. All I'm saying is that each of us has our story to tell. Even the most boring of people."

"We do, but that's just it. We don't even know if he was boring! Only, that he seems to have been elusive - or should that be reclusive - in broad daylight? I just find it hard to believe that a man of nearly fifty has left behind such a bland trail; so few clues for us to go on. I'm thinking that every small detail, however insignificant it might appear at the time, will be like gold dust in this enquiry, or a precious needle ..."

"DS Flowers did remark one day, sir, that some people just drift through life with very little substance to show they'd ever been there at all like shadows ultimately failed by the sun."

Harcourt is genuinely bemused. "Did he indeed? And there was me thinking the two of you only speak in shorthand! Well, the sun's just gone behind the clouds so let's see if we can find anything substantial in Frank Fairhurst's story."

They spot the two tatty petrol pumps ahead. A large, overweight man in brown overalls is driving away in a dirty green van offering food 'so fresh you can taste the dew' as they approach the forecourt. Harcourt grimaces, feeling the dryness around his eyes, and hopes the produce is cleaner than the proprietor.

They spy a heavy-set man in jeans and a red cable-knit sweater heading back into the gloom of the dilapidated garage's 'service bay.'

"Frank Fairhurst?" Taylor asks, holding up her warrant card as she does so.

The man stops and half turns towards them. His grey hair and whiskers look as greasy as no doubt his world beyond them is.

Harcourt notices the fleeting look of panic on the man's face before also holding up his card and confirming his identity.

"I'm Stuart Fairhurst. He's my dad. He's in the back."

They move towards him, but he doesn't move. Not exactly hostile, he is not exactly welcoming either.

"What's all this about?"

"We just wanted to speak with him - and you - about the events leading up to a man's body being found on the footpath just up the road from here."

"Andrew? That was an accident?"

"You seem very sure about that!" Taylor walks nearer but still, he gives no ground.

"Why would it be otherwise? The man was drunk - an accident waiting to happen you might say."

"We might. But, then again, we might not." Harcourt doesn't like the man's apparent disrespect for the death of another. 'Apparent' usually implies something unseen though, in his book.

"We were all in the pub that night. Andrew had come down for Grace's birthday. He'd had a few too many. Ale down here's much stronger than that watered-down stuff up there."

Harcourt is also unimpressed by the man's grasp of geography. "So, he was drunk when he left the pub that evening?"

"As a lord. We all saw it." An older, harsher voice answers the question for him.

"Mr Fairhurst?"

"Frank, yeah."

An older man in a tatty green anorak which seems at least a size too big for him walks slowly into view. Taylor notices the scuffed boots and crumpled jeans. She also takes in the stubble on the new arrival's chin - more disorderly than 'designer.' While there are undoubtedly some facial similarities between father and son, the same shade of brown eyes especially,

Frank's face is thin and drawn, like he hasn't eaten, or is being eaten from the inside.

Harcourt has also spotted the multiple liver spots on his gnarled hands as well as the shuffling gait, or is that just a morning thing? Though they remain outside, he is assaulted by the sour odour of stale alcohol fighting to be released from the man's skin. "We understand that you were in the pub that evening?" It almost seems like a rhetorical question.

"I was."

"You were celebrating the forthcoming birthday of Grace Beech?" Taylor lays a little trap and watches his response carefully.

"I was not."

Slightly disappointed, and not just at his monotone responses, Taylor continues calmly, trying to ignore the way he is looking her up and down in mild disgust. "But you were aware that there was a celebration going on."

"Couldn't miss it. There were only about a dozen of us in there at the time."

"What's this got to do with anything?" Stuart Fairhurst is either anxious to get on or move on.

"Just background information." Harcourt adopts the same calm approach as Taylor, even smiling benignly. He turns back to Frank. "You knew Andrew Patch though. His father sold you his garage didn't he?"

Fairhurst sniffs disparagingly and Harcourt fears he's about to spit on the ground between them. "Years ago."

"Did you not want to talk with him, find out what happened to his parents once they'd left Castle Upton."

"None of my business, was it? Our business was done."

"And how is business these days?"

Stuart Fairhurst once again steps in, keen perhaps to show who's really in charge of the business these days. "It's steady. Should start picking up now."

"Tourist season?" Taylor offers.

"You got a problem with that? People visiting, spending their money here; better than spending it on the 'worldwide web' on rubbish they don't need."

Taylor notes the sarcasm behind Stuart Fairhurst's feeble attempt to show that, though it might not be a high-tech hub, the internet has indeed reached the Cotswold Hills. She turns back to his father.

"Did you buy Grace Beech a birthday card?"

Frank looks up sharply. "I haven't got money for that sort of thing."

"Maybe that's why Grace didn't want you to be part of her birthday party?"

Stuart Fairhurst moves towards Taylor but his father, almost imperceptibly, signals a halt to the advance. "Why would you say that?"

Noting the colour rising in his hollowed cheeks, Harcourt decides to take him on. "It just seems strange to us, that's all. Here is a man returning to the village he used to live in, close to the garage his father used to run before selling it to you; visiting a woman who still lives here and is clearly friends with your son and daughter-in-law, and yet you show no interest in him whatsoever - or Grace Beech's big day come to that?"

"And that's a crime, is it?

Harcourt notices the older man's fists clenching and unclenching. He might have expected it in the son rather than the father. "Of course not! We are treating Andrew Patch's death as suspicious at this stage and are consequently exploring every angle. Did you leave the pub before or after Mr Patch?"

"After."

"And went straight home?

"Must have done. I was in my bed in the morning."

"You can't remember?" Taylor offers, helpfully.

"Being in bed?" He doesn't even favour the woman with a glance, even as he mocks her.

"Getting home?"

"It's only a few steps. Call it muscle memory!"

"And yet you had no problem at all in remembering that you left the pub after Mr Patch rather than before?" Harcourt' voice is firm now, not friendly.

"I can vouch for that." Stuart makes a point of confirming the fact but he has missed the point of Harcourt's observation completely. "We walked Dad home then went straight home ourselves. We didn't see

Andrew again."

Harcourt concludes the conversation more enigmatically than he would have liked. "Neither did anybody else."

***

Half an hour later Lisa Fairhurst gets a call on her mobile and answers it, unsure at first if it is an automated message she is hearing; that is before she recognises the voice.

"You just do exactly what I say. Say what I'm about to tell you. There's no need for the deaths to keep on coming. This can be an end to it. All of it. Understand?"

She has never understood it. Not all of it.

CHAPTER FIVE

He changes down through all the gears as they descend the hill - only a one in four but with a nasty left-hand bend thrown in to throw cocky tourists off their stride (or position on the road itself).

The Herefordshire countryside is so familiar to him, rolling hills of lush green with cows and sheep living alongside each other more harmoniously than many of the people who share this land with them. The extensive wire trellises are still in place for the hop plants to climb, although oast houses in the county have been largely relegated to 'country lets' these days.

Charlotte had called it 'hillbilly' country when he'd first taken her to the little hamlet of Marcombe – the place where he'd been born and brought up. Nestling into the southern slope of the lovely Frome Valley, just a few miles from Bromyard, where his father had been the resident pharmacist in the local chemist's shop, he had thought she would find it peaceful and carefree - as he had once done. Sadly, she'd failed to see the natural beauty beyond the small-mindedness and generally closed nature of the people themselves. Not exactly unwelcoming, they had made it clear from the outset that she didn't (and would never) belong there.

Her brother - Fergus - had, on the other hand, adored it the moment he had been invited down to a family get-together just before Daniel and Charlotte were married. Or perhaps he had been seduced by a wealth of human material he could work with. Unfortunately, he had found out quickly that change comes slowly here, if at all.

After his mother had joined his father in the local churchyard, now presided over by Fergus, Daniel preferred to stay away. He's seen his mother once since, but only once - and that was many years ago. It isn't that he doesn't get on with his brother-in-law either, although his wife, Lucy, always seems to have a huge chip on her shoulder. He just feels that he's moved away - moved on - much as Charlotte has reminded him quite frequently lately that he hasn't moved very far at all.

The vicarage is, naturally, the largest house in the village: a rambling, dark stone edifice below Welsh slate. On a cold, wet day it gives the impression of hopelessness and despair. On a fresh, clear day like today perhaps the end of the earth is a few miles further on after all.

Lucy is already walking around the side of the house as they get out of the car.

"Lucille; it's been too far long!" Charlotte is so much better at this than he is, or maybe she's just learned to do it more naturally. After all, in the latter years much of her job had involved advising people who were about to lose theirs, and being terribly nice about it.

The two women air kiss at a safe range of about two inches, then Lucy turns and quite abruptly leads his wife away, ignoring Daniel completely. As per his gloomy thoughts, nothing much has changed here.

Fergus is dressed in his usual brown, cordy pullover and crumpled dark trousers. He is seated at the wooden picnic bench - though Lucy would no doubt have described it as a 'rustic lawn seat' - with a sheaf of papers beside an empty teacup. Daniel is momentarily reminded of the actor Colin Firth in the film 'Love Actually' whose hapless writer character momentarily loses pages to a gust of wind. This is not Portugal, though, and there isn't much love actually. Fergus is trying to tuck his particular offering below a tea tray.

"There's not much point in doing that is there?" his wife, all silk chintz dress and showy silver earrings, chides him, before seating herself and trying to iron out her folds of skin with short, dumpy fingers.

Daniel isn't sure if Fergus's words or the resting position of them has been deemed pointless, but he shakes the older man's hand warmly and takes a seat beside Charlotte, who could be re-considering her decision to wear jeans and a comfy cashmere sweater.

"Tomorrow's sermon?" He enquires, watching Lucy lift the tray, meanly, and head off to the kitchen, still failing to even acknowledge his existence. Charlotte quickly follows her.

"It is," Fergus confirms, wearily. "What good it will do, God only knows."

"I thought that was the point!" Daniel is smiling, not wishing to be controversial in any way. At least not here, not now.

"Ha! Well, yes, you're right of course. The days go by, don't they, and the years too come to that? How is my sister coping as a lady of leisure?"

Daniel has tried to put the text to his wife out of his mind, but now it returns, character by character. "She's fine, I think."

"You think?"

"I don't keep tabs on her every minute of the day; she goes out walking a lot - in the hills, mainly."

"Alone?"

"Naturally, alone. I still have my work."

"Ah. Your work."

"Our pensions don't kick in for a few years..."

"Perhaps you should try spending more time with her; talking to her?"

"Yes, well you know your sister tends to do the talking, while others listen."

"It wasn't always like that, though, was it? You were at that wretched newspaper. Night after night. Much good that did you in the end."

Daniel stares in disbelief at the man's insensitivity, not that it is a new trait.

"I'm sorry. I'm sorry. I didn't mean that, but just look at what's right in front of you - staring you in the face. Remember, she gave up her career in London to move up to Winklers in Birmingham – or Moseley Village, wasn't it? Not even a top-six firm in the second city. Just to be closer to you; closer to 'home.'"

"I don't remember Woodhouse & Partners trying too hard to keep her!"

"Maybe not, and I do realise that she was making a new start with you anyway. But she just looks so lost these days. It's hard not to have a career."

"Is that really how you feel, Fergus?"

Fergus ignores the fully intended slight and is galvanised by it perhaps. "It gave her a structure, especially when she was doing so much of it on her own - apart from young Claire of course. I would have thought you'd want to make it up to her now that you can. Surely you can read in bed, like the rest of us."

Daniel knows that it is impossible to explain proofreading to one who sincerely believes himself to be in possession of The Truth - where proof is simply not required. To a man of such elevated ideals, the word is always on message even if the grammatical disciples fall by the wayside.

He has to admit that he does enjoy the peace when his wife is absent as much as she appears to. Charlotte doesn't seem lost to him. She seems very much aware of where she is - where they both are.

Perhaps he'll surprise her one day by following her and then suddenly appearing - like a genie offering her three wishes, or sandwiches, a flask of coffee and a hopeful smile? Maybe a little variety would be no bad thing, take her mind off the endless, empty years ahead that may well be bothering her. Fergus might have a point, for once.

"You could be right. We both have more time on our hands these days. Thanks for asking."

He tips his head back, mollified, or is he just being a little bit smug? "It's what families are for. Being interested, concerned even."

Daniel wonders, not for the first time today, whether Fergus and Lucy resent the fact that they haven't visited since before Christmas, a visit that ended with a shouting match between Charlotte and Fergus over their mother. They could just as easily have come to Wood Lench, he reasons. It's only taken them forty minutes today. No doubt Fergus would argue that his parishioners might need him and he wanted to make himself available at all times. Presumably, this is also why so many religious men fail to travel far into the real world, especially from Herefordshire where the Worcestershire border to the east seems every bit as daunting as that with Wales to the west.

"And Lucy. Still lunching out I assume."

"Shhh. For Heaven's sake don't let her hear you call her that. I know that you do it on purpose - a little game of yours designed to rile her, but I have to pick up the pieces afterwards. She does a lot of good work in the parish; always has done." He frowns, the furrows forking across his forehead.

Probably too deep to be smoothed out now, thinks Daniel, as he surveys the portly figure whose grey hair is unacceptably long now. The John the Baptist look is beginning to look a bit silly. Fergus has always been a little unpredictable though. Daniel remembers well him organizing a summer solstice celebration, complete with bacon sandwiches, which had been ambushed by a pro-life group of pensioners from Leominster who had worthily brought their plant-based picnics with them. Fergus had called it a parable. Lucy hadn't.

He ventures further while retaining general platitudes as a safety net. "And how have you been? Has life been treating you alright?"

"Better than many, I imagine." Fergus clutches the papers and sits back in his seat. "You never quite know what's going to happen next, do you? One of my parishioners told me a story about his neighbour a couple of weeks ago. Not that this happened a couple of weeks ago, you understand, the story took place years earlier - in the Fifties I think…

Daniel is relieved not to be hearing, let alone reading, tomorrow's sermon. He nods his head, encouraging Fergus to continue (quickly if at all possible).

"I only found out about it then. Anyway, the neighbour - an old gent in his eighties I think, or was it seventies? Anyway, he mistook a handful of daffodil bulbs for onions. Fried them up and promptly dropped down dead. The coroner advised death by daffodil poisoning! Who would have thought that something so beautiful could at the same time be so deadly? I mean the banks on either side of the garden - especially down by the apple trees - like beds of bright yellow they were. Can you imagine?"

"I'm sure he can." Lucy has returned with a plate of butterfly cakes, each seated on an individual white doily. "It's what you do, isn't it Daniel: daydream your life away?"

"Lucille!" Fergus raises an arm, forgetting that he is holding whole words in his hand. The papers fall out of his fist and land in a muddy patch of lawn - the wrong (right?) way up of course.

Charlotte comes to Daniel's if not her brother's rescue. "Daniel doesn't daydream, Lucille, he seeks to correct those who do. Sees things that others don't."

"That's very well put!" Fergus beams, clearly unsure whether his sister is being ironic or not.

"If I saw everything, I'd be God!" Daniel quips.

"Not quite," Fergus interjects, sitting upright now. He is glad to be on firmer ground. Ground that he understands. "You are just an observer, Daniel, nothing more. God sees everything - including all things that are yet to happen."

"I'm so sorry," Lucy's unlovely rouged lips remain parted from each other in mock surprise. "I thought it was a gift he had, not a vocation. So, you're little more than a fraud dear brother-in-law. A charlatan."

"No more so than one who married for heavenly status because she had no hope in hell of getting there through any good deeds of her own." Daniel cannot believe what he has just said, or that it has taken him such a short time to do so.

"My mother called it at your wedding." Lucy sniffs disdainfully. "She said that Charlotte was throwing away not just her career but her whole life. No wonder she's so frustrated the whole time."

"I've been thinking about 'first love.'"

Daniel isn't sure whether his wife is trying to tactfully change the subject or laying a trap for her brother which she knows he will fall into eventually. He sits back to admire the sport, like the little dog from the nursery rhyme.

"What about it?"

"Not 'it' I suppose; more the people it affects. That feeling when two strangers just know they are meant to be together."

"Like you two, I suppose!" Lucy's sarcasm laces the confessional, like a bored priest in an adjacent wooden box.

"Not necessarily." Charlotte is still staring at her brother, ignoring the unholy spirit in her midst. "Can it happen twice? I mean I know that you can fall in and out of love, but can you ever experience that blissful feeling of first love more than once?"

"You're assuming he even felt it once." Lucy chuckles unpleasantly.

Daniel hasn't a clue where this enquiry is going but feels uneasy about the path it is taking.

Fergus responds slowly and thoughtfully, which usually means he hasn't any idea either. "I would have to say that first love is often synonymous with young love. That's not to say, of course, that beauty is bounded by age. Not at all. No, I think it may be possible, but the subsequent feeling may be one of recognition of a feeling that has been felt before, rather than the dizzying ecstasy of something felt for the first time. It may not be any the less satisfying for all that."

"Indeed." Charlotte comments, enigmatically. "And what happens if you go to Heaven but, at that point, were in love with someone other than your wife or husband? When they also die are you expected to hook up with them again - for appearance's sake?"

Fergus is looking for tell-tale signs of drink or, God help him, drugs, but, seeing none, he does his very best not to flounder. "Well. Well. First of all, God sees everything so appearances are never deceptive to him. The sanctity of marriage is confirmed by vows made by man and wife at their wedding ceremony, and this cannot be broken in God's eyes. So, with nothing broken, there must be an expectation that constituent parts must come together again whenever and however they have been parted... "

"So, you can't have a lover in Heaven then? I thought it was supposed to represent paradise. Sounds more like an unliving hell to me!"

Fergus is horror-struck but, before he can escape indoors to consult volumes he hasn't opened once in all the time they've been sitting on the shelves of the dining room, patiently waiting, he is unexpectedly 'saved' by his wife.

"A good time for me to make some tea!" Lucy addresses Charlotte. She doesn't like mysteries, which is why she prefers a divine gin and tonic on a hot (or cold) afternoon to the theology her husband would love her to engage with.

"While you're handling that long, warm and very hard kettle spout in the kitchen, wouldn't it be a good time to have a good, long shag!"

Nobody speaks. Even with mouths slightly open, no words are formed. Charlotte's rebuke is met, quite literally, by the sound of silence. If there is anybody there - any other being - they say nothing, do not intervene.

Neither Daniel nor Charlotte discusses it or anything else following their much earlier-than-planned exit.

Later that evening, Charlotte is lying on top of her husband in his bed - naked and quite exhausted - agreeing with him that the regulation family catch-up had been ghastly. For him, at this moment, there is nothing but glorious transparency. No words are required.

***

"Good morning, everyone." Harcourt breezes into his office, glad to be back at work, blissfully aware though he is that for most people it is the other way around. "Good weekends?"

"Not bad, sir. Thanks" Taylor never likes to give much away. He suspects that includes weekends.

"Flowers?"

Flowers has been reading something on his computer screen, intently (or at least pretending to, intently). His head jerks up to attention. "Very nice, thank you, sir. We went to the Fleece in Bretforton yesterday."

"You and your mum?" Like Taylor, Flowers keeps his home life very close to home, but Harcourt likes them to at least think that he is interested - in touch with each member of his team, something Hunter-Wright would no doubt dismiss as too 'touchy-feely.' He perceives the slightest of hesitations from Flowers. Nicholas Parsons would have pounced on this, but he knows this would just result in Flowers going back into his shell. Besides, long-running radio programmes such as 'Just a Minute' are considered suitable only for the undead now, aren't they? He still tunes in regularly, though, as he is trying to do now.

"That's right. It gave us a nice run and the days are getting a bit warmer now."

"I've only ever been there once - in the pewter room? The pies were delicious, as I recall. Was it busy?"

"It was. I think they make more on a Sunday than almost any other day, what with the food and so on. They're already full on with the Asparagus Festival."

"Asparagus?" Taylor screws her face up in mock disgust.

"Big thing in Worcestershire," Harcourt explains. "They have an annual festival at The Fleece every spring. There's also a local psychic who uses Vale of Evesham asparagus to predict the future. An 'asparamancer.' The only one of her kind I believe."

"That, I can believe."

"She calls it a gift: inherited it from her aunt who used to read tea leaves."

"Lots of people still read *The Sporting Life* despite all the evidence – gathered daily – that it's a completely pointless exercise, sir. What is the connection between asparagus and Worcestershire anyway?" Taylor looks far from convinced.

"You wouldn't expect asparagus to do well here actually; it normally prefers sandy soils. For some reason, Evesham clay does the trick. I think they do auctions during the festival too. It's become more popular since celebrity chefs started including it in their recipes."

"How do you know all this, sir" Flowers is more impressed than his colleague is.

"I remember reading about it when we visited the pub. The pub itself is from the early fifteenth century - belongs to the National Trust now - and predates the Beaver in Castle Upton by about a hundred years. So much for all their oldie worldly tradition! At the Fleece, you might have seen soldiers heading off to fight in the War of the Roses ..."

"It's also reputed to be the most haunted pub in England," Flowers adds, helpfully. "Lola Taplin. She was the landlady there until she died in 1977, just in front of the fire in the snug. Logs from the fire often seem to be spat out onto the floor, and her spirit is quite often seen about the place."

"Ok. Enough!" Taylor closes the conversation which, in her view, has already gone on for far too long. "Asparagus is bad enough, but ghosts and spirits leave me cold."

"I should think they leave everyone feeling cold!" Flowers grins at Harcourt and is thrilled when his effort is reciprocated.

"So," Harcourt sits down behind the vacant desk opposite them both, "Do we have any updates before you two head off for a chat with Grace Beech?"

"Tox in, sir?"

Harcourt waits momentarily to see if Flowers is enjoying a play on words or just the usual shorthand. "Go on."

"The lab reports on Andew Patch are complete now, sir. They just had a slight delay over the stomach contents."

"Should have had a plate of asparagus!"

"Taylor!" Harcourt admonishes her, but she and he know that he is not being serious; he is in a pleasingly good mood.

"There was indeed alcohol present, sir," Flowers is reading from his screen again, "But only a couple of units - maybe a pint or a glass of wine. Otherwise just water-based fluids. No other significant elements; could even have been just water."

"Not enough to impair the performance of an otherwise healthy middle-aged man then?"

"No, sir. Dr Graham says he would have been well within the limit had he wanted to drive."

"And he was just visiting the village yet was somehow unable to walk very far at all."

"Or someone brought that walk to an end?" Taylor expresses what the three of them are all thinking.

"SOCOs?"

"Nothing more to add to their first findings, sir. No sign of any kind of struggle and nothing of any particular interest from the fingertip search. They restricted that to the immediate area only though, as per your orders."

"And no sighting of Andrew Patch from the moment he left the pub to when he turned on to the public footpath, Gabby?"

"Uniform have finished door-to-door, sir. There weren't many houses to visit, to be honest. No, no one appears to have seen anything untoward."

"Or anything at all it would seem. I find that odd in itself! So, the only thing that makes this suspicious is the marking and contusion on the body originally reported by the good doctor. Were it not for that, we'd be saying this was an accidental death. But, because of that, it moves from accidental to unexplained, as it stands. The Superintendent won't like that, and neither do I."

***

Grace Beech is sitting on a dark, cast iron bench to the side of her bungalow, facing the late morning sun, as they draw up. Her black dress almost blends in with the seat, suggesting a much larger, continuous form than the diminutive lady she is. Flowers takes in the sunburnt face and deduces either a winter sun holiday or this being a favourite seat - of many, it seems - in her garden. He settles on the latter.

Taylor is ahead of him, introducing them both, and sitting on the edge of a similar bench, at right angles to Grace's, but closest to her. Flowers realises that he won't be able to see Grace's face properly if he sits next to his DS, so he remains standing, citing a back problem that doesn't usually improve with bending or sitting.

"How can I help you?" Grace's voice is soft but calm. She hasn't leapt up to make tea or coffee, which so many people do when police officers come to visit; less down to hospitality, and much more to do with buying time. To collect thoughts perhaps?

Taylor leads, as per the unarticulated assumption that a woman-to-woman conversation might prove more fruitful in the first instance.

"Thank you again for agreeing to see us today. We are just making general enquiries about the death of Mr Andrew Patch last week. We understand that the gentleman was known to you?"

"He was, yes."

Flowers takes in the green eyes that do not blink.

Another man might quite easily have fallen into them altogether. Grey-haired and fifty years old she might well be, but she has an allure that must have been almost overwhelming when she was younger. Even the large silver cross, lying brightly but silently against the upper reaches of her high-collared dress is somehow mesmerising.

Taylor is less interested in allure than in advancing the conversation beyond staccato answers. "He had travelled from London, we believe, to celebrate your recent birthday?"

"That's correct, yes."

Taylor notes that the woman continues to stare straight ahead, not looking at Flowers either. It's as if avoiding eye contact with either of them will also enable her to somehow avoid giving too much (anything) away. "Did you know Mr Patch as a child?"

"I did."

"And you'd stayed in touch?"

"He'd stayed in touch. He sent a birthday card each year. I never contacted him."

"Was there any reason for that - you're not contacting him, I mean?"

"I didn't need to. Andrew's family moved away when we were just children and, as I've said, he used to send me a birthday card each year."

"Wasn't that a bit strange?" Flowers does bend slightly now, as though to make himself part of her vision, or at least to be heard more clearly, although there is no need to as no car has passed on the road since they've been there, and the birdsong from the nearby woods is hardly going to drown him out. "I mean children do stay in touch for a while when their school friends move away, but it's usually a fleeting thing isn't it? Children quickly make new friends."

"I don't see how the making of new friends necessarily requires existing ones to be jettisoned."

Both Flowers and Taylor have picked up on the slight but discernible hardening of her voice and the crossing of her legs.

Taylor continues. "I think what DS Flowers is getting at is that it's unusual for an exchange of cards to continue beyond childhood or school years; certainly not every year for what, thirty years?"

"Thirty-nine. I hadn't seen Andrew since he left the village."

"Did his cards ever contain letters, tell you what he was up to these days?"

Grace turns towards Taylor now, still calm, still unblinking. "I have no idea what he was 'up to' as you so quaintly put it and have no interest in knowing any more than I did when he was alive."

"How did he seem to you in the pub? It must have been strange seeing someone after all these years, especially as you'd been so young when you last saw him."

"I wouldn't have described it as strange. I would have

recognised Andrew even if he hadn't told me he was coming; he wouldn't have been able to surprise me."

"You seem very sure of that" Flowers again, searching for any non-verbal clues that might explain their interviewee's evasiveness.

"I am. Age does not alter memories, constable. They may become impaired - lost even - but the memories themselves are as good as photographs, even if you've mislaid the album in which you filed them away."

"What did you talk about?"

"Our lives, since we last saw each other; there was a lot to catch up on."

"It seems that Andrew lived a fairly quiet life in London," Taylor interjects, leaning forward slightly.

Grace makes no outward sign that they are getting closer. "Not everything is as it seems, Sergeant."

"And you have never moved from Castle Upton? I assume you saw no need." Flowers again.

"I thought it was the policeman's job to assume nothing, believe nobody and challenge everything? Or is beginning with that ABC too Clouseau ... or Julie Andrews?"

Taylor can see that her colleague has no idea who Clouseau is. He is also inwardly seduced by Grace's use of language. She's seen this quite often in the past, though hasn't raised it with Harcourt who, if she were being unkind, which she rarely is, has his own long-winded issues to deal with. "Do you remember when he left the pub that night?"

"I do."

"Can you remember if anyone else had left earlier?"

"Duncan Harewood, I believe, though I can't be certain of that. It was quite noisy in there at the time. Andrew said he was too hot and needed some fresh air, so he left. I never saw him again."

"Was there any disagreement before that? We understand there might have been raised voices, shouting even."

"As I said, there was a good deal of noise, but I don't recall any disagreements as such."

***

"You talked last time about your life in London. That's where you grew up, right?"

"South London suburbs - not quite Croydon thank God. Morden, right at the end of the tube line though. Might as well have been the end of the world."

"You didn't like it?"

"There was nothing particularly wrong with it. We lived in a smart enough, mock Tudor house - that tells you everything."

"Does it?"

"Mummy seemed to love it but only really because our father did."

"She didn't get to choose?"

"She wouldn't have opposed anything he said or wanted, and that's just how he liked it?"

"It was, but I don't want you to think I had a bad childhood; that isn't where this all comes from. I can assure you of that right now. He didn't treat my mother especially well but neither would he have done anything to hurt her either. He was just frustrated with life. Disappointed I suppose."

"Because of not becoming a doctor? We touched on this last year."

"He didn't get the grades to get into medical school, but it didn't all turn out bad for him. He set up a physiotherapy practice, and his patients called him 'Mr.' They thought he must have been some high-powered medical consultant before setting up on his own. He did nothing to disabuse them of that, of course, but he knew the truth; always had done."

"Was social standing important to him?"

"Not as much as it would have been for my sister-in-law's parents, I imagine."

"Lucille?"

"The same. Her father was a middle-ranking civil servant, don't you know."

She smooths her new blue skirt, bought especially for the occasion.

"Rather like Daddy he never quite made the grade, but he and her mother lorded it over everyone. She - Alison - filled Lucille with all kinds of ideas above her social station. She belittles everybody; is determined to make everyone else feel bad about themselves to achieve superiority. It isn't an unknown tactic. I came across it quite often, professionally (when people paid good money for them to be mean to others). That's probably why she continues to give Fergus a hard time to this day; while he just remains hard."

"She's sexually repressed?"

"Not sure about that but certainly repressive. In a rare moment, after slightly too much gin, she admitted that she keeps my brother very much at arm's length (and that doesn't include hands)."

"It's not such an unusual reaction to male dominance in childhood. In later years, if the woman has managed to build an otherwise independent platform for herself, sex can bring back all of those feelings of helplessness – of submission and losing control. Lying on your back with a man on top of you isn't just about physical weight; it's about the mind recalling mental pressure too."

"I've found that I've often been either too tired or too busy for sex."

"Have you used that as an excuse for not submitting to it?"

"I'd never refer to it as a submission. Even if your theory is right, my father has never entered my head when I've been enjoying sex (or any other part of my anatomy, I'm pleased to report), and I've never seen it as some kind of power struggle. Little and often has always worked for us."

"Quality time!"

"Indeed."

"Have you ever played much sport?"

"An interesting segue!" He doesn't return her backhand return so she searches for new balls. "Not often. A bit of tennis at Uni when we knew the boys would be ogling us in the sunshine I suppose."

"But nothing involving consistent head trauma. No impact injuries as such."

"Unless you count the corporate jostling for position akin to banging your head against a wall on a semi-regular basis, no."

He must have decided that going off-piste wasn't going to work after all. "Do you visit your brother and his wife often?"

"Not often, but we did at the weekend."

"How was it?"

"Same old. Daniel feels belittled by them both, and I loathe just about everything they stand for."

"Did Fergus heed the call at an early age - in Morden I mean?"

"Fergus didn't have a calling. Nobody rang the bell, so he went into the church."

"That's very harsh. I can see it still makes you angry."

"It does, but it isn't a rage I've just embraced. It's always defined our relationship."

"Has it, though, or is that just your perception of your relationship now? We often circle the real issues - wrap ourselves up in invisible layers because we think that will keep us safe from the cold outside. Sometimes we do so in order to present ourselves as comfortable in external surroundings while trying to move further away from a chill within our inner selves - in our true hearts.

When we are forced to unravel those protective layers - or concentric rings if you like - there is often nothing toxic or icy at the centre at all. It's similar to the plaque on your teeth. Your teeth or tooth may feel uncomfortable (and you worry that other people will notice it) but once the plaque is removed, the tooth underneath is in good health, even if it's not as shiny now as it might once have been."

"I cannot remember Fergus and I ever having a healthy relationship."

"So, back to Daniel. What has defined your relationship with your husband."

"That's so much harder to discuss."

"Why? Because it touches a nerve that is more exposed?"

"Because it's a much more complex situation."

"So, simplify it for me."

"I do still love my husband. This could never be something it isn't."

"Sounds like a phrase he would approve of!"

"And yet he infuriates me now far more than he ever did before. I look forward to seeing him - sometimes I long to feel his arms (or legs) around me - but then he will say something that, even though I know he's right and it's probably harmless, gets right under my skin. There's no reason for my being as unreasonable with him as I am. He hasn't changed."

"Do you mean that he is pedantic; corrects you?"

"He's a proofreader. I think it probably comes with the territory; but there you are: it always has done. Ever since I met him, he has always been in the same profession, been pretty much the same as he is now. We both left our respective jobs within a few weeks of each other; both of us were 'retired;' me early and him earlier than he had expected."

"Yes, you said in one of our earlier discussions that you missed him when he worked late; it must generally be much nicer now that you can be together so much more."

"You'd think so, wouldn't you? It could be that I had to adapt and perhaps became even more independent because of spending so much time on my own, but now we sleep in separate rooms and wake up to days spent apart."

"Has he ever mentioned that he is hurt by this? Maybe he is just confused by your behaviour and needs the structure of language to fall back on. It would reassure him that all meaning is not lost. That could be why he comes across as being 'schoolmasterly,' if you like. He may be feeling a little out of control of the human situation whereas 'you can always rely on books?'"

"I'm sure he does. I often think he loves them more than he does me. As I said, it's complicated."

"And the law firm - the London firm I mean - did you leave there on good terms?"

"Financially, yes. I think they saw that I was my father's daughter; that I was never quite going to make a partner. They made me a Senior Associate of course."

"Based on post-qualification years?"

"I'd done nearly seventeen; they didn't have much choice. It would have looked bad to prospective clients to have someone so old working in a senior role who hadn't gone up or out of the firm. For my part, I had also seen from an early stage how frustrating that would have been."

"Not getting the big promotion?"

"No. No. Getting the title. The name above the door."

"Presumably the internal promotion did give you a share of the collective responsibility."

"In case I said or did something contrary? Yes, like an Associate Director of a company – 'we recognize what you've done and want you to stay, but we don't think you're good enough to be a Director. Stick around for a few more years and we'll see if someone dies: there may be a vacancy then.'"

"Again, a bit harsh?"

"I had a friend whose children were getting bullied

at the primary school they attended. The school had resolutely refused to accept it was happening and had done nothing about it. One day, my friend – Anna – started to talk about it to other parents in the playground. About a week later Anna was invited to stand as a Parent Governor of the school."

"To keep her quiet?"

"Anna thought that if she got on the inside track, she might be able to do something about it. In hindsight that was just foolish. The Governors' meetings were shrouded in red tape, meaningless buzzwords and established processes. She didn't stand a chance."

"Did they ever do anything about the bullying?"

"Not a thing. They did spend the year-end budget on a glossy pamphlet detailing their anti-bullying policy."

"And Anna's children?"

"Left and went to High School. The eldest (I can't remember his name now) works in a supermarket. I think the youngest is a cleaner, but it's a long while ago now and we've lost touch apart from Christmas cards and a little update sheet she tucks inside it each year."

"How about your colleagues in the law firm? Did you find any kindred spirits?"

"There was a chap called Simon. He was very gentle and empathetic. Sadly, the Partners associated meek with weak and moved him on quite quickly. There was another lawyer there - also specialising in redundancy cases - from Scotland. Amy Whiteman. Whereas I felt let down by the partner overseeing us, she didn't care. The bigger the client's restructuring, the more redundancy cases and sometimes tribunals as a result, the more she was in her absolute element."

"She never saw the little people beyond the big bucks?"

"Something like that, except she was inconsistent too. A friend of a friend had a son - Nabeel - who had just graduated in computing. I think you'd call his specialism 'software engineering' today, but then it was just plain old computing, and it was as plain as day why he hadn't been able to get a job."

"Too many computer graduates?"

"That, and the fact that he was lazy. Couldn't be bothered. It wasn't that he couldn't fix things and he certainly helped us tighten up on our data security - again, before that became the big issue every consultant wants a piece of."

"You suggested the firm let him go?"

"I was just the mouthpiece; others felt precisely the same as I did. Before I knew it, she was suggesting I had racist tendencies. His family were from Lahore and quite well-to-do, I think. Mind you, the generation that had settled in Lewisham was hard-working, and his siblings were too. I suppose every family has a bad apple - a bit like me in mine I suppose."

"Did you feel threatened by her: this Amy?"

"Not threatened, no."

"Perhaps you wanted to be more like her then, and it

upset you to know that you couldn't be or wouldn't."

"Let me be absolutely clear. Sorry, that did sound a bit Margaret Thatcher, didn't it?"

She allows herself a brief smile and the action instantly relaxes her other muscles too. "Amy Whiteman was an absolute bitch - and I have the luxury of being able to say that without fear of being labelled 'sexist' as well! She was little more than a jumped-up legal secretary who saw her main chance: repeating the right thing here, borrowing the right comment there; ingratiating herself with those she thought could push her up the pole."

"Presumably you wanted to push her off!"

"She had nothing original about her, just thrived on others' weaknesses, whether it be a slightly crumpled blouse or a skirt that hadn't been properly pressed – that sort of thing. Trivial matters pursued by a small-minded person who just wanted (and knew) how to get under your skin. She was the office gossip, which is dangerous enough in a law firm, but she also took sides against others on her team."

"Including you?"

"Yes, including me. I couldn't advance her career could I - apart from leaving. Besides, she was effectively 'sponsored' by the Managing Partner, Trevor Brainsfoot. He thought that what she was doing was amusing. 'Character building' I think he once called it. Not that he was in the office very much. His family had a smallholding in Norfolk, and he was always up there shooting and fishing with clients."

"You must have hated that?"

"Not really. I still felt in control of the situation. I was good at my job, even though I didn't revel in treading all over others. I was organised, meticulous even. I remembered every detail of every case and, of course, clients loved me for it. They used to call me 'Dotty' or just, plain 'Dot.' It was them being ironic, you see, as the nickname was the opposite of everything I represented to them."

"I'm still not entirely convinced that you have dealt with that; you were a lawyer and these were injustices, plain and simple, right? How could you just let that go?"

She wishes he wouldn't say 'right.' It sounds so mid-Atlantic, certainly not authentic. She doesn't particularly remember him using this phrase before. Perhaps he's been reading a paperback, or another woman has since rubbed off on him? Maybe she's just too hot? It had been cold when she'd first come in and she'd asked him to turn the heat up.

He hasn't noticed. "Most people would have been upset, angry even?"

"You learn to let things go, don't you? You must look forward to the next case all the time, especially if you lost the last one. I learned at an early stage that our mock Tudor was mocked by most of them – in Amy's case, often to my face. Besides, I've had plenty of time to come to terms with it."

"Do you keep in touch with anyone from those days?"

"No, but I do think of them from time to time. I was

there for a good twenty years and not all of it was bad by any means. Amy died last year of heart disease."

"Did you go to the funeral?"

"No, I didn't, but I was intrigued to discover that she'd had a heart."

***

He sees them coming from a long way off. There are two of them, just like before. He knows that one of them - probably the woman - will do most of the talking and the other will just stare at him, looking for tell-tale slips in his story, little cracks, chasms even.

The older one has asked him where he was that Wednesday evening. The younger, prettier one pretends to be writing notes but he isn't; he is listening. Drawing a simple sketch and then making it much more complex; creating a completely different picture. Painting by numbers his mother had always thrust on him when he was small. But, even back then, he could never be constrained by a digital world he still lives doggedly outside of.

"I was in The Beaver until late, then I left and walked home."

"Who were you in there with?"

"With other people. They don't just open it up for me you know." That was a mistake. It showed them an energy they'll try to exploit. Just breathe. Think of the trees on the hillside flowing in the breeze; be the lake in the woods: even if there are hidden depths, the surface must always remain calm. That's what she'd told him, wasn't it?

The older one doesn't even flinch. Perhaps it's alright then. "You are in there most nights, I believe?"

"It gives me a routine."

She nods thoughtfully as if she's thinking of something, someone who isn't there. "Did you speak with anyone - on Wednesday evening I mean."

"Only to order two glasses of cider."

"Did you see any strangers in there or, at least, anyone you didn't recognise? It's a small community, isn't it? I imagine everyone knows just about everyone else?"

"No. Nobody I didn't recognise." Wasn't that the truth of it?

"So, you finished your drink at, what, around closing time? And then you walked straight home?"

Now he had to be careful. They hadn't believed the truth before - preferred their version of it - so why would they believe an untruth now?

"In a manner of speaking?"

"What does that mean?" The younger one has looked up, his long eyelashes failing to hide the intent in his eye. They want to trap him - always had done.

"I mean that I went straight home. I didn't stop to do anything or speak to anyone."

"You took the footpath just before Grace Beech's bungalow then? That's the most direct route to here from the pub, isn't it?"

"It is but I decided to take the long way round. Down Wickham lane and across the fields."

"I thought you said you came straight home?"

"I did."

"So, why go for a walk in the middle of the night? It must have taken you much longer and would have been dark?"

"Moon came up just after eleven, as I knew it would. Besides, I don't need light. I know this part of the world inside out."

"Did you see anyone at all? Not just people you knew; a stranger or strangers perhaps?"

"I didn't see anybody or anything. I came straight home."

"It still seems strange, though," the younger one again, "You have a few drinks and then go for a wander in the middle of the night, unless you were drunk and weren't sure exactly where you were going?"

"I always know exactly where I'm going." He knows that they want to lead him astray.

"What if you had drunk too much? How would you have got home? Taxi would have cost quite a bit, given it has to go out of the village, travel, what, two miles down the road before turning back on itself to climb up the winding track through the woods to here?"

"I've never taken a taxi in my life. I used to stay over at the pub sometimes but that was because of bad weather not bad judgement on my part."

"You paid to stay there?" The older one has finished gazing around his hut, barely able to contain her surprise at how little there is to see. They're all the same.

"I used to have a camp bed they let me use in my mum's room. She used to work there and lodged above."

"Was she not there on Wednesday night - you weren't tempted to stay over?"

He really must stay calm. Don't give them anything they can break and put back together incorrectly. "There was no need for me to stay. She wasn't there in any case."

"Where was she?"

"She'd just been buried in the earth of St Benedict's graveyard."

He watches them walk back down the footpath until they too are out of sight.

**

Lisa Fairhurst is flustered, which is of the utmost interest to Taylor. They are sitting on wooden stools at the 'breakfast bar' in Lisa's small-scale kitchen.

Blushing unnecessarily as Taylor introduced herself, she has thus far busied herself with making them coffee in incongruously pink mugs which now sit, steaming, in front of them both, Taylor's version swirling around with little undissolved granules on the surface, like untended children swimming above a whirlpool.

"As I said, I don't believe I can help you."

A strange and very defensive opening statement from someone who has hitherto no idea what help might be required. Or has the village grapevine already turned wine into water?

"That's fine." Taylor hopes she sounds reassuring, but with just that little bit of needle that might get under the woman's skin. "This visit is just a formality. As part of our routine enquiries when something suspicious happens, we're required to speak with all of those who may have seen or spoken with the person or persons, before an incident has taken place ..."

"Suspicious? Do you mean them finding Andrew's body? I don't know anything about that I'm afraid."

Taylor watches her pretending not to be stealing glances out of the kitchen window which, though its sill is adorned with the greenery of trailing spider plants, provides a good vantage point over the crumpled tarmac drive leading down to the road.

"Did you know Andrew Patch?"

"Yes. Well, no, not really."

"Sorry, was that a yes or a no?" Again, a deep blush appears on the woman's unlovely, flabby face.

"He was a friend of my husband - Stuart. Years ago. Andrew's family moved away when they were little. I didn't know Stuart then. We met at secondary school."

"Andrew had come back for Grace Beech's fiftieth birthday party; is that right?"

"Yes. We met in the pub: The Beaver. Obviously, Stuart hadn't seen him since they left."

"Why obviously? Grace had kept in touch with him all these years."

"No, she hadn't!"

That was interesting. The needle was making good progress.

"I"m sorry, we understood that they exchanged birthday cards each year."

"No. They didn't exchange cards. He sent them to her, not the other way around. He kept in touch with Grace, but nobody kept in touch with Andrew. That's why Stuart was nervous about seeing him again."

"Nervous?"

Now she is on edge. Taylor watches her walk to the window and back again, smoothing down her shapeless pink kitchen overalls before twisting a plain, gold wedding ring around and around her finger.

"Nervous is probably the wrong word. Just ... you know what it's like when you haven't seen someone for a long time! You don't know if they're going to be different, do you? People change, don't they?"

Or maybe you hope that time does change them, thinks Taylor. Whose character did she want to have changed by now: Andrew's or her husband's? And, much more importantly, why?

"How did Andrew seem - on the Wednesday evening

before his body was found just across the road?" Taylor was probably turning the screw a little too tightly - or too quickly - but there was a hole in the wall of silence that Lisa Fairhurst was so obviously struggling to fill.

"He seemed OK. I didn't talk to him much. Neither of us did once Grace arrived."

"We understood there may have been a bit of an argument in the pub before Andrew left; voices raised, that sort of thing?"

"No. No, I don't remember anything like that. It was just a normal night out."

Except that it wasn't, was it? Not unless 'normal' nights out in Castle Upton often involved returning villagers from forty years ago who never managed to leave for a second time.

CHAPTER SIX

Daniel is cursing himself, not for the first time, after leaving the Tesco store in Evesham. It isn't that he wanted to stay there. He hadn't wanted to go in the first place, but they hadn't been able to get an online delivery time until the end of the week. Although Charlotte was remarkably insouciant about it, he hadn't wanted Claire to do without either cereal or fruit. She needed all the fuel she could get, he considered, especially as breakfast seemed to be the only 'real' meal she was eating at the moment. He can barely remember that bottomless pit in his stomach whenever exams approached, but he can appreciate how she is feeling now.

The local shop in Harvington would no doubt have stepped into the breach on both counts but, as Charlotte has kindly pointed out for years, the precious Tesco points contribute to their holidays. Not that they've enjoyed a holiday since she retired.

He pretends to know exactly where he has parked his car among the rank and file of metal bodies while edging tentatively towards the first row. Before he is even halfway across the zebra crossing a car approaches from his right and beeps its horn. Daniel swings around angrily, like a wild animal being threatened by something more powerful. The blue Renault is being driven by a lady who, thankfully, he instantly recognises. How primitive we are, he considers, that such a primal reaction can be tempered by simple recognition. He often considers things like this.

"Let me just go and park!" The driver yells. He watches her narrowly avoid two elderly shoppers with silver trolleys piled high with white, plastic bags, as she dives into a space just large enough for her to slide out of the driver's door, providing she allows her ample bust to be temporarily flattened against the side of the car.

"Hello, stranger!" Kate Shelbourne half walks, half runs towards him.

"Kate. How lovely to see you." He is genuinely pleased to see her, and genuinely delighted that he's remembered her name.

"Where have you been?"

"I've been shopping," he nods towards the vast building behind them both.

"You know what I mean," she laughs, her long hair trying to fly away in the breeze, "I haven't seen you for ages."

"Probably not since I left the paper?" He is very pleased to see her, but, for some reason, he cannot yet identify, is equally keen not to show it.

"I can see that you've done your shopping - last of the big spenders eh!"

"Just a few bits to keep us going," he smiles easily, and it feels so good.

"Are you rushing home, or do you have time for a

quick coffee? There's a Costa just on the left there ..."

He doesn't even make a play of looking at his watch and they are soon installed behind a skinny latte for him and a mocha for her.

"You're looking well!"

"Oh, thanks." She beams. "So are you. Are you still living up at Wood Lench?"

"We are. And you in Evesham?"

"I am. Still on the Journal too, before you ask."

"Out on the road looking for juicy stories."

"That's what it still says in the unofficial job title."

He admires Kate, even though he hasn't seen her since an awards evening almost seven years ago now. 'Time flies.' Isn't that what you're supposed to say? Not for him it hasn't. She's put a few pounds on, to be sure, but he probably has too. Too much sitting – that's always been his problem. Maybe he will take up walking again. He can smell her perfume; listens to her as she runs herself down, just like she did that night until he'd kissed her for the first and only time.

"How about you? How's freelancing?"

"It's fine. Steady. That's the problem!"

She laughs again and sips her drink, the dark line of chocolate remaining on her lip, momentarily. "Did you hear about Eddie Worth's wife? You worked with him didn't you."

"I did. I saw him last week, but he didn't mention

anything."

"Hit and run. Just a few yards from her house. It happened at the weekend. She's in Worcester Royal and the prognosis is not good."

Daniel feels a familiar coldness at the top of his spine. "Poor Linda. I'll have to give Eddie a ring."

"He's at the hospital 24/7 I think, so you might have to keep trying. How about Charlotte? In good health, I hope."

"She is. She misses work I think."

"A bit like you?"

"Yes, but although it's not a work environment, at least I'm still working - she only really has her memories. She does walk a lot, which helps to fill her time."

"You don't go with her?"

This is the second time in a matter of days that he has been asked a similar question. First Fergus and now Kate, who he barely knows. Is it such a crime to prefer peace and quiet?

"Sometimes, but she generally prefers to wander alone; clears her head."

"What is it, Daniel?"

What can she sense that others don't? He has played the same straight bat at her questions, just as he does with everybody else. And yet. And yet something inside him wants to confide in this woman. He ignores the little voice in his head, telling him that this is exactly how journalists get people to say the things they don't want to say. She is sufficiently far removed from his family and friends, and, after all, she has always been kind to him.

"She just gets so angry. Please don't get me wrong: there are times when we are how we used to be. It's lovely when it's like that. It really is. But then she just explodes for no apparent reason, often over something so trivial that it doesn't seem worth the effort - at least not to me."

"Is it always aimed at you? Have you sought any kind of professional help?"

"No. No, I haven't and wouldn't know where to start. Besides, it isn't just me. She's started yelling at Claire more and more. The poor kid doesn't deserve it and certainly not at the moment."

"A-levels?"

"GCSEs. I do what I can to keep her focused, but I can't keep apologising for her mother's behaviour or ask her to understand when I don't understand it myself."

"You said that it isn't like this all the time though?"

"It isn't, no. Something has fundamentally changed. I do know that, and I don't think it's just us growing old or 'familiarity breeding contempt.' It's little things. When I walk into a room she doesn't even look up; no acknowledgement at all that I am there. It's a silly example, I know, but it's often the small details that describe the bigger picture isn't it?"

He can feel his eyes watering. Perhaps he's drunk the hot drink too fast. If Kate has noticed this, she chooses to diplomatically ignore it. Perhaps she's nice with everyone.

"You mentioned her retiring. Do you think she left too early?"

"Probably, but I thought it was work that was getting her so uptight. I thought she would be better when she left them. The last nine months of her time there were pretty tough, but two years have passed since then. Instead of finding peace, she's found war."

"I guess you just need to keep talking to her - or listening - as best you can, for your daughter's sake as much as anybody's, and hope it blows over. It might well do, you know."

She has placed her right hand on his left in a gesture of support. Thankfully he can still lift his coffee glass with his right as he has no desire for her to move it.

"I hope so. I tell everyone that it's just a period of change and I have to hang on to that; I suppose we both do."

He doesn't tell her that he and Charlotte have made love twice in the last week - which is more than they have done for a very long time - or that she had flown at him the day before for re-arranging the plates in the dishwasher. He has always done this automatically, but this time Charlotte seemed to take great, personal offence at his actions. 'If I'd wanted a dishwasher, I wouldn't have bought a machine' she'd screamed at him.

Even Claire had hurried downstairs, her glasses smudged beyond tired eyes, to see what crisis had taken her away from Neville Chamberlain's best efforts during the 30s.

Kate does now remove her hand but only to reach inside her jacket pocket and hand him a card.

"You know you can call me at any time ... off the record, naturally."

They both laugh.

He wonders whether to confide in her about his wife's texts. It seems a step too far, even though it would be a weight off his mind. Maybe next time - if, as he sincerely hopes, there is a next time. They can go further then if it feels right.

Besides, this is the first text he's spotted for a while, and he does feel a bit ashamed at going behind Charlotte's back. He's probably reading far too much into those few characters. It isn't like last summer when they seemed to be coming through every other hour. Charlotte's explanation at the time had been that an old school friend from Surrey had moved to Malvern and wanted some help to find out about shops, doctor's surgery and so on: stuff she didn't think he'd have been interested in. Charlotte had spent a lot of time away from the house during those hot weeks and seemed to head for the shower as soon as she returned.

He's never actually met the friend. Perhaps she'd found what she'd needed help with because the texts subsided (or Charlotte buried them more cleverly). Is this a new friend?

"At least you've got your health". Kate is continuing. "Did you read the piece about that poor man in Castle Upton?"

"I did. Found dead on a footpath, wasn't he?"

"He was. The police have been all over the village collecting DNA from each of those who saw him last. They were in the pub - The Beaver, do you know it?"

"I don't, I'm afraid. I've seen the signs to it off the main road though."

"Very 'olde worthy' and aimed at the tourists. Except that the person who died wasn't a tourist. He'd come back to celebrate a birthday with a lady he was at school with more than forty years ago."

"Poor chap. Do they have any idea how he died?"

"There were some strange markings on the front of his face and also his neck."

Daniel raises his eyebrows. "I won't ask."

"Good, Because I won't tell. Suffice to say my sources are extremely well-placed."

"Of course, they are. Go on."

"It doesn't look accidental; put it like that. Except there appears to be nothing else for the police to go on so they've drawn a bit of a blank. I'm not sure if they've explored the historical angle to see if there is any connection with this case. We'll soon find out because there's another piece going out tomorrow morning."

"What historical angle?"

"The Julie Beech disappearance in 1977."

"The little girl? The children who were playing hide and seek in the woods?"

"They'd been playing in a quarry. I was only eight myself – the same age as Julie. I remember my Gran crying her eyes out over it."

"That's it. They found blood splatters on some stones but no body. I thought I remembered a series of stories about it from the time but wasn't sure if my mind was playing tricks on me. They never did find out what happened to her, did they?"

"They didn't. She might still be alive today. The detective in charge of the enquiry - Cummings - never got over it, apparently, and certainly didn't manage to clamber any further up the greasy pole. Did you ever come across him? He was based in Worcester?"

"Oh yes. I remember him very well; no need to question myself about that. When you're young - just starting out - you tend to remember the people you first come into contact with, and he was up there, believe me!"

"Sorry. I'd forgotten you'd had history. Well, the really interesting thing is that one of the children who was questioned at the time about whether or not he'd seen anything was Andrew Patch - the man who has just lost his life."

***

"Duncan Harewood didn't appear to be at all inquisitive as to why we were there. He also told us that he 'didn't see anybody or anything.' Why would he say that? Why would someone with absolutely nothing to hide rule out his seeing 'anything' without even knowing what the something is that we're investigating?"

The three of them are sitting around Taylor's desk, Harcourt having wheeled his chair out to them as there was barely enough room in his booth for them to come to him.

"Perhaps Harewood just isn't the inquisitive type?" Flowers is trying not to look too relaxed but can't help sitting back in his chair and rotating very slightly. "His appears to be a very simple life. I didn't spot a TV or radio in his house, and the only books on display were on birds and British wildflowers. Apart from that it was pretty much just an empty shack. Must get mighty cold in the winter, especially if it's a bad one!"

"Maybe he is just at home in his immediate environment, and that's enough for him?" Taylor doesn't sound convinced or convincing.

"I always worry when people who live remotely or in isolation appear to be completely cut off from the rest of the world. Man is by nature a social being and to have so little interaction with the outside world seems unlikely to me."

"But that is the real world to him, sir; he doesn't need

or want to go beyond that!" Flowers sits forward again. "His home in the woods and his regular trips to The Beaver might be pretty much all he has ever known. How would a man like that broaden his horizons? Presumably at his age he never will?"

"On that subject, what did we find out about his mother?"

Taylor opens a database record on her screen and navigates down to a notes section she had been updating when Harcourt arrived. "Lettie Harewood, sir. She worked at The Beaver for over fifty years. Again, a local girl who doesn't appear to have strayed very far at all. Duncan took her name. She was never married and there is no father listed on Duncan's birth certificate. She died a couple of weeks ago. Pneumonia. She'd had a weak chest for years; bronchitis most winters."

"What is it with these people who are prepared to just accept what they've got, pretty much all that they were born with - no ambition to venture further afield?" Harcourt still isn't convinced that this is a natural default. "Castle Upton is nice enough but surely you only really get to appreciate that when you've got somewhere else to compare it with?"

"Security, though, isn't it, sir?" Flowers is really on it today. He'd left Rob in a great mood earlier and feels as if he's on something of a high (even as they discuss death). "They might have seen people leave for greater things and just as quickly return to what they know best; the grass isn't always greener. That sort of thing."

"Andrew Patch didn't come back did he - not for

decades?"

"No, he didn't. But not sure Gunnersbury Park was a heavenly paradise either."

Paradise? Harcourt wheels sideways towards Taylor once more.

"So, nothing else to add about Lettie Harewood?"

"No, sir. The funeral took place on the same day that Andrew Patch travelled down from London."

"Patch was not coming down for that then? He'd have come down at least a day earlier if that was the case."

"Yes, sir. There doesn't appear to be anything to connect Patch with Duncan Harewood at this stage, or any of the others we've spoken with, beyond a childhood association with Stuart Fairhurst. It does seem that Grace Beech's birthday celebration was his only reason for coming back to Castle Upton."

"It seems a long way to come for just a couple of days though, doesn't it?" Harcourt gets up and walks slowly around the small office space, very quickly ending up where he started. "By everyone's accounts, he hasn't seen Grace or been back for the best part of forty years. I know that fifty years old is quite an achievement - well worth a celebration - but, I mean, in reality, it was just a drink in the pub, wasn't it? No marquee on the lawn or even a social event in the village hall. It all seems a bit flimsy to me."

"And why wouldn't turning fifty mean anything to the rest of the village? Flowers sits up but immediately sits down again, hemmed in as he effectively is by

Harcourt's chair and his own desk. "She's lived there all her life and yet hasn't enough friends who would want to have a proper party."

"That's a very good point, Ian. a very good point indeed."

Flowers grins from ear to ear, not just because he'd come up with something useful but because the DI had used his Christian name. It was as rare an occurrence as it was welcome.

"You both said that Grace Beech was hard work? Or, at least, I think that's how you described her?"

"She certainly was sir. DS Flowers and I felt it was like getting blood out of a stone. I thought at first it might have been that 'Saint Grace' thing, you know - where people adopt a very calm, holier-than-thou approach to keep quiet about the things that do matter to them. During our short time there, though, I watched as her eyes darted all over the place and there was a noticeable tightening of her facial muscles at certain points in the conversation."

"She was all there then?"

"Without a doubt. She was tuned in and, more than that, it was as though she was anticipating us asking her things, having already rehearsed her answers, and knowing full well when to close down the interview altogether."

"I agree with DS Taylor, sir." Flower is nodding sagely. "Grace Beech was extremely defensive for no single reason that we could work out. Yes, we seemed to strike a nerve here and there, but her whole outlook was borderline hostile."

There is a sudden crash as the only door to their office bursts open, completing its sixty-degree rotation and recording another permanent marker to join the many marks and dents on the wall adjacent to it.

"So sorry to spoil your cosy little chat!"

They all stand up - Flowers a little ungainly as his bottom is pushed so far back in the chair it takes him a couple of movements before he can scramble out of it – as Hunter-Wright strides towards them.

"I suppose you're expecting me to say, 'at ease' or something like that!" He thunders. "Unfortunately, this is not the armed services and you lot can count yourselves very lucky indeed that I'm not armed."

"How may we help you, sir?" Harcourt is trying hard to keep the wobble out of his voice - for the sake of his team members as much as himself.

"'How may I help you, sir'" Hunter-Wright mimics him, hunching his shoulders in a submissive fashion as he does so - to enhance the effect. "We're not bloody shopkeepers, Harcourt; we're the police. Other people help us as we detect and then inform. We do not 'help'"

"Sorry, sir!"

"And we never apologise for what we do or how we do it unless forced to do so by the bloody media. Understand!"

They all nod in unison, although Taylor and

Flowers are more confused than subdued. The Detective Superintendent is well known for his outbursts but doesn't normally share them with mere foot soldiers.

"How precisely did we miss this?" He holds up a copy of the Evesham Journal, folded to page three. "Forgive me for being old-fashioned and a not very PC PC, but page three used to be something you looked forward to revealing. Not today, it seems."

Taylor has moved her face very slightly sideways as if it has received a slap. Each of them awaits further information.

***

Frank Fairhurst is reading aloud at the kitchen table, even though his wife has already read the article and is curled up in a comfy chair at the far end of the room, trying hard to concentrate on the latest in a series of fictional novels featuring Thomas Cromwell.

... memories of the tragic case of Julie Beech, the eight-year-old schoolgirl who disappeared late one evening in 1977. She had been playing hide and seek in the now-disused Vale Quarry with her older sister, Grace, who had dutifully counted to ten but then couldn't find her anywhere. After an hour or so she rushed back into Castle Upton to raise the alarm and a search party of friends and family was formed before the police even arrived at the village. All of this was to no avail as Julie was never found, although blood splatters - later confirmed as belonging to Julie - were found on stones to one side of the quarry.

Andrew Patch, whose body was found in Castle Upton last week, was a close friend of the Beech girls and was routinely questioned as part of the police enquiry, but no evidence was ever produced that put him at the scene. Similarly, Stuart Fairhurst later claimed that he had seen Duncan Harewood - a seventeen-year-old labourer who worked on his father's farm on Piddle Road - walking past the quarry that evening but, again, nothing came of it.

No motive was ever put forward for foul play as such. Mrs Angela Rogers - her class teacher - described Julie at the time as 'a bright and popular girl.' The officer in charge of the original case - DI Cummings - who has since retired, said at the time that the case would remain open and that the police would 'never give up on the Beech family.' Until an actual body was discovered, they would 'continue to work tirelessly on the assumption that she was still alive.'

It is unclear whether the police are linking the two incidents or, indeed, whether any crime took place in either. Naturally, the suspicious nature of Mr Patch's sudden death has brought back unhappy memories for many in the village who have had to live with 'the unexplained' for far too long.

He slaps the paper down, noisily drains his mug of coffee, and turns to Anabel, completely oblivious to the fact that he hasn't been reading to her at all.

"All things come to an end then!"

She looks up with as much disinterest as she can muster and replies, enigmatically. "Is it the end, though, or just the beginning?"

He glares at her before lifting his heavy gut off the stool, walking out of the room and slamming the front door behind him.

***

Harcourt is feeling tense now - as though all of his joints have been tightened by an invisible screwdriver. It isn't Hunter-Wright's latest eruption that has done this, it's something from the past: his past. After a short pause, he answers the question regarding their original sin.

"There was nothing on file about this, sir. No link to any cold case in the area."

"You did search, presumably?" He is glaring at Flowers now. "Billy Whizz kid over here turned up nothing?"

Flowers feels as if he should say something if only to try and reduce quite so much blood building up in his cheeks. "I did all the usual cross-checks, sir."

"You're a policeman, not bloody cabin crew."

"No, sir."

"So how did we not make the connection when some hack did? No wonder the people you've interviewed were so reticent. They were probably grieving all over again for the little girl who went out to play and never came back, or they were waiting for you to at least indicate to them that you knew what you were doing. Grace Beech was most likely expecting some kind of sensitivity, which might have been the key to other secrets rather than downright suspicion! Nothing you've told me so far suggests you've got any further with this case than Cummings did."

"With respect, sir, we do have a body this time."

"And much progress you've made since a paper boy found it for you!"

They each wait for him to calm down. Taylor hasn't uttered a word for several minutes, looking downwards and averting the Superintendent's furious gaze.

"Right. Well, firstly, we did make the connection. Agreed?" He glares at each of them in turn, watching Harcourt blush and the others simply nod. "We chose not to pursue it as a first line of enquiry for fear of upsetting the villagers when there was no obvious connection to the Julie Beech case. We can play that one out as our modern commitment to sensitive policing. Put it on file and backdate it, OK?"

Flowers glances at Harcourt, then back at Hunter-Wright but says nothing.

"Well!" His voice echoes around the small room which is becoming smaller by the second, like an interview room for those with one thing to hide.

"Yes, sir." Flowers bows his head, out of shame rather than courtesy.

What is it with this pretty boy? Hunter-Wright is far from impressed. 'Don't you know you're driving your mamas and papas insane?'

"At least then we'll have it on file, and this will confirm that we were ahead of the game played by those bloody scribblers. We have collected all DNA samples?"

"Yes, sir." Harcourt feels slightly more relaxed now,

police procedure filling the void of helplessness and self-doubt, though institutional deception is not what he had signed up for. None of them had.

"Including Pinky and Perky from the farm who were in the pub?"

"John Orfield and Peter Farnham. Yes, sir. Nothing on file for either."

"Oh, laddie managed to do a 'cross-check' did he?"

"Yes, sir." Harcourt knows that there is nothing more he can do until the storm dies down; not until the full weight of the force has dissipated and Hunter-Wright remembers that they are in this together. They are the force.

"What about the woofter's 'partner' from the cafe?"

Taylor notices Flowers visibly flinch and steps into the breach. No need for him to have to deal with Neanderthal Man. It's bad enough being a mere woman. "Jo Silva, sir. He broke up with Steve Pateman about three years ago. We haven't managed to get his DNA, but I can assure you that he wasn't involved with the death of Andrew Patch."

"Oh, and how precisely can you draw such a conclusion, Sergeant?"

"Because he moved to the States just under a year ago, sir. The Wisconsin sheriff's office has established a sound alibi for his whereabouts that evening."

"Go on."

"He was at a 'spring harvest' celebration with several

of their officers. There is a strong Christian bond between police and the local community there."

"God, give me strength! At least that's one person from the recent past we can rule out then. You now need to start digging much deeper. See if our villagers are upset or uneasy. There's a big difference between the two. Harcourt, get over to the pathologist's office. We need to understand better what the markings on Andrew Patch's body mean."

"With respect, sir, Jenny has already told me that there's not much more she can tell us."

"Well, with respect, DI Harcourt, ask 'Jenny' again and find out what little help she can be. You two need to go and see this Mrs Rogers who's mentioned in the article. Go gently with her. I've no doubt Cummings will have given her a rough time during the original enquiry. He's far less subtle than me."

"Yes, sir" Taylor and Flowers move to leave the room.

"Harcourt, you need to speak with this Harewood chap - see and hear for yourself what he's like. Make your own mind up."

Taylor bristles at the intended slur. She's not always right in her character judgements, but she rarely gets it wrong either.

"And we'll need to talk with Grace Beech again?"

"Of course, sir."

Of course or off course?

"Again, kill her with kindness. She lost a sister and

time may have done little to ease the pain. You know how it is when families haven't got a body to bury: the grieving process can never be properly completed, especially as she was just a child when it all happened. She had everything to look forward to - they both did - but, instead, she's probably never stopped looking back."

He breaks off, suddenly, as if trying to recall something; fails and moves on. "I'll speak with Cummings directly. He must be well into his eighties now so not sure how selective his memory will be. By all accounts he was an irascible bastard then and I don't imagine he is so very different now. He left the force soon after the Julie Beech case - he was only 40 - but, as we all know, police officers never really leave the scene."

"Will this be referred up the line, sir?" Harcourt is also relieved at having something to do.

"Up the line? Over my dead body. Without motive or evidence in either case, or any obvious link between them, the coroner will have no choice but to leave the case open or, worse, ours will just be ruled 'accidental' and everything else will be buried again. There would clearly have been no DNA from back then. It must have been a good nine or ten years before that little gift was given to us. So, we have very little to go on, but we are going to revisit all of it. Understand?"

"Yes, sir. I'll request the files from storage immediately."

"I'm aware that we're running things on a shoestring here. This team should be at least twice as big as this. If we do need extra bodies, I'll second them from somewhere."

One body would be good, thinks Taylor, naughtily. She detests Hunter-Wright with a passion, both for what he says and what she believes he stands for. She had at first assumed that she was invisible in his presence, only to quickly realise that he had seen her and made his mind up on that initial glance in her direction, and that alone, about who she was.

"Given that the media have been so helpful to us, I want to reciprocate by ensuring nothing else goes into the papers without my say-so. I shall be heading this enquiry from now on. I want answers, and explanations, not contact reports that social services could have written."

He turns to leave but stops just before the door, still wide open to reveal bent hinges.

"And all of you need to remember, as one old fart said to another: 'Hope I die before I get old.' We don't know for certain whether Julie Beech's hopes were ever realised, or her fears. By solving the mystery of Andrew Patch's death, we may go some way to understanding what happened all those years ago. Now that's something I would gladly encourage the papers to print."

***

Jenny Graham is sitting in her small but perfectly adequate office, sipping lemon tea from a white china cup. She looks up when Harcourt is escorted in by Ted, one of her clinical assistants, but otherwise doesn't move.

"Dr Graham!" Harcourt seats himself on the long white bench adjacent to her remarkably tidy desk. Everything in here is as though it's been hermetically sealed, he thinks, including Jenny Graham herself.

"You wanted to see me, Inspector, though why the sudden desire to make house calls is beyond me."

There is a gentle knock on the door. It's Ted again. Tall, gangly and fighting a losing battle against acne he asks, politely and almost soundlessly, whether anyone would like a drink.

"We're fine, thanks, Ted." Dr Graham continues sipping whereas Harcourt is just relieved that the automatic door has closed behind Ted. The overwhelming smell of disinfectant and other chemicals that took the opportunity to creep in reminds him of the horrors at the other end of the corridor.

"I just wanted to ask you again about the contusion and markings on the body of Andrew Patch."

"You mean you wanted to hear me repeat myself - in person - as opposed to over the phone!"

He tries not to look into her eyes but can't help taking in her small face below her short, cropped blonde hair and wondering what it would take for her to smile - just once.

"You maintain that this wasn't a simple accident?"

"I never said that so it's difficult to maintain it." She smiles, but it isn't the kind of smile Harcourt was dreaming of.

"The markings on his face: you said they seemed odd and inconsistent with a simple fall, after which, everything else led to a cardiac arrest as cause of death."

"They are unexplained, yes, but you've got the latter part of the diagnosis correct. It appears that something had been pushed into his face, but I'd rule out a man's fist - or a woman's. Neither was it sharp as there is no tear in the skin, just extensive bruising.

One of his rear neck muscles was also torn. Technically we'd refer to it as neck strain or a 'pulled muscle' had we been dealing with a live patient. In this case, the Trapezius muscle was damaged. For someone so interested in flying kites, I can confirm that it is the kite-shaped one running from the neck's base, down the back and out towards the shoulders.

The injury could have happened as a result of the fall itself - where his head came into contact with the stone and possibly flipped up. If that had been the case, though, I'd have expected front muscles to also have been damaged, but they were not."

"So, you think the sudden movement into his face was the trigger for everything that came after?"

"I don't think it, I'm certain of it."

***

Daniel is half-listening as his wife and daughter discuss some arcane aspects of mathematics downstairs. He is vaguely aware that it concerns co-ordinates, but the example Claire had shown him earlier involved far more than finding a simple point on a map.

He is up in his wife's room, the contents of her handbag strewn over her bed. He picks each of them up in turn - purse, hairbrush, a battered silver strip of ibuprofen tablets that look as though they lost their protective cardboard box years earlier - before returning them to the bag. He feels nothing. He picks up her mobile phone again. There had been another text that morning, confirming a time for the following afternoon: 3.30. He scans for notifications on the Home Screen that, similarly, do not require it to be unlocked. There is nothing there.

He hears the murmur of voices growing louder as he descends.

***

Angela Rogers greets Taylor and Flowers as if they are old friends. She is dressed in a grey, knitted waistcoat atop a pink blouse and matching grey skirt which fans out as she walks, covering almost everything in its path, including a considerably overweight tabby cat which shows surprising acceleration in hurtling outside before she can shut the front door. Red-faced and stout, she is the embodiment of a jolly hockey teacher who entered teaching in the late 1950s and undoubtedly informed and entertained two generations of children in equal measure.

On the latter front, the detectives can't help wondering how she obtained a black eye patch over her left eye and wondering for how long either of them can avoid mentioning it.

"Come in. Come in!"

They are led into a comfortable front room of a pink chintz sofa and younger armchair cousins. Their host sinks into a comfortable well-upholstered chair in one corner, a small table to one side of her hosting both a silver laptop and crystal glass on its dedicated circular mat. The laptop pings as she does so.

"Please do excuse me for one second!"

The detectives sit at either end of the sofa, watching her type: not the one-fingered plonking of keys that might have been expected of a woman in her eighties, but swift and decisive.

Taylor glances around the bright and airy room. No photographs but some nice Capodimonte figurines on the windowsill and Lladro monks praying for forgiveness behind a locked glass cabinet. This certainly isn't a woman who struggles on a pension, but neither is it ostentatious as such. It all seems to just fit comfortably with someone comfortable in her own skin. Her mum would have loved this room. No wooden 'A Present from Ironbridge' coasters here, precious though they were to her.

She notices also that the chairs on which they are sitting are much too close to the small glass coffee table that separates them from Mrs Rogers. She deduces that the occasional chairs are only used very occasionally; this probably isn't a room which sees many family gatherings and visitors might be few and far between. Mrs Rogers' chair represents 'mission control' and there are few orbiting satellites to get in the way of that.

Mrs Rogers hits the RETURN key with a flourish and looks up.

"Ah, you've made yourself quite at home. Excellent. Let me get you both a drink."

Taylor holds up her right hand in mock protest. "Really. There's no need. We won't take up too much of your time."

"Are you quite sure?" She looks questioningly at Flowers who follows the party line of abstinence. "I hope you don't mind if I have a top-up?"

With that, she leans into a small wooden cabinet on the other side of her chair and selects a bottle of Glenmorangie whisky. Two-thirds full she pours herself a generous measure into a crystal tumbler before carefully placing the bottle back in its (almost certainly) temporary home.

"I know it's a bit early but I have a busy evening ahead."

Flowers surreptitiously checks his watch to confirm that it is, indeed, just past half-past one, while they both wait politely for her to elaborate.

The 'pirate' image would have been complete had it been a glass of rum. Taylor thinks it; Flowers articulates it, sort of. "Your partial eyesight does not appear to affect your speed around the keyboard…"

She smiles. "Everyone wonders, but few have the courage to ask. Good for you, young man!"

They wait, on tenterhooks, while she empties most

of the glass before proceeding. "It was eighteen years ago during a darts match: the Wychavon Inter-Village Championship, Third Division South. I was a keen player and they were keen to have me as I could work out the scores like lightning. '301 down' held few terrors for me. They used to call me 'double and out' as I could quickly calculate the best route to win; could see it in my mind, never mind this patch. I also had plenty of doubles from the bar afterwards to celebrate the wins. I loved the competition, you see."

"What happened?" Flowers is spellbound by this quite unexpected character reference.

"We were down at Elmley Castle – *The Nelson's Arm*. An arrow bounced off the metal surround of the board. I was going for double seven – always trickier for a right-hander – and overdid it. Meant it as a marker but it flew back into my left eye. I never did get my sight back; well, not all of it. Right one's fine, praise the Lord."

"That must have been quite a talking point for the schoolchildren?"

"It was. Lots of giggling, parrot references and 'we don't see eye to eye, miss' comments. I've heard them all. All good fun, apart from those whose minds were less developed. Their stares were more sinister and long-lasting. Children have the capacity to be very cruel from a very young age. Most grow out of it, of course."

The grown-up (ish!) child in Taylor feels vaguely ashamed as she takes the lead. "Thank you for agreeing to see us today Mrs Rogers ..."

"Angela, please!"

"Sure. Angela. We are just investigating the unexplained death of Andrew Patch last week and, naturally, following up on any possible links to the disappearance of Julie Beech in 1977."

Mrs Rogers takes another large gulp of whisky. Not that she seems at all perturbed by anything in the present or the past. "Lovely children - both of them."

"You remember them clearly?" Flowers is concerned equally about the stimulating or subduing effects of alcohol.

"I do. Of course!" She smiles. "They say that a good teacher never forgets any of her pupils - not just those who go on to become mass murderers!" She throws back her head and laughs heartily.

Seeing the blank, if not slightly mystified, faces staring back at her, she continues quickly. "Sorry. Sorry. In bad taste I suppose. Yes, I remember all of them. Julie was eight at the time of ... and Grace – her sister – must have been at least a year older. Grace's birthday was in the April. I do remember that because it was very close to Easter one year and we wrapped an extra egg up for her birthday. Julie's was later. End of August maybe?"

"Were they close - as sisters I mean?" Taylor is trying very hard not to think about chocolate.

"Yes. Very. In fact, there was a little group of them who teamed up. Grace and Julie along with Stuart Fairhurst and poor Andrew Patch."

"Nobody else in their gang?"

"I wouldn't call it a gang, my dear. That rather conjures up various dark images of violence or coercion or, at the very least, bullying, doesn't it? I think these children were just happy to be children which seems to be a state of contentment - of equilibrium - by-passed by so many today, sadly."

"They were good friends!"

"As far as I could see, which was usually the wall at the end of the classroom with the map of the world on it. Their world was much larger I think."

She takes another large gulp of whisky which appears to have no effect whatsoever on either her speech or attention to detail. "I don't know if others were allowed to join in their games. Children can be quite territorial once they've formed their cohorts, can't they? On playground duty we would often come across shy little things leaning against the wall, hoping their loneliness would not be noticed, yet knowing at the same time that to try and join in (or break into) others' circles was futile. Not that everything was rosy in the garden."

"What do you mean by that?" Taylor is striving to keep the conversation on track, aware that whimsy is very often a bed partner of whisky.

"Nothing specific. Just that we often look back at our childhoods or those of our parents through rose-tinted spectacles, do we not? Everything is pretty straightforward when you're a child, isn't it? Uncomplicated. Anything else you usually leave to your parents to sort out. The problem for Grace was that her parents didn't sort things out for her - they weren't in any fit state to do so. I don't think they ever really got over Julie's death, so poor Grace effectively lost a sister, a mother and a father - her whole family."

"And best friend too - if Julie and Grace were close that is?"

"I'm sure they were. No doubt there were lots of petty jealousies and squabbles as well - the Beech girls certainly had their moments, like all sisters - but 'soap operas' on television try to persuade us that these only occur in adulthood ... when we reach 'maturity.' Grace was off school for the remainder of the summer term. I do remember that."

Flowers also senses that Mrs Rogers is peering into some kind of chasm. What was it that Rob had called it? 'The irony of oversight.' He tries to drive her away from the edge.

"And Stuart and Andrew, what can you tell us about them?"

"Stuart was a larger child, and larger than life. I suspect he led the others astray whenever he got the chance. Andrew was quieter - in thrall to the others perhaps - but the cleverest. He wasn't a practical child but always came out at the top or nearly top of the class in pretty much everything else."

"His family left the village quite soon after Julie died?"

"They did and I was very sad to see him go. A bright spark can often ignite the flames of others. His father struggled, I think. Since then, they've put a lot of effort into making Castle Upton more tourist-friendly ..." she screws up her nose in distaste, "so he might have done better these days. He was a pale, thin man - Andrew's father; always looked as though he had the weight of the world on his slender shoulders."

Flowers turns back several pages in his notebook. "We met a Mr Duncan Harewood. Do you remember him at all?"

"Duncan! Of course. The poor child came to school in rags most days, not that he played truant - unlike some. I could have understood it if he had. The others teased him endlessly, but he seemed to rise above it. Always one for the outdoors, Duncan. He loved it whenever we worked outside in the playground or went on nature walks. He knew the names of the butterflies and wildflowers better than I did!"

"He didn't live in the woods then, surely?"

"I don't believe so. I'm not sure, to be honest. I wouldn't keep seed potatoes in that shed. He'd certainly been living with his mother - Lettie - over the pub. Not that it was a much more suitable place for a young boy. I suppose she had little choice."

"The father was unknown?"

"I suspect he was known, young man, although whether or not she ever told anyone who he was, I wouldn't know. He certainly wasn't on the scene throughout Duncan's childhood."

"He was older, wasn't he?

"Older than?"

"Sorry. The children - Grace, Julie, Stuart and Andrew."

"He was. Duncan was a strapping young man at the time of the incident. He'd left school the previous summer. He had to put up with a great deal after Julie's disappearance. Papers from London got hold of the story - thought it might be the beginning of another Moors Murders scenario I suppose: 'Cotswolds Killer or Kidnapper?' That was one of their more tedious headlines. Of course, they knew no more about what had happened to Julie than the rest of us.

They did seem to think Duncan was somehow involved though. I never really understood why that was. Mr Sutcliffe - our Headmaster - believed that someone was feeding them false information in return for money. I'm not sure if that was true or not. Mr Sutcliffe was an English teacher after all; they're always blessed with vivid imaginations."

"It must have been terrible for Grace - and her parents. Not knowing what had happened to Julie. Newspaper stories can only have made it worse?" Taylor has lowered her voice as if in deference to the dead (or at least the missing).

"Of course. I suspect all their worlds were completely shattered. Tom Beech - the girls' father was a greengrocer. His shop's long gone now. A pity really - his cabbages were delicious - and it would have fitted the 'traditional English village' brochure now, wouldn't it? He had a heart attack only a few years later and died in hospital. I didn't know her mother - Evelyn - very well.

Well, you don't, do you? You see the man, not his wife. She moved away after that. I'm afraid I couldn't tell you where to, but I do know that she died too. Annabel Fairhurst told me so."

"Poor woman!"

"Which one: Evelyn or Annabel? Evelyn went to her grave not knowing if her daughter was still alive or not. Annabel will go to hers no doubt wondering if she's ever really lived."

"Because of her husband?" Taylor is quite shocked by the old woman's assertion.

"Would you like to wake up next to him every morning?"

Taylor feels even more uncomfortable now, a little vulnerable even. "And Grace. How do you think she would have coped with Julie's absence all these years?"

"She refused to talk about it for a long time. The 'experts' tried to get her to write stories or draw pictures as a means of letting her thoughts out. I don't think it did any good. Grace and her sister used to spend hours with their crayons. 'Quiet play' we called it. It allowed their creativity to develop with no bounds you see. The National Curriculum would probably call it 'developmental mindfulness' these days, though how the nouveau kitsch would measure it I have no idea. Not that they do either of course! How we ever managed to teach without them providing rear mirrors I'll never know."

"Do you think Grace has ever come to terms with

what happened?"

"Again, difficult to know for certain isn't it? Equilibrium is such a terrible word - should never have been let out of science labs - and I don't know if 'balance' is appropriate here. Is a balanced individual on the surface better equipped to face life than one with an inner drive to do something, believe something ... be something."

"You think she's still expecting Julie to walk in one day?" Taylor has seen other victims of loss fight tooth and nail against acceptance of the facts, even given the most compelling evidence presented to them.

"I think as a child she thought that, yes. Anything can seem possible when you're a child, can't it? She tended to spend less time with the boys after Julie's death. I saw her heading into the woods a few times on her own. I caught her unawares once - quite close to Duncan's shack - and she was a bit embarrassed, I think. She told me she was looking for Julie. Poor child. After her father died, it was as if all hope died with him.

Grace has been grieving ever since that terrible evening in the quarry and you'll find that she's usually dressed in black still; all the colour drained from her life as a child. Hard to even begin to fill that kind of gap, isn't it?"

"Indeed. I'm sorry if all of this brings back bad memories for you - and to all of those who lived through it I imagine."

"At least we did live through it; we're still here. We don't know where Julie is."

There is a sudden ping on the laptop. Mrs Rogers almost leaps off the sofa before opening the lid of her laptop and tapping several keys.

"Excuse me one moment ... ah, excellent." She starts tapping again - with much more than a flourish this time - before closing the lid again and turning back to them both, a broad grin on her face.

"Another good result. Let's hope you have similar success."

"Are you some kind of online trader, Angela?" Taylor's curiosity is piqued now.

"Not exactly, though all my dealings are online, yes." She pours herself another, even more generous measure of whisky (to celebrate?) and sits back, clearly very pleased with herself.

"What I do involves understanding and anticipating other people's behaviour patterns. I suppose you could say it is an extension of teaching - though that was many years ago now - in that observation is everything. No point in teaching granny to suck eggs if her mouth's stitched up is there?"

CHAPTER SEVEN

By his poor standards, Harcourt has slept even worse than usual. From memory he was first awake at about two o'clock - just an hour after putting his book down - and then his mobile phone told him it was three, four and five, without even ringing him to let him know.

Naturally, he may well have been asleep for some of the intervening time, but he could just as easily not have slept at all. He certainly feels more wrecked than revitalised, and coffee is surely going to face an uphill struggle all day to keep him in a vertical position.

Debbie was seemingly unaware of his restlessness - or pretended not to notice - but she is stirring now.

"What time is it?" Even half-asleep she can still snap as crisply as a crocodile.

"Just after seven; go back to sleep. I'll bring you a cup of tea up when I've had my shower."

"No point. I'm awake now!"

"OK. Well, I'll go and make it now then."

"That isn't what I meant, and you know it. I never get back to sleep once you've woken me up."

He ignores the unfounded accusation and the strange logic within it.

"I didn't wake you up on purpose."

"No, Martin, you never do! Was it her again?"

"Yes. But I'm dealing with it."

"Except you're not really, are you? Each time you get involved with a case like this it's going to bring it all back."

"I can't help it. I wish it wouldn't."

"I know that, and I do understand, but I've suggested time and time again that you seek some kind of professional help and still you refuse to do so. Everyone says that talking about it – sharing it with someone else – is the first step to recovery."

"I'm not everyone, and I think that would just make it worse - going over it all again."

"Like you haven't spent the night doing just that? She's not one of your victims who's going to be content to remain buried, is she? You must face it."

"I know. Sleeping has just been hard work lately."

"If you're going to just talk rubbish…" She turns away on her side, crossly, and dragging most of the blankets with her - for comfort, but also to cocoon herself from him.

"I just can't resolve it in my mind."

"It's not always about the difference between right and wrong."

For him, it is though. For him, it always will be.

***

"Morning sir. I've discovered why Julie Beech's cold case was not linked to our current enquiry."

Harcourt sees how enthusiastic his acting sergeant is but finds it difficult to respond in kind. Whatever Flowers has now turned up, mistakes have been made, and Harcourt doesn't like mistakes - especially when he is the one now having to take responsibility for them.

"Go on."

"Whoever wrote up the original report on file, misspelt Julie Beech's name, sir. It's down as Beck."

"Surely there's more to it than that?"

"Yes, there is, sir." Flowers can understand his superior's frustration but doesn't yet understand why he's being quite so aggressive. "The contact report filed by DI Cummings's team was on the old system. When our new network went in four years ago and all the files were transferred, the address of the incident was listed simply as Evesham, not Castle Upton. Because of that simple lack of cross-referencing, we failed to make the connection."

"Maybe we needed to be more sophisticated - like the Evesham Journal? Presumably, their systems and their people talk to each other. Perhaps they use Google Maps while we're still relying on dog-eared atlases."

Taylor has been listening to this increasingly heated exchange. "It's not our fault that DI Cummings's team messed up, is it sir? Or that the techies didn't match all the address fields properly when the old records came across."

"Try telling that to a prosecution lawyer or a fifty-year-old woman who's spent the best part of her life wondering if she'll ever see her sister again?" He hears his words reverberating around the small room and immediately regrets it, if not them: that way Detective Superintendent Hunter-Wright lies.

"There is one piece of good news, sir." Flowers is as red in the face as Harcourt is.

"That would be welcome." He is calmer now, better.

"The photograph Andrew Patch had in his wallet has been matched to the one of the young Julie Beech on the file at the time of her sister's disappearance. It was a copy of a school photograph taken in 1976."

"Why would he have that? I mean, why would her parents have paid for an extra school photograph? They cost money, which was tight at the garage. They would surely have only been to give out to other family members?"

"Could they have been childhood sweethearts, giving one to Julie, who in turn passed it on to Andrew? Perhaps he too was holding on to the hope of one day seeing her again?" Taylor offers, tentatively.

"Possibly. I wonder if he had her picture in his wallet all the time he was married, or only since the divorce. What would he have told his wife? Just someone he happened to know as a child? Seems a bit far-fetched to me unless Andrew Patch did know what happened to her, and this was a reminder to him - and his former playmates - to never allow her to be forgotten?"

"You mean like some kind of scourge to punish himself with?"

Harcourt glares at Flowers as he would at any Jesuit priest who might have advocated such a monstrosity.

"Only if he felt guilty in some way for what happened! My reasoning is that if someone was lost - dead or just missing - you would want to keep their memory alive if they were special to you, wouldn't you? It's all too easy to forget people; what they looked like, what they said and how they said it - the individual you knew them once to be."

Neither of them replies immediately, leaving Harcourt with a young girl's photograph of his own, indelibly printed on his mind.

***

"What do you mean: 'I'll give you a lift.'"

"Exactly that," he is surprised not by her reaction, but by the severity of it. "I have to get some notepads from Messenger's and fancy a break."

"Why can't you order them from Amazon like a normal person?"

He reflects on the little stationers, fitting snugly into a square with other independent artisan shops and the warm and very welcoming cafe run by a gentle giant of a man who'd spent much of his young life confined to a prison cell. He often used to pick up a coffee and panini from there before heading back to the newspaper.

"I can't find the same ones and there's something about the quality of the paper in the ones I use, I can't explain it..."

"I'm sure you can't because there's probably no good reason for it," Charlotte replies crossly, completely ignoring his desire to get out of the house and, even more so to spend some time with her. She was all set to leave when Daniel announced his intention to accompany her – and then chauffeur her - at least as far as Worcester.

"I thought you did everything digitally now - all PDFs and track changes?"

"I do, but I still find it helpful to make notes on paper. Sometimes thoughts flow more easily that way."

"And yet, you're paid not to think, aren't you? You're there to make sure the words that have been chosen are spelt correctly and follow the same grammatical rules that we all have to live with. Only a writer sees a world beyond their words - something you'll never be however much you wish life could have been different."

She knows him better than most people and therefore how to hurt him the hardest. He did indeed harbour thoughts of becoming a writer when he was a student at Aberystwyth - that's why he'd chosen English, after all - and he'd hoped his initial placement on the paper would lead to something more formative. It hadn't. Although he'd stayed, the unarticulated creative ambition that had driven him in his early years slowly gave way to the assurance of a technical career path, leading him through sub-editing and now simply proofreading.

"No doubt you still make notes using that pen they gave you as well?" Like one of the Fates, she has him on a string, yet she doesn't look that old, just knowing.

"The Parker. It's a beautiful pen."

"You should have put a cartridge of blood in it, rather than ink, after the way they treated you!"

He isn't sure if this is some kind of latent anger, referred from her own experience, but she appears to be calming down slightly.

"It was disappointing and true, I hadn't seen it coming... "

"Like erectile dysfunction perhaps?"

"I was 60. There was a contractual clause."

"I think I do understand how the process works, thank you so much! My point is that they chose you, or rather they didn't choose you as one of the people they wanted to keep on. You just accepted it and walked away - without a word. You're supposed to be good with those, but I saw no evidence of it then. I thought I'd married a man, not a moorhen, content to cluck happily in some backwater. Why can't you stand up for yourself?"

It is almost a rhetorical question. There hadn't been any obvious reason not to keep him on. His work had always been good and no sign of any mistakes creeping in; errors he might not have spotted. It didn't make sense but there seemed to be little point in trying to argue with the irrational - there or here.

"I am perfectly capable of driving myself, you know. I don't need a driver all of a sudden, and I'm buggered if I'm going to hang around for you."

Wrong. "That's fine. I wouldn't have expected you to. I can go for a walk by the river, maybe pop into Brown's for a coffee. I'm in no rush."

"Oh, how considerate! I won't be rushing either. I don't see them very often and I'm going to make the most of it. You might want to order a three-course meal for yourself."

"Is it a friend from work?"

"Work? I had no friends at work. Why can't you get that into your shitty little head? That was then and this is now. Unlike you I do need to get out now and again; is that so wrong?"

"Not wrong at all which is why I said I needed a break too." He rails inwardly at Fergus's suggestion that he try and spend more time with his sister. If this is the reaction he's going to get then, yes, perhaps sitting down with a good (or bad) book would be preferable.

"I just need some space and don't require you to start filling it, thank you very much."

"Alright. Alright. You've made your point. I'm going in anyway, so it seems pointless to take two cars."

"Senseless."

"I'm sorry?"

"Senseless. Isn't that a better word to use in this context? Making a point and then almost immediately referring to something as pointless would seem to suggest a fairly limited vocabulary. Oh, bloody hell! I'm turning into you!"

***

It hasn't escaped Taylor's attention that Flowers has been very quiet since they left the station." They don't mean it, you know?"

Flowers barely turns towards her from his passenger seat. "Who? Who doesn't?"

"The DI and the Super. Well, certainly not the DI."

"I don't know what you're talking about." His voice is much softer than usual, barely a whisper.

"When they shout, let off steam. It's probably because they have something else on their minds completely - maybe not even about this case at all. Certainly, nothing personal for you to worry about."

"You don't know that for certain."

"Not for certain, no. I don't have evidence or a case file but call it a woman's instinct, or gut reaction if you like."

"I hope your guts are clearer than they were yesterday!"

That breaks the silence, just as her flatulence had done the day before after she'd allowed herself to believe that one sausage roll from Gregg's is never enough.

"Any more thoughts on our Mrs Rogers?" Taylor can relax her grip on the steering wheel now.

"What she was up to on her computer you mean?" This time, Flowers does turn towards her, uncrossing his arms. Less defensive now and ready to move forward.

"That and her general demeanour. I couldn't believe she was 82."

"Not sure she'll see 83 if she carries on drinking at that rate either!"

"Agreed, yet the place was clean, and tidy wasn't it and..."

"A lot of money there?"

"Exactly. She was also so totally in control - of us and whatever it was that she could see that we couldn't. Most people are either downright nervy when we turn up or over-confident to compensate for the nerves they're trying to hide. She was neither of those things, just naturally confident."

"To be fair, she was a teacher for many years. You have to cultivate an air of self-confidence to get away with that, don't you - especially when you don't know what you're talking about. They say that those who can, do; those who can't, teach, and those who don't know the difference become Local Councillors!"

"Not sure that's right but I'll go with it for now." They laugh, easy in each other's company.

"Besides, if she has nothing to hide, there isn't anything for her or us to worry about is there?"

"What do you think she was up to online?"

"Not sure, but she must belong to some kind of private network she didn't want us to know about, for all her self-confidence."

"You don't think she's some kind of white witch?" Taylor can hardly believe she's voiced the thoughts she's had since waking at dawn that morning. She knows too that it won't go any further if she asks her colleague to keep quiet (much as a white witch might ensure!)

"What? Like in Narnia, you mean?"

"No, no. More like a woman with spiritual powers - a kind of healer from the olden times, maybe."

"I think the only spirits in her house are likely to come out of a bottle."

"Seriously though. She was so controlling. I wouldn't have wanted to get on the wrong side of her as a child."

"Maybe not but look around you, the trees are in blossom, and we have daffodils on every verge. If she does have special powers, she hasn't worked her way up to being able to freeze the world over."

Taylor giggles. "I think I'd rather live in your fantasy world; besides, my wardrobe's falling to bits: hardly 'fit for purpose' as they say."

***

Daniel parks the car in the Cornmarket and heads off

to the pay machine. Charlotte is standing by the closed passenger door, checking her 'phone and no doubt still irritated with him.

"What time is your friend expecting you?" He asks, innocently enough, but his suspicions were raised even further when she failed to clarify who he or she was.

"Eleven-thirty."

"That's very precise."

"It's part of being in the digital world, or did you suppose that PDFs were vaguely electronic versions of beautiful sheets of paper?"

"Which way are you walking?"

"Past the station."

"I'll walk with you as far as the Hop Market then."

"You'll need to walk quickly then, or I'll leave you."

Shouldn't that be 'leave you behind?' He is trying not to overthink things - has been endeavouring to do so since the texts started up again but hasn't been very successful so far. He can feel his heart beating inside his chest; the same heart he had given to her voluntarily all those years ago.

The grey afternoon is reflected in his mood as they head up Queen Street and turn left onto St Martin's Street, her a yard or so in front of him at all times, just to emphasise that this is not a friendly stroll and that she hadn't asked to walk with him by her side. It begins to spit with rain as the terracotta bricks of the old Hop Market tower above them, He stops, dutifully, at its side entrance. His wife keeps on walking at the same pace, leaving him behind and quite alone.

"Text me when you're ready to leave!"

He thinks at first that she hasn't heard him, but then she half raises her left hand in acknowledgement. Not turning. Not for him at least.

He waits outside for a few moments before walking slowly to the end of the road. Foolishly he considers taking off his shoes and socks to minimise the sound until a van passes him noisily and he realises how ridiculous he is being.

He has never done anything like this before, either in real life or online: following somebody on Twitter is one thing, but at least they are aware of it. He tries to avoid the term 'stalking' as that sounds altogether more sinister, but isn't this what he is doing? Not only that, but she is also his wife. What does that tell you about the level of trust he still has in her - in their marriage?

Despite a lack of conviction which could easily fall over into self-loathing, he does feel an adrenaline rush not unlike many years ago when seeking out someone who was trying to hide. But they were just games.

She has crossed Foregate Street and is about to walk under the great railway arch of the Hereford and Worcester railway that has been carrying unnamed passengers from Worcester's station since 1860, despite its name changes, including the West Midland and Great Western Railway ('God's Wonderful Railway': the originators of 'Railway Time' back in the 1840s).

He checks himself. Why is the name of a railway company or its history at all relevant? What possible use can all that knowledge be put to here, now? Is it his OCD that is really transporting her away from him or is he just choosing any distraction that comes his way to take his nagging, anxious mind off what might lie ahead?

Exasperated with himself he follows her along The Tything at what he considers to be a 'safe distance.' Thankfully he hasn't got a newspaper with him or the results of his hiding behind it would have been far more tragic than comic.

Up ahead on the same side of the road, he spots the unmistakable red clay bricks of St Oswald's Hospital and the Royal Grammar School buildings beyond. A newspaper article he'd proofed what, fifteen or twenty years ago, unexpectedly comes into his head. The hospital was named after the Bishop of Worcester and was at least thirteenth century, but an excavation was underway that might have placed its origins even earlier in history - in the tenth century? If proven, they would have been the oldest surviving almshouses in the whole country.

He wonders what happened. As with so many pieces of research he'd been involved with, he had intended to follow it up later but, of course, he hasn't. It would have been easy to blame the pressures of time and work, but those comfortable bedfellows alone could not be blamed for life's consumption of him.

Charlotte turns left. Still, she fails to look behind her

(though how many people do when walking from A to B?), walking briskly, determinedly. He holds back a little before following her into Britannia Square - one of the most affluent addresses in the whole city - and watches as she approaches a grand, white Regency building. She walks up a grey path bisecting an impossibly green lawn and enters via a smart red door that must have been unlocked and waiting for her.

From behind the front hedge his heart is pounding, but nothing to do with the gentle pace of the pursuit. Standing on tiptoes he glances up and down at the building's three storeys and, before he can look away, sees a man of maybe mid-thirties, wearing rimless glasses, a white shirt and a dark tie above khaki chinos moving towards a first-floor window. He is looking out into the square but failing to see the steadily falling rain beyond the pane.

Presumably, he doesn't expect to find anyone out here, certainly not a middle-aged husband. A bookworm who knows a bit about old buildings and railways. Someone who feels secure only when surrounded by words that don't mean anything to him. How much easier it is to see the past. Maybe that's where Daniel truly now belongs?

Carefully staying out of sight he watches as the man slowly and quite unselfconsciously pulls the white Venetian blinds together. Daniel realises that his mouth has gone completely dry and his hands are shaking slightly. Is it the element of subterfuge or simply that he cannot see anything now? Not what is going on inside his wife's head nor, much more worryingly, her body?

***

Phone in hand, Hunter-Wright surveys the walls of his 'study' while waiting impatiently to be connected. It isn't a study of course - he doesn't do studying and he's never been that studious. It is a room on the ground floor that wasn't quite big enough to call a sixth bedroom and presumably the estate agent couldn't describe any other use for it. That must have been a landmark moment: when an estate agent's vacancy matches that in the brain of an architect. Two tribes.

They didn't and still don't need another bedroom. They only use one. Miriam won't admit it of course and he isn't that insensitive that he would bring the subject up for no good (or new) reason. Seven years and ten now, yet still he cannot think of any mirrors he might have accidentally broken or spiders deliberately crushed to set things in motion in the first place, even as they were being immobilised. All of them.

The walls are bare. Not for him awards or certificates of 'achievement' any more than the trappings of 'status' he has always railed against, despite his wife's love of trinkets. It's different for her, he supposes. She has very little else.

She won't return yet, with her snappy little retorts formed by the recriminations that seem to drive her these days. She's stopped asking him to join the Bridge Club now, praise the Lord. It had always been one too far for him.

"Cummings."

A real voice has interrupted his reverie. A confident voice with a Birmingham accent. A voice not to be messed with, as used to be the case. He holds the phone even tighter to his ear than is strictly necessary, not wanting to miss a thing; not wanting to give the outside world any chance now of getting in the way.

"Hello. It's Hunter-Wright from West Mercia. I'm sorry for intruding on your time."

"I hardly think you're intruding unless it's against my wishes." The voice at the end of the line is not remotely the old and doddery one he had anticipated it becoming. On the contrary, it is clear and firm. Years of police training hadn't been altogether wasted after all.

"Thank you. I'll still be as brief as I can be."

Only silence encourages him to fill in the details of their latest case for the former officer and await his response.

"So, Andrew Patch, or should I say the 'death' of Andrew Patch is your only link to my case?"

"It is, and he's not going to be much help with intelligence-gathering now."

Hunter-Wright is thoroughly aware that Police Standards today would have been right across the Julie Beech case in terms of how it was conducted and how an 'unexplained' result came to pass. From reading the file, he can see how sloppy the investigation had been and why Cummings might have jumped when he did. He only has two years to go himself, and the same thing is very definitely not going to happen to him - even if he has to hang Harcourt out to dry.

Any hint of 'incompetence' on his gravestone is not acceptable, though other similarly discouraging words about him might get through the net.

"You're only really looking at the previous Castle Upton case because you've come to a dead end with this one?" Cummings seems to be relaxing now - possibly because it isn't going to involve too much raking up of dirt after all.

"We're still keeping an open mind…"

A chuckle acknowledges this hackneyed phrase so Hunter-Wright desists. The man may have had his failings, but he had been a policeman after all.

Hunter-Wright starts again. "We're not sure if the two cases are connected but it's an angle we have to cover. We're talking to everyone who was around at the time. One of the obvious issues we have is that several of them were merely children."

"Merely children!" Now there is a smirk, easy to imagine. "Have you seen what children are capable of? How they can destroy lives in an instant. You… we don't even know that Julie didn't choose to leave the village of her own free will and ran off with someone else. It may have been a game to her, but maybe she just didn't want to be found. I'd have thought that would have caused just as much pain as if we'd found an actual body."

Hunter-Wright is listening intently but visualising a different scene albeit with the same sequence of possible events. Tears have formed in his eyes, but he blinks them away impatiently.

"Are you still there?"

This is a question he has asked out loud many times when the forces of loneliness have gathered all around him. "Yes. Yes, of course. Apart from the blood spatters, did you find any evidence at all of a struggle - flattened bushes, broken branches, that sort of thing?"

"None. Although the villagers had speedily formed a volunteer search party which may have inadvertently caused that kind of damage anyway - especially as night had fallen by then. Crime scenes weren't dealt with as efficiently then as perhaps they are now."

"They were ahead of you!"

The silence confirms that the police had indeed been slow off the mark, unlike Julie's family and friends.

"We did what we could. Because it was a child the whole missing persons protocol was escalated. We searched that area for three days solid but found nothing at all. It was as though she'd vanished into thin air."

"The children that she was playing with: you got no further clues from any of them either?"

"They were traumatized; especially the sister, Grace. Struck dumb she was. Her parents were in pieces. It was very, very difficult."

"Was anybody else playing with them?"

"Possibly."

"Meaning?"

"It was forty-odd years ago, remember."

"I do. You've done very well so far though."

"Oh. Thanks very much. Worth letting my Horlicks go cold then?"

Hunter-Wright worries that his slightly patronising response may have been inappropriate and stopped Cummings in his tracks. He mentally slaps himself for it but this is becoming more and more difficult for him too, as he knew it would be.

Fortunately, Cummings has agreed to cooperate further. Maybe he is so thick-skinned he hadn't even noticed? "As I recall - and this should be in the case notes; apologies if it isn't, everything was in a bit of a mess at the time - Stuart Fairhurst initially told us that he was playing hide and seek with Julie and Grace. However, when we went back to the village a few days later he'd changed his story slightly. He said then that he had been playing with them but got bored and headed home before the incident. He did say that he passed Duncan Harewood on the way though."

"Did he change his story again after that?"

"No, He decided to stop twisting at that point."

"Which version did you believe?

"My senses told me that he was there at the time when Grace had finished counting and came back to the quarry. I think he was with her then. The look in his eyes told me that he'd seen something no child should ever see. Whatever it was, it had freaked him. Not that I imagine modern policing gives much credence to unmeasurable feelings such as 'gut instinct.'"

"You'd be surprised!"

"I doubt it."

"Do you think someone got to Stuart for some reason?"

"Either that or he just got frightened and pretended to have left earlier. It must have been scary for a simple game of hide and seek to so quickly turn into a search party - especially when it concerned his best friends."

"His father was a bit feisty, allegedly."

"It was a tough time for him, with the farm and everything. It had been in the family for generations and Frank was trying to fight an inevitable decline."

"Why inevitable?"

"Asparagus takes a very long time for a crop of any significance to be produced – and, even then, the weather can do it in. That's farming in a nutshell! I think it takes about three years from seed to harvest but the rot set in during the war. Because no new beds were sown then, they were behind the curve. He did buy a few sheep but that didn't work out well for him either; kept getting out of his field, he told us.

It all seemed a bit caggy to be honest, like a last throw of the dice. I may even have felt a bit sorry for him had he not been so angry at everything and everyone. I remember his father - Stuart's grandfather - telling me that passing the farm on to Frank was a bit of a poisoned chalice. Joining the EEC in '73 didn't help matters really - not that either of them would have admitted it if it had - so I wasn't surprised when Frank sold up."

"This is the underlying cause of prickliness - his anger?"

"I assume it must be a contributing factor. It must have been pretty galling when celebrity chefs started using the 'Gras' in their various recipes later: it could have been the saving of Frank's farm, but too late I'm afraid. Much too late."

"And Andrew Patch. He claimed not to have been there at all?"

"He did. His Dad was a bit funny about it though. Very protective you might say. It wasn't easy for us. You have to understand that we had a job to do but, at the end of the day, they were just kids. If we'd known about waterboarding then, we still wouldn't have been able to use it."

He chuckles. Hunter-Wright does not join him. "Patch's father was worried for his son?"

"Worried about life itself if you ask me, much like Frank. I think he just built on his learns and threw in the towel. Life was a struggle for those guys in the Seventies."

The colloquialism momentarily takes him back to his youth. He can almost smell the cordite that had hung in the air for days.

"It must just have weighed heavily on you - as with

the parents and sister of course - the not knowing."

"I hardly think me doing the job I'm paid to do can begin to compare with the anxiety of parents who don't know whether to grieve for their child or carry on hoping that one day they'll be at the back door, in time for tea."

Hunter-Wright's silence encourages Cummings to similarly bring their conversation to a close.

"The child was lost, and so were we. I was encouraged to use all kinds of outside resources to get a result. Just imagine that: the police force, set up to protect everyone within its area, having to ask for help from so-called 'specialists.' I'd had enough of that by then. Self-serving mavericks at best, sad little voyeurs at worst.

We'll never know if Julie Beech would have been found, but I wasn't prepared to let the lunatics in. The parents had suffered enough madness. I may not have been the tidiest of detectives - I may have run down a lot of blind alleys and taken others with me - but I did it by the book, which is more than can be said for many of my colleagues from that era."

Long after the call has ended and Cummings is reassigned to the history books, Hunter-Wright is staring at the blank walls again. The thumping bass of 'White Riot' by The Clash is bouncing off them.

He ignores the irony of the words he is listening to, simply absorbing an energy he no longer feels. He had been young once: full of ideas about self-determination and rebellion. Why is it that so many lose their way?

***

The late afternoon sunshine is pouring through the windows now, although she can still see the wavy patterns left behind by raindrops. For some, the weight has been too great and their decline to the foot of the windowpanes has been speedy. For others, there is still an appreciation that, although they cannot possibly hope to rise again, their zigzags sideways offer time to think - for tears to dry.

He is talking in the same soft tones as when they first began.

"... which is why it is my belief that we have come to a natural end."

Panic. How can he possibly want to stop this? Isn't what they have - have had for months now - precious to him too? Even as she climbs off the bed, she knows that her face is flushed. Not with shyness or modesty - they have moved way, way beyond that. No, this is a passion far stronger; far more forceful.

"You surely cannot be serious?" Even as she utters the words, too quickly as one in shock, she perceives her foolishness. He is serious. Softly spoken and gentle, yes, but never casual, relaxed. Perhaps it is this intensity that has always attracted her - something her husband has somehow lost over the years, though she doesn't blame him for that. Life has not always been kind.

"I think I am. We've been meeting here for around eighteen months now..."

She thought it had been longer, much longer. Life

before him seems misty, inconclusive.

"... and we have talked at length about your childhood, university years, life in the City and then here in The Midlands. We have talked about your father, your brother and, of course, Daniel. In each of our conversations, I have been looking carefully for unresolved conflicts, real and possibly imaginary. I have examined you for signs of anxiety in the same way as trying to understand what makes you happiest."

That part of the discussion was always hard, she reflects, never having managed to find an answer within her grasp.

"Because we have visited and re-visited general and specific themes – as well as physical activities - without any new information being forthcoming, I have to conclude that I do believe (and I completely accept that this is going to be difficult for you to come to terms with) that we have now passed a threshold."

She is physically shaking, not with fury, but with fear. This sounds much like the Head of HR telling her in similarly calm terms that the life she had dedicated to the law firm was now at an end."

"Anger management is very often about sufferers overthinking," he has noticed her physical response but continues to address himself to her mind, "Especially when the need to take a broader view of the world is necessary. I don't see that with you at all. I cannot find any psychological basis for the symptoms of anger you are both feeling and expressing. To that end, I'm afraid I have no choice but to refer you back to your GP for further clinical tests."

***

"But how do you know that for certain? It's all very well saying 'she'll be fine' but what if she isn't?"

The spring sunshine had flooded the garden and filled her heart with thoughts of good things. Now this.

"I've said so, haven't I!" He is as belligerent as ever. "We've come this far; we're not going to let things slip now."

"Depends on what you're holding on to. We used to climb to the top of the poles in the playground, didn't we? Proper cocky we were. Still fell off though - eventually."

"We were just children."

"Yes. That's the point. You can get away with almost anything as a child."

"She knows what she's doing. It's like riding a bike to her."

"We often fell off them too."

He looks back down at the screen in his hand and carries on typing.

***

She watches them watching her. There's nothing so very different about this. Most of the villagers have been observing her from a distance - waiting for some unexpected move - for most of her life. She has disappointed them by doing precisely the opposite. She grieved, as expected. Never married, as expected. Never left the village... as expected.

"... and we do appreciate that this may be difficult for you." The woman has finished talking.

The young boy just stares at her, fiddling with his notepad. After a while, he turns away, as they all do.

"I'm not sure how this is going to help you discover the cause of Andrew's death."

"We have to explore all angles."

"Your colleague didn't mention it when he invaded my privacy the first time."

That blow landed. The worn suit and crumpled blouse have no answer for it.

"We were hoping not to have to discuss it at that time out of respect for yourself and the others who witnessed such an upsetting episode."

"Witnessed?"

"Well, not witnessed as such. Got caught up in your sister's disappearance."

Had that been a trap? She'd better give them something. "Not everyone was quite so sensitive."

"I cannot comment on other officers' methods I'm afraid."

"I might not have been referring to other policemen." She lets the silence speak for her and then continues, slightly more charitably. "Having said that, it was a different era. People behaved differently if they could get away with it. I suppose they most likely did. I've had many years to deal with it in my own way, quietly and away from the public's gaze."

"But you still talk with Stuart Fairhurst and his father I suppose? They still live in Castle Upton too."

So, the young one is allowed to speak after all. Interesting.

"Occasionally. When I met Stuart in the pub - on the night of poor Andrew's death - it was the first time for ages."

"And his wife?"

"I've never really spoken to her."

The older one has moved forward slightly. Maybe she thinks she is 'on to something.' No doubt they'll congratulate each other later on great teamwork. "Why is that? Do you not get on for some reason."

"No reason at all. I don't know her. She's the same age as Stuart and I but once we all went to school in Evesham things changed. You see horizons beyond the limitations of a small village."

"And yet you never left?"

"It never left me."

The young one writes something down as the woman pretends to look through her notes. "Stuart was playing hide and seek with you, on the night that Julie went missing?"

She allows the question to lay there for a

few minutes, for the room to empty itself of all contemporary sounds.

"I'm sorry! I'm sure this can't be easy for you."

"It isn't."

"We're just trying to see if there is any link between the death of your friend, Andrew Patch, and the horrific time you all had as children."

Horrific? Yes, it was. That word described it then and has defined her life ever since.

"We were all playing together but the sun was going down and Stuart had promised his parents he'd be back before dark."

"He left to go home?"

More scribbling in an official-looking notebook.

"I was counting by the tree, my back turned to the quarry where I'd left Julie. When I turned around, she'd disappeared. Well, you'd expect that, wouldn't you? You can't hide in the middle of a quarry. I looked everywhere for her - under bushes, up trees. It was getting dark, and I knew it was useless. I yelled out for her to show herself; to admit defeat. That usually did the trick, but there was nothing. Even the birds had gone to sleep by then. I suddenly felt quite alone and scared that I might not be. I ran home and told Dad what had happened."

"And you've never heard or seen anything over the years to make you think that your sister might still be alive?"

"Some people prefer to live in hope. I'm afraid I found

that more exhausting than grief."

"Your father (I'm sorry again to have to raise this) never got over Julie's disappearance?"

"He was beside himself - they both were. My mother just cried all the time."

"And you think this led to his heart attack?"

Simple cause and effect. No wonder so many crimes remain unsolved. Why can't these people think outside of the box, just once in their lives? Praise the Lord that they don't.

"I don't suppose we'll ever know for certain. It was made worse for him in a way because he lived and worked in the heart of the village. He had a greengrocer's shop and there was nowhere to hide. People kept bringing the subject up, long after it had happened and even after all the newspaper people had given up and gone home.

Would you believe that they hid in our garden? A good job I didn't go to school for a while. Each had their unoriginal little theory on what might have taken place. They do that, though, don't they? People must have ready explanations on hand for things they don't understand. Doesn't matter if it's done by the 'Hand of God' or someone or something altogether more evil."

"You're not a believer, I take it?"

"'Fain I would to Thee be brought' Not for me I'm afraid."

***

"No offer of tea!"

"Or, more importantly, biscuits."

Taylor adjusts the car's sun visor as they pull out of the drive, but the sun is still too low, glaring at her futile attempt to see the road right in front of her. She sits up in her seat and slightly sideways for now, blocking it out as best she can.

"You'll be alright in a minute; once we turn left, we'll have it behind us." Flowers offers helpfully.

"I think it was so dark in that room, my eyes haven't adjusted yet!"

"It was like being in a cave, wasn't it?"

"Yet it didn't feel like a shelter. Do you know what I mean? Gave me the creeps, to be honest."

"Impenetrable darkness!"

"Is that one of Rob's?"

"Sorry. Oh, no. It was just an observation on her...it."

She smiles disarmingly. Her colleague can still be too temperamental at times. "What she said about the village - 'it never left me' - what do you think she meant?"

"Maybe just that wherever she lived, she'd never be able to properly get away from what happened. I suppose finding a body might have made it easier. She could then have more easily left it and everything else behind her."

"Or maybe she didn't want to leave. I wonder if she felt that by staying, she'd remain close to her sister. Almost as if she expected her to appear one day, despite what she said about giving up hope. What I wanted to ask her was how close they'd been as sisters, but it didn't seem right somehow, given how on the edge she seemed to be (and the Superintendent's voice in my head). She was definitely less assured than the last time we spoke to her. If the girls had been inseparable, I'd have felt even worse than I already did. If they hadn't got on, she might have thought I was implying some kind of foul play."

"It's tough, isn't it? At least we now know that she's no 'Saint.'"

"How do you mean?"

"She told us she didn't believe in God!"

"So why does she wear black all the time?"

"I know that's what people did in the past - lit candles and all that stuff. For me, it's hard to hard to imagine someone grieving and yet still believing at the same time." He thinks of his mother and is a little ashamed as if he's betrayed her all over again.

"Did you believe her?" Taylor skillfully unwraps a chocolate bar while keeping both hands on the wheel.

"That she's grieving? Maybe. Or it could be that it's the way she's always coped with it. She saw what living in a goldfish bowl did to her father, so I can understand why she'd want to keep people at a distance, whatever it took."

"She clammed up when I mentioned Duncan Harewood's name."

"I noticed that too. Not sure about him, but we've got nothing on him now, any more than Cummings's lot were able to thrash out of him back then."

"Do you still think Grace is hiding something from us?"

Flowers tries to ignore the chocolate stain on his colleague's chin. "I'm not sure. It does all feel a bit like she's tried to throw a security blanket over everything. People aren't usually as two-dimensional as that are they? Yes, she had a few family photographs dotted around that old doll, but it was as if they were watching everything, looking out at her, rather than Grace looking at them and remembering – which is the point of them isn't it?

Could you live in the past for forty years anyway, however lowly or lonely 'society' made you feel? You certainly couldn't preserve it, even if that kind of trauma kept taking you back there. Besides, there was a spanking new iPad on the table beside her chair. Wouldn't have happened in Jane Austen's time."

CHAPTER EIGHT

Daniel is reading without seeing the words or the punctuation or the meaning. It isn't that his glasses are still misted up, though he's polished them several times that morning already.

He simply cannot process what he saw or why he didn't see it coming. He of all people! True, his wife has struggled continually since she retired and, contrary to her brother's unsolicited advice, Daniel had felt it better that she be left alone to vent her anger on the countryside and its inhabitants that couldn't answer back. It didn't always mean she was calmer when she returned to the house – at least from what he could make out - but it was no worse.

Despite their largely separate working lives - especially when she was based in London during the early years of their marriage - he has never, ever suspected her of being unfaithful to him. How strange that word sounds now. It's a word Fergus would use without thinking, as with so many others.

Sex hasn't ever been a problem and still isn't, or so he had thought until a couple of days ago. Has it not been good enough, or simply enough? Since that lonely walk back from Britannia Square he has tried to re-evaluate everything about their relationship which, in reality, means that he has overthought it - all of it, including those parts that have never (and still aren't) in doubt. He's 62 now and while she might not need him anymore (and almost certainly won't in two years' time!) he hasn't considered the possibility of her leaving him since their very first few fumbling days of discovery.

He has no proof of course that what he saw amounted to anything other than a meeting of friends. However, when he'd first dated a girl - a different girl - the sentence he'd feared most in the world was: 'Let's just be friends.'

***

"Duncan Harewood?" Harcourt holds his badge up automatically, no matter that the afternoon sun behind him would have made it almost impossible to read. Most people barely scrutinised ID cards anyway. No wonder unscrupulous door-to-door salesmen see career paths beckoning.

This giant of a man - probably enhanced by the dark gloom behind him - does read it though; for much longer than is necessary. He seemed to be studying it, remembering the details in case he needs them in the future.

"May I come in please?"

"Do I have a choice?"

"Of course. You're not under any suspicion, I'm just following up on the discussion you had with DS Taylor and DS Flowers."

"We'll sit out here," he motions the policeman towards a rickety wooden pew that sits outside the shack. Once much darker, it has been lightened by sunshine and almost blends in with its new surroundings, though Harcourt isn't sure if it will bear his weight.

He sits down gingerly, moving his bottom back quickly from the edge as a slight splintering sound sends a couple of swallows twittering into the safety of the woods that surround them on the other three sides of the clearing.

"This must have taken some shifting... up that hill. Is it from the church in the village?"

"St Hilda's, yes. She was the patron saint of learning - probably still is, I don't know. I sit here in the evenings sometimes and read."

Undeterred by the strangeness of the man sitting next to him or the fact that he is wearing a dark hoodie and what looks like yellow pyjama bottoms, Harcourt quickly continues, not wanting to end the engagement. "Before you go down to the pub?"

"No. Later. I have a lantern here, see."

"Is it a paraffin lamp?"

His host gives him an incredulous look. "Out here! Surrounded by trees and bracken. Of course not. It takes three AA batteries."

Harcourt suddenly feels very small; not because of the other man's height but because of how much in control he is of his surroundings, his piece of land in the woods meant for all.

"I wanted to talk to you about an incident, if that's OK, that took place near here."

"I told the others everything I know. I walked the long way home because it was a pleasant evening…"

"No. No, let me stop you there. I'm talking about an incident from much longer ago - almost forty years ago."

"You mean the girls in the woods?"

"Julie and Grace Beech, yes, and possibly Stuart Fairhurst too."

"I didn't see them, not on that particular evening anyway. I said all this to the police at the time, but they didn't want to believe me. There was a big man, loud and rude he was."

"A man called Cummings?"

"That was him. All bluster and a sweaty head. Lots of shouting. Used words I didn't understand - not in those days anyhow."

"He gave you a hard time. Why do you think that was?"

"I didn't know then but I've had plenty of time to think about it since. It's a mystery to me. He just wouldn't listen when I repeated my answers to his questions or believe me when I said I was speaking the truth… the whole truth."

"But you do like to walk out in the woods in the evenings?"

"Course I do. Why wouldn't I?"

"Except you didn't on that particular evening?"

"Mum wasn't well. She used to have problems with her chest. I'd only been living here for a few weeks, but I moved back in with her for a while to look after her?"

"The pub?"

"Yes. I suppose it's been like a second home to me. We had a small flat at the back when I was little but then they gave her a room upstairs. I suppose they thought that was all the space she needed. To be fair, Mum never had very much."

"Did DI Cummings check all of this at the time?"

"I assume so. Police were all over the village, weren't they? He kept coming back, though. It was like my answers didn't match with his and until they did, he'd be on the pub doorstep every day. At least that's how it felt. I guess that's how they did things in the Seventies?"

Harcourt sidesteps the historical context for once. "Surely there were plenty of other people there at the time to give you an alibi? What I mean is…"

"I know what an alibi is. As I said, I like to read. Not as much as I used to, mind, not with the mobile library finishing."

"Where do you get your books from now?"

"I have a friend in the village who helps me out. A lovely lady - a good person."

"May I ask the name of that person?"

"I'd rather not say if you don't mind. It's our little secret: that's how she puts it."

Harcourt can do discretion – for now. "No problem. So, back to the pub."

"I felt trapped inside there. Mum was much better and all I wanted to do was come home, but they'd have followed me all the way back."

"The policemen?"

"No. Well, maybe, but I was thinking more about the reporters. Set up flashlights and all sorts outside. Frightened the rabbits and deer half to death."

Harcourt feels his stomach wrench on hearing this wooden shed being described as 'home.' This man doesn't even have a mother to go to now, pub or no pub. It seems as though his lines of escape haven't become any clearer as he's grown older.

"If not on that night specifically, did you ever see the children playing? In the woods I mean. One of the paths leads right past your door?"

"I'm not funny like that if that's what you mean." He moves to get up, clearly upset.

"I didn't. I don't!" Harcourt is mortified. "I simply meant they must have played up here a lot - especially in the spring and summer months."

Harewood takes a few moments to respond. Harcourt thinks he has lost his trust and will just clam up, but he is in luck - an opportunity to make up for his schoolboy error.

"They were up here quite a lot. Not usually after dark though. Four of them there were. I used to think of them as the Famous Five without the dog."

"But Andrew Patch was the fourth child - the man who sadly died last week?"

"His dad owned the garage where I now work, part-time like."

"I guess they were a tight-knit little group."

"Most of the time."

Harcourt turns slowly sideways to get a full view of his confessor. "Why do you say that?"

"Nothing really and I only saw it once - about a month or so before that evening everyone seems determined to keep talking about."

"Saw what? Who?" Harcourt is excited but knows he needs to proceed equally cautiously; such is the fine line they are drawing here.

"The girls. Julie and Grace Beech. Arguing at the tops of their voices they were, in the hollow beyond the line of trees you can just see down the hill there. I walked down the path to see what was going on - all out in the open, not secretive at all as I didn't want to frighten them. I saw Grace first, red in the face and extremely angry. She had a stick in her hand and swung it towards whoever it was behind the tree. Luckily, she caught the trunk first, giving the other girl the chance to get away."

"And the other girl was her sister: Julie"

"Yes. Proper frightened she looked. Ran right past me.
"

"And Grace ran after her?"

"I thought she would but, no, she didn't. She turned in her direction alright, but then she caught sight of me and just smiled."

"Smiled? You're sure about that?"

"You can't misunderstand a smile, can you?"

Harcourt knows differently. Call it the curse of being a detective.

**

Later that night, Grace Beech is lying in her bed. The room is bathed in moonlight, just as it was then. She's weary from going over it all again - both face-to-face with those wretched police officers and the seemingly endless conversations on the phone.

No matter how many times she's asked, they'll never understand, not one of them. Her life - the very essence of her - was lost that evening and, though she has done what they said for all these years, she might just as well have gone to prison. It couldn't have been worse than the one she's woken up in every day, gone to bed in - if not to sleep. How could she find peace when her flesh and blood was out there: cold, lonely and dying for revenge?

**

Hunter-Wright is nearly back at the house. His

early-morning walks take him on different routes, but the start and end points are always the same. In between those fixed markers, the rolling Worcestershire countryside takes him through the ups and downs of life. Lost in thought he can sometimes barely believe he has returned so quickly. A good job Miriam has never allowed dogs; he'd forget to let the ball or stick out of his clenched fist.

The Malvern Hills away to the west provide their usual canvas on which the sunlight begins to paint the day ahead, tentative sketches at first and then much bolder strokes. His old boots traverse the dewy grass and irregular piles of rabbit droppings - proof of life if he chooses to see it. And he does. Oh, he does.

Barren patches of blonde stubble lie alongside the rich brown soils of their neighbours which have been ploughed and planted. Discarded and dried out now, the wheat would once have been nurtured and encouraged to grow too. The fallow and the plenty, side by side.

"Who presides over all of this?" he thinks out loud. "Who survives and who is destined just to fall along the way? Is there a body out there, buried under the earth, or is it just a spirit that remains: a hollow carcass of what was or what might have been?"

***

"Morning sir. I've uncovered something odd."

Wonders will never cease, thinks Harcourt grimly as he surveys the young pretender before him.

"Go on."

"I've been going through Lettie Harewood's bank statements, as you requested.

"Yes." What do they want: commendations for proving that they can follow basic instructions? He must calm down; it will pass.

"The bank was a bit iffy at first because they had her (their customer) down as dying from natural causes in their records."

"Which is perfectly true!"

"Exactly. Because of data protection, they weren't sure on what grounds I felt we had any authority to investigate, especially as no crime has been formally registered."

"So you told them that, as the coroner hasn't yet held her inquest, we are still obliged to look at the incident from all angles."

Flowers looks pleased with himself. "I did sir, and it worked!"

Harcourt alternates each day between porridge and Weetabix - unless Tesco substitutes the latter for some kind of trendy wheat product which looks so promising from the outside packaging, but much less so the more layers you strip away.

Today he should have had blueberries with his porridge; he knows it was a mistake not to. Debbie gets them for him because they're supposed to be good for his eyes - better than carrots for breakfast he supposes. It's just the whole rinsing them under the tap thing...

especially when you're in a hurry. It interrupts the semi-conscious flow of cereal preparation at the time of the morning somehow.

Faced with what is already turning into a long morning, he now wishes he'd taken the plunge. 'Happy Harry' is continuing.

"I went back three years. There's been a regular amount coming into her current account each month via Standing Order. Never fails, apart from the day of the week changing slightly when it falls on a weekend."

"How much?" Harcourt is tired, as usual, but marginally more awake now.

"One thousand pounds."

"Sizeable. Did you go further back in time?"

"Not yet sir. We'll need something more substantial before the bank will release them. This is like a set period they initially agree to, though it's a grey area; all banks adopt slightly different criteria when making their decisions."

"No matter that a man lies dead on a mortuary slab and a little girl who went missing forty years ago has never been found. Still, good to know the banks are the ones making the decisions."

His sarcastic retort metaphorically slaps his sergeant around the ears, which are quickly turning red - a sure sign of embarrassment (he hadn't needed to be a detective to work that one out).

"Excellent work!" He hears his kinder self say out

loud. "We now need to work out who they were coming from."

"Ahead of you, sir!"

Better. Much better.

"They were made from one Frank Fairhurst."

***

Only her mother calls her Gabriella. If she'd had a sister, would she have called her that or 'Gabby' like everybody else? She'll never know now. She walks slowly through the small kitchen of her house to her front room and back again, the mobile phone seemingly glued to her right ear. It takes all of ten seconds.

"He's better now he can get out more," the voice at the other end had continued unbroken; neither spatial nor temporal awareness coming into it, "He gets me fruit from the corner shop. Every day he goes out to fetch me fruit. I tell him we can get it delivered directly, but he knows - and I know - that isn't the point."

"At least you'll be getting your Vitamin C intake!"

"While you're stocking up on Vitamin D in this lovely spring sunshine we're having. You're getting enough to eat though, aren't you? I know what you're like when you get your head stuck into something."

She glances over at her cutting board, covered in sliced peppers, onion and mango.

"Mum. Have you ever known me not to eat?"

The two ladies chuckle relaxed in each other's virtual

company. It's always been like this; the same with her Dad, though he is a bit more reserved. Still the 'head' of their three-person family.

Her mind wanders back to Julie Beech, as it has, off and on, since they became aware of her cold case. How would her father have coped if she - the Gabby they dote on - had gone missing? He'd have had to look after her mother, who would have gone to pieces, as well as himself. Her father has never been in poor health exactly - just chesty and prone to colds in the wintertime - but nothing in his life would have prepared him for that kind of mental anguish. Julie and Grace's parents must have been in torment until they died, not knowing whether to believe any more.

"Is it concerning that poor girl who went missing? All those years without a body to bury."

"We don't know for certain that she's dead. We've never known what happened."

"But it was her blood they found, wasn't it? The paper confirmed it."

Taylor smiles inwardly. It must be true then if the paper confirmed it.

"She must have been killed. No little girl would just run away and leave her parents hanging like that for all these years."

"You know I can't talk about it, Mum."

"I know. I know. I told your father I'd ask but he said the same thing. Said I wasn't to get you into any kind of trouble."

Again, they laugh, before her caller becomes altogether more serious, brooding even.

"We shouldn't laugh though, should we? People hurting each other. Seems to still be happening everywhere, especially around here. My mother told me that Myra Hindley had taught everyone a lesson - herself included. Children walking home from school on their own, doing paper rounds on dark mornings. They even tried to turn back time for a while to give us more light. That didn't work though, did it? Young men are stabbed or shot; girls are still being hurt by gangs. Whatever happened to 'don't ever get into a stranger's car?' My father drummed that into us - sometimes with his belt."

Taylor remembers her grandfather: old and wise and terrifying.

"We could do with Grandpa Holding on our team!"

"He would have loved that, Gabriella - he never missed an episode of *Softly Softly* - but he would never have fitted in, would he?"

***

Flowers is dreading the debrief, not just because of how he expects Hunter-Wright to act but because of what he is trying to pluck up the courage to suggest.

They are seated in the meeting room next door which offers up a white screen, grey chairs and lots of multi-coloured pens for colouring in the many gaps that have led them there in the first place.

Taylor seems preoccupied as she spins a pencil on the glass conference table they are seated around. Fully transparent, there should be no secrets between them. Harcourt is sitting nearest to the screen, tense and white-faced - like a suspect who knows more than they do.

Hunter-Wright enters from a door at the far end of the room which immediately feels much smaller. They all sit up, straight like ballet dancers who have been told umpteen times that they can still grow another inch or so if they try.

"Good morning, everyone."

His voice is soft. Is this a good sign or a new tactic?

They respond simultaneously, crisp voices waiting nervously to individually answer the teacher's register call.

"You spoke with Frank Fairhurst, I take it?" He motions to Harcourt to appraise him.

"We did, sir. We asked him about the regular payments to Lettie Harewood. He confirmed what his bank wouldn't: that these payments have been made each month for nearly forty years."

"Did he offer up any plausible reason why this was so? I mean, here is a man who has presided over the decline of the family business until he sold up. The man who bought a garage which can do little more than wash its face. And yet he finds a grand in his back pocket every month to give to a barmaid."

Taylor shuffles her feet but leaves her boss to speak. There's teamwork and there's teamwork. She glances across at Flowers who seems even paler than usual, although the Detective Superintendent does tend to drain blood from bodies as effectively as any murderer.

Harcourt is on his feet now, although there is nothing to write on the board, no new theory to project. "He was as irascible as ever, but he isn't a stupid man. I could see that we'd struck a chord immediately."

Flowers nods his agreement. A pointless gesture as Hunter-Wright simply looks at him with distaste, as though observing a nodding dog on the back shelf of his car.

"He admitted to an affair with Lettie Harewood. Said it had 'just happened' one evening."

And kept on 'just happening' thinks Taylor. She'd heard Harcourt tell them already that Fairhurst had blamed all of it on drink and none of it on himself.

"I asked if his wife knew of it, but he was non-committal."

"Did you believe him?"

"About Annabel Fairhurst knowing?"

"Probably more usefully about the affair - as a reason for the payments. It's an obvious answer, isn't it? If you were going to make a pre-emptive strike, that's the angle you'd take, surely? Lonely barmaid seeks rough sex. The fact that a man like him takes advantage of and treats her like a prostitute would fit. The only real issue is the size of the payment. It doesn't mean anything; doesn't hurt anyone etc etc

Taylor cannot do it. Cannot stop herself.

"Except he did hurt someone, sir. His wife and Stuart, his son. Whether they knew about it or not, he deliberately went ahead with his balls rather than his conscience, knowing there was a good chance they actually would find out about such a sordid affair one day. Notwithstanding that, as you alluded to, sir, I am sure his family could have made good use of that kind of money - especially when Stuart was a little boy."

"Firstly, DS Taylor, I do not allude to anything. Secondly, I am not sure from what personal experience you draw your knowledge of being a parent facing financial difficulties?"

His chilling retort causes each of them to bow their heads over invisible notes in invisible notebooks while he continues. A soft voice, true, yet harder than ever.

"I neither condone what Fairhurst alleges that he did, nor that Lettie Harewood was some kind of passive victim 'asking for it.' I am merely trying to imagine what picture of him Fairhurst would have considered we had already drawn. All he had to do then was some careful shading."

"You think he was just reinforcing a stereotype, sir, the one we had pre-conceived?" Flowers is animated now, colour returning to his young cheeks.

"Possibly. He would know all about prevailing winds, wouldn't he? He was a farmer for God's sake. Go against the grain at your peril. Much easier to hide in broad daylight."

"But you think there's more to it than this, sir?" Flowers again.

"I don't think that laddie, but am merely suggesting we all consider it as a possibility. What if Lettie Harewood was blackmailing Fairhurst?"

"Because he raped her?" Taylor is not relaxing like her colleague; if anything, she is more tense now than when all this began.

"That is indeed a possibility. What if she was blackmailing him for a quite different reason?"

Like Hitchcock behind his Director's monitor, Hunter-Wright loves to build up the suspense, watching as, one by one, the members of the audience at this private screening suspend disbelief.

"What if she saw something on the night that Julie Beech disappeared - or knows somebody who did? How much would that be worth to keep silent? Rather more than a regular fumble under the sheets I'd wager."

The more recent, sordid image is quickly replaced in all of their minds by an imaginary scene from much earlier.

"You're suggesting that Lettie Harewood and Andrew Patch might have been acting together?" Harcourt is no longer nervous, a different kind of adrenalin hurtling around his body and leaping over hurdles like a steeplechaser.

"It does seem convenient that Lettie Harewood should die just as Patch is making his way back here after so many years?"

"I've seen the medical notes, sir. They do confirm that she died of natural causes." Flowers is more than a little deflated that the balloon might have burst before it had any real chance of flying.

"It still seems convenient." Hunter-Wright remains calm. "And it would explain why Frank Fairhurst appears to be both angry - to hide his fear of exposure - and so apparently indifferent to Patch's arrival... and departure."

"He's had plenty of time to kill Lettie Harewood though?" Taylor isn't convinced.

"And we've had plenty of time to discover Julie Beech's body, but we haven't, have we? The passing of time might appear to make things less likely to have happened, but it doesn't of itself erase actual facts, does it?"

"So, you think... are asking us to consider the possibility that Frank Fairhurst might have seen the opportunity to kill two birds with one stone, sir?" Flowers is on a roll now, and not necessarily downhill. "He worries that Patch is coming back to Castle Upton to meet with Lettie Harewood and turn the screw on him. At the very least it would rake up old history about Julie Beech that he'd want to have long since buried.

So, he somehow kills Lettie Harewood and manages to make it look like natural causes - he'd know full well about the long incidence of chest infections and so on. He then attacks Andrew Patch and manages to make it look like an accident. He's then free, isn't he, of both his problems in the past and the present."

And therefore, all we need to do is catch Colonel Mustard red-handed in the library with the lead piping. Hunter-Wright would once have admired the young man's enthusiasm. "Except that, despite the best efforts from each one of you, we have uncovered no new evidence to comprehensively explain what happened to either Julie Beech or Andrew Patch. Nothing new! Nor have we found any evidence to link the two cases. We cannot press Fairhurst any further unless we charge him; we cannot do that as we haven't even so much as a stain on his toilet roll, let alone his character. Detection and discovery have led to nothing more than conjecture."

They all recognise a summing up of the stalemate they now find themselves in, rather than a fresh call to arms.

"We've gone back over the original case of Julie Beech's disappearance with the benefit of fresh eyes and new technology. We've re-interviewed the main characters who were around at the time of that case and who were also around at the time of Andrew Beech's death, along with a consideration of all the extras who may have lived or worked in Castle Upton. Nothing.

Frank Fairhurst and/or Lettie Harewood and Andrew Beech may well have had motives for doing what they did - even if we had evidence to support whatever that was - but two of them are dead and Frank Fairhurst is never likely to give us anything.

We have a body in the present where the cause of death is inconclusive and no body at all from the past. We have a possible motive but there is a chasm between 'possible' and 'likely.' The icing on our sad little cake is a complete lack of evidence to support any theory conclusively - as DI Cummings also found - so that too has melted away our prospects of the CPS ever agreeing to take this on."

"You think we're at the end of the road, sir?" Harcourt can hear the wobble in his voice, based on disappointment rather than fear.

"I don't think we've made progress even as far as the junction between these two cases, Inspector. We might get an 'unexplained' result but that's almost as useless to us as 'accidental.' As I made clear before, it makes all of us look bad in the eyes of the public and little more than hopeless to any remaining family or friends of either Julie Beech or Andrew Patch."

Flowers has been listening patiently, waiting for his moment. Now he swallows hard as he leaps into the abyss of the unknown. "Sir. I did have one thought."

Only one? He must try harder to remember how it was to be a younger man; how he used to be. "Do go on, Sergeant."

"Well, sir. Looking back through all of the old case files, I came across a link to another girl who had gone missing just a year earlier. A case which DI Cummings also worked on."

"Did that remain unexplained also?"

"No, sir, but it took outside help to find her..."

"What precisely do you mean by 'outside help?'"

"The incident took place just over the border, sir, but West Mercia helped West Midlands with the enquiry, given that the girl's home was on our side. This was way before the various alliances between the forces. As with our case, a little girl went missing, but this time some witnesses saw her snatched from outside a supermarket. Both forces threw everything they had at it but were completely stumped. DI Cummings was convinced her disappearance had something to do with a gang operating out of Birmingham, but a bit like in our case, there was no evidence to support it."

"So, the breakthrough eventually came thanks to this 'outside help' you still haven't explained. What was it, an act of God?"

Harcourt and Taylor smile but Flowers can see that the Super is being deadly serious. "Not exactly, sir, but there is an out-of-body element to it."

The silence in the room is at once deafening but also inviting, so he accepts the unspoken invitation to break it. "DI Cumming's boss - DCI Hargreaves - had a contact at Worcester News at the time who had witnessed one of his colleagues having a psychic episode."

Taylor is the first to react. "Haven't these people been largely discredited, sir, " She turns to Harcourt first for affirmation. "I remember reading about a case in the US – Salt Lake City – I think it was. No credible information was passed through."

"And there have been several others – in Australia too." Harcourt is as unimpressed as his colleague. "There's also the little matter of confirmation bias where things are somehow retro-fitted to what we do already know."

"Isn't that what we, as detectives, do every day of the week?" Hunter-Wright is rigid - with scepticism or anger, it is difficult to tell. "Besides, what is 'gut instinct' if it isn't some intangible feeling whose origin is unexplained?"

Not sure whether he is outnumbered or not, Flowers continues, hesitatingly. "The guy was a sub-editor on the paper - only young - but had this gift for looking back at events in the past, as well as sometimes in the future. Well, they had drawn a complete blank over the little girl's whereabouts, so Hargreaves insisted that Cummings speak to this... this psychic person. He wasn't happy about it apparently - or at least that's what his notes at the time suggested. But the thing is sir: it worked. They eventually found her."

"Dead?" Incredibly, Hunter-Wright's bottom lip is trembling.

"No, sir. She was alive."

"And this man - the 'psychic' person - what was his name?"

"His name was, is, Daniel Reed, sir. He still lives in the area."

They each await the jagged streaks of lightning and

eventually the thunderbolt that normally follows a situation where the temperature in a room has built to such an unbearable degree it is forced to explode. The very idea of them following such a route is ridiculous, practically unheard-of, despite them hitting the buffers not once but twice in Castle Upton.

Not only this, but Hunter-Wright's personality is that of a driver. There is no room for 'amiables' or 'expressives' in his book of personality types any more than there is for 'analysers.' He understands that the latter are a necessary evil, given that police forces these days must work on data gleaned from searching rather than good, old-fashioned coercion; but still, for him, sensitivity resulting from unseen happenings below the surface is strictly restricted to his teeth.

It is therefore as astonishing as it is refreshing when his response is restricted to two simple words - and not the two they were all thinking of.

"Call him."

CHAPTER NINE

"There you go, Frank." Grady places another pint in front of his tetchy customer although, to be fair, he has been much more relaxed in the last couple of weeks.

"Ta." Fairhurst drinks thirstily, as though it is his first pint of the evening, when, in fact, it's his seventh.

"How's trade?"

"Better now summer's here. You?"

"Rooms have been fully booked since April. Looks like we're covered until early September, though people find it easier to cancel online (no need to pick a phone up and speak to an actual human being) so you never really know. Bar's picking up now that people can sit at the tables outside again. Same again Pete? Won't keep you a minute."

Frank waits for the barman's return before continuing, with just the slightest of slurs. "Amazing what a bit of publicity can do!"

"It is. Not just the ancient history vultures either. I assume you've heard nothing about our gentleman from London?"

"Patch? What would there be to hear? It's all blown over just like it did before, thank God. We can get on with our lives without police or reporters writing down our every word. Bloody women eh!"

Grady is certainly not going to be drawn into that kind of debate, even though there are no other women present. Besides, though she never usually enters The Beaver, he feels sorry for Grace Beech, as all the other villagers do. He respects women even if he can't find a way to love them. Why wouldn't he? "Except he can't, can he? Patch, I mean. He can't get on with whatever life he was leading."

"No. No, I get that." Frank aims for the nearest beer mat and misses spectacularly, landing his pint glass too firmly, the protesting froth spilling over the top of it and forming a small puddle on Grady's immaculate bar which is now more sticky than slick. "Police came up with nothing though, so it must have been an accident like some of them at the inquest argued for. I reckon they just looked for a link with that little girl's disappearance because they'd run right out of clues. You can't always connect the present with the past, can you?"

Mopping up the mess with a towel that is always to hand, Grady considers this an odd thing to say, even though Fairhurst is about to cross the sober/smashed parallel, beyond which he usually falls quite rapidly (or falls over). A bit like the border dividing the two Koreas. "Surely we're all products of the past in some way - even a newborn baby starts with a nine-month history?"

"Yeah, but what if you can't remember things that happened in the past - or choose not to?

"It doesn't mean they didn't happen though, does it? Sometimes we have to go backwards to go forwards."

He notes the look of confusion on the older man's face whose ignorance has quite often turned similar comments into unnecessarily violent responses. He adds quickly: "What I mean to say is if you don't have your memories to fall back on, it must be very hard to make any kind of sense out of the present, let alone what's still to come."

Fairhurst takes a long gulp of beer before replying, ever more sagely (thankfully): "But if events in the past didn't make sense to you then, how can you ever expect to grow normally? Your foundations are flawed aren't they, or stunted at best? You're damaged... like each one of those children I expect?"

Not for the first time Grady - and certainly not just with Frank - questions his judgement in starting a philosophical debate with one of his customers whose grip on reality has been loosened by the products he's been so keen to sell them. The only element in the ensuing haze that's real is usually the ale and that never lasts for long either.

"I guess you're right. That was all before my time of course."

"Terrible time for everyone, particularly Julie Beech's family. You've seen what it did to Grace, the poor woman. I was only 37 myself at the time, about your age?"

"Actually, I'm 36."

"All I can say is that you've aged better than I had. Quite knocked me off my feet it all did. Still, we'll all be long gone in another forty years, won't we?"

A tall figure looms up behind him and plants an empty pint glass on the counter, almost knocking Fairhurst's over.

"Same again please, Mike."

"Right you are, Duncan. Are you keeping well?"

Grady knows that his polite enquiry will elicit no response - it never has done - and yet an answer is beginning to form in his mind. An answer to a nagging question he has been asking himself since the unfortunate Andrew Patch last left his pub.

***

Harcourt and Taylor are on their way back to the City of Worcester. It's a journey they've completed often in the last few weeks, and much warmer now than when they began, hence the air con on max and both in shortsleeves, jackets hurled onto the back seat.

A row of bedraggled-looking fruit trees falls into a line beside the road.

"Have they got some sort of blight; do you think?" Taylor contrasts them with the many others that have recently been seen in brilliant pink and white bloom.

"Not necessarily. They may just have stopped producing fruit – past their prime you might say."

She smiles at the female inference, knowing that

Harcourt is about as far away from being an 'alpha male' as DS Flowers is.

"Why don't they just cut them down then?"

"It's illegal in the Vale of Evesham to cut down a fruit tree until it's completely dead – 'grubbing up' I think they call it around here.

Taylor is encouraged to continue with the horticultural theme. "So, is the grapevine functioning correctly, sir?"

"Hard to say unless you tell me which message we are or are not talking about?"

She is staring straight ahead now but can still see every new worry line on her boss's face; how his eyes have lost their brightness. She wonders if it's hay fever - though the pollen count isn't as bad today after last night's rain - or something less superficial.

"The new DS?"

"Ah. I thought Flowers might have been the first to ask, not you!"

"So, it's true then?"

"That she's joining our team, very pretty or both?"

His weariness seems to have abated slightly, leading her to wonder what he had thought the station gossipers had been whispering.

"You do not have to say anything..."

"Ha ha. I haven't met her myself but, yes, DS Linda Farren will be joining us soon. She's coming over from uniform, so getting up to speed before making the leap."

"Of faith?"

"Something like that. Flowers will continue to act up for now, though, at least until the return of DC Hanrahan."

Taylor knows he has been worrying about the lack of progress in this, their latest enquiry, so changes tack (or is that too nautical in their decidedly landlocked circumstances?)

"Have you made contact with Daniel Reed yet?"

"He might be psychic, DS Taylor, but I believe we humans can still make contact using normal channels of communication. I sent him an email."

"When was this, sir?"

"Last week when the Superintendent asked me how I was getting on with our new 'helper.'"

So that was it. The DI had been dumbstruck by the idea of them using such a person outside of the force and even more so by Hunter-Wright's endorsement of such a 'left-field' approach. No doubt he'd put it off for as long as he could, but Hunter-Wright had caught up with him - as he always did, eventually.

"You didn't think it better to talk with him on the 'phone; get a better feeling for who he is?"

"No, Sergeant, I didn't think that getting a better 'feeling' about someone was more important than laying out the facts."

"Sorry, sir. Did he come back to you?"

"Over the ether, yes."

"Sir?"

"He sent me a text. We're due to meet at the end of the week."

***

"How did it go?"

Sunshine is flooding The Lenches today. Daniel looks out at the familiar, dark grey silhouette of the Malvern Hills, a slightly lighter grey mist above them today, failing to convince him that the hills are even more elevated than they are.

Housman's 'Blue Remembered Hills' of neighbouring Shropshire fills his head with verse but he decides to keep it to himself, just as he did when first reading it way beyond even those peaks, looking out over Cardigan Bay. Exhilarated, it had felt then as if it was his discovery and his alone: something to keep private and re-read when all around him had forgotten what it was like to be young and carefree, and, in his case anyway, slightly afraid of the infinite possibilities that lay ahead.

He and Charlotte are sitting at the kitchen counter, each with slate-coloured mugs of coffee in front of them. Had one of them not drunk much faster than the other, they might have been in perfect harmony.

"It's one of those." Claire throws her jacket onto the kitchen sofa and climbs up onto the vacant wooden stool between them both. "I thought it went OK but then you start worrying, don't you? To be honest, I think I'd rather come out thinking it was terrible and then realising that I did get a lot of it right after all, as opposed to now doubting myself."

"I remember O-level Chemistry. I just couldn't get my head around valency numbers. I think I managed to mismatch so many elements I ended up with more acid than in a car battery."

Claire laughs out loud, even though they both know that he has told her the same story many times before. Post-exam nerves he supposes.

"Still managed to pass though!"

"That's all I want, as you know. Apart from History, RE and English, just getting through the rest of them will do. It's not like I'd want to do A-level Chemistry either. Triple Science is bad enough."

Charlotte has been smiling benignly, quite relaxed. She has been quieter lately, seemingly more at peace with herself and with them, apart from the nightmare of two nights ago when she'd sat bolt upright in bed, eyes seemingly wide open, and screamed. Neither Daniel nor Claire - who had also rushed into her mother's room, which smelled damp with sweat - had been able to calm her for several minutes. Neither of them is any the wiser about what abyss she'd been looking into - not even in the safe harbour of daybreak - but it had undeniably terrified her.

"Uncle Fergus is coming to see us tomorrow, don't forget!"

Claire looks awkwardly at Daniel.

"It's fine. He'll understand your needing to get back to your books. He's just coming for tea, isn't he?"

His wife nods. "He invited himself. How did he describe it? 'A nice bridge between the dead and the living!'"

Daniel explains this to his daughter who unofficially gave up on religion when puberty hit her. "He's presiding over a funeral service in Flyford Flavell. An old lady who used to live in Bromyard before moving here. He'd got to know her quite well after her husband died and helped her quite a lot - by listening, presumably. Anyway, her family asked if he'd come over to do the business."

"Is Aunt Lucille coming too?"

"I think she prefers to bury the living as opposed to the dead."

"Daniel!" Charlotte feigns mock outrage.

She hasn't mentioned her 'friend' since that wet afternoon and, apart from one outing to the GP for 'women's needs' she has barely left the house. He prefers not to question her, still afraid of the answers she might give him. He changes the subject.

"It's English tomorrow morning, isn't it?" He knows it is.

"Certainly is. An afternoon with Romeo and Juliet beckons."

"I love Prokofiev's ballet score to that."

"If music be the food of love, play on…" Charlotte adopts a mock-serious pose at which they all laugh.

"Now that was an opening line!" Daniel loves to see this more relaxed version of his wife but is simultaneously uneasy about how long it will last.

"Twelfth Night?" Claire grabs a pile of books from the little table by the window.

Daniel watches her with a huge sense of both love and pride that she has come this far, relatively unscathed by the demands and expectations of her contemporaries, never mind the poisoned chalices handed out to teachers of an ever-changing school curriculum. He smiles at the young pink and yellow antirrhinums dancing in the breeze beyond the glass. They have always been his favourites. Their common English name might be 'snapdragons,' but he takes much more comfort in the Latin.

***

She loves to see him walking up the garden path. He exudes an air of unadulterated optimism, completely oblivious to the light rain that is falling, matting his hair that is so much nearer the clouds than most people judge his mind to be.

He taps tentatively on the utility room door, though there is far more to him than the simple utilitarian they take him for.

"I got your text."

"Great. Let's get those wet clothes off before you catch a chill."

He stretches his long arms upwards as she pulls the threadbare jumper over his head.

He smiles down at her. "Mum used to do that! She had the same turn of phrase as well: chills and snuffles."

"Well, she would know. I imagine she had a lot of those to put up with."

He smiles again but a sad smile this time.

"How did you get on with *Sister*?"

"Immeasurably better than my own daydreams!"

"It's an interesting read, isn't it? It was her debut novel too - six years ago; how time drags."

"Not for her. Everything was ebbing away, wasn't it? I loved the way we were drawn into the mystery, only for that twist to explain everything that was right in front of us all the time."

"An ambiguous ending though - open-ended even?"

"It was but I think it was far more about the journey she went on, lamenting the time she never had with her sister - to understand who she was. That line: 'you are my sister in every fibre of my being' reminded me of Kathy's obsession with Heathcliff in *Wuthering Heights* when she says 'I am him... as my own being.' The suicide versus murder debate was one I made up my mind about quite early on though."

"Wow, I didn't; or at least I didn't pick up on the clues

that I can see now were liberally dotted about. You'd have had to be psychic to see for certain what was going on, I think?"

She loves the enthusiasm they share for literature; just talking about books. There is a book club in Castle Upton, but she's never felt able to join it. It isn't that the participants aren't friendly enough and, indeed, of a similar age to her. No, it's more that she wouldn't fit in: 'Long-suffering wife of aggressive garage-owner and ex-farmer - always wearing that dirty anorak - who discovers a love of books later in life.'

She can picture them now in their casual clothes which are finer than her smartest outfits. Seated on well-stuffed chintz sofas, gathered round glasses of Prosecco and bowls of exotic nuts from Waitrose with names she couldn't pronounce. All the time they'd be nodding sagely at her unsophisticated observations while furtively examining her boots for signs of mud. And, of course, they all knew what had happened; a less-than-original plot line for any story.

"And yet, as you say, the clues are all there, laid out for us then hidden again, like a stain in the forest covered with leaves." He is continuing without blinking; with that strange stare he has when concentrating hard on something he can see right in front of him or way behind.

"Come on," she beckons, leading him to a different place, "You can write in here where there's plenty of light. I'll make us coffee."

He rejoins her later and sits down beside her. How

she longs for him to rest his great head on her slender shoulder. She turns to him and smiles instead. "I have a new story for you to read." She half whispers this as if it is a secret to be shared between just the two of them. "It only arrived on Monday, but I finished it last night."

"You spend far too much time on your own you know."

"Says he! I think you'll like it. It's about a young man discovering who his family are, where they came from. Set in the Lake District."

"I've never been there."

"It's beautiful, though I've only really done the tourist places like Coniston, Ambleside - Windermere of course."

"I read that there are much quieter parts, remote, like?"

"Most of it is, but more difficult to get to."

"Makes the journey more worthwhile though!"

She stands back to admire his stature, as she hands him the paperback. "Maybe we'll give it a try one day?"

"I'd love that."

"Treat it as your first piece of research then! You can text me when you've finished, and come and write your review of this one next. We need to keep you going."

"This is my favourite part of every week."

She smiles outwardly. Inwardly she is beaming. She looks forward to his arrival even more than her husband's departure now. "You have a reputation to uphold now that you've become such an online star! You got more than two hundred new followers again last week."

"If only they knew who I was..."

"Wouldn't make any difference: it's what you think, what you say, and how you say it that counts, no matter who you are or where you've come from."

He leaves her then. A son she never had. She watches as hope clicks the garden gate shut and despair quickly fills the space left behind it.

**

Fergus navigates his hatchback up the narrow, winding road past the black and white timbers of Rous Lench Court. He wonders momentarily what it must have been like to live there in the sixteenth century – it is roughly the same age as his church in Marcombe, but much more accessible.

A large container lorry meets him at the top of the hill. He respectfully slows down to let it pass, while its porky driver waves a half-eaten sandwich at him with one hand as he grips the steering wheel with the other. Not for the first time, Fergus praises the Good Lord that he drives such a small car; not that he was ever going to be blessed with the need for anything larger.

He passes a sign to Dr Chafy's Tower - a brown-bricked folly surveying the beautiful surrounding countryside like a watchtower - and turns left to Wood Lench. Nothing much seems to have changed here since he last came, just before Christmas. Mind you, he considers, it probably takes far more than the coming of Christ to change anything much in this part of the world.

"Is Lucille not with you?" His sister's opening gambit had been rather abrupt, or maybe he is just out of practice.

"No. She finds funerals all a bit too gloomy; like life in many ways, I suppose."

Daniel arrives from his back bedroom (or 'study,' 'library' or whatever he chose to call it this week). His enigmatic response seems to have eluded both of them as Daniel ushers them through to a room that seems square and sparse, like so many modern houses. At least it's light on a day that has threatened rain pretty much since dawn.

"She's alright though - Lucille?" Charlotte persists.

What is this preoccupation with his wife? Isn't he the one who is visiting them? Is he then just a marker for a more important absent soul, like John the Baptist perhaps?

"Nothing an apology from you wouldn't improve. To this day I've no idea why you were so rude to her."

"Nor me!" Replies Charlotte; her turn to play the enigma card.

He sinks into a well-worn armchair as Daniel produces a plate of fairy cakes that will surely be harder than they look (like all fairytales) and then busies himself with the kettle.

"How was it? Worse than usual or about what you expected?"

His brother-in-law makes a funeral service sound more like a football match report, except that there can be no score draws, only defeats.

"It went according to plan, thank you. Monstrously sad of course but I like to think I gave them just a little bit of hope for the future. You never can tell, but it gives them something to hang on to. Unfortunate if the deceased died through suicide from hanging…"

His spontaneous attempt at gallows humour seems as inappropriate to him as it does to them. Fortunately, his niece joins them at that pivotal point in his discourse and pecks him on the cheek. "Hello, Uncle Fergus. How are you?"

Finally! Maybe not all youth is lost after all. "I am very well, thank you, my dear, all things considered."

"Auntie Lucy"

Christ!

"No. No, nothing to do with your aunt. I have just been conducting a funeral which can leave one feeling bereft; one questions oneself deeply at times such as that, as if one was a mourner oneself."

"At least one doesn't struggle with the unexplained."

Is she mocking me too?

She is continuing, full of self-confidence. How he envies her. "If one has a faith, I mean. Anything that seemingly makes no sense in this world can be blamed on someone pulling the strings in another, can't it?"

She remains standing, right in front of him, as does his sister. Now Daniel comes to join them. Looking up to one person leaves him feeling outnumbered; with three of them, it is a positive massacre.

"Are you studying RE at school by any chance?" His rather smug response will catch her off guard. Catch all that self-assurance and squeeze every last drop out of the Inquisition.

"I am but I had an English exam this morning, so more make-believe than made-up." She smiles nicely at him and then: "Please excuse me, I have to get back to 'The Plague.'"

"I'm sorry?" He can usually deal with riddles; they are pretty much unavoidable in his line of work.

"Camus!" Daniel saves him. "They're introducing elements of literature into the French GCSE curriculum whereas it used to be the preserve of the A-level."

"He saw the world as absurd I believe?"

Daniel sits down beside him. Never a good sign. What's more, he seems to be pleased to have someone to talk to on a different level.

"He did. He never went along with the existential view of the world in full but, for him, it was all down to individual actions that made them authentic."

Fergus must change the subject, and quickly. This could go on for hours otherwise. He addresses

Charlotte. "On the subject of individual actions - or the absurd, you choose - our mother was asking for you again last week. She insists on knowing when you will be visiting her again."

"Who knows."

"Well, I for one don't. Then there's Mother - that makes at least two."

"She won't remember me if I do go to see her, or even that I've ever been."

"You know that, and I know that. I just think you should make much more of an effort. It's not an exact science, Charlotte. We don't know whether some small thing could trigger a memory and make a big difference."

"It won't."

"Won't what?"

"Make any difference."

"You don't know that for certain. Besides, she's old. Death's inevitable tentacles are wrapped around every part of her body and soul; the end surely cometh soon and life's great mystery shall be solved at last."

That was quite good he thinks, not entirely sure that it isn't original. Predictably, though - like Fate itself - instead of congratulating him they ignore his talents. They always do. Even the sons and grown-up grandchildren at this afternoon's internment couldn't wait to get away from him.

"Talking of which, Daniel is going to be helping the

police again."

Charlotte seems proud. What on earth is there to be proud of about that?

"Not with their enquiries?" He laughs at his small witticism.

"Yes and no."

Daniel smiles back up at his wife. Ghastly. "I'm not in any kind of trouble if that's what you mean? They've just asked me if I'd help with something the coroner has ruled as 'unexplained.'"

"People used to attend church for that sort of thing," his tart response fills the small room. "Not that the authorities ever believed in much more than how to gain or retain their power over ordinary people. They'd try anything. Still do."

"Man-made allies then!" His sister is insufferable. Perhaps he should have gone straight home to face the tyranny of an empty kitchen, after all; its empty plates resolutely remaining in their cupboards.

"If you say so… where did the crime take place?"

"Well, that's just it, you see: they don't know if any crime was committed - then or now. That's why they need to think outside of the box."

"I hate that phrase, especially after a funeral. Didn't you do this sort of thing before?"

"Way back, but well remembered. I'd just started on the paper at the time and a little girl had gone missing then too. They did eventually find her, but it took a while. The police got there just in time."

"Based on your extraordinary expertise?" He chooses his words carefully whenever describing the supernatural beyond the prayer book.

"It was but they never gave him credit for it. The policeman in charge didn't believe him for a long time." Charlotte has placed her hand on his knee, for Heaven's sake.

"Ah. The barren field of non-believers increases one by one…" He hasn't heard his sister defend Daniel for a long time. It makes a pleasant change from her being simply defensive.

"Which means they effectively haven't used him since." She hands him a cake on a small china plate.

"Your incredible powers have been on hold!" He mocks as he chews. "Where did these unfortunate events take place?" Best to show some kind of interest if only to fill time. The cake is surprisingly good.

"A village called Castle Upton, about eight miles south of here - towards Pershore."

"I know it well. One of my parishioners resides over that way! Well, not her exactly. Her sister lives in Leominster but her parents worshipped with me for many years. The father took me aside - must be twenty years ago. Just before he died anyway."

"That's all very interesting, Is there some great moral behind this little homily, or even a point?"

Charlotte should have studied sarcasm as a major,

rather than law, he acknowledges.

"The point is simply that she lived in Castle Upton. Her father was concerned about her gambling addiction. The sister was too busy being afraid of her husband and his unpredictable temper, so I got the task of coming over to see her."

"That must have been a nice surprise!"

Has his brother-in-law always been like this or is his decline in tune with his sister's anger? Nature versus nurture again, he supposes.

"Something of a shock, yes. Quite brazen about it all though. Didn't try to hide it or see anything ungodly in logging into such a website night after night."

"What was the site called?"

"Not one I'd advise you to dabble with. In any case, I'm sure it's long gone by now. What do they say these days: 'The bubble has burst?'"

"So, what did you do? Offer yourself up to her as an alternative?"

"Charlotte!"

Daniel's warning follows the warning signs. Venus is about to erupt as Vesuvius again, her alter ego. Best ignored for now, or is that what they said at the time?

"In any case, she told me she had everything under control and showed me her bank statement as proof. She had more than a million pounds in an offshore account in the Canary Islands. Talked about retiring there after reaping its tax advantages - not that I know very much about that world you understand."

"Alright for some!"

"But not for the many I'm afraid. You cannot possibly appreciate the number of addiction cases I have to deal with on a weekly, even daily basis sometimes. It isn't always that they are in denial either; many are quite open to the hopelessness of their conditions and do sincerely wish to change their lives around. The bonds that bind all of them together are formed by a shared darkness. The unfounded promise of glory drives these poor souls from within, while the glittering future slowly rusts from without."

"What was her name - this gambler extraordinaire?"

Charlotte has always been the mistress of rhetorical questions to which she seemingly has no interest in the answers. She'd have been deadly as a barrister if she'd gone on to be called, as their father had so dearly wanted.

"Her name was Rogers: Angela Rogers. She was a teacher in the local school. Her sister Maureen died much too soon. Probably saw much too much in that house."

"Did you keep in touch with her after that first meeting?"

"Sadly no. I reported back to her father that there was little he or I or Our Father could do other than pray that she might one day see reason. He was terribly concerned when I told him I thought she was lonely (thus helping to feed the gambling) but even more so on hearing her remark that she could buy anyone she wanted... or buy them off."

***

Harcourt's hands are sweaty despite the station's air conditioning. The latter has never worked properly, recycling the unwelcome smells of cooked meat, with its associated effects on body parts, in an endless loop. A shared history of long hours and the need for instant gratification from food means that their canteen would never be able to boast about its personnel appearing on *Masterchef*.

However, it would have made no difference today. Harcourt's nerves might have single-handedly melted an igloo. He has been putting off this moment for as long as Hunter-Wright's not asking about it has allowed. Yesterday, he asked why no appointment had yet been made and, being a detective, had seen through the 'heavy caseload' and 'lack of staff' excuses immediately.

He has been through all of DI Cummings's case files (or rather, DS Flowers has worked late into the night doing precisely that) but found only one instance of his involving Daniel Reed in a live enquiry. The same match that Flowers had picked up on originally.

He is curious to know why that was. It will be his first question of the man claiming to have special powers. If they're that special, why were they harnessed only once? After all, it had seemed to work; or did they all just get lucky, especially the little girl in question?

He glances up at the old analogue clock in the corner.

Unfortunately, its timekeeping is as good as any digital newcomer. Harcourt stands, looks around the empty office, and heads off for the interview room where Reed is already sitting, having arrived five minutes earlier than the allotted time. Perhaps he is nervous too, thinks the DI, as he makes his way slowly down the scuffed marble stairs, his footsteps sounding more like those of a condemned prisoner than a jailer.

"Sorry about the short notice and late hour!' They shake hands across a bare table. Reed looks fairly normal, but you never can tell. By the same token, does the middle-aged man sitting in front of him already know that he deliberately arranged the meeting for the early evening as he didn't want his colleagues to be present? Didn't want them to see a real-life 'psychic' and draw early and uninformed conclusions as to his likely effectiveness, although that is precisely what he has done – and he isn't optimistic.

"That's fine. My time is very much my own, Inspector, so I can be flexible."

He seems quite relaxed or perhaps he's in some kind of meditative state? Who would know?

"You worked with this police force before, I understand. Can you tell me a little more about that please?"

The man smiles slightly and is the epitome of calmness - unlike most of the others who sit on the other side of this table, in this room. "You surely don't need any special powers to look back through your case files. All of that would have been a matter of public record. I remember my colleague editing an article in the paper giving most of the details."

"You're right of course; I just wanted to hear it from you. DI Cummings was not the best of note-takers and maybe there are other details that you can recall but he might choose not to."

"You've spoken with him again recently?"

"We have. That is to say, my colleague has, not me."

"It was more than forty years ago, so that would put him into the mid to late eighties. Perhaps it's less a case of selective memory than memory loss? That would be quite understandable, wouldn't it?"

Thank goodness this man isn't a suspect. Harcourt hasn't noticed the slightest flicker of emotion in the man's eyes nor muscle twitches in his face. Body language doesn't always throw up clues as to what a person is thinking, but this man might just as well have been a corpse.

"I came across an internal note from DI Cummings, suggesting that we shouldn't revert to, er, 'external sources' in future... and yet, you got a result."

"He 'got a result.' I merely helped him to see what wasn't on the surface. I'm not at all surprised at that prognosis as it chimes with his behaviour at the time."

"He didn't believe you?"

"Yes and no. He didn't believe in me."

"Please. Just take me back to the beginning." Harcourt's patience is running thin, but he finds that he doesn't want Reed to put him in the same box as Cummings.

"The origins of such species?"

Whether he is tuned in to all this or not, the 'psychic' gives nothing away. He simply smiles again while raising the two index fingers from his hands that are clasped, to form an arch-like entrance he is finally allowing Harcourt through.

"OK. Your colleagues had been investigating the disappearance of a young girl - Mary-Jane Boyle. Her father had made his money from wastepaper recycling, long before each of the political parties, in turn, claimed that they thought of it first. He was a wealthy man, Mr Boyle, but a bit close to the wind (and I'm not talking about green energy here)."

"How so?"

"It was a cut-throat business, operating on fine margins. Boyle didn't quite fall into criminal activities - or at least nothing in your records showed that he had."

Harcourt recognises the familiar trails blazed - and sometimes incinerated - by some of his colleagues from that time. "Reading through some of his working hypotheses it does seem that Cummings saw connections all over the place with organised crime in the West Midlands. He would quite often jump to the same conclusion whenever a body unexpectedly turned up in a skip - usually low life."

"A mother's son or a child's Daddy nevertheless."

He's not exactly smug or especially worthy, but this

man has an otherworldly, non-judgmental air about him (or is that perception derived from Harcourt being told that Reed possesses a 'gift?'). Either way, he is already beginning to get under the detective's skin - no matter that the methods and motivations of some who wore the uniform long before he did were questionable at the very least.

Reed hasn't missed a beat. "Cummings quickly came to the view that the whole distribution business was some kind of cover for narcotics. None of this was ever proved at the time. I'm not sure if they - you - have uncovered anything since then. You've certainly had plenty of time."

Harcourt makes a mental note to ask Flowers to check this out. "And the daughter? They assumed that her disappearance was a kidnapping?"

"Cummings did, although there was no evidence of that at first. She just seemed to have vanished into thin air."

"How old was she?"

"Seventeen." Reed pauses to smile at the Inspector, knowing what he is thinking: a seventeen-year-old girl goes missing in the mid-1970s - probably not a top priority for any police force at that time, no matter how rich her parents were.

"Neither the parents nor police heard anything for three days or so. They had no leads as such - no sightings of Mary-Jane since she'd left the Tech College where she was studying for her A-levels. She was supposed to be attending a dance class that evening in

Droitwich - where the family lived - but didn't show up. According to her parents, it was the thing she looked forward to most each week and wouldn't have missed it for the world."

"No one out of the ordinary she'd met; no rogue boyfriends?"

"No boyfriends at all. She had her head in her books most of the time, rather than the clouds most girls of that age prefer."

"What happened next?"

"A note was put through the letterbox at the family home, demanding a ransom of £250,000. Boyle had money tied up in investments all over the place but could have got at the cash. His wife was out of her mind and urged him to pay off whoever had taken their daughter. She was an only child, so I imagine that only made things worse."

"But the father held out?"

"More that Cummings urged him to do so. The DI felt that this was his best chance of a lead into the kind of crime syndicates he'd been trying to prise open for years."

"But nothing at the time suggested organised crime was behind this at all, did it? It could have been a business rival - traumatic enough for everyone concerned but on a completely different level to those guys!"

"The simple fact, Inspector, was that they didn't know who was behind the kidnapping. Boyle was persuaded not to pay up and there was no further communication either way. We shouldn't forget that this was a girl - a young woman - who wasn't at all streetwise. The mother was frantic over what they might be doing to her daughter. Starving her was almost the least of her worries."

"So, presumably they brought in all the usual suspects for questioning; looked closely at Boyle's business contacts and his main competitors, and anyone who might have a quarter-of-a-million-pound grudge against him, or debt to settle?"

"I assume they did all of that. I wasn't part of the investigation at that point. They only asked me to help because they had exhausted all the other lines of enquiry. I wasn't party to what they quite rightly wished to remain confidential. I expect it's all on file though."

"And how did you come to be involved with the enquiry?"

"I was 21 and had just started at the paper as a trainee sub-editor. Consequently, I was always in early each day and usually left quite late too. At that point in your career, you'll do anything to impress won't you?"

Harcourt allows himself a small smile of recognition.

"It was a Thursday morning in early March."

"1976. The drought year?"

"Yes, all that came later. Well, the rain didn't. Not for a long time. I'm surprised you remember it, Inspector?"

"I don't. I was only one!"

Daniel is genuinely surprised. He had assumed that the DI was around ten years younger than he was; not expecting a gap of nearly twenty. His attempt at a compliment had just backfired more badly than the motorbike they'd just heard from the street outside. "I do beg your pardon, I ..."

"Not at all. You look pretty young for your age whereas I'm just old before my time. You could blame it on police work but it was probably also the case when I too turned 21!"

Daniel laughs but just as quickly returns to the drought year. "I just remember it being sweltering in the office. There was no air conditioning, but, as it was my first job, I naively assumed that those were normal working conditions. Anyway, on the nights immediately before that March morning, I'd been having panic attacks (you know when you're not sure if you're awake or not, but the anxiety feels completely real?)"

Harcourt knows that feeling much too well and, even now, feels his chest tightening as Reed continues.

"They always took the same, confused form: cannons lined up to fire at approaching trains - modern trains. Completely incongruous of course but I saw two sets of railway carriages - one quite empty and the other packed with people. What stressed me was that I didn't know which one the cannons were going to aim at. Yet it was up to me and me alone to somehow make that decision."

Harcourt is aware for the first time of the silence hanging around them. "What did happen on that morning?"

"As I said, I was in early and there were only a couple of journalists and one of the other sub-editors there at the time. I remember swivelling around in my chair so that my back was to my desk. I stood up and must have shouted something because suddenly they were all on my side of the room. I suppose they thought I was having some kind of stroke.

I was sweating all over - I don't recall that part of it too much because my mind had suddenly made sense of it all: an early-morning train packed with commuters was approaching Cannon Street station in London with a bomb on board. I saw everything as clear as day but the people who were screaming were not on that train but another one passing - the much emptier train I had dreamed about."

"Whatever did they say - your colleagues?" He remains patient but eager to know what happened too.

"Even for a provincial paper the journalists had plenty of contacts in London and they swung into action - the Met, colleagues on the big papers, British Rail as it was then. Nobody took it seriously, but the police did eventually report back to them that a ten-pound bomb had been detonated on a train at the Cannon Street terminus. Thank goodness it had just emptied. There was a handful of casualties on another train which was passing but clearly, they'd got their timing wrong, or it could have been much worse."

"You say 'they' - did they find the people responsible?" Harcourt feels suddenly cold - and nothing to do with the air conditioning in their much more modern office either.

"Not too difficult, Inspector. The IRA had been targeting trains in London that spring. An even bigger bomb had been defused in the underground station at Oxford Circus about a month before, and there were further attacks at West Ham and, I think, Wood Green. None of these compared to the bombings in 2005 of course."

"Nevertheless, this was the first time you'd sensed something like this - something yet to happen?"

Reed remains impassive. He has shown no flicker of emotion, even while relating such a traumatic tale. "I had always known there was something there. I usually pick up on things from the past, although, like most of us who have these heightened senses, we sometimes see things that are about to happen too - or at least they will occur if nothing can be done to prevent them from happening."

"And someone in your office told Cummings about this... this 'event.'

"One of the journalists - I never knew which - was close to one of the guys in the local CID and so I suppose that got passed through to Cummings."

"You didn't actually 'see' it though?" Harcourt regrets the slightly sarcastic, more than suspicious insinuation as soon as it has left his mouth. "I'm sorry. I'm just finding all of this quite hard."

"I understand completely. It's an entirely common and pretty understandable reaction, Inspector. Please do not worry. We don't by any means see everything. It is very far from being an exact science: that's rather the point."

"But you were called in and presumably led the police to Mary-Jane?"

"Not at first. My particular gift is something called 'psychometry.' The term was first used by an American physician from Cincinnati in the mid-nineteenth century. When I handle objects I can very often sense the energy lines associated with those artefacts, and sometimes then see where they have been and what has happened to them in the past - and the people handling them before me."

"Don't you people sometimes have to wear gloves - to stop the flow as it were?" Harcourt is quite pleased that he remembered one thing he saw on TV some time ago. It would have been some drama Deborah had chosen. He only really does documentaries and the News.

"Though quite uncontrollable, my gift is not quite that advanced, Inspector. I'm not at all sure that it is for anybody who has it. Besides, it would be difficult to be a proofreader wearing gloves."

"I'm sorry. I didn't mean to be rude..." Back on the back foot.

"No offence taken. I don't do pendulums either; I tend to entrust their use to clocks, nor do I wear outlandish waistcoats! We're not all 'freaks.' Some of us can appear to be quite normal. It's the gift that is special, not us."

"I'm so sorry. Pre-judging on such a grand scale is quite unforgivable." He is genuinely remorseful in the face of such a modest, gentle soul

"Except that it is, because I forgive you! To continue, although there were no clues written down on the ransom note itself for the police to investigate, there was a pulsating force to it. After I finally managed to persuade them to leave me in an office alone for a while, I managed to form a picture of a young girl, locked in quite a small cream-coloured house in a residential area nearby."

"And you were able to give them sufficient detail for the police to act on this?"

"Yes and no. Cummings already had someone lined up for the kidnapping, though he had no actual evidence to support it. I don't know who he was other than that he was involved in drug dealing of some kind. Unfortunately, this man also lived in a cream-coloured house - a semi-detached house on a residential street.

I tried to persuade them that the house I had seen was small but detached and looked out on wasteland, with what looked like the large, round tower of a gas holder in the distance. Cummings wouldn't listen. He had been sceptical of my abilities from the outset - much more so than yourself, Inspector - and just saw the big chance he had been waiting for. They raided the house but found nobody there."

"Did they blame you? I imagine someone like

Cummings would have tried to do so: attack as the first form of defence and all that?"

"I think he might well have done, had it not been for one of the junior members of his team: a sergeant whose name escapes me I'm afraid. He sat with me and plotted where nearby (I knew she wasn't far away) gas holders were situated; all on a paper map of course. No GPS to help in those days, just a spirit guide."

Reed smiles, causing Harcourt to sense a happy ending to the story. He finds himself relaxing slightly too - for the first time in the 'interview.' "The police swarmed around several neighbourhoods. I went with them - all the time Cummings assuring everyone that would listen that it was a complete waste of time - until they found a street on the outskirts of Wolverhampton that seemed to fit the picture in my head. They found the girl in the fourth house that they searched."

"Alive?"

"Only just. Because of all the hours that the police had wasted, she was barely conscious and almost completely dehydrated. It seemed that her abductors had just left her there to die, once they knew there was no money coming."

"However, your intervention made all the difference! I am impressed."

"Don't be. Cummings's superiors were aware of the earlier, failed raid - maybe through the same sergeant who had listened more carefully and trusted what I was able to tell him, I don't know. They took the view that he had acted irresponsibly and almost contributed to the girl's death, rather than the 'hero of the hour' he wanted to be."

"And he never forgave you for that?"

"Not even a word of thanks. He made quite sure that I was never called to help them with any enquiry again - hence why I had no involvement with the Julie Beech case a year later - at least not until now."

"You said that your gift enables you to better understand things from the past. Have you had any other visions of things yet to happen - like the Cannon Street episode?"

"A few. Nothing major, apart from when I visualised another bomb exploding, about ten years later."

"Where was that?"

"Over a small town in Scotland called Lockerbie. Nobody listened to me then either."

CHAPTER TEN

They have finished dinner - or 'tea' as Deborah usually calls it when it is just the two of them (which is most of the time). Harcourt is loading the dishwasher. Equally, as usual, he tuts out loud at the way she has placed bowls at ridiculous angles in the top half, meaning there is no room for the glasses. As he has told her quite a few times, the small glasses are much more vulnerable and likely to be damaged alongside the large plates below, but he knows that the same pattern will follow tomorrow and the day after that.

"I can't believe you've stooped so low."

He listened to her ignoring his 'tut' so knows that this is nothing to do with the dishwashing procedure. "In terms of?"

"The psycho!"

"Psychic."

"Same difference."

No. They are almost certainly going to be completely different.

"Well, for a start, it wasn't my decision to bring him in. I'm not sure we were quite on our knees, but things certainly looked grim. Without any real evidence of any kind, the CPS wouldn't have given us the time of day."

"And you think this man will be able to help you: to find the evidence you haven't been able to find for yourself."

"Me and the rest of the team you mean?" Harcourt is frequently irked when his wife seems to take police failure personally, even when he doesn't. "We simply 'don't know' would be the honest answer."

"And the dishonest one?" She is looking at him quizzically.

"I don't do dishonesty. I see far too many people who specialise in it. No need for me to join them."

She swirls her remaining half glass of red wine around the glass (which will most definitely be destined for the top tray of the aforementioned dishwasher) before tipping it up and gulping it down in one go.

"But you must have some idea after talking to him for so long."

Indeed, they had chatted for nearly two hours - about the Julie Beech case mostly, during which Harcourt had brought Daniel Reed fully up to speed.

"He doesn't give anything away."

"Helpful!"

"What I mean is: he is thoughtful, self-contained I suppose. He has a lot of information to absorb, and quite quickly too. The Detective Superintendent wants him in Castle Upton tomorrow.

"It must be difficult for you."

"How so?"

"I know you don't believe in any of this stuff yet you have to go along with it because Hunter-Wright orders you to. I wouldn't have thought he'd have much truck with any of this mumbo jumbo either."

"Nor me. The fact remains, though, that we have practically nothing else to go on. What we mere mortals can all see is not enough to take us forward. If we're not careful, in another forty years we'll be no wiser about the cause of Andrew Patch's death either."

"Did you talk with him about getting help?"

"Help?"

"Don't be obtuse, Martin. You've told me often enough how stretched you are."

Harcourt cannot help but feel relieved. She's talking about bodies on the ground, not the celestial versions they're hoping to meet. "The new DS has been approved and they have somebody in mind."

"Much like your new shrink, then."

"Let's give him the benefit of the doubt before labelling him with failure."

"You approved them appointing this new sergeant, even though you knew it meant that your own promotion would have to wait, I suppose."

He sighs. This, again, is not a new bone of contention between them. "I got the pay rise and am effectively acting up even though I haven't got the title yet. The budget is fixed. My hands are tied."

"Not behind your back though, are they? Perhaps you should act up, make them notice you're not just going to be trampled all over for the good of the department?"

"Or the good of the general public!"

She pauses, preparing her second serve. "At least Andrew Patch was good enough to give up his body for medical science!"

"I think you've probably had quite enough to drink."

"Unlikely. I'm out with the girls shortly. This is just pre-pre-drink time. Don't look at me like that, Martin; I did tell you."

"I'm sure you did."

He is sure but doesn't remember it. In truth, the whole Daniel Reed involvement has unsettled him. The man seemed nice enough - genuine even - but Harcourt doesn't believe in meddling with the unknown. The world of spirits and ghouls. Looking for clues on the ground is often difficult enough in piecing together what has happened above it, in the past.

Talk of predicting events yet to happen or 'seeing' events in the past that nobody else manages to witness doesn't sit easily with him. Maybe he just lacks imagination? His teachers back at school in Cambridgeshire used to regularly moan at his parents about that (apart from Mr Hesketh, the History teacher, who was quite pleased).

He mulls over this later, while walking along the country lane leading from their housing estate into green fields that are still in a tense standoff with the developers. With the clocks going forward, it is quite light again, albeit a bit chilly. He zips his jacket up - like an old man - and breathes in and out deeply.

Young lambs bleat for their mothers. Harcourt is watching them scurrying across the grass when a thought unexpectedly comes into his head. He may not be psychic, but it does feel like a lightbulb moment.

***

"Oh, bad luck!"

No matter how many times Welbourne says it, or however hard he tries to make it sound sincere, it grates on him every time. Insufferable little man.

"Thanks. Maybe next time?"

"Definitely. Make it happen!

Loathsome and vaguely ridiculous in his red striped trousers, below his yellow golfing jumper, he looks like an inverted Rupert Bear.

"I'll certainly give it a go."

When did he settle for such platitudes? The man was a dentist for Heaven's sake. OK, so he makes holes on the greens as fast as he used to fill them in his surgery, but a healthy dose of anaesthetic wouldn't go amiss.

Hunter-Wright is almost at the end of his round on The Vale golf course. It makes for a pleasant walk across beautiful Wychavon countryside - and this afternoon has been a particularly fresh and sunny occasion - although it has clouded over menacingly now. He should feel invigorated, but he just feels tired.

They play twice a month when he can get away - which is increasingly easy these days. His playing partner today sold his practice a year ago so neither money worries nor frustration at work affect his swing or putting action. To be fair, both had always been superior to Hunter-Wright's technique, but it hadn't seemed to matter before. But then he hadn't felt that flutter in his chest before. It has happened twice today, each time on the long par fives.

Ever since Hunter-Wright had moved to Worcester, Welbourne had been trying to persuade him to join his Lodge, which he has fought against - usually through a healthy show of indifference but sometimes through direct, unambiguous rejection. The man has now taken a different tack, talking about all the influential people he knows, that his beaten friend will never now have the pleasure of meeting.

"Of course, he can't have had much change out of two million, not if Hampton's got their price. Would have been nearer five in the Home Counties I suppose. It's a nice place - eleven bedrooms and all that, but, I ask you, what can he want with forty acres? Oh, I know there's an indoor pool, sauna and all that stuff but that's just for show, isn't it? To entice the right kind of guest perhaps? Given his lifestyle, I assumed a simple en-suite with a two-way mirror was more to his tastes if you know what I mean!"

Thankfully, the smirk is whipped from his face by a nasty pull into the woods down the left side, giving him very little chance of finding his golf ball but a very great chance of him being stung by the giant nettles or his dressing-up clothes being snagged on one of the plentiful low-lying branches.

Hunter-Wright tries not to hide his satisfaction as his own ball flies nearly two hundred and eighty yards down the middle of the fairway, lush and green before the onslaught of summer's sunshine. There are usually four of them but the other two have cried off, turning their four into a two (though, gratifyingly, Welbourne has shouted 'fore' in case any rabbits are crouching in the undergrowth).

The other two are Hunter-Wright's real 'friends.' Happy in each other's company, the three of them played regularly until about a year ago when Wright introduced Welbourne to the group. Wrong move. Wright was still part-owner in a local restaurant so could be forgiven (just a little) for wanting to invite one of his regular customers. Unfortunately, the tips that had been there on the table had quickly migrated to the golf course and now none of them seemed to know the best way of getting rid of him. He grimaces. There is something about being a serving police officer that makes that sentiment sound all wrong.

Neaves on the other hand is happy just to play, no matter the vocal interference that is offered up so willingly, via those perfect white teeth. Older than the rest of them, Neaves suffered a minor heart attack five years ago and was prescribed plenty of walking and fresh air. Not for him fresh air shots though. On the contrary, he is the most talented of them out there. At the same time, seemingly happy-go-lucky as well as fiercely competitive, he is rarely one to lose his nerve on the greens, yet the first to genuinely commiserate when someone else chooses the wrong line. He had been a well-known bookkeeper in Evesham before having to hand the reins to his oldest son. With just the right balance of conversation and focus, he was beating the odds each day and seemed in better health now than he had ever been.

Welbourne hasn't stopped his charmless charm offensive for even a second. "We're off to the Collingwood-Smiths for the weekend. Do you know them? No, well he made his cash out of real estate, but his wife was already well-endowed. Nudge. Nudge."

Now he is feeling really tired and just wants it all to end.

"That should be pleasant for you."

"Pleasant! What a passive little word. He keeps a great cellar so should be a dam sight more exciting than that!"

Hunter-Wright doesn't respond; simply can't be bothered. He has never been that fond of fine wine, which normally leads to a fine mess of humanity. Miriam has never seen the point of it, apart from at the Queen's Silver Jubilee when for some bizarre reason she'd asked the restaurant waiter for a Babycham as an aperitif.

She was also the one who warned him against the modern-day fraternity of Freemasons. Her own father -

like his - had stood on the wrong square and had never really been able to step off it.

Oh great, now it has started to hail - in April!

"I hear you've got some kind of nutter helping you with your enquiries? Isn't that how you phrase it for the plebs?" Welbourne seems oblivious to the small pieces of white ice bouncing off his cap. Perhaps there's little left of the grey matter below it to register them?

"The 'nutter' or the enquiries bit?"

Welbourne laughs noisily but hasn't found his quip in the slightest bit funny.

"It's true then! I note that you're not denying it?"

"I didn't realise that I was under caution! The police have always used whatever means they have at their disposal to solve crimes and execute justice."

"There you go again... 'execute justice.' Wouldn't that lead to anarchy?"

'In the UK' and especially within the luxury development where you try to lord it over everyone else.

"I'm just saying that it's not as unusual as it may sound."

"I thought other forces had used shrinks in the past and been led down the garden path as it were, with or without actual footprints! A hit or miss affair which is usually a miss?"

God. He's turned into David Jacobs.

The shorter man laughs at his attempted wit. With

a solid three wood and a fair wind, he could obliterate that laugh for the good of man, forever.

"It isn't something that gets widely publicized, and I admit that it's unconventional, but surely the public would rather we try to think laterally now and again for us all to then move forwards - especially where a missing child is concerned?"

"She would hardly be a child now though, would she?" Welbourne scoffs as he heads off towards the trees. "I mean, you've had forty-odd years to think outside of the box, haven't you? Smacks of desperation if you ask me."

Hunter-Wright feels a cold wave of hatred for the man sweep across his entire body, warmed only by the thought of his perma-tanned face being sliced open by boughs which haven't yet learned how to bow.

***

Harcourt places the phone back in its cradle and closes his eyes momentarily. Jenny Graham has just confirmed that his late-evening epiphany could indeed lead to judgement and, hopefully, to justice.

Sitting up and seeing the world around him once more, he is aware that Flowers is by his side, his long eyelashes fluttering nervously as usual.

"What is it?"

"Sorry to interrupt you, sir..."

"I was merely thinking, Sergeant. If you deduced a snooze in there, I'll be sending you back for basic training."

He has meant it to be light-hearted; indeed, he feels light-hearted all of a sudden. However, shyness can be such a barrier for so many. "Go ahead; how can I help you?"

This is the straightforward language his subordinate understands as he launches into a revelation of his own.

"I've just taken a call from Mike Grady - the barman at The Beaver in Castle Upton."

Well, congratulations, both on being able to use the telephone and remembering where the pub was. He must stop this; must be more tolerant. Flowers has improved so much during the last 18 months – either because of or despite his tutelage - he sometimes forgets how much the young man still wants to please everyone, especially him. Thankfully, he is showing signs of developing a harder exterior now and at least he is using proper words rather than text 'speak.'

"Go on."

"He was quite cautious at first and I thought he was going to ring off again, so I tried to gently encourage him by remaining quiet, allowing him to take his time."

"Excellent!"

"He seemed to be in two minds as to whether to talk or not, but then he must have resolved what was going on in his head because he told me quite quickly that he had remembered what was troubling him about that night when Andrew Patch was killed."

"Or just died."

"Yes, I know we are keeping an open mind but..."

"It's fine. We just have to be careful how we phrase things sometimes, regardless of what we are thinking or even know."

Harcourt doesn't mean to sound patronizing but he has seen far too many cases where barristers have torn cases apart because of the presumptive language used and where a presumption of guilt - evidenced and documented comprehensively - has been simply shunted aside. Detection is only one part of the process: delivering articulate, neutral findings where the jury is quickly led to compelling evidence leaves defence lawyers with far fewer words to play with.

Flowers looks deflated but Harcourt knows from experience with the lad that his point will have hit home and he will remember it, and learn from it.

"So, what is it that Grady has remembered?" He hopes he sounds encouraging and that the news is too.

"Duncan Harewood, sir. When he left the pub - Grady still can't remember whether it was before or after Andrew Patch did - he was hunched over strangely. Grady knew that something wasn't right about it. He's now worked it out: Duncan didn't have his stick. He leaves it in the copper urn they use for umbrellas, just inside the back door. Regular as clockwork. Grady has never seen Duncan walk in or out without it."

***

"No, you're fine, "Steven Pateman sits down opposite her, a latte in front of her white mug of black tea, dividing them. "Nice day, though, so it might get busy again later."

She looks up and out of the window as though she hasn't noticed the weather up until that moment. "I'd have come out even if it had been raining. Sometimes you've just got to make the effort, haven't you?"

He doesn't reply. She hasn't made much of an effort with her appearance, which is remarkably like when she'd come in a few days ago – soon after the Patch incident. A lot of women come into the café to talk; some with prams in tow, others just towing the socially-acceptable line which requires them never to turn up at the school gates without a takeaway coffee in hand. Chai latte is the accessory of choice, even though he watches them sip as they leave his café, barely disguising their distaste.

"I just needed to get out of there. I've started seeing the four walls around the garden now too!" She throws out the words as if they are only ever meant to form a throwaway comment.

He understands the truth of individuals. He makes a study out of it every day. He also knows that talking really can cost lives. As soon as Andrew Patch had told him who he was and who he had returned to see, Steve Pateman was on the case. It hadn't taken him very long at all to smell danger above the once-enticing aromas of sausage rolls and coffee beans. It had excited him and he can admit to himself if, for obvious reasons, to nobody else (and especially not the police) he flirted with the man fairly shamelessly. They'd arranged to meet the following day – and did, sort of.

"Stuart has always been quiet. I knew that from years back. It's just that he snaps at me whenever I try and talk to him these days. Honestly, I can't open my mouth without him wanting to jump down my throat."

"Have you spoken to Annabel about this, or maybe even Frank?" He sips calmly at his latte (definitely not Chai) as her tea goes cold.

"Annabel still has him up on a pedestal, doesn't she? As for Frank, who talks to Frank these days?"

It's hard to argue with that, he has to admit to himself. The man had quickly made his mind up about Steve's masculinity when he'd first moved to the village. Nothing and nobody is going to change his mind about that now, but he'd have expected better from people of his own generation.

***

Daniel glances across at Harcourt who is driving them to Castle Upton. It is a fresh, sunny morning but the car seems too warm - stifling even. He has asked the DI if he could turn the heating down a notch and he has willingly responded, but the air remains heavy.

They pass a road sign indicating a 'public weighbridge' ahead.

"You'd think Weight Watchers clients would want to be more discrete, wouldn't you?"

Harcourt laughs out loud. It breaks the tension between them, or maybe the detective is just very focused on his job. Daniel does though perceive a damaged aura around the man - a sadness that belies the no-nonsense persona he has tried to project so far.

The long, straight stretch of road they are motoring along (Roman, according to his driver) inevitably ends with a bend to the right ahead. Daniel sees the funeral cortege as it slowly processes around the bend, two formidably dark hearses despatched by Hades. He also glimpses the small, pink coffin before the glassed vehicle offering no light turns towards them.

"Even worse when a child is involved," he murmurs.

"I'm sorry." Harcourt swings around even as he pulls out to overtake a slow-moving tractor, seemingly oblivious to the doom approaching.

"Look out!" Daniel grips the front panel of the car, sitting upright and bracing his legs for the inevitable collision. There surely won't be enough space or time to complete the manoeuvre.

"What? What is it?" Harcourt swerves left, cutting the tractor driver up and incurring the wrath of his horn. Who knew that tractors had horns?

"I don't know how you managed to miss it."

"Miss what? Nothing was approaching us."

Daniel watches in the side mirror as the last car passes them in slow motion, and knows that something was. He lets out a deep breath and re-arranges his seating position, turning sideways towards Harcourt who is staring at him intently, alarmed for a quite different reason.

Knowing that he needs to return them to some kind of equilibrium, Daniel enquires: "Are you from Worcester - originally I mean?" (Well, it beats asking about the weather!)

"No. I don't think we'll ever be classed as natives." Harcourt has relaxed a little, glad not to have to discuss the near-death experience of his passenger. He even manages a smile, probably recognising the familiar foothills of an interrogation when there exists a mountain to find out about. "We're from Cambridgeshire. My wife was born in Cambridge itself and I'm from Chatteris - about 12 miles to the west of Ely."

"With the... octagon tower?"

"The Lantern Tower, yes. You're very well informed!"

"My father loved cathedrals, although he found their present custodians rather shallow."

"Your father could see through things too!"

"Ha. Ha. Not exactly. Most people thought him quiet and a bit dull I suppose. He didn't miss much though."

"Best way. Did you visit Ely then?"

"I was only small, but I remember him marvelling at the way the lantern seemed to float overhead."

"The original Norman construction had collapsed at that central point of the building - something to do with new foundations, I think. Like everywhere else in The Fens, the ground is soft so they removed the original stone pillars and used the narrowest struts that they could get away with - that's what makes it appear the way it does. I wish I could say it was designed with effect in mind, but much more due to cause I'm afraid."

"Everything about it just seemed huge to me, but, as I said, I was only five or six at the time which probably accounts for it."

Harcourt laughs again; an easy, relaxed laugh which fills the car before a sudden,
shocked silence pushes it out of the windows. He brakes suddenly, bringing the car to a shuddering halt.

"I didn't expect this!" Daniel gasps, pushing himself slightly forward to ease the restraining seatbelt which has pinned him to the passenger seat.

Both men watch intently as a deer with red-brown fur stands in the middle of the road, watching, waiting quite calmly for their next move. Its three-pointed antlers quiver slightly as it turns to face the hedge from which it seemed to explode just a few seconds earlier. A smaller, younger version then appears, tentatively at first, before gaining confidence to cross the road quickly behind the other. Once safely across, the first deer joins it and they see two heads bobbing up and down as they race across the open field to their right.

"What was that all about?" Harcourt is still slightly unnerved.

"A father putting himself on the line for his son I guess," Daniel reassures him, "I imagine he would do anything to protect him."

Harcourt moves the car forward once more, also tentatively. Daniel moves to change the subject and lead them both to safer ground.

"When did you transfer to Worcester?"

"About three years ago." The reply is abrupt; the smile has gone completely now.

Daniel witnesses a tightening of the facial muscles - feels an instant darkening of his mood. He wants to keep the conversation flowing. If he's to work successfully with this policeman, there is no room for silence between them. There were no quiet times with DI Cummings either - his voice seemed to fill every void.

"How do you find Worcestershire?"

"Hilly!"

The eyes are smiling again. The moment of jeopardy has passed.

"And you? Have you always called this area home?"

Home. A word that means so much more than a place. Daniel considers the quiet stillness that has befallen most of the previous few days. He is relieved that Charlotte's anger itself seems to have hit some kind of relief. At the same time, he knows from unhappy recent experiences that this can change in an instant. He also pretends that they are trying very hard to give Claire some quiet in which to do her revision for the few exams that remain. But is it home? Will it ever be home again?

He needs to reply. "I was born on the other side of Worcester, then went abroad to study."

"Indeed. The Grand Tour no less!"

"Wales!" They both laugh out loud again. "Aberystwyth - to study English!"

"Any particular reason why you chose to go there; apart from it not being too far away of course?"

"I think our careers advice in the sixth form ran to all of ten minutes. They'd gathered three or four university prospectuses and I liked the cover of the Aber one."

"And you enjoyed your time there - I know you'll have spent all your time studying, mind!"

The detective's eyes are properly shining now but not in reflection. Daniel senses that Harcourt has never enjoyed the college experience.

"I did - have a good experience - and then came back here to join the local rag; stayed there until they felt they had an abundance of riches and 'let me go.'

Harcourt nods sagely as he takes the turn for Castle Upton. "And your wife: is she local too?"

"From London originally. South. Very definitely not 'Sarf London' though. She then worked in Birmingham for many years before she retired. I met her at a friend's thirtieth birthday party in Droitwich."

"That place always conjures up a vision for me - no pun intended - of my old Dad listening to a huge, black wireless set we kept on a shelf in the kitchen. The dial was always set to Droitwich (or Radio 2 as it's become). I think the radio masts there are all used for long-wave these days."

"The devil horns of Wychbold!"

"I'm sorry?" Harcourt subconsciously brakes again as he tries to process Daniel's latest broadcast.

"The red lights on the masts - to warn aircraft of their existence - that's what some people call them. They glow in the dark you see."

Seeing the wary look in the detective's eyes, Daniel quickly continues with his story. "Nice memories, aren't they? Anyway, Charlotte had helped this friend out with an unfair dismissal claim. Seems to be the backdrop to our life together. Her brother - Charlotte's I mean - lives in the village where I was born. My parents (both dead now) invited him to join us one Christmas when Charlotte and I were first going out. Fergus fell in love with it and moved over there as soon as he could. He's a vicar."

"And your father was OK with that?"

"Although my father's disappointment with the clergy was deep-seated, he always tried to give people a chance - to prove him wrong if you like?"

"And did he? Did your brother-in-law prove him wrong?"

"I doubt it!"

The conversation ends with Harcourt yanking up the handbrake and switching off the engine. Moments later they are standing outside the front door of Duncan Harewood's modest home.

Duncan leads them around to the same old pew that Harcourt has so recently sat on. Remembering the precarious nature of it, he remains standing as Daniel seats himself at one end while Duncan joins him, a little further along.

He has explained - in very broad terms - who Daniel is and why he is helping them with their enquiries into both Andrew Patch's death and Julie Beech's disappearance.

"As I said, this won't take very long, Duncan. I did have one further question for you though."

Both men watch as the big man raises his head, as if after silent prayer, and looks up at Harcourt, expectantly.

"Witnesses have told us that when you left the pub on the night of Andrew Patch's unfortunate demise, you did so without your walking stick - the one with the curved handle?"

Duncan continues to stare at Harcourt who, like Daniel, can see that he is searching for an answer to the question, either the correct one or an alternative.

"Why would you need witnesses? Do you think a crime has been committed then: in both cases or just Andrew's?"

The man's articulate response throws Harcourt a little. It seems more than a little incongruous out here in the woods, coming from a man who is as wonderfully unkempt as he is strange. Daniel smiles inwardly. The man next to him has nothing to hide; he is sure of it. Quite unlike Harcourt.

"Could you just answer the question please, Duncan?"

"It wasn't where I left it."

Harcourt is relieved that he isn't denying it. His speech speeds up slightly as self-confidence and excitement merge to dispel the discomfort he feels at being in Duncan's presence. "By the door - the back door - of The Beaver?"

"That's right. When I came to leave it wasn't there."

"Did you look for it?"

"Why would I do that? I could see with my own eyes that it wasn't in the little pot. I always leave it there; no point in looking elsewhere."

"Did you ask anyone about it?"

"There weren't many people left by then; besides, what could they have told me? If I didn't notice somebody else taking it, why would they?"

Daniel smiles again at the man's perfectly understandable logic.

Harcourt isn't smiling. Rather like a few minutes ago in the car, a switch seems to have been flicked. "And yet you told us that you went for a walk in the woods that night, rather than coming straight back here? I find that hard to believe, Duncan!"

"Why would you find it hard to believe? Nothing's changed, I just didn't have my stick, that's all. I use it more as a kind of crutch, to be honest."

"A crutch not a crook?"

"A what? Not everything's about cops and robbers you know."

"No. I mean a shepherd's crook! You didn't use it to hook Andrew Patch from behind, causing him to fall backwards, hit his head and never regain consciousness?"

"No. No." He gets up quickly, practically squaring up to Harcourt - not angry exactly but certainly unwilling to accept his latest theory. "I told you. I went the long way home. I never saw Andrew Patch again after I left the pub that night. I don't need my stick for walking, I just like to have it with me."

"And you didn't think it worth mentioning to myself or my fellow officers?"

"Well, I didn't mention it to anyone at the time so why would I think to do so later?"

"You have a bit of a stoop, Duncan - may I call you Duncan?" Daniel, still sitting, considers it a good point to intervene and allow Harcourt to pause for thought.

"Of course. That's my name." Duncan sits back down beside Daniel, who notices the slight tremble in his fingers as he puts his hands to the side of him for balance.

"How did that happen: the stoop?"

"It's not old age if that's what you're thinking?"

"I wasn't! You're only a few years younger than me I should think, and I don't have a stoop either."

Duncan looks across at him to see if he is playing with him or not. Satisfied that he is being earnest he explains. "There's a quarry just over that hill there. When I was little, I used to love climbing up the sides, though my mother always warned against it - said it wasn't safe. She was right of course. She was right about most things. I slipped one evening and a couple of biggish stones were disturbed by my sliding down. Fell on top of me, both of them."

"That must have been painful!"

"Not as painful as the lesson itself. My mother never did stop the teaching of it."

"Have you replaced the walking stick, Duncan?"

"Of course; whittled and turned it myself. It's on the end there."

With a nod, he indicates to the end of the pew, just beyond Daniel who, in turn, looks to his left and sees the newly varnished stick hanging there. He puts his hand out to pick it up but catches the wooden armrest first and feels an immediate shock up his arm to the top of his shoulder - as though he has touched an exposed live electrical wire, and almost certainly where its predecessor had resided.

He closes his eyes as usual and sees Duncan's stick being thrown through trees - giant, skeletal fingers try to catch it, but none of them does. He concentrates, really concentrates, even as he hears voices shouting - urgent voices.

He cannot see who has thrown the stick, even though he tries and tries again. Tries so hard. It must certainly have been a strong throw as the stick arced up into the night sky - caught momentarily in the moon's searchlight - before plummeting back to the earth. He does though feel spots of water from a small stream as the handle end bounces on its rocky bed and out of it again, finally coming to rest, half-hidden in the undergrowth of leaves left for dead by the previous autumn.

"Daniel! Are you alright?"

He opens his eyes (or is it the other way round?) to find Harcourt crouching in front of him, alarm describing each fold of the skin on his white face. Duncan remains sitting next to him, quite unmoved - physically or mentally it would seem.

"I'm fine. really. Thank you. I'm fine." He turns slowly to Duncan. "I've found your old stick. I'm not sure if you'll still have a use for it, but I'm sure DI Harcourt will."

***

Daniel knows that the house will be empty, even before he puts his key in the lock. He was already aware that Claire would be out, spending the night with her friend Joanne as a treat for finishing her final exam that afternoon. He's received a text from her to say all went well and has responded to say he hopes that the evening does too! What he hasn't anticipated is Charlotte's absence. He knows she is not just out for a walk: she is much further away than that.

Her black and white travel case is missing from the bottom of the wardrobe in her bedroom and a few toiletries must have accompanied it on its journey. Otherwise, apart from the room being unnaturally tidy, there are no other signs - no messages for him. If there are any unseen clues, he is as frustrated as ever that he cannot read them, given that he sometimes manages to decode others' mysteries.

He defrosts a 'Paella made with natural ingredients fresh from the Atlantic Ocean' wondering idly when seaweed became a constituent part of frozen 'meals for one' before sitting at the kitchen table which suddenly seems absurdly large. The food is hot and tasteless but at least satisfies his immediate need and places a lining on his stomach. He sits back and pours himself a glass of the silky Merlot he has become quite fond of (or at least that's what Charlotte told him quite nastily the previous day; probably only because she prefers white wine). He wonders where she is. Who she is with?

Moving into the lounge he sinks into the settee whose old springs always make him think of the wear and tear they have had to endure together. He considers the trip to Duncan Harewood that afternoon. How do people like that survive? Not just the hardship of the climate - especially during the wet or freezing winter months - but the isolation. He needs to be quiet a lot of the time - most certainly when he is working and paying attention to detail (something he has to admit he rarely does when Charlotte is talking to him) - but at least he has people around him or the radio or the television to turn on.

On the one hand, he admires Duncan's ability to find all the company he needs in the simple nature surrounding him, but, on the other, he knows that all humans are social beings at heart, albeit on an accepted scale or spectrum. They require contrasts and comparisons every bit as much as a school essay; conflicts and harmonies that require courage to overcome or accept. Even Ben Gunn needed cheese which no desert island could supply.

He had his dream about the apples in the orchard again last night - just out of reach, no matter how high the lady managed to raise her pale, white arm. On his way 'home' he had wondered whether there might be some connection with Duncan's stick - being thrown through trees that could easily have been fruit trees - but there seems to be no correlation between the two. None that he can see anyway. From his extra sensory experience (unlike detective work based on actual evidence), this is unlikely to change. The scenes he sees can certainly become more detailed as he focuses more intently on them, but if they take place on different pages, albeit of the same book, they will usually remain so.

He has to admit that DI Harcourt is a far cry from Cummings. Though callow youth may well have rendered him far too sensitive and thus infinitely more susceptible to the previous detective's loud and laddish jibes and unkind comments in front of his fellow officers, Daniel feels a connection with Harcourt. He doesn't yet know what it is, but he does know that this policeman hides behind rules and regulations to protect himself every bit as much as the public he serves.

A ping from the kitchen disturbs his thought process. It could be that he didn't press the switch on the microwave fully or, much more likely, it is the announcement of a text - a toned-down version of the trumpet fanfare that might have heralded the arrival of news in days gone by.

The message fills the screen of his phone, though it contains just 25 words (shortened or otherwise): "I'm going away for a few days. When I get back, we need to talk. There's something important I need to tell you."

A fine sheen of sweat has formed on his forehead, and probably not caused by fruits of the ocean. His fingers are also shaking slightly as he hits the standby button, obliterating the message - killing the 'messenger'. This isn't merely a text, it is proof that there is indeed a subtext.

Daniel's troubled mind shifts to the minimalist Ernest Hemingway who relied on subtext, naming it the 'Iceberg Theory.' He felt that deep meanings suggested by characters or implied by plot turns should reside below the surface in the same way that the majority of an iceberg is floating beneath the water's surface. Hemingway was famous for his blunt, straightforward prose which Daniel would have little problem with as a proofreader. As a mind reader, he can't help feeling that somewhere a bell is tolling: a mournful portend of doom.

***

"Well, keep looking. It must be there somewhere. I just know that's all! If you need to move further away from the footpath then do so and, when you do find it, treat it with the utmost care until forensics get there."

Taylor watches through the office glass as Harcourt ends the call and throws his mobile phone down on a desk increasingly covered by the inexorable march of paper folders. She pops her head around the open door.

"Don't forget that the dead boy's parents are coming in later this morning, sir, to make a statement."

"I won't. I was going to say that life goes on, but it doesn't does it? Death is the real constant. Here we are with yet another unexplained death - a teenage boy drowns in a lake after 'getting into difficulties.' How could that happen when he was surrounded by his friends? This is going to have to take priority now and the powers that be are going to want to see some movement on it very soon.

Flowers is down there again this morning but we're struggling with it already and going to have to close the file on the Andrew Patch death in the meantime - and the Julie Beech disappearance - neither of which we managed to successfully explain. I know the files will remain officially 'open' but that's just a word, isn't it? 'Failed' would be a more appropriate one. The Super has finally authorised the new DS to join us, but, honestly, what's the point if we can't explain what's right in front of us now?"

"I'm sure the search team will come good on the missing stick, sir. It was late when they started last night. With daylight, it will be so much easier for them."

Harcourt is sitting back in his chair with his hands clasped behind his head. He shakes his head slowly while beckoning her to sit down on the hard chair opposite. "It isn't that. Well, not only that. We're just so desperate to find it - anything - that will help us to move on with this case that I wonder if we are losing our way at the same time."

"Sir?"

"Just think about what I said on the phone just then: 'It must be there somewhere.' How do I know that - really 'know' that? Daniel Reed claimed to have seen a stick being thrown up in the air through some trees. What if he didn't? He knows about Andrew Patch's body being found on the footpath leading through the woods and he saw Duncan's new stick. What if this is nothing more than the 'confirmation bias' I was so afraid of at the beginning?

Cummings talked a lot about this in his notes, though I suspect scepticism and doubt were passed down and shared around by pretty much every officer in the station at that time. What if Mr Reed is making his 'sightings' fit with what he and we already know? I could be wasting valuable police resources on a completely hopeless wild goose chase and yet I am effectively telling them with a fair degree of certainty that I am already trusting a man with 'psychic powers' more than my intuition, and certainly following no evidence trail whatsoever!"

"It's what we have to do, though, isn't it sir?"

"I'm sorry?"

"Well. We have to be allowed to think outside of the box in just the same way as we carefully place evidence into it which will lead to answers and ultimately a successful conviction, don't we?" (She's surprised herself by that one!). "Police procedures and the usual 'linear' approaches are very successful in most of our cases but, when they don't work, we have to try something different. Surely the end does justify the means."

"I'm sure Karl Marx meant well but he still ended up in Highgate Cemetery surrounded by large houses owned by the rich."

Taylor knows that behind his flippancy her point has been well made and that he has appreciated it as such.

"Perhaps DI Cummings was looking for a scapegoat - for his failure to solve the disappearance of Julie Beech, I mean. Daniel Reed - especially the younger version of himself as he was then - would have been an easy target if they'd asked him to help them again, wouldn't he, sir?"

"No policemen like to accept defeat. Sometimes that stubbornness, or 'determination' if you read the manuals, can eat away at you for the rest of your life. I don't intend that to be the case here and so, yes, I'm prepared to consider other 'skill sets.' The problem I have is that once you step away from a known way of doing things you've trusted for all your professional life (even if it's for all the right reasons, as you say) it feels very unnerving. It's as though all boundaries have been crossed - like taking a detour from the road you've always driven down, only to go off-roading without brakes.

I know that this is why so many people find ventures into the 'unexplained' so difficult, disturbing even, and why the likes of Cummings seek to disparage those with special gifts as loudly and convincingly as they can. I'm not one of those people but I admit to finding it hard. I wasn't expecting to go with it at the speed I have or accept the leaps of faith so readily. That in itself is unsettling: we're normally following the science, but now we've very quickly turned to 'second sight' or the 'third eye' instead. It doesn't add up does it?"

"Only because the fear of the unknown can't be quantified. We're all with you on that one, sir. I'm equally certain though that anyone who cared for Andrew Patch would thank you for putting yourself out there, not to mention Grace Beech."

"I guess we'll find out this afternoon when I accompany Mr Reed to the aforementioned Miss Beech."

CHAPTER ELEVEN

Ian Flowers glances up at the window, behind which he knows that Rob is now sleeping. He beeps the lock on his red Astra and climbs in, slowly. There has been a ground frost and he waits while the windscreen clears, quickly deciding that he doesn't need to get out again to scrape the thin layer of ice off his side windows.

Rob had just wanted to talk last night; not about anything in particular, though they'd discussed their respective days over a nice dinner of meatballs and rice. He'd been keen to talk about their plans and they'd talked late into the night, or at least that's what Flowers's red-rimmed eyes are telling him each time he looks in the rear-view mirror to see if the back window is clear yet.

He'd read some of Rob's favourite Wordsworth poems, always with the same effect of inspiring him to want to write poetry of his own, but driven to familiar inaction with the acute self-awareness that he could never hope to raise mere words to such heights - so why bother writing at all?

He must admit that he likes the certainty and the security of police language - all the key expressions they have to use when dealing with the public, and key phrases when dealing with their superiors. But none of it is him; not really. It is a job he enjoys, and he certainly wants to make the world a better, safer place for both Rob and his mum. But he also longs to express himself differently, freely and fully.

He has only met Daniel Reed - the 'special one' - once but it isn't his 'gift' that Ian Flowers takes issue with. While Harcourt happily polices the rules of grammar, Reed, as a proofreader in his day job, preserves them. How many authors have sought to express themselves with purity, only to have people like him vandalise their beautiful prose? It isn't preservation, it's prohibition.

He blinks back tears of frustration while reassuring himself that his eyes are simply watering because of the cold start. They'd talked about holidays, each picturing themselves lying on a warm, empty beach; Rob listening to an audiobook on his headphones while Ian writes hungrily beside him. Despite the unconditional love between them, he knows though that this will never happen - neither the creative expression nor the sand between their toes.

Rob understands all of this. He always has done, living in the moment as he is forced to do. Perhaps it is because he is such a pure water soul himself? What place could he possibly have in a world where men might commit suicide in lakes?

***

Grace Beech greets them as though they are Jehovah's Witnesses. She leads them silently into her small but tidy front room, overlooking the road out of Castle Upton. A red van is speeding up through the village, having made its delivery to one or other of the independent shops. Not the Royal Mail then. The window frames rattle but their host, smoothing her dark grey dress beneath her, seems oblivious to it and them. Presumably, no amount of double-glazing would keep out the sounds from her past anyway, Daniel muses.

He is sitting on a small stool opposite Harcourt who has plumped for the armchair adjacent to Grace. Harcourt is explaining their presence and introduces Daniel as a 'missing person expert.' He could have told her that Daniel was the long-lost brother of Sherlock Holmes for all the acknowledgement she affords him. Grace Beech seems to be barely present, yet Daniel senses that she is: tuned in and listening very carefully.

"What makes you believe that you can find my sister after all these years, Mr Reed?" She turns her eyes towards him. Staring and unblinking he sees the inevitable doubt but also something else. Fear maybe? Perhaps she is afraid of him raising her hopes after so long; far more comfortable in accepting absence rather than presence.

"I always believe in hope, no matter how hopeless things may appear to be."

"Hope" She scoffs noisily. "What can you possibly know about hope and the tricks it plays? You sit there talking to me about hope after more than forty years. You might well be some kind of 'expert' but, believe me, I've become a specialist in denial."

"I'm sorry, I..." Daniel begins, but Harcourt holds his hand up slightly, allowing Grace to continue.

"Have you the slightest idea of how all of this shaped my life? We're not just talking about Julie's hopes or my hope of one day hearing her telling me what they are again. What about my hopes? For myself?"

Daniel can see that Harcourt, listening benignly and calmly, expects a dam to burst at any moment, one that was presumably constructed a very long time ago. He looks around the room for any family photographs but finds none. Perhaps that is part of the dam?

"I've no idea what my life would have been like - whether I'd have achieved anything of any significance - but it would have certainly been different from the one I was forced to lead. You have no idea how such a traumatic event can scar a child. They certainly didn't in those days, and I doubt very much whether their fancy therapies with fancy names would uncover all the details now. All the details!"

She metaphorically hurls her last comment in Daniel's direction. In return, he now sees only anger. Fear and worry have long since left town. He says nothing, taking Harcourt's lead. He doesn't need to as she has barely drawn breath.

"My parents never came to terms with it, of course, but they died relatively early. I'm still here. In the village which I've never left. Unlike her."

"You always believed she'd left - or was taken?" Daniel allows himself a small halt to the flow.

"They searched the whole area repeatedly. What credible conclusion could there otherwise have been? If the police hadn't found something, no doubt the papers would have done. Reporters were camped out here for weeks, with their endless coffees and tabs at the pub."

Daniel isn't sure whether Harcourt is aware of it, but he senses a subtle difference in her attitude towards them. It had begun with scorn and doubt, moving surprisingly quickly onto a wave of obviously deep-set anger and resentment. Instead of receiving any form of early catharsis from finally expressing her feelings, she has surprisingly become wary - even a little defensive. As if to prove his point, she suddenly leaps up and leaves the room with only a cursory "Please excuse me for a moment."

Daniel scans the room once more for anything that might explain not just events in the past but seemingly the present too. If there is any connection here with the Andrew Patch case - a link which he knows Harcourt is increasingly desperate to make - the room is relatively bare and uncompromising; defiant.

A car horn suddenly sounds from outside, making him jump. Another horn responds with several beeps. Road rage is not confined to towns and motorways it seems. As he imagines angry drivers exchanging raised fingers or whole fists, he spies an old rag doll on the window seat just behind him. Tatty and a little grubby it has a strange, crooked smile that wouldn't be out of place in a witch's coven.

He reaches out for it and picks it up gently, its head flopping forward as he does so. He closes his eyes and allows himself to leave the room. He is close to Duncan Harewood's shed, but Duncan is not there. Unlike the other day, the shock is much less acute - a trickle rather than a surge - but it is still there: old yet familiar.

He opens his eyes again and regardless of the late afternoon sunshine flooding into the stark little room, shivers involuntarily. Grace has returned and both are gazing at him as he places the doll back in its place, almost reverentially, by the window, though its eyes have long since lost the power of sight.

"This was Julie's, wasn't it?"

Now there is a resignation about her. Perhaps there always has been in the face of her sister's fate. Grace Beech slowly nods.

***

About twenty minutes later Daniel and Harcourt are sitting in the corner of the 'Cotswold Kettle' having walked the short distance from Grace Beech's cottage. They are the only ones in there apart from a young woman with two much younger girls. One of them is possibly a friend of her daughter, all of them out for a teatime treat - especially the mother who looks tired and drawn.

Steven Pateman sidles over to them. He is less than pleased to see Harcourt again and asks them rather officiously for their order.

"Just tea for two please." Harcourt smiles but it is not reciprocated.

"How nice! Just to remind you that we'll be closing soon." Pateman's gruff delivery is in direct contrast to his smiling encouragement of the young family who he visits on his way back to the counter. The little girls have requested further scones. Perhaps his official opening and closing hours do not apply to them.

"I'm probably the last person he'd hoped to see today - and nothing to do with the timing," Harcourt speaks in a low voice to Daniel who has taken the cafe owner's rudeness in his seemingly implacable stride as usual. "No doubt he and all the others hoped this enquiry would go away, much like Andrew Patch."

"I guess it's just money for them, isn't it?" Daniel moves forward so that he can hear the other man more easily. "He's no doubt charged for each of those little notes and cards to be pinned to the cork board over there, despite it being labelled the 'Community Hub.'"

"No doubt about it!" Harcourt grimaces. "On the subject of doubt, you're sure about this? Your face was ashen when we left."

"I am. I saw a place with a lot of stones and maybe gravel - close to Harewood's place."

"Could it have been a quarry?"

"It could. Easily, except that it was completely overgrown. I don't think it had been used for some time."

"And it wasn't Harewood that was there?"

"No. It wasn't him, but there was somebody else there, just out of camera shot if you like. Not a nice presence. Not evil exactly but certainly not passive and friendly."

"Tell me again what you saw, if that's OK?"

"Of course." Daniel now lowers his voice to a pitch he is sure only Harcourt can hear, breaking off momentarily as Pateman places a tray of assorted white cups and saucers in front of them, so heavily that tea spills out of both spouts of the matching teapots simultaneously. He leaves them to sort out the mess.

"I saw Grace and Julie Beech as children, arguing. Grace was trying to pull a doll - the one in Grace's cottage - out of her sister's hands. Julie was clinging to it and started screaming. For some reason, Grace suddenly let go and Julie fell backwards, hitting her head on some kind of boulder. I saw blood but it wasn't necessary to confirm that the blow to her head killed her outright."

"And after that?"

"Very little I'm afraid. Grace is just standing there as a little boy runs to join her. Then everything fades out - like the dissolve at the end of a key scene in a film. Maybe the defining one."

***

Claire is standing in the kitchen as he walks in, finishing a glass of orange juice. She is in a smart new beige jumper and jeans, clearly on her way out. He is strangely relieved to see that though her hair is newly washed and shining, she is not wearing make-up. It shouldn't matter, of course, and doesn't really. Nevertheless, he does take comfort from this small indication that the little girl she once was hasn't completely disappeared. Perhaps the events of the afternoon had sharpened his senses even further.

"You look tired, Dad." She is pleased to see him (as she usually is) and comes over to give him a generous hug. "I hope the police aren't working you too hard. Mum was a bit worried that they might."

"It's fine. I'll make sure they don't charge me overtime!"

They both laugh out loud. It is so nice to be home. 'Home.' Passing through Upton Snodsbury earlier, he noted at least two 'For Sale' signs - from a local agent called Cornell's. Is this what lies ahead of him? Selling their house and then a small, poky flat?

"Have you heard from your mother at all?"

"Only a text last night to ask if we were both alright. She thought she would be back by tomorrow."

"That's good," he replies, even though he's already thinking that her return might not be. "We've managed OK though haven't we?"

"Of course, we have. I had my tea earlier as I'm off to the pictures in Evesham with Joanne."

"Would you like a lift?"

"It's fine, thanks. We're going to get the bus down and Joanne's Mum is picking us up afterwards. I didn't know what you'd want or what time you expected to be back, but I checked and there's plenty in the freezer."

"Then that shall be my very next port of call," he announces with a flourish and a bow.

"Bye Dad," she grins while unsuccessfully trying to roll her eyes at the same time.

He watches as she passes the kitchen window and almost skips down the road until she is out of sight. He thinks of Grace Beech and her sister, Julie: out of sight but never out of mind.

He picks up his phone to check on any emails that may have come through. He is expecting an acknowledgement of the latest piece he sent back to the publisher that morning. Nothing yet, but there is a text. He must have missed its announcement thanks to the radio filling the unwanted silence in his car on the journey back from Worcester.

It is from Kate Shelbourne and simply reads: 'Can you ring me when you get this, please? XX Kate'

His eyes linger on the two kisses - substitutes for words that convey so much - rather than the words themselves, then pulls himself together and dials her number.

She answers after just two rings. "Kate Shelbourne. How can I help?"

"No. How can I help you?" It's good to hear her voice again but he quickly perceives that she hasn't recognised his. "It's Daniel - you sent me a text."

"Hi, Daniel." If she is at all embarrassed, she doesn't show it, or perhaps her professional training kicks in as a default. "Thanks very much for phoning me back so quickly."

"No problem at all."

"It's just that I wanted to give you a heads-up. We've had a tip-off from a source who's usually pretty reliable that the police have called in a psychic to help them with the Andrew Patch case - and probably Julie Beech's disappearance too."

He hesitates before replying. This isn't what he was expecting, although he isn't entirely sure of what it was he was hoping she would say either.

Kate takes his silence as an affirmation and continues quickly. "I know of only one other such person, but they live in Carlisle now, so I thought it unlikely they'd bring someone down from Cumbria, especially with the cost of travel and overnights etc..."

"Kate. Let me stop you there." He speaks gently but firmly. "Your source is correct and so are you. I am helping West Mercia on both cases, though we're still not sure if they are linked or not. I can't give you any details - even off the record - but I can tell you that we (they) seem to be getting somewhere now, although we're still a long way off."

"They approached you I assume?"

"They did."

"And after your previous experience, you're OK with that?"

"I think so. It feels different this time or maybe it's just that I am a lot older!"

"You're only as old as the woman you feel - or so one

of my colleagues told me after much too long a lunch last week."

"Yes. Well, I'm not feeling it at all, as my daughter might phrase it."

"Charlotte still acting strangely?"

"More so than ever I'm afraid, but you didn't get in touch to hear all about that."

"Actually, if you wanted to meet up and talk about it, I'd be happy to get a Chinese in."

Daniel sits upright, leaving the support of the comfy chair behind. Charlotte has made it quite clear where her feelings lie, or at least that they no longer lie with him. Why, then, does guilt throw its usual safety curtain across the stage? Hiding the players. Preventing any further action. Is this why he hesitates?

"That would be great, Kate" he is breathless, excited at what he has just said but then hears, "But it's been a long day and I'm not sure I'd be much company."

"Maybe a nice relaxing evening is what you need; what you deserve?" She purrs and he wants to lap it up, all of it. He can tell that she is as disappointed as he is. He can't do it. For whatever reason, he just can't do it.

"I'm sure you're right but maybe another time?"

"Maybe. You know how to get hold of me."

"I do." He does; would like to so much.

"I just thought you should know about the police thing."

"Thanks. I appreciate it and, Kate…"

"Yes." He can almost see her gripping the phone as indeed he is.

"I'd appreciate it even more if you could keep it out of print for now. I promise they will give you an exclusive if and when there's more to say."

"Do you always keep your promises though, Daniel?" She has relaxed, the warmth in her voice returning, playful.

"I do." Sadly, I do, he thinks as he hits the Red Cross on his screen. He doubts that even they could successfully come to his aid right now.

***

Flowers hands Harcourt a plastic cup of coffee and they both look at each other hopelessly.

"This environmental thing isn't working is it, sir?"

"You're not wrong. I worry that people of your age and below will make as little progress as we did, despite it becoming the flavour of every month on the news.'

"Any kind of flavour would be good! Poor farmers the world over are harvesting perfectly good coffee beans, and we have to settle for this. It's just not right."

Harcourt cannot retain his 'serious' face any longer and they both laugh out loud as they make their way slowly back along the corridor.

Taylor looks up from her desk as they enter the operations room and is pleased to see the smiles after so many weeks of frowning and scowling.

"Are you going to let me in on the joke?"

Flowers raises his cup, to which she shakes her head in resignation. "That's not even a little bit funny!"

A ping from Flowers's mobile alerts him to the job at hand.

"PC Pearson, sir. They've found what they think is Duncan Harewood's walking stick."

***

Daniel had started to work on his next proofreading project after finishing his call with Kate Shelbourne. He'd needed to focus on something away from real life. Thankfully, the new book is rather good. Written in a pleasingly pacy style, it is set on the Norfolk coast in the late 1960s and concerns a man looking back over his life and finally grasping the fact that there are far more unexplained gaps than he'd been aware of.

In the middle of the night, that thought had come back to him. Had there been periods in his own life where he had missed more than he'd thought? Yes, there were undoubtedly many late nights when he and the other subs had enjoyed a late-night drink once the presses were rolling. Yes, he had missed a lot of homework deadlines but thankfully they had been Claire's not his.

It wasn't that these thoughts had come back to 'haunt' him, though. It wasn't even the nagging concern about Charlotte: where she was sleeping, and who with. No, the image that stood before him was a change from the blood-red fruits of the apple trees that had tormented him for so long. It was of an elderly, scruffy man writing. Hunched over an A4 pad he was scribbling away furiously - probably without much in the way of punctuation - head down, concentrating.

***

"And there's no doubt?"

"There is always an element of doubt, Inspector, you know that perfectly well."

He can easily picture Jenny Graham, dressed in immaculate white, with no time or place for human error. He can barely hide his excitement but knows her to be the least excitable person he has ever met so opts to proceed with caution. "Alright. Let's just focus on probabilities then – percentages. I know you prefer those."

"I always play the percentage game, both inside and outside of work."

Harcourt has never been quite sure whether she is mocking or coming on to him in some weird way. She is an enigma for certain. "The DNA you were able to examine from the stick; let's start there."

"A very good place to start. At the foot of the stick (i.e. at the opposite end to the handle) we were able to isolate a small collection of hairs. They were most likely left due to the person holding the stick's hands being slightly sweaty as well as their holding or gripping the stick particularly tightly. Thankfully, some of the hairs still had their roots attached and from those, we were able to extract DNA."

"Excellent!" He is tempted to say 'good work' or some similarly inappropriate pat on the head comment. Thankfully, he doesn't get the chance as Jenny (Dr Graham of course) is moving meticulously down her list of related findings.

"We checked against those 'background samples' you sent us, taken from individuals known to be in the vicinity of The Beaver on the night of Andrew Patch's death. There is a distinct and significant match of the DNA found on the stick to the DNA of Frank Fairhurst. The probability of this sample not being from the same DNA source as Mr Fairhurst's sample, given to you voluntarily, is less than 0.1 per cent."

"Thank you so much, doctor. This really could be the breakthrough we've been looking for, though we still need to establish a motive for the attack on Andrew Patch."

"I don't mean to dampen the flames from the obvious furnace in your belly, Inspector, but, before your volcano well and truly erupts and spills over, we have only ascertained that one man's DNA has been found on another man' stick, albeit one discarded in the way it was - presumably to hide it or at least buy some time? You cannot place it definitively at the crime scene."

"Although we did find a DNA match between saliva found on Patch's body and that of Frank Fairhurst as well?"

"Indeed we did, as we did for his son and Lisa, his wife, as well as Mr Grady the barman. Droplets of saliva can be easily passed on through talking, sneezing and, in particular, from one person shouting at another, especially in a relatively confined area. I believe you mentioned that there had been just such an altercation on the evening in question."

"It was suggested, yes, but nobody can confirm whether or not that did happen or, if it did, who was shouting at whom."

Though somewhat deflated, his mind is spinning unscientifically in multiple directions, seemingly all at once. He sits down at his desk as though that will slow them down, allowing his thoughts to be directed. He hears a familiar voice and quickly comprehends that Dr Graham is continuing to speak through the device still clamped to his right ear.

"If it helps, such a stick could have been used to pull another person backwards - whether just as a cautionary action or a deliberate strike. Pulling someone in that way could easily have caused them to fall backwards, hitting their head on a stone. The muscle tears that we described and the lesions on his head could certainly fit such a scenario (not that I deal with scenarios). What is much harder to discern is whether the act was a deliberate act of aggression or an unfortunate accident."

"How could it not have been meant deliberately?" The fog in his head is still swirling around the scene on the footpath.

"You misunderstand me once again. I hope it isn't becoming a habit!"

"I'm sorry. Please do go on."

"When I say 'deliberate' I mean that the action of reaching out with a stick towards someone who is walking away from you and hooking them around the neck to stop them moving is, indeed, deliberate. The point I am so laboriously trying to make to you – and one a Court of Law would certainly need addressing – is that such an action might not necessarily have been made with malicious intent.

It could have been the action of one person reaching out to another to protect them from some danger that they knew lay ahead. An act of kindness. Alternatively, perhaps the person walking behind Andrew Patch merely wanted to stop him for a moment and listen to what he had to say, even as Patch was moving forward. It doesn't in itself prove that Patch was trying to get away from them, or that they were a pursuer as such, does it?"

"Or that Frank Fairhurst's intent quickly went beyond conversation? What if he did intend from the outset to cause him actual bodily harm?"

"Well then, that is the deliberation you will have to conduct. I am merely a scientist."

"I believe you to be much more than that."

"Greater than the sum of the parts you mean? Not mathematically possible I'm afraid."

"Possibilities. That's what my life is all about until they finally become extinguished."

"Or extinct? That volcano soon burned itself about!"

He smiles down the phone and hopes it reaches her. "Just gone back underground; it hasn't gone away."

"Are we still talking purely professionally?" Her voice remains as expressionless as ever.

"Everything above board and visible."

"As long as that's the case, I may be able to help you further, though I appreciate things could become even more confusing before they become clearer."

"You've found something else; or somebody else?"

"When I tested against those same background samples, obviously Stuart Fairhurst came up as a direct match to Frank; the Y Chromosome was almost exactly the same, so no mutation there. He is undoubtedly Frank's son. But Stuart's DNA, based on the required number of centimorgans of DNA, also had a 24.7% shared match with somebody else in the same pool."

"Stuart has a half-sibling?"

"Indeed, he does. There is 98.8% proof that Stuart and Duncan Harewood are half-brothers, who share the same father. Frank Fairhurst, without any reasonable scientific doubt, sired both of them."

***

Daniel clicks the button on his steering column, ending the telephone call, and silencing Harcourt. He muses on Frank Fairhurst who he hasn't yet met. The tractor pulling the yellow, industrial digger ahead of him shows no sign of pulling over and certainly not of speeding up. This gives him and everyone else in the mid-morning queue plenty of time to think while in low-level (certainly low-gear) processing.

Harcourt has told him about the payments being made to Lettie Harewood - Duncan's late mother - and so the first conclusion to jump to would be that Frank Fairhurst is merely supporting his son and lover, though that suggests a certain altruism at odds with the inspector's character assessment of him. The second leap would be that Lettie was blackmailing Frank. What could she have had over him? It doesn't seem like his marriage to Amanda Fairhurst is particularly harmonious so the threat of exposure seems unlikely. Or perhaps Lettie knew something that none of them has yet discovered.

Either way, the interview planned for this afternoon promises to be interesting. He gratefully pulls off of the Rous Lench road, happy to lose his place in the procession, and is soon walking back into the house.

As he opens the door, he sees Claire, in her faded, pink dressing gown running up the stairs. To see her running is one thing; to see her up and about at this hour of the day - and ascending rather than descending - is something else altogether.

"Are you OK?' He smiles as he asks, mindful of the irony of his slightly humorous concern.

She turns momentarily and he quickly sees that she has been crying. Her eyes are red and her cheeks mottled where she has been trying to rub them and the remaining 'sleepy dust' away. A long-ago scene assaults his senses. She is still tiny, and he is trying to reassure her that the prickling feeling around her eyes isn't really salt and pepper at all. She isn't smiling now though. Something has upset the lovely girl she has grown into.

"Claire. What is it?'

"Leave her. She just needs a bit of space."

Charlotte's voice from the kitchen is soft but firm.

He hadn't noticed her car in the drive but then, tuned in as he still was to the extended Fairhurst family, it was hardly surprising.

"Is it a boy?"

"Yes, I'm fine; thanks so much for asking. I've missed you too during the last three days!"

"You chose to go away, and you also chose not to tell me where or why."

"And Claire is more important to you. Yes, I know."

"That's not what I said, and it certainly isn't true. She is our daughter, though, and I can't bear it when she's either ill or upset - or both."

"And what if I was ill, or upset, or both?"

"Then I would find that equally hard to bear."

"This isn't a novel that you can correct, Daniel. You can't just change the names of the main characters; highlight grammatical errors or advise the author to change the ending to one which you like or think works better. This is real life. These are the facts."

He thinks about reminding her that fact-checking is also part of his profession. Facts are facts no matter in what context the reader encounters them. However, he is entirely unsure as to where all of this has come from or where it's going. Charlotte still seems angry, but her outburst is much more one of resignation than rage. She has a story to tell, and he prefers to wait for her to begin.

"I do have something to tell you - something original although it might well sound like an adaptation of a tale you've read or heard many times before."

"Where have you been Charlotte? Physically for the last three days and metaphorically for much of the last three years?"

"The first answer is straightforward enough; the second will take a little longer. I've been staying with Fergus since Monday."

"I'm surprised Lucy didn't lock you in the watchtower and throw away the key."

Charlotte smiles. It's nice to see - warms him at least - but it also shows how thin her face has become. He hadn't noticed the crisscross of worry lines bisecting her forehead either. Perhaps they weren't there before, or maybe he simply hasn't looked hard enough."

"Lucille was on her annoyingly best behaviour: insufferable politeness while wanting to be sure that I knew at all times the battering her pride had taken."

"She hasn't forgiven you then?"

"She has now. Now that she understands. Besides, I

took myself off to the Welsh hills each day - even drove up to the Black Mountains on Wednesday - so she didn't have much of an audience to perform to."

"I remember us heading up there via Abergavenny. Old Mrs Evans and her Guest House rules…"

"'… and do not forget: the door will be locked at 10.30 sharp!'"

They both laugh before Charlotte continues.

"I imagine she's long gone now."

"I should jolly well think so. She was about a hundred and twenty-five then!"

"Nice memories though. Where would we be without them?"

She has grown sad again and, somewhat horrified, Daniel can see that his lovely bride - the woman he married for life, regardless of whatever plot twist in their story together he knows to lie ahead - is on the verge of tears.

"I just needed time to think. To process things. Isn't that the vernacular these days? The truth is that I've been seeing a consultant."

"Seeing? In what way, seeing?" His own eyes are beginning to prick around the edges now.

"In a professional capacity." She plainly understands the context of his question. How her statement could have been so easily misconstrued? "He is an anger management specialist, based in Worcester."

"Oh. Whereabouts?"

"Just up past the station. A lovely old house that was his father's I believe. Old money."

Daniel beams. He can't help it; can't hide it. He is not just loose change after all.

"I don't know why you're smiling!"

"Just be happy that I am."

"I wish I could be. The trouble is that I think I'm about to tell you something that might well ruin your life, as it has done mine."

He leans forward to grasp her hand. It is usually warm to touch but now it is icy cold. Although he experiences no special feelings - no coldness around his heart for example - the hairs are standing up as they would on the back of any concerned life partner's head.

"Is it something that the consultant discovered?"

"No. No. He was first mentioned to me before I retired. Joe Bryan thought I needed an outlet for my anger (he reasoned that no reasonable person could be so angry for so long and that I needed an outlet. His was Birmingham City apparently...) I've been seeing the specialist for almost two years now, but it didn't work. He couldn't pinpoint any definitive cause of it either and so, naturally, couldn't prescribe any further course of action that might help."

"What did you do?" Daniel is still holding her hand, hanging onto her every word.

"I went back to the Royal in Worcester for more tests, including an MRI scan." She grips his hand hard at this point. "The fact is..."

He puts her arm around her and pulls her in close, breathing in the scent of her lovely hair and knowing that they will never be so far apart again.

"I'm not very well, Daniel. I have a disease and it's only going to get worse. They say there's no cure - well not yet anyway. A lot of research is going on so you never know: that's what they told me."

The last few words have poured out; the dam of silent contempt is finally broken it seems.

"What have they diagnosed? Is it... is it?"

"Not cancer, no. Thank God. But it is terminal all the same. I have a form of dementia called Pick's Disease. At least that explains why I've been such an awful bitch to you..."

"No. You could never be that - have not been that." He is overwhelmed now, initial joy turning so quickly to the cruel inevitability of fate.

"The good news is that I should become calmer - a bit nicer to live with again, though they don't know enough about the disease to give it a sensible timeframe. The first couple of years are by all accounts characterised by aggressive behaviour. They think I must be approaching the end of that phase at least."

"And the bad news?" He almost wants to close his ears, but it seems that he has been seeking answers for so long that he has to take his medicine now, if not 'like a man' then like the husband he always wanted to be.

"The bad news - the perfectly awful reality that they, unfortunately, can predict without any doubt at all - is that dementia will gradually follow like a fog slowly sweeping in off the sea on a clear day. Unlike with Alzheimer's, the loss of memory and the confusion doesn't happen straight away - it sets in after the rage (some medical experts think it is actually at the heart of the anger which is otherwise unexplained). You know how these people talk? All rhymes and riddles to decipher.

"How did Fergus react?" He grips her hand tightly.

"I couldn't find the words to tell him. Instead, I said that we'd had a falling out. I hope you'll understand… I'm afraid he blames you for everything."

"I thought he wanted God to be our judge?"

"Well, the jury's still out on that one."

"I'll be there with you. You won't be alone with this."

"Thank you. I know you will; always have done. There may be flashes of sudden, dramatic memory loss then there could be weeks, even months of 'normality', but probably not years. What it all means is that one day I won't be able to remember who you are, let alone how I failed in my marriage to you."

"You haven't failed me." An image of the man at the window in Britannia Square flashes in front of his eyes. "You have been a wonderful wife - kind and understanding - and the best mother to Claire you could possibly have been."

"It will be even harder for her in some ways, she's much too young to be a witness to such decline. Thank goodness her exams are over."

"Did you tell her everything?"

"Just that I had a disease and was so sorry to have to tell her that I wouldn't be getting better; that I was going to need you and her to be even stronger than ever because I'm not feeling very brave myself right now."

"We will! We'll be your strength. We will help you to see a way forward through all of this." He holds her face in his hands and stares again into the eyes through which he had once seen a beautiful life together. This is not the end of that story; he would hide all full stops if necessary so that they couldn't be used. "You're not to worry."

She smiles back, weakly but honestly. "But I do worry, Daniel. I've never been so frightened about anything in my life before."

CHAPTER TWELVE

"He came in of his own accord?"

"He did, sir. DS Flowers left a message on his mobile and he phoned us back about an hour later."

"So, the wife doesn't know he's here?"

"Not unless he told her so himself, sir. Out of respect for both her and her son, we are treading discreetly - especially as everything remains circumstantial - even at this late stage."

"He quoted some poetry at me the other day; did I tell you?"

"DS Flowers did?"

"Well, I'd hardly place Frank Fairhurst in the running for Poet Laureate! Flowers had visited Tintern Abbey, down on the Wye. A day trip apparently:

'... wreaths of smoke
Sent up, in silence, from among the trees!
With some uncertain notice, as might seem
Of vagrant dwellers in the houseless woods,
Or of some Hermit's cave, where by his fire
The Hermit sits alone.'"

"Very evocative, sir."

"Wordsworth's words, not mine. It was a gothic masterpiece in its time you know. It evidently meant more to Wordsworth than Henry VIII. Or maybe he was like a lover in later life: can see the woman for the beauty she once was, and even after she has been effectively ruined by some man."

Harcourt makes a mental note to have another word with Flowers. Lateral thinking is all very well, but daydreaming is decidedly suspect. He waits patiently for Hunter-Wright to get to the point, which, sensing no discussion of literature, architecture or history to be forthcoming, he duly does.

"You don't seriously think that Duncan Harewood was involved in either incident, do you?"

"I don't. Daniel Reed thinks – 'saw' - the two little girls playing alone, although he sensed that someone else was nearby. We have Fairhurst's DNA on the stick and proof that Duncan is his son, which might account for the payments to Lettie Harewood. Beyond that, we have no reason to suggest Duncan is (was) involved in any of this."

"And no doubt about Duncan's lineage?"

"None at all. Neither Frank nor Lettie had any brothers or sisters so no possibility of the DNA linkage being based on Stuart and Duncan being cousins; besides Dr Graham did not doubt that Frank was the father."

"Then Duncan could have been supported by fatherly money if not fatherly pride? Just a gentle soul living out a quiet life in the woods."

"Indeed, sir."

"Ripe for framing though."

"Sir?"

"When Julie Beech went missing. People in close-knit communities fear outsider involvement in almost anything - that's why they're usually so hostile to incomers. They'd have preferred that Julie's death was somehow caused by someone they knew; then they could have closed ranks - contained it - or simply expelled the perpetrator, like a child called 'out' in the playground. Who could be better than the misfit from the forest? The simpleton who is known to walk the woods at nighttime."

"I wouldn't describe Duncan Harewood as 'simple' sir. Far from it."

"Nor me. Smoke signals spelling loneliness, not guilt. You just have to separate them from the fire in ignorant villagers' collective bellies."

"Or at least douse the flames!"

"Perhaps poetry is the answer after all: a reminder that we are not all alone in the world."

A few minutes later, Harcourt and Taylor are sitting in front of Frank Fairhurst. Dressed in the same dirty anorak and freshly-stained jeans they had seen him wearing previously, he has decided not to dress for the occasion.

"Thank you for coming in Mr Fairhurst. We just wanted to ask you a few follow-up questions."

"Ask away." Intermittently shaven, the man's face has the red glow of one who spends most of his life outdoors or indoors worrying about high blood pressure. He folds his arms in a slightly defensive move, but his eyes are open to suggestion: worn out rather than wary.

"During our investigations, we discovered that you had been making monthly payments to Lettie Harewood for many years. Those payments have now ceased."

"She has ceased hasn't she?"

"What do you mean by that" Taylor leans forward slightly.

"Deceased - is that what you call it? Dead. I'm not going to carry on paying a dead woman, am I?"

"What were the payments for?" Harcourt senses his colleague's hackles rising.

"What's it to you? I'm not the one under investigation and you mustn't have got anything on me because you haven't even cautioned me."

"And, as I said, we're grateful for your co-operation. We are still looking into possible motives for the death of Andrew Patch and possible links back to the disappearance of Julie Beech."

"Which in plain words means you're no further forward with either!" He leans back, pleased with himself, smiling at DS Taylor who studiously ignores him.

"Was Lettie Harewood blackmailing you?"

"Over what?"

"Was she?"

"She wouldn't have had the nous."

Taylor drops her pen on the table between them, possibly by accident. "Is that why she was such easy prey for you."

There is a sharp intake of breath - from Harcourt rather than Fairhurst. The older man replies though. "Is that what you lot think? A quick shandy and a shag, is that it?"

Harcourt has recovered sufficiently to be pleased to see that Fairhurst has been well and truly riled. "Nothing of the kind, Mr Fairhurst."

"No. It wasn't. Lettie and I were very young and... inexperienced. We thought we were in love. When I married my wife three years later I realized that it had just been lust."

Tell me about your son's stick."

"Stuart doesn't use a stick - doesn't need one." There is a pleasing flash of confusion now in the otherwise rock-solid defence.

"Not that son," Harcourt continues evenly, "Your other son."

"Oh, so that's it. Been playing Cluedo again, have you?"

"We do know, beyond any reasonable doubt, that Duncan - the one who does need a stick - is your son."

"Why are you so obsessed with his stick?"

Later, Taylor will consider how strange that question was, in the context of his having been exposed as (or at least that the police now know him to be) the father of an illegitimate son. Instead of protesting his innocence or showing any signs of guilt about it, the man focuses, with laser-type accuracy, on a detail of their conversation which would otherwise have been incidental at best.

"Obsession is a strong word." She can see that he has been needled. "Would you describe yourself as obsessive, Mr Fairhurst?"

Fairhurst's face is redder than before. Before he can answer, Harcourt goes for it.

"We've found Duncan Harewood's stick, Mr Fairhurst."

The hard stare betrays no reaction.

"And your DNA is on it."

Now there is one of palpable relief. "Well, that's easily solved - I should be in your job. In answer to the earlier question, I am a little bit obsessive – I think they call it OCD or some such. Stuart did tell me once. Duncan always left his stick in the pot by the door of the pub. I have been known on several occasions to re-arrange it and various umbrellas so that they stand upright rather than leaning over."

"Aha. Interesting."

"Satisfied?" Now there is the hint of a grin.

"Not quite. You see your DNA was found, not on the handle, but at the base of the stick. As though you had been holding it upside down. Hardly fits with a profile suggesting OCD."

The grin has vanished.

Taylor cannot resist. "Perhaps you used it as a weapon before you threw it away."

"I don't know what you are talking about, or what substances you two have been taking."

"You hooked it round the neck of Andrew Patch, didn't you?" Harcourt can feel his heart pumping now. "Did you pull him backwards deliberately, causing him to fall and hit his head?"

"Got witnesses to this little fantasy, have you?"

"Why were you trying to stop him? What was it that you wanted him to keep quiet about?"

"So, the answer is no. You have no proof. No motive and nobody saw any of this."

"Were you protecting Duncan in some way or trying to throw the blame on him, like you did when Julie disappeared? Was that the action of a father who cared?" Taylor senses that this is getting away from them again. Duncan's stick might just as well have floated downstream and out to sea.

"Going to tell him, are you?" Fairhurst half stands and

points a finger at Harcourt. "Feeling nice and smug now, are you? Found a family tree but still can't see the woods for it!"

"We have no reason to share any of this with anyone, do we?"

"If you mean my wife, don't trouble yourselves. She's always known. Always understood my needs."

Taylor visibly shrinks backwards. "And the needs of your son?"

"I've never shirked my responsibilities. Don't you worry about that."

"We're very glad to hear it." Harcourt finds it difficult to disguise his obvious contempt.

"Are you though?" With that, Fairhurst stands and walks to the door. Before leaving, he turns to make a parting comment as an actor might do at the dramatic high (and end) point of a scene. He glares at Taylor. "You want to be careful. Not everyone around here is as tolerant as I am."

***

Daniel has shared Charlotte's bed again for the two previous nights, not wanting to let her out of his sight. They'd held each other close and on each of the following mornings, he'd woken to her tousled head nestled in the hollow of his arm. It felt good, natural. Nothing else was required nor words to be spoken. Last night, though, Charlotte had developed a nagging headache that saw her go to her bed earlier than either him or Claire.

The two of them had crept upstairs to look in on her just before midnight, ready to offer platitudes and paracetamol, but she was already asleep, lying on her back and snoring slightly.

They'd returned to the TV police drama, which had paused, holding its breath while they investigated, and decided at just after one-thirty that even they'd had enough streaming for one night.

Claire and he had not spoken at length about Charlotte's illness yet. His daughter had kept herself unusually busy and he knew that it was just her way of taking time to process things. When she was good and ready, they'd have a good talk about it all. For the moment she was as alone with her thoughts as he was with his.

Either due to the lateness of the hour or late-night caffeine or worry over Charlotte (or all three) he had fallen into a fitful sleep and woken up several times. Once, he had tiptoed across the corridor to check on his wife: she was on her side now, sleeping soundly. This had offered him little subconscious relief though. The apple trees he had been seeing previously were still laden with fruit that couldn't quite be reached but now a rope had been tied around the highest branch.

He thought at first it must have been a rope ladder, up which some enterprising fellow would soon climb determinedly, forcing the forbidden to submit. But it wasn't a ladder. The familiar noose dangled menacingly below in the breeze before concrete block walls grew up all around it, the sky disappeared, and somebody unknown switched the light out.

***

"The Superintendent agrees that we're unlikely to get any further with Frank. Yes, we have his DNA on the stick that was almost certainly used to stop Andrew Patch in his tracks - but accidental or deliberate we'll never know. The CPS would laugh in our faces and no jury is going to convict him, however badly he's likely to wind them up with that belligerent attitude of his.

Yes, we've been able to prove a biological link with Duncan Harewood, but we have no way of proving the reason for the financial one. It doesn't help that Lettie Harewood is dead."

Taylor looks across at Harcourt and raises her eyes slightly. "I don't suppose it helps Duncan either, sir!"

"I know. I know. That was harsh."

"Do you think Duncan knows about his father?"

"Difficult one, isn't it? He worked as a young lad for Frank's father and then Frank took him on as a casual at the garage, so he might have worked it out for himself. I see no reason why Frank would have told him. Maybe Duncan did know but didn't like what he saw - either Frank as a father or as his mother's lover. Not that he had any choice in the matter. Clotho, Lachesis and Atropos up to their usual tricks."

"Sir?"

"The Fates."

Taylor never did Classics. Unsurprisingly, they

weren't an option at her school. Nobody could opt out though. "It's led Duncan through a solitary life, and yet I'm not sure he's exactly unhappy - more like the wise old man in the woods."

"Or the Fool on the Hill?"

"Not fair is it, sir?"

Harcourt shakes his head in agreement. "But what's equally unfair - though understandable I suppose - is that we've now got two days left before we have to file all of this downstairs and let the whole case go into deep freeze again. That doesn't seem like justice to me for either Andrew or Grace - or Julie of course."

He glances in the mirror to see Daniel sitting behind Taylor, seemingly exhausted or maybe just deep in thought. "Thanks to Daniel we were able to retrieve the stick and also now believe Julie to be dead." He attempts to engage with the other man while slowly pulling up at traffic lights, but there is silence, broken helpfully by Taylor.

"With respect, sir, and to you, Mr Reed, many people will have assumed Julie was dead all along. There were no signs of struggle, apart from possibly the drops of the blood retrieved at the quarry; no subsequent sightings of her, no messages and no obvious strangers in the village who may have sought to cause her harm."

Reed seemingly has no comment to make at this point, so Harcourt engages the clutch on amber, and continues. "I just sense that there's a connection there somewhere - a motive that will fit with the little evidence that we do have. It bothers me that we've let everyone down: Andrew Patch, and Grace Beech for a second time."

"I'm not sure you should beat yourself up about Grace, sir. She can't have held out much hope after all these years and hasn't exactly been what you might call 'helpful.'"

"The years have certainly been unkind to her, I agree. I suppose the initial pain becomes less acute, but it never really goes away. Why would she be friendly, or welcoming - to anybody?"

Reed is stirring from his reverie. He rubs his eyes with the back of his hand.

"Too much late-night reading?" Harcourt jokes.

Reed doesn't smile, "Something like that. Mind you, that old chap with the beard looks as though life has crept up on him in a hurry!'

Both Taylor and Harcourt look around them, seeing nobody.

***

Quaint nineteenth-century cottages come into view as Castle Upton belies its secrets.

"Lisa Fairhurst was pretty unhelpful last time. What makes the Superintendent think she will be any different now, sir?"

"Divide and rule I guess. Stuart appears to be welded to his father - metaphorically and almost physically - so we're not expecting much joy there in the time that we have left. Nobody is ever as defensive as you said she was without some reason. With a bit more pressing we may find out what it is."

The three of them stand patiently on the doorstep porch, shaded from the mid-morning sun and, more pertinently, from the strong wind that has been building in the south.

"Just our luck that she's not in!" Taylor's low expectation of the return visit has quickly turned to frustration.

"Maybe we could come back later?" Reed's voice is even, without expression beyond the language itself.

"She could be gardening round the back?" Taylor remembers the dirt under Lisa Fairhurst's fingernails and how she hoped at the time that it was from garden soil.

"Then why are the tools lined up underneath the front window here?" Harcourt eyes the motley collection of rakes, trowel, and an ancient hoe."

Suddenly, there is a crash from the room next to the front door.

"I'm no expert," Reed speaks softly, "but I'd say our interviewee is already in conference with her plants, judging by the gap that has just appeared on the windowsill."

Harcourt has had enough. The ticking clock set him by Hunter-Wright allows no time for games of hide and seek.

"Police. Open up please!" He yells through the letterbox. Shortly afterwards the door opens, and Lisa Fairclough resplendent in a slightly different but still bright pink housecoat stands aside to let them pass, defeated - out for the count.

After Harcourt has introduced himself and Reed he proceeds quickly.

"You didn't know Andrew Beech personally?"

"Not until I met him in the pub for the first time, no."

The two men are seated in uncomfortable armchairs, opposite Lisa Fairhurst, also in padded discomfort. Taylor is perched on a badly stuffed piano stool that presumably parted company with its musical partner long ago.

"You said previously that your husband - Stuart - had known Andrew at school. Did he talk about him - Andrew I mean?"

"Never. Well, not until he heard that Andrew was travelling down for Grace's birthday celebration."

"He'd kept in touch with Grace I believe?" Harcourt pitches forward slightly and is pleased to see Lisa lean back by the same number of degrees.

"Yes. A card every year. He never missed her birthday."

Harcourt decides that it's time to take a chance. "Was it just a birthday greeting do you think? Or could it have been a reminder to Grace that Andrew was still around?"

"I don't know what you mean. What are you suggesting?" She crosses her fat legs awkwardly. Both men are relieved that she is wearing an old pair of oversized cream shorts below the coat.

"Was it a warning card? Did Andrew know something about Grace, or Julie, or Stuart perhaps?"

Taylor takes in Lisa's rumpled clothes. Not exactly dirty, there is little in the way of cleanliness about her either. Instead of making direct eye contact with any of them, she has been focusing her attention on the fake Indian carpet on the floor that has never been east of Smethwick. Now she is fiddling with her faded (and fake) silver watch strap, twisting it first one way and then the other as though she is trying to stop time and then reset it on its way again.

"Was Stuart involved in Andrew's death in some way, Lisa?"

The panic button did its job. "No. Why would you say that? Stuart knew nothing; knows nothing."

Her wide-eyed denial reflects in Harcourt's steely, focused eyes. "Everyone knows something, Lisa," he responds in a dramatically low voice, "And some people know much more than they are prepared to admit. Andrew knew what happened to Julie didn't he?"

"I don't know. I never knew Andrew then. He was Stuart and Grace's friend - and Julie's too."

"Maybe Andrew came into contact with Julie after her disappearance. Maybe she didn't want to see Grace but wanted her sister to know at the same time that she was still alive?"

"No. No that's not what happened."

"Because Julie is dead." It is the first and only contribution that Reed has made to the conversation.

"You don't know that."

"Oh, but I do." Reed's assurance is exactly that: final and indisputable.

Taylor watches sweat appear on the other woman's forehead, a watery veil that offers her no protection. "You can't possibly…"

"Can't possibly what, Lisa?" Harcourt feels the adrenaline pumping around his veins now. He'd felt flat when he'd woken that morning, resigned to lack of closure. Little did he imagine then that such an unexpected opening would appear before them.

She opens and closes her mouth for a few moments then closes it without replying, a slightly pink stream bending downwards at either end with nowhere left to flow.

"Did Stuart kill Julie Beech?"

"No. He didn't kill her, it was…"

"Who? Who are you protecting if not your husband?"

"Come on Lisa," Taylor backs Harcourt up, "This has gone on long enough. Stuart killed her didn't he, and Andrew saw what happened."

"It wasn't like that. Stuart wouldn't hurt a fly."

"So, what was it like?"

"It was an accident. A terrible accident. Stuart found Julie lying there at Grace's feet. He's never got over it. That image haunted him for years though he never talked about it. It was only when I was trying to get pregnant that it all came out and he made me promise never to mention it again."

"Why then?" Taylor is gentler now and doesn't want Harcourt trampling over women's things.

"They said we were unlikely to have children as Stuart had a low sperm count and couldn't be persuaded to, to, you know, often enough."

"Doctors told you this?"

"At the fertility clinic." Her voice has lost its hardness, as tear clouds gather. "Dr Latham. He kept asking us about stress and whether Stuart had ever experienced major trauma. Apart from his dad losing the farm, I couldn't think of anything and, of course, Stuart didn't say anything. Well, not then. Only later on when I couldn't stop crying, he must have decided to tell me. I don't think he'll ever get over it."

"Who else was there, on the evening of the accident?" Reed speaks gently but as one who knows irrefutably that there was somebody else at the scene.

"Stuart never said. It could have been Andrew though. Stuart told me that Andrew had chased Grace into a corner of the playground once they were back in school (it was closed for a few days after Julie's death while everyone joined the search party) and put his arm around her while whispering into her ear that he had 'seen everything.'"

"You think he saw Julie's head hit the rock?"

"He could have done. Stuart was never sure. They hadn't invited Andrew to join them, but he was always hanging around. This was before I knew them."

"If Andrew did see something, do you think he was blackmailing Stuart – or Grace - if not for money but for the satisfaction of them knowing he knew what he did?"

"I suppose it's possible. I don't really know."

"Because that would also give someone motive for silencing Andrew Patch!"

"You don't think…"

"What happened to Julie's body after the accident had happened? I understand that no trace was ever found despite an extensive search - especially by the standards of the 1970s?" Daniel hasn't changed his tone of voice in the slightest. If he is excited or bored, few people would ever know.

"I've no idea. Stuart never told me. It was like those soldiers that came back from the war. They never talked did they, not properly I mean? Stuart has always been a bit like that."

"But Stuart knows."

"I'm not sure that he knows all the details, but I do believe him when he says he never saw Julie's body again after he'd left the quarry. Please don't let him know that

I've told you any of this. Life hasn't always been easy, and this could throw him over the edge."

"He sounds quite fragile – Stuart." Harcourt makes to stand up.

"He is. Far more than people will ever know."

"There was some kind of fracas in the pub that night - the night that Andrew Patch died. Do you remember what that was about?"

"I don't remember. It was late."

"Did someone upset Stuart, or maybe Frank?"

"I just remember it happening quickly and then it was done. Andrew had left us."

"What do you mean Lisa?" Again, Taylor is playing the good, 'sympathetic cop.' "Are you talking about inside the pub or later?"

"Inside. Of course. Andrew was describing how he'd come home earlier than unexpected and found his wife in bed with some man he'd never seen before. He said she was just lying there, not speaking. Then Frank - Stuart's dad - began shouting at him. I guess he must have been sitting behind us, listening in on the conversation. He was extremely angry. I've seen him angry on lots of occasions, but nothing like that."

"And that caused Andrew to leave?"

"He had a strange look on his face like he was amused by it all. Said he needed to get some air and left the pub by the back door."

"Who followed him, Lisa?" Harcourt is standing over her now. A looming figure.

She just shakes her head defiantly, examining the carpet for clues on what not to say next.

As the three of them leave a still tearful Lisa Fairhurst sitting in her chair, Harcourt closing the door gently behind them, Reed notices that the garden tools have been blown sideways. He moves to stand an ancient shovel upright. As he does so, he sees a figure digging a hole by the sharp bend of a quiet country lane. Someone he hasn't yet met, but he knows who it is and why he's been dreaming about apple trees.

***

DS Flowers hears the CSI call come over the radio as he is driving back to Worcester. He has had a harrowing afternoon: their new case looks like being every bit as challenging as those of Julie Beech and Andrew Patch if, indeed, those two are connected. His boss had been tight-lipped about it when they'd spoken earlier but they'd been walking through the woods - Harcourt, Taylor and Mr Reed - and the signal had broken up several times. He hadn't been sure if Harcourt was excited or even more frustrated than he had been for these last few weeks.

At least the dead boy in his new case had been found quickly, even though he was lost forever. Parents should never have to bury their children - Harcourt had told him that often enough - and informing them of that forthcoming ordeal was by far the hardest part of their job. Thankfully WPC Tina Brewin from Family Liaison had accompanied him and would stay with the family for as long as they needed her. She couldn't replace their son though – no woman could.

Another young life full of promise ended tragically early. His left hand shakes as he shifts the gear lever, overtaking a battered old motorhome in the slow lane of this short stretch of dual carriageway. Perhaps that is the only alternative for all of those who don't die young, he considers miserably.

***

Harcourt's reaction hadn't been as positive as he would have liked.

"How do you suppose we're going to find these particular fruit trees? This is the Vale of Evesham!"

Thankfully, it was Daniel who had first spotted Duncan walking towards them. Later, he wondered whether the two men shared a connection that nobody in authority could possibly have forged; followed the same signs.

"It's down there you need to go," he had pointed, knowingly, "I've many a time seen Frank sitting in the far corner of the field, beyond the ditch, talking to himself."

It is only a few yards from the quarry which is, itself, just down the hill from Duncan Harewood's shack. No wonder the connection had been made by so many at the time, only for time to effectively try and dismiss it.

Daniel is staring at the baby buds on the branches of the trees: the promise of new life from old. They had followed the track down to where it joined the narrow lane which would eventually take them back into Castle Upton. Just a few paces along the lane, they saw the ancient, red triangular sign indicating a right-hand bend. The hedgerow had gaps in several places where deer had forced themselves through - either in flight or out of curiosity. Daniel isn't curious, just seeking confirmation.

There are five trees in total, forming a circle and marking the spot; they must have been planted deliberately to ensure that the tractor's plough could get no nearer to it as the regular cycle of planting, growing and harvesting continued while Julie slept, oblivious to it all, perhaps.

Digging between the forty-year-old roots might prove difficult, he thinks, but it is somebody else's job now. As Claire might phrase it for him: his work here is done.

***

"What are we going to do?"

Annabel Fairhurst looks back at her daughter-in-law's tear-streaked face; at her chubby fingers clutching at the kitchen surface. She remembers the angst of years ago when Lisa and Stuart had traversed their bad patches. It was always Lisa who had appeared at her door though, not her son. Her real son doesn't have anything like the same trust in her as Duncan does.

She has never really understood why Stuart chose to confide in and have faith in Frank, though she acknowledges it as an unbreakable bond forged years ago. Certainly, no links in that particular chain had ever been meant to connect her to them. She recalls - as she has done so many times - how her son had arrived on the doorstep, panting from running, white as a sheet. He wouldn't tell her what had scared him, just ran upstairs to bed without any tea. Nothing like it had ever happened before or since.

Almost two hours later her husband had also returned. His face was scorched red from a day in the fields. He had nothing to say either but, just a few hours later when a collection of torches, held high by those who believed themselves to be on a rescue mission, passed by their window - when her husband left the house again to join the search party - she too was scared.

"Annabel?" Lisa is wringing her hands together. Now.

She needs to act - now. For too long she has been watching from the sidelines.

"What did they say?"

"They were asking about Andrew at first and then Stuart."

"Stuart? Why were they asking about Stuart?"

"I don't know!"

Lisa bursts into tears and Annabel rushes around the kitchen island, puts her arms around her and holds her close. She smells her dirty hair and the faint smell of body odour but still, she offers close comfort. Eventually, the sobbing ceases and a piece of kitchen towel soon mops up the wet patches on her cheeks (though this is not a widely advertised example of its usefulness).

"Now, I'm sure there's nothing for either of you to worry about. They're probably just fishing. It's obvious that they've got nothing to go on or they'd have been round again long before this."

"You're probably right," she sniffs in reply, "But they've got this other bloke with them now. Tall and thin. Really scary he is. His eyes don't move, just stare right through you."

"Who is he then?"

"Don't know - they didn't say. Just that he was helping them. He seemed to know things though - about Julie's death. If Stuart was involved in some way, I think it's only a matter of time..."

Annabel shushes her gently, heading off another flood. "I don't know for certain what happened back then either, on that evening. All I can say is that Stuart was never the same again. I hardly know who he is now, whereas once upon a time I knew everything about my little boy. It's never made him happy - whatever he did or didn't do."

"Or Frank. I've never known him not to be angry."

"No, but that set in before this. That evening in the quarry was a turning point for the whole family."

"The whole family?"

"The whole family, yes." She emphasises the word again and feels complete in a way that, strangely, she has never really felt before. "Does Stuart know about the police visit?"

"No yet. I went straight round to the garage after, but it was closed. Neither Frank nor Stuart was there."

"In the middle of the day?"

"That's what I thought. What if they come after Stuart?"

"If they do, send them here. This has all gone on for far too long. I effectively lost one son and very nearly another. It's not going to happen again."

"What do you mean?" Confusion has taken the place of concern on Lisa's face.

"You don't need to worry. Let's not wait. I'll contact the police directly."

"Why. Why would you do that?" Horror has arrived now, sweeping all before it.

"Because I can tell them something that they definitely won't have been aware of; not yet."

***

Flowers has joined Harcourt, relieving Taylor to head home for some rest. He sees Daniel Reed, standing upright by the trees, beside the huge white tent that has been erected at the scene.

"Do you think it's her, sir?"

"Daniel is sure of it and therefore so am I."

"He wasn't..." Flowers hesitates. It isn't just what Daniel Reed represents to him, but who he is. He hasn't warmed to the man, though, to be fair to them both, he hasn't exactly had any kind of in-depth conversation with him either. Perhaps he's afraid to engage with him; afraid of what Reed might see?

"Go on, Sergeant."

"Sorry sir, but he was wrong last time, wasn't he?"

"The stick. He got that exactly right, as though he'd taken a video of it all."

"No. Sorry, sir. I mean when the other girl was kidnapped. Years ago. He got the wrong location, didn't he?"

Harcourt is tired and hungry, easily confounding the best efforts of the chocolate bar he found in his pocket just over three hours earlier. He turns slowly to face Flowers. "He didn't. No. The police didn't believe him then. I believe in him now. I thought it would take me longer but it didn't."

Suitably silenced, Flowers looks up at the moon as wispy ribbons of cloud scuttle away, out of its spotlight. It has seen it all before, he thinks. Is it only the poets who truly understand this? We wax and we wane and, all the time, most of us ignore the most important message of all: to cherish simply being alive.

Shortly after midnight, there is a sudden incomprehensible shout that sounds like a bullet crack resonating across the slumbering countryside. The arc lights are moved even closer to the hole and seem brighter than ever in the surrounding gloom. Harcourt can see the head and shoulders of a fellow officer, just above the ground's surface: PC Arbon he thinks, but he isn't sure.

"Sir!"

The news is now articulated in letter form, though the exclamation mark would have been quite sufficient on its own to convey the meaning of the sentence.

He crouches down beside the hole and sees quickly that it has turned into a grave. A small skull sits on the earth, eyes unseeing as they have failed to do for more than forty years. A single bone leads to some kind of material, below which he laments that a framework built for life's many challenges lies broken. She might once have looked forward to growing up into a young woman - daydreamed about finding true love and maybe having children of her own one day. It was just a fairy tale without a happy ending. She had been let down - by all of them.

PC Arbon has climbed out and two Crime Scene officers are photographing from every angle. Their flashes barely make an impact in the bright light overhead. Is that what Julie Beech saw in the last seconds of her life, he wonders sadly, or is that just make-believe too?

"She looks like she's been covered by some sort of sack, sir." One of the officers is talking to him. He doesn't immediately know which one it is, much less know their name. "It looks like it's preserved things quite well; surprising given the soil content. There's also some wording on it but we'll have to examine it more closely. We're unlikely to be able to tell you more until we've moved it, I'm afraid."

"She! Moved her!" Harcourt knows he is being unfair, but since when did fairness live on the same street as his job? "Treat it like a shroud. We'll find the words later."

***

"And you thought this was odd. Why?"

DS Taylor is wide awake now. Two chocolate croissants and three cups of coffee had failed to make any kind of impact, but now it's ten past nine in the morning and the confessional is an earlier riser than caffeine it seems.

"Because he never does that. I'm pretty surprised that he even knew where the washing machine was."

"Did you query Frank about this?"

"Why would I have done that? It would only have led to another argument and prolonged absence without leave in the pub."

"But you were suspicious enough to remove the jeans and place them in this bag - which you'd hidden in the utility cupboard until now?"

Taylor knows that all links are important - especially in the light of Harcourt's startling and disturbing report from the previous evening - but some often require piecing back together gently if they're to form a complete chain of events which can be presented later.

"I wouldn't say I was suspicious exactly - not then, anyway. It's only after I heard about Andrew Patch's death that I began to wonder."

"Because of the bloodstains?"

Annabel Fairhurst looks up. She appears to be far less tired and emotional than Taylor is, and yet she is knowingly turning over evidence that is very likely to incriminate a loved one (once upon a time, at least?)

"I didn't - don't - know if they are bloodstains. It was just that he had never just come home and stripped his clothes off in the kitchen before. Even when he was madly drunk and…"

"Abusive?"

"Yes. Even then he would just have been boorish and unpleasant and - insistent I suppose."

She takes a breath rather than a gulp of air, Taylor notices. This woman is on a mission. She waits for her to continue, which she quickly does. "This was completely different. I brought a load down to wash the following morning and found his stuff already in there. I did wonder about the stains - they weren't like anything I had seen before apart from…"

"Apart from?" Taylor is still trying to be gentle, but a rising excitement is making her patience harder to control. However, she resolves to remain as calm and impassive as she possibly can.

"Apart from years ago when he'd tended to a young ewe that had become impaled on some barbed wire. That's why I thought the stains might be blood. But not from a sheep this time."

"So why did you bring this to us now? It's been several

weeks since Andrew Patch's body was found?"

"I know. I know. And I'm sorry. I wasn't sure whether I was just imagining things. I didn't want to waste your time."

"You were hardly imagining dirty clothes dumped in a washing machine late at night; the same night that a man died. You didn't imagine the stains either."

This has come out far too harshly and Taylor is immediately aware of the fact. So much for calm.

"That's what Duncan said."

"Duncan Harewood?"

"Frank's son, yes. Oh, don't pretend you didn't know! Or didn't know that I knew. Call it a woman's intuition if nothing else. You must know yourself that there is always a certain knowledge between a mother and her son - even if it isn't proven in any visible way. It's a certainty that stretches way beyond facts stored way in encyclopaedias or feelings expressed in books. You'll know exactly what I mean if you have children of your own?"

Taylor flinches at the question; cannot even find a suitable answer. Certainly not here. Not now. She finds solace in police procedure, as she has always done - as she believes DI Harcourt does. A kindred spirit in a way.

"Duncan thought I should tell you now. He said it could be important."

"While also helping to put him in the clear, presumably?" Too hard, again. She needs to hold this together.

"Duncan? You surely couldn't have suspected him of any involvement in Andrew Patch's death?"

Taylor notes that Annabel Fairhurst is far more animated - angry even - about the insinuation that Duncan Harewood could be in trouble than seemingly any blood relation.

"Or Julie Beech's death?"

She is angry now, without a doubt. "Firstly, you don't know for certain that Julie Beech is dead, and, for seconds, none of those rumours they came out with about Duncan at the time were true. Not one of them. Most were put about by the reporters."

Taylor knows that the discovery of the body is still classified but she can't resist a final turn of the screw:

"Aided and abetted by your husband?"

"He was upset. We all were. Nobody could explain Julie's disappearance and you people were clueless."

"Or the clues were very carefully buried?"

"Perhaps. The whole village went along with rumours because they're what rural communities like ours substitute when there are no known facts, don't they? Sometimes they upgrade them to 'myths' and 'legends' for the amusement of others.

Taylor stands up and Annabel Fairhurst follows suit. The interview room seems much smaller now than when they entered it just fifteen minutes or so ago.

"Thank you for bringing this to our attention," her voice is far stiffer than the legs struggling to hold her upright, "We'll get it checked out. I'm sure DI Harcourt will want to speak with you again - and other members of your family."

"Good luck with that, Sergeant."

***

Hunter-Wright has gone back in time - much further than he normally allows himself:

"'There's no time to lose" I heard her say
"Catch your dreams before they slip away
Dying all the time
Lose your dreams and you will lose your mind
Ain't life unkind?'"

He clicks the mute button as Harcourt enters.

"We've found them, sir, they were in an old shepherd's hut on the far side of Fladbury; used to be owned by the Fairhurst family but not much left of it now.

"You say you 'found them.' Were they hiding?"

"Difficult to say, sir. They were just sitting together on an old bench when we moved the corrugated iron aside - a makeshift door. Did not seem surprised and did not attempt to escape."

For once, Hunter-Wright ignores the nervousness in the younger officer's delivery, taking in the obvious mental exhaustion instead. He beckons him to sit opposite, which Harcourt gratefully does.

"Fathers and sons eh!" He hopes to appear upbeat but appreciates that the words are tinged with the sadness he feels inside.

"Indeed, sir. The DNA on the clothing Annabel Fairhurst brought in is unmistakably that of Frank Fairhurst and also matches tiny particles we have been able to retrieve from Julie Beech's grave."

"That's impressive after all these years. Dr Graham must be expecting house points!"

Again, the forced jollity fails and both men simply remain miserable.

"We believe that the material remnants in which Julie Beech's body was originally buried, was some kind of sack. We've managed to isolate two words from one part of it: *Piddle Peat.* DS Flowers has been researching this and we think it came originally from a local firm that would have supplied many of the farms around here. The peat would have been mixed with the existing earth to give it more nutrients - like a fertiliser. In our case, it helped to preserve everything remarkably well. The positioning of it right in the corner of the field meant that no ploughs got that close to it either, so no danger of discovery there."

"And too early for cadaver dogs?"

"Sir?

"They were only just discovering their capabilities in the 1970s. Even had they been further on with their training, officers would have had to have been pretty certain of where to lead them to look. I suppose he planted the trees to complete the deceit - just in case?"

"That is our understanding, yes, sir. Traces of Grace Beech's DNA were also found, and we were further able to analyse DNA taken from other the roots of hair samples at the scene; quite a lot of them. These are a match for Stuart Fairhurst."

"He always admitted that he was playing there with Grace and her sister, just that he never actually saw what happened to Julie. It's still circumstantial. The sack could have been Frank Fairhurst's - hence the DNA - but they were adjacent to Fairhurst land, so no great surprise there."

"And no firm motive in either case - none that the CPS would be prepared to prove anyway. Accidental death is much easier to live with."

"Is it though?"

"Sir?"

Hunter-Wright does not pursue it. He too can stick to procedure when he chooses to. "At least Julie Beech is no longer missing. Have you told Grace yet?"

"Her bungalow is all closed up, sir, although there was a pint of milk on the doorstep this morning when we called - it looks as though she left suddenly."

"Hardly, Inspector."

"Sir?"

"If Daniel Reed is to be believed - and, Lord knows, I have no reason to doubt him (not after all of this) - Grace Beech knew all along what happened to her sister, even if Stuart Fairhurst didn't. What happened afterwards, we may never know. Andrew Patch may have seen what happened, or he might not have, despite what he chose to tell Grace Beech in the playground. If he hadn't returned to Castle Upton when he did, he might still be alive today, and so might our file on Julie Beech."

"Suffer little children."

"Children can be malicious too, Inspector, far more spiteful than Mr Fox in stories their parents may have hopefully read to them. What is important is that the others – Stuart, Frank and certainly Grace - believed that he had witnessed what happened. Grace hasn't been waiting all her life to find Julie; she's been waiting for her to be found."

***

"It just shows you, doesn't it, that you can hide in broad daylight for all those years, but the truth will eventually find you out?"

Not for the first time in recent weeks, Daniel gazes admiringly at his daughter and how articulate she has become. She probably always has been if he'd taken time to look up from his dictionaries and books on grammar a little more often. She is rinsing glasses, while he arranges the next round of salmon canapés on the large dinner plates they usually only use at Christmas.

"Not necessarily the whole truth though."

"You're beginning to sound like that policeman."

Harcourt had popped over that morning to give him

an update on the latest events but had just as quickly departed when he had seen the preparations being made for that afternoon's 'small gathering.'

"All I'm saying is that we'll probably never hear the whole story; there are several plausible endings. All we know is that the girl died in an accident and was buried very near to the scene - at least until now."

"What will happen to Stuart Fairhurst – the son?"

"They'll never be able to pin it on him one way or another in terms of what happened on the night that Julie died – he was a minor at the time anyway. No court would believe that he could have stood up to his overbearing, aggressive father. Frank may have been prepared to make a witness out of Grace Beech – to protect himself later through little reminders or even blackmail if she got flaky about it - but not his son. Whether the CPS decide to pursue a case of perverting the course of justice against him is also, I would say, unlikely."

"How do you mean?"

"He told the police that he saw Frank Fairhurst straight home on the night that Andrew Beech died. He clearly didn't and was lying to protect his father, whom he thought was under threat. That's very different to lying to prevent justice from taking place though. He may not have known about Frank pursuing Andrew – a pursuit which ended with him dying, certainly, but inconclusive as to whether it was an accident or not. Stuart coming clean would not have changed anything: it wouldn't have erased the intent in Frank's head."

"Do you think they'll tell Stuart about Duncan being his brother?"

"I'm not sure what purpose it would serve. Once you compare yourself with someone else, especially someone you've known all your life, you can become either jealous or vain - usually one or the other. If you believe in destiny, you should perhaps stick to the path it's set out for you?"

"I think 'destiny' is a bit of an easy excuse where human behaviour is concerned!"

"I did wonder why you'd stopped listening to Destiny's Child…"

She aims a playful punch in his direction, which he backs away from, almost colliding with the fridge as he does so.

"You must be so pleased to have been able to help, though. They wouldn't have got this far without you."

"You did. For much of the time."

He dodges a half-hearted attempt at another punch, but only just this time. She has grown quite a lot taller as well.

"I don't think 'pleased' is the right adjective anyway," he continues, even as he pops open another bottle of Prosecco. "Far too many people's lives have been on hold because of a game that went so badly wrong."

"I overheard you telling the policeman to keep a close watch on Mr Fairhurst!"

"Let's just say I'll feel happier when he's released."

"So that's where you two are. We thought you'd gone for another walk!" Fergus Colfax strides into the kitchen, resplendent in a flowery white shirt and beige chinos - like an ice cream that's never been licked.

"On your sister's big birthday! I think not, although I do seem to remember you telling us to get out more."

Their saintly guest takes it all in good humour. "With Charlotte - not without her!"

"Well, in that case, we'd better stop filling her up with fizzy wine or she won't see 61."

Daniel is relieved that the party is going well. In truth, he feels deathly tired, but close friends and family can sometimes be the perfect antidote to that.

"Come on Uncle Ferg, let's go and find Mum." With that, Claire leads him out into the garden where he is received with far more applause and genuine good cheer than in a month of Sundays.

A few moments later, just as Daniel is retrieving the latest batch of rolls that were once half-baked from the oven, Charlotte seems to float in through the patio doors. In a nice white dress and with a small garland of fresh flowers in her hair (courtesy of Claire no doubt). She has been in a somewhat dreamy state for a few days now, and he recalls her telling him that her GP felt the diazepam pills would help her 'to adjust.' The reality is that they have just made her sleepy.

"How are you?" He folds his arms around her and

pulls her close.

"I'm having a lovely time," she whispers, "But I wish you'd do something about that old stray cat that's started coming in: I keep thinking that Claire's dropped her orange scarf and forgotten about it!"

**

"Please tell me it's not true."

Harcourt is barking into the 'phone, even as a dog is trying to gain everyone's attention a few doors further down. He listens and then allows his head to drop to his chest. Debbie sits up and places her hand on his shoulder, trying to hear the voice that is coming from just a few miles away.

In Worcester's central police station, the sergeant is holding the desk phone firmly to the same ear that has been getting a bashing for the last few early morning minutes.

"We can only do our best, sir... no, no, I appreciate that on this occasion it wasn't good enough but..."

"Mr Reed was very sure about it. He was worried for the man's state of mind."

"I appreciate that, sir, but, if you'll forgive me, not all of us believe in those sorts of people. Call us cynics if you like, but that's the basis of police work isn't it - believe what you can see. At least he left a note for everyone to read."

**

'I've always wanted to explain. You've got to believe

that but I'm no good with words. Not like you. I wish I could have seen beyond the covers of all your lovely books. I suppose they weren't meant for me. You'll probably say that I'm no good at anything and I wouldn't argue with you. I've always known that what we did was wrong, but you have to believe me when I say I did it for the right reasons - at least in my head.

Stuart came bolting out of the woods like he'd seen a ghost. He said that he thought Julie was dead. After I'd calmed him down, he told me that he'd been hiding but neither of the girls came looking for him, long after they must have counted to ten. So, he went looking for them instead and eventually found them back in the quarry. He said that neither of them had moved and that Julie still wasn't. I took him back there and, sure enough, Julie was lying on the floor and Grace just stood over her - not angry or even frightened. Just quietly standing there.

I felt for the little girl's pulse and knew she'd left us. I didn't want Stuart involved in any of it - you've got to believe me, Annabel. I sent him home and he tore off. I'd been planting in the field just on the other side of the wood so went and got one of the sacks from the trailer. Grace helped me wrap the body up - still silent, like her sister - and we took it across the ditch to a patch of the land that was quite moist. The rain always used to run downhill into that corner, so it was easier to dig in than the rest of the field. I'm used to digging holes – been doing so for my whole life, haven't I? I just dug down, getting hotter and hotter until I reckoned I must have been near enough at the core of the earth itself. We then went our separate ways.

A few days later, Stuart told me what Andrew had said to Grace. Thankfully they moved out of Castle Upton soon after, but he would keep sending Grace birthday cards, not that she ever remembered when his birthday was. She thought it was him taunting her, all-knowing and like. When he came back and started talking about a girl lying there, not speaking, I knew I was right. I went after him and caught up with him at the end of the village. I'd grabbed Duncan's stick and hauled him back. He lost his balance and fell over. I suppose you could say it was history repeating itself, in a way.

I never meant to hurt him, just frighten him off once and for all. Same as happened with young Julie: I think Grace just wanted to frighten her, but she turned her into a ghost that has haunted us ever since.

I didn't tell Stuart that I'd buried Julie, just that he didn't need to worry. I did want him to know that. I did what I thought was right, Annabel. If he didn't know the truth, then he couldn't be a part of it, could he? I wanted to protect my family. (I know I did wrong by Duncan, but I made it up to him, didn't I? Saw he never really went without anything these past years. Julie dying did that to me. Made me realise how precious a child's life truly is).

I didn't want to fail them you see. I'd let everyone else down: you, Dad, Grandad. Everything that was good, I'd managed to ruin. This was my last chance to put it right and do the right thing for once. Now I'm going to do so again. I can't live inside these four walls. Do you remember the rope ladder I built for Stuart - out in the woods? Well, when you've worked with animals, it's strange how you remember how to fold and knot material, even if it is the shirt off my own back. I would have given that to you once - happily - but now I reckon you'd just throw it away.

Please believe me, Annabel, even if you didn't believe in me in the end.

Frank'

She folds the piece of paper back on itself so that the words can no longer be seen. She hasn't committed them to memory yet, but she knows that, when she has, they will become just that: as vivid and vulnerable as a memory.

The End

ABOUT THE AUTHOR

Mark Rasdall

Mark Rasdall was born in Peterborough in 1960 and brought up on the edge of the Cambridgeshire Fens. He is a writer of fiction and history, with a professional background in content creation, curation, and online search in London's advertising sector. He is based in the UK, in a small village on top of a hill in the beautiful Worcestershire countryside. For a few years he ran a sweet shop on Worcester High Street with his wife Michelle.

Now retired, this is the first in the series of Inspector Harcourt crime novels set in a changing rural Worcestershire, nestling between the Malvern Hills to the west and the Cotswolds to the south.

You can visit his website at www.markrasdallwriting.com and follow Mark on Facebook, X and Instagram.

MAILING LIST

If you enjoyed this book please look out for the next title in the series:

Water, slaughter everywhere

Also, join our mailing list for the latest news, including about forthcoming books in the series:

https://23e39b8f.sibforms.com/serve/MUIFANz0yGHzWd78toV2l8aQF4W9OEv6OK0gKWoa-Gj_LjT9GSzpHGYX1GZwsXLSNxUGcQezK_H6jsvjgnPYBvhl8ctfHQAvxgVvCJuQNos4F2bRHEYFYH-kgQwGBlyUisLxTZPgufZAQLICtjX5mM83Cf-osZw3dmXqTi-1JvRa9dIBPgcaePmVrm8DnlEhBrWJHSqRbJ9LKKuC

Printed in Great Britain
by Amazon